W9-CHD-409

OBJECT OF DESIRE

DAL MACLEAN

OBJECT OF DESIRE

DAL MACLEAN

An Imprint of BLIND EYE BOOKS
blindeyebooks.com

Published by:
One Block Empire
an imprint of
BLIND EYE BOOKS
1141 Grant Street Bellingham, WA 98225

All rights reserved. No part of this book may be used or reproduced in any manner without written permission of the publisher, except for the purpose of reviews.

Edited by Nicole Kimberling and Anne Scott

Cover Art by KaNaXa

This book is a work of fiction and as such all characters and situations are fictional. Any resemblances to actual people or events are coincidental.

First Edition: 2018
Copyright © Dal Maclean 2018

ISBN: 978-1-935560-54-8 (print)
ISBN: 978-1-935560-55-5 (digital)

To N and J as always. And to Penfold, for always having my back.

"Dead? Come on, that's...of course she's not dead."

"She is." Nick's voice. Choked and shaky, at the other end of a poor phone line. "God, Tom. She really is."

"But...I saw her yesterday," Tom insisted. "Catriona. At the office. She was fine."

His stunned gaze skittered over his surroundings, trying to clutch on to normality.

Grand, white colonnades, bleached render, yellowing grass, scorching July sunlight—Greenwich Riverside—with the glass and metal towers of Canary Wharf looming across the Thames.

The gorgeous photographer Tom had been idly chatting-up when he answered his phone, breaking down his gear a few yards away.

An assistant waiting for Tom by a fold-up table, holding a bottle of makeup remover in one bored hand.

Two gulls, startling white against startling blue, wheeling and crying over the river.

"She's on the bed." Nick's unwanted voice again, worming in his ear. "And...there's so much...blood. She's *cold*."

Tom drew in a sharp breath through his nose. "Have you called an ambulance?"

"Christ, Tom, of course I have! Please. Please, I need you to come now. She..."

Tom squeezed his eyes tight shut, until he saw sparkles behind his straining lids.

Don't say it. Don't. You. Fucking. Say it.

"She's killed herself, Tom." Nick's voice broke.

Tom opened his eyes.

•••

Tom's hastily arranged cab arrived at Catriona's Clapham townhouse, seconds behind an ambulance that had clearly struggled to get there too. It was close to four o'clock, after all. Saturday. People driving home from the shops.

All the way from Greenwich, sitting impotently in the back of the cab as it hit traffic snarl-up after snarl-up, Tom had cursed the fact that he hadn't brought his bike to the shoot. But maybe it was as well; he was in no state to make split-second judgments.

Tom and the taxi driver stared out for uncomfortable seconds at the obvious signs of crisis surrounding the house. The front door, wide open; the police car outside. Tom's stomach was a tight writhing ball of dread. Then the driver shook himself back to business.

"That's…um…thirty-one eighty-five, mate." He sounded awkward, as if he felt embarrassed asking for payment in the circumstances. "Actually. Just make it thirty quid, ay?" His voice was gruff with sympathy.

The ambulance had double-parked beside Nick's black Porsche, and two crew-members were already out on the road, equipment extracted, heavy doors thudding closed, as the men headed toward the house.

Tom fumbled two twenty-pound notes out of his wallet, shoved them through the open glass partition into the driver's startled hand, and scrambled out of the cab. Then, he raced up the short path and into the house, hard on the heels of the ambulance crew.

A young uniformed, first-response police officer stood in the sunlit hallway, but she wasn't quick enough to notice that Tom wasn't a paramedic too. So he was able to belt up the stairs behind the team unimpeded and follow them through the open doorway at the top.

The smell hit him first, a thick, cloying blend of expensive perfume and corrupt, metallic fruit.

He saw Nick, hunched against a far wall, body shaking with silent grief, eyes closed.

Then he took in the rest.

An all-white bedroom—glamorous and totally impractical, designed like something from a magazine, so that every dot of color looked shocking. A painted wooden desk stood by the window, holding a silver laptop; the signature light-green-blue of a Tiffany box; a stack of envelopes tied with a red cord; five little, glass, medical bottles lined up, with matching purple bars on their labels. A familiar light-blue dress lay draped over the arm of a padded armchair, a tiny tangle of lacy pink underwear on top.

White walls, furniture, carpet, bedding. Everything was absurdly neat and clean, save the most demanding splash of color—the huge stain which covered the fluffy duvet like crimson dye. A palette of shades of red, in fact, as if the pool had dried gradually from the outside, into the dark and clotted center.

Catriona lay on her side on top of it, in the middle of the wide bed, facing the doorway. She was naked but utterly sexless, her skin like bleached ash against the wet, red cloth. Her beautiful, blank profile, eyes decently shut at least, rested on the purity of her pillow.

Tom saw the guilty kitchen knife lying on the blood-pool beside the upturned palm of her right hand; the mangled, meaty churn of her inner wrists. Then, the dark hole, visible through black-blood-clotted ash-blonde hair, where her ear had been. The shockingly recognizable auricle resting near her fingertips.

One of the paramedics called sharply, "Hey! You shouldn't be in here, mate!" just as the uniformed police constable materialized behind Tom, to pull him, unresisting, back into the hallway and then, down the stairs. At the bottom, Tom slurred out his name and address, and the reason he was there. He didn't sound like himself at all, he thought distantly, but the officer noted it all down.

Finally, she left him to perch on the pristine linen sofa in Catriona's airy sitting room. And he found himself stupidly anxious not to crease the fabric or mark its snowy perfection.

He'd never been in this room before. In fact, he'd never been inside the house.

The door into the hallway lay wide open, allowing Tom to see the bustle of comings and goings in the hallway, as the procedures surrounding an unexpected death snapped into place. All things he'd heard recounted before, but never—actually—witnessed.

The first-response officer, out of his eyeline, was speaking to her radio. Someone—a man—shouted instructions from upstairs as one of the paramedics barreled past the open door and out of Tom's vision, as if his urgency still had some point.

Movement, back and fore. Voices outside. Inside. Tom forced desperate focus—made himself identify what was happening. Who was who, as they passed.

First onto Tom's little stage—a man he suspected to be the divisional pathologist, followed by a group of SOCO officers, silent and eerie in hooded white suits, ready to pick over the scene for evidence of anything that might turn out to be suspicious.

Then, less than a minute after they disappeared, two men, clearly plain-clothed police officers. They stood in front of the open sitting room doorway, pulling on those same white forensic suits and overshoes, and Tom was almost certain they'd be the advance Homicide Assessment Team, from whichever murder investigation unit happened to be on call. Tom didn't recognize either of them—a dull, distant relief.

Part of him was riveted, because after having heard it described so often, casually and not, it felt unreal seeing everything actually happen, like a dramatic performance put on, specially for him. But as the two

HAT officers moved out of Tom's vision, another white-clad figure came in behind them, and as he passed the open sitting room door, he glanced in and caught sight of Tom.

The man stopped and blinked.

For a moment, Tom felt an audience's shock at having been acknowledged, and he shifted self-consciously under the man's startled stare. Then, as that stare turned to wide-eyed disbelief, Tom felt suddenly, horribly aware of how incongruous he must look. His golden tan, his glossy, pale-blond shoulder-length hair; his long body, clad in an on-trend brown suede shirt and perfectly cut jeans; his obsessively precise grooming. A peacock, sitting at the edge of a tragedy.

It took whole seconds for Tom to understand that the man's reaction wasn't puzzlement; it was recognition. And finally, even under that disorientating, tightly drawn white hood, Tom recognized him in turn.

Each man stared at the other as if a monstrous apparition had manifested in front of them.

Des *fucking* Salt.

Through surging panic, Tom took in the man's once-familiar sharp features; his densely freckled skin, almost as white as the forensic hood concealing his wiry red hair. How the fuck hadn't he recognized him? Was it just the oddness of that hood, framing Salt's narrow face like a nun's coif?

The relief Tom had felt just minutes before sneered at him now. Because…yes, Tom had known there was a small chance they'd be involved—of course he had—but how unlucky did he have to be?

His face felt scalding hot, his guts skittering with a kind of death-row anticipation. And, inevitably his gaze shot to the hallway behind Salt.

Because always, with DC Des Salt, came DI Will Foster.

Tom's eyes fixed on that empty space like a mouse in front of a stoat. But nothing happened.

He snapped his attention back to Salt, but Salt had turned away and walked out of Tom's field of vision. He could hear hushed voices though, as Salt presumably asked the uniformed PC by the staircase what the fuck Tom was doing there.

When Salt appeared again in the doorway, his expression had fixed into professional neutrality. He extracted a notebook from inside the opening of his forensic suit, pulled down his hood and walked in the room.

"Mr. Gray," he said. It was stupidly shocking to hear his voice. Perhaps Tom had hoped it was all a lurid dream.

Then he registered, *Mr. Gray*. They were going to pretend they didn't know each other, then. Fine by him. But he couldn't help looking compulsively toward the open doorway before he focused again on Salt.

"I'm DS Salt with Southwark and Peckham Murder Investigation Team."

Southwark and Peckham. That was new at least. And so was the rank. He'd made Sergeant. Salt's Northern Irish accent sounded as strong as it ever had, but Tom unwillingly noted tiny changes in him. New, fine lines between his ginger brows. His unfortunate moustache had gone, as had that shy, awkward niceness he'd exuded once, so out of place on a policeman.

"Don't be alarmed, sir," Salt went on blandly. "This is all routine procedure in a case like this."

Of course it was. With all that blood.

Tom involuntarily squeezed closed his eyes, and the image was starkly there, like a high-res photograph dropping in behind his lids. He thought he would never stop seeing it.

His eyes sprang open.

That was what mattered. What lay upstairs. Not some soap opera from his past.

Sick with himself, he forced his attention back to Salt.

"I know," he said.

Salt raised an eyebrow. "You told the officer that you're here because Mr. Haining—Mr. Dominic Haining—requested you come to support him. When he found the body of his wife. Catriona Haining."

Tom nodded, then said, "Yes." Aloud, as if he were being recorded.

"And, what's your relationship to Mr. and Mrs. Haining?" There was no one here to witness any recognition between them, but still, Salt's tone remained that of a stranger.

"I—Mr...and Mrs. Haining own one of the modeling agencies I work with. Echo...it's called."

"This is Mrs. Haining's home. Mr. Haining no longer lives here, is that correct?"

Tom tightened his jaw. "Yes."

"You must be a...close friend as well as a client?" Salt began to write in his notebook. "For Mr. Haining to have called you here at a time like this."

Tom's mind darted around the question of how much total honesty could complicate things for Nick, but in the end all he said was, "Yes."

Salt glanced up, brown eyes narrowed. And Tom was sure Salt must be making those damning connections in his head.

Tom and Nick Haining. Nick and Tom.

Nick—whose wife had just killed herself. Of all people to judge him, it had to be Des.

Salt though, didn't try to push him on it. Instead, when he finished scribbling his notes, he left the room until he could return with a forensics officer from the scene upstairs to take Tom's fingerprints, a swab of his cheek for DNA, and a print of his boot. For elimination purposes, Salt assured him. And all through the process, though Tom ignored him, he could feel Salt's narrow observation, as if he was taking mental notes.

All the better to report back to his guv, Tom thought viciously, about what a wreaker of havoc Tom continued to be.

"Right. Thanks for your cooperation, Mr. Gray," Salt said, when the process ended. And that appeared to be it. Salt gave a curt nod and turned to the door, and he still hadn't acknowledged their acquaintanceship.

Tom stared at his retreating white-clad back, and he realized he had to have some certainty, rather than wasting even a second, on top of everything else, fearing something that might not happen.

He blurted. "Who's your SIO?"

Salt halted and peered over his shoulder. He was frowning, as if, for some reason, that wasn't what he'd expected Tom to say, then, understanding visibly hit.

Salt's lip curled. "If this turns into something, it'll be DCI Lawson, *sir*."

Tom could hear his contempt. *You're safe enough.*

DCI Lawson.

Tom didn't have a fucking clue who he was.

He felt a nauseating rush of emotion, anticlimax perhaps. Shame. All easily overwhelmed by a tsunami tide of relief that in this, at least, his luck had held. That, on top of this catastrophe, he wouldn't have to deal with Will Foster.

That was the moment he heard the first sounds of Catriona's corpse being manhandled down the narrow staircase.

Dull obscene thumps, subdued curses, a quiet laugh.

He moved in a daze to the open sitting room door, and stood beside Salt, watching, agonized, as the zipped lumpen body bag was carried on a graceless stretcher through the hall and out into the glorious, glorious sunlight.

•••

Tom sat in Catriona's drawing room, still waiting.

It felt like hours since the ambulance had left with Catriona's body, and his mind remained fixed compulsively on the image of the obscene black bag. The uninterested hands carrying it. What was left of Catriona, flopping inside.

The last time he'd seen her—styled as always like an old-time movie goddess, sashaying down the corridor in her tight baby-blue sheath dress. That delicate, glacial elegance of hers; everything around her—fastidious and impeccable. Like this room, before it had been smeared with brutish black forensic powder.

In the cab over from Greenwich, trying to prepare himself for what was coming, Tom had imagined he could predict how Catriona would have staged a final exit. He'd expected…a carefully set scene of beautiful, useless tragedy. Grace Kelly as Ophelia, with or without the flowers.

And he couldn't bear that she'd chosen to punish herself with such ugliness and indignity at her end.

He rubbed a desperate hand over his face, trying to silence the chaos of guilt and regret in his mind. His palm came away with traces of melted foundation, a touch of dark mascara. The makeup assistant had given him wipes to get off the worst of it in the cab, and he'd tried, blind, but clearly he hadn't done that well. Salt must have thought he looked like a melted clown.

He hadn't looked in a mirror for hours, he realized with a needle-jab of self-contempt. Must be a crisis, then.

Maybe—the thought struck treacherously from nowhere—maybe it actually wasn't such a good idea to hang around here anymore. Now everything had sunk in, surely Tom would be the last person Nick'd want to see.

Perhaps he should go home, he told himself with a little, shameful flip of hope.

"Tom?"

Tom's eyes jerked up to the doorway.

Nick stood silhouetted against the brightness of the hall. For a moment, Des Salt was a white ghost at his shoulder, before he turned and moved out of Tom's sight.

Nick's short dark-blond hair was still somehow in place, combed back off his forehead. He always carefully maintained a fine, golden stubble, which set off his firm chin and gentle features, and beneath his Versace suit, he had a tanned gym-honed body that could give a swimwear model a run for his money. He was seven years older than Tom, and very, very sexy with…something indefinable. Confidence, success, power, will, determination, protectiveness…any of them.

Tom had never imagined seeing him like this—haggard and dazed.

There was an awful silence, and Nick seemed to be waiting, as if he expected Tom to say something. The right thing. But now the moment had come, what could possibly fit?

I'm sorry? I'm sorry we drove your wife to suicide?

Tom felt his face twist, almost spasm, with distress, and he had to fight his expression back to neutrality. But Nick's eyes remained fixed on him as if he were the only beautiful thing in an ugly landscape.

Well, Tom told himself numbly, as he rose to his feet, at least he'd made the right choice in waiting.

"Seriously," Pez said, from behind his new-season Marc Jacob shades. "I still think I'm having some kind of lucid nightmare. It's actually yesterday morning, and I'm going to wake up and swear I'll never drink tequila again."

Tom gave a wan smile and took a sip of coffee.

They sat at a small two-person table on a quiet pavement, shaded by a white canvas canopy. Café Oto, their usual haunt for daytime meets in good weather, not that far from Pez's flat in now-trendy Dalston.

It had been Pez's discovery. Italian Vogue had once dubbed it "the coolest café in Britain" and that had been more than enough for him. But though Tom would have been just as happy at a Costa, he never said it out loud, because he knew these things should matter more to him, the way they did to Pez. As much as he tried, he'd never quite managed to get genuinely invested. In clothes. In trends. In image. He just managed a reasonable facsimile of caring.

Two nights before, in another life, Tom and Pez had had been on the tear together, and for Pez, tequila had definitely been involved. But Tom felt distantly as if those reckless memories belonged to someone else, as if he were watching the world through a window now, rather than living in it.

He'd spent the night in Nick's flat in Notting Hill, in Nick's bed—the two of them lying side by side like a couple of naked corpses on a slab, holding hands. Tom hadn't slept. And in the morning, as Nick left to begin to tackle arrangements for when Catriona's body would be released, Tom canceled his scheduled session with his personal trainer and texted Pez, desperate to meet.

"There's going to be a postmortem," Tom said, and that was actually one of the least traumatizing things he and Nick had talked about the night before. "It happens for unexpected and violent deaths."

Tom even managed to sound matter of fact.

But the truth was that, for all he tried, he couldn't convince himself of the intellectual case that it didn't matter to Catriona. She was an object now, an "it" kept on ice, waiting for the knife. It shouldn't matter that she would lose what was left of her precise feminine dignity, gutted like a beast on the mortuary table. But Tom felt, with preternatural sensitivity, the light, warm breeze on his skin, and he smelled the scent of the city and tasted bitter coffee on his tongue—and he felt greedily, guiltily alive.

"I still can't believe it," Pez repeated, filed-off South London accent nipping in around the edges. "I mean…" He sighed and trailed off as a thought visibly struck him, and pulled off his shades to peer into his capacious leather man-bag.

There was no denying that Pez was a striking guy. His dark hair was cut short at the sides, and ferociously styled and gelled on top, and his large olive-green eyes were discreetly mascaraed and lined. He had a neat, plush mouth; a small, wide nose and flawless winter-pale skin. His features, put together, were interesting rather than beautiful, but his looks had won him work with plenty of indie brands and magazines in his time. A quirky, editorial model's career was nearly always short though, and Pez had been far too smart to wait for the axe to fall, so he'd talked his way into booking and managing at Echo, and he was brilliant at it.

Pez had actually been the one to spot Tom, playing football shirtless in Hyde Park, the summer he was supposed to begin his postgrad. He'd taken Tom's very first polaroids: *Lower your chin. Look up. Don't smile.* Tom still wasn't sure why he'd gone along with it.

Pez had shown Catriona the test shots and called Tom to come in to the office to meet her the very next day. And Tom could remember in perfect detail his first sight of her: what she'd worn, what she'd said, and how she'd said it.

"A truly successful model is…an object of desire, Tom," she'd told him. "Do you understand how subtle a concept that is to project? You have to create someone that people can't help but want."

How impressed he'd been by her Hitchcock-blonde aloofness and stylized elegance, her bored cut-glass accent—all so different from the girls he knew from uni. How sparing she'd been with her flattery, and how much more any approval from her—relayed exclusively through Pez or Nick's sister Jena—had come to mean to him.

Pez on the other hand, had always been the opposite of sparing. He'd bullshitted relentlessly about Tom's potential and managed to persuade him, on spec, onto a plane to New York City and an open call for what turned into his first major jeans campaign.

Most male models started their careers broke and in debt to their agency, but Tom hadn't had the chance. He hadn't even had the chance to think it through. He'd signed to a big agency in New York, as well as Echo, he'd managed to catch and—importantly—hold, the interest of a slew of major brands, and he'd long since deferred his postgraduate place at University College London.

Genuine friendships were rare in their business, but Tom and Pez weren't just model and manager, using each other. They were the closest of friends, who guarded each other's secrets. Maybe it helped that they were both gay, and also had excellent sex together when either of them needed it, or wanted it. But whatever the reason, it worked. They loved each other, and they were both on the same page. None of the complications of romance, no would-be love affair.

"I know I fucking brought it," Pez muttered, still rifling through his bag, and Tom began to drift, so tired, he was ready to finally nod off right there.

His phone, as if it had read his mind, began to buzz and jump spitefully on the table in front of him.

Tom groaned, and when he saw the name on the display he was more than tempted to ignore the call. But something…a craving for normality perhaps…prompted him to pick it up.

"Hey, Dad." Tom thought he sounded pretty much as usual.

"Hi, Tom. Are you working?" His father's voice was warm and deep, unaccented like Tom's. Tom glanced up and caught Pez's eye.

Pez grimaced. And Tom found he couldn't bear to tell his father what had happened. Couldn't face the concern, the questions, the unspoken, *How could you?* The parallels that had just struck him forcibly, between his father and Catriona.

"No, I'm…with a friend. Are you up to anything? Any plans?" It was blind distraction without expectation, but his father surprised him.

"Well, actually…Bernie and Joan have invited me for dinner at their new place next weekend. An overnight stay. It's in Kent. Staplehurst. And you know what?" Tom's father said with bright defiance. "I think I'll go."

Tom suppressed a weary sigh. "That's great. And maybe you could ask Joan to invite a single lady friend too."

"Tom," his father said, with fond reproach. And he didn't need to go any further. They both knew Alistair Gray had no interest in saving himself, or in moving on.

It felt, as always to Tom, as if they were reciting lines from a bad play, and he couldn't miss any of his cues.

His father didn't miss his either. "I have some mail for your mum. Have you heard from her?"

Tom let his head fall back until he was looking up at the underside of the white linen umbrella, minutely spotted with dark mold.

"No, Dad," he said. "Not since she called from Nice. I told you, she said Richard wanted to try Monaco."

His father laughed shakily, trying his useless brave face. "I'd never have imagined your mum on a boat. She doesn't like the water much."

But she liked money, and glamour, and excitement and deception. As she'd proved over and over again.

His father sniffed quietly and Tom couldn't stand it. "I have to go, Dad, sorry. I'll ring you soon."

He listened to his father's startled goodbyes, then cut the call.

Pez gave him a "poor you" moue. He knew all about Tom's parents.

"*Anyway...*" Pez nudged Tom's hand hard with the side of a small box-shaped package he'd finally extracted from his bag. "Someone left this for you at Reception." The parcel had been wrapped neatly in classic brown paper, tastefully stained navy blue.

Tom eyed it with apathy. He got a lot of presents. A lot of samples.

Pez prompted, "Well?"

Tom shrugged one shoulder.

"Oh for fuck's sake! Give it here." With an irritated *humpf* Pez snatched up the package and tore off the paper. "If your fans send you stuff, the least you can do is take a look. I will *never* forget the box of cheese that French guy sent you after Fashion Week last year. Which you left in the office unopened till Jena had to break into it, because it smelled like a corpse." Tom flinched, but Pez was focused on the box that his deft fingers had pulled from the paper. Robin's-egg-blue embossed with black. "Oooh. Nice! Tiffany." He shoved the box over to Tom. "Open it then!"

Tom stared at it, repelled, seeing that same splash of Tiffany blue in Catriona's white and red bedroom. He blinked hard and forced himself to pick up the box and pull off the lid.

It revealed a broad, brown leather cuff, with a large sleek fastening in what looked like copper. Beautiful.

"That's the Paloma Picasso line," Pez breathed with reverence, because there wasn't a trend in the world he wasn't on top of. "The rose gold design. Tommy...that's two thousand quid! Who's it from?"

Pez scrabbled first through the wrapping paper, then reached for the box. Tom watched his urgency with no excitement of his own to offer in return.

"No card." Pez pulled back with a pout of disappointment. "Who pays that kind of money without trying for a shag?"

Tom rubbed the tips of his fingers across his brow. "No one does. It's a fake."

The metal of the bracelet glowed softly in Pez's hand as he held it close to his face and scrutinized it, like a gems dealer sizing up a dodgy diamond. "It looks real. The gold looks real. Hang on, there's an inscription!" He raised his eyebrows and handed it wordlessly to Tom.

There were small italicized letters engraved on the metal fastening: *I want you more.*

Tom rolled his eyes and shook his head as he dropped the bracelet back into its box. He just couldn't be bothered—not today—with blind adulation from people who imagined they knew him through photoshopped images and the odd, sanitized interview. From what his social-media manager posted for him online.

"I can't accept that. If it's real, it's too much. And that inscription…I don't want to encourage…whoever it is."

Pez gaped with exaggerated shock as he latched on to the one part of Tom's protest that seemed to matter. "Too much? *Darling!* You're a model!" He huffed an impatient sigh as Tom failed to react. "It's totally you! I mean you could have bought it for yourself," he coaxed. Tom thought his belief in his own subtlety was almost endearing. "Go on, Tommy. A piece like that's a little symbol of success."

Tom nodded because he couldn't be bothered arguing, and when Pez handed him the box, he took it. He'd put it in a drawer when he got home.

There was a short, waiting silence.

"So. Are you all right?" Pez asked, and at long last it seemed, they were going to talk about it properly. The very large elephant in the corner of the room.

"Me?" Tom scoffed, and perversely, his immediate urge was to deflect. "What about you? You worked with her every day for years."

Pez sighed again. "Tommy, come on. She liked me well enough. But we were just colleagues and…you know how she was. She could give Nuclear Wintour a run for her money."

But Tom could see that his eyes were slightly bloodshot, slightly swollen. Pez had cried for her, he just wouldn't admit it.

Tom never had paid much attention to the hot gossip in Echo. He was away so much, walking in shows in New York, Paris and Milan; doing castings and shoots around the world; having deliberately pointless, or deliberately useful, flings. Schmoozing with the photographers and casting directors and editors and designers whose goodwill helped smooth his path to the very top.

When he came home to London, he'd listened absently to Pez's tales of the weirdly intense marriage between the ice queen who'd overseen the beginning of his career, and the hot boss he'd seen in passing a few times. But it had meant nothing to him then.

Pez pushed his full, dark-pink lips into a tentative pout. "Seriously though, Tommy…"

"How d'you *think* I am?" Tom snapped. "How could I have been so fucking stupid? You *told* me. And I didn't listen."

Pez blinked, then he said loyally, "Well I might have succumbed myself, on the receiving end of that campaign, sweetie. Nick really meant business."

Tom's mouth twisted. "I didn't exactly fight him off, did I?"

"Well…" Pez seemed to be choosing his words carefully. "You held him off for a while. A decent interval."

"A decent interval? What's that, when someone walks out on his marriage on the off-chance you're going to want them back? I just…"

Pez looked down at his coffee cup. "You didn't know that when you agreed to go out with him. And no one knew she'd taken it this badly."

No. And Tom hadn't known she'd been self-harming either, until Nick had told him last night. Which had blown Tom's comfortable image of Catriona—of icy self-possession and glacial toughness—to smithereens. Because he'd just let himself…assume she was handling her dysfunctional marriage the way everyone around him now handled the end of their relationships. With indifference; perhaps a modicum of pique; occasional drama. He'd even believed the reason she'd taken to blanking him was annoyance that he'd been crass enough to start seeing her ex.

But Nick had kept his wife's secrets all the way, even from Tom, and Tom couldn't share them now.

He said, bitter and hard, another truth: "I was the moron who misjudged everything."

He'd thought at the beginning it would be a bit of fun—easy and mutually enjoyable. Scratch an itch, since he'd fancied Nick, in an idle sort of way. He'd honestly believed that Nick would be allergic to serious, given he'd just stepped away from a long marriage. And Tom had made it totally clear that he didn't want anything exclusive or heavy with anyone. He didn't care what Nick did, or with whom, while Nick, in turn, knew how his relationship with Pez worked, and about the other men Tom got together with when the mood, or the job, took him. Nick knew where Tom stood.

But then Nick had confessed, several months in, that he hadn't just been conveniently single; he'd left Catriona to begin wooing Tom. Which was the moment Tom should have run for the hills, as Pez had been urging him to do from the start.

Except. *Except*, that over the two months of Nick's campaign to get Tom to go out with him, and the subsequent months of their sexual relationship, Tom had slid into liking and caring for Nick. It was hard not to care for someone who listened to every word he said, who was fascinated by what he thought, and what he enjoyed, who didn't try to change him. Who focused all his considerable determination on making him happy.

But that was all the more reason to have ended it, before any more damage was done.

Instead, to Pez's relentless disgust, Tom had dithered, and—he had to face it—apart from a reluctance to lose the rare emotional connection he'd allowed himself with Nick, there had also been the very simple fact he'd dodged away from the confrontation and the complications of dumping his boss. Maybe he'd hoped Nick would get tired of the novelty and go back to Catriona. Stupid, fucking *cowardly* reasons.

The look on Pez's face was familiar—a fraught mixture of sympathy and frustration. "You can't let this distract you anymore, Tommy. You're in the Global Top Five now. You'll make the Top Three if you get the Armani fragrance campaign. You have to focus on your career. You know you have to be ruthless."

Tom looked away, the lump in his throat growing larger and more jagged by the word. Pez never had wavered from that hardnosed booker's bottom line.

"Tom!" Finally Pez's natural impatience burst free. "It's not your fault he left Catriona."

"If I hadn't gone out with him, or if I'd finished it…" Tom's face scrunched into open distress. "They could have made up. She must have hated me so much, Pez."

"We always blame the other woman, sweetie," Pez said with reflexive cynicism, but Tom could see that he was grasping for a strategy. Pez gave a dramatic sigh. "I should have your problems, though, you bitch—a hot, bisexual millionaire totally in love with me…"

Tom smiled humorlessly. "Don't give me that shit. You're even worse at this than I am." And Pez really was. Tom was the closest to a stable relationship he had.

But Pez's relentlessness was one of the attributes that made him so effective at his job. His slender hand pressed Tom's where it lay on the table, the whiteness of his skin tinged almost purple-blue in the cool morning light, against Tom's pale-gold tan.

"You can't let him get in any deeper, Tommy."

"Are you talking as my friend or my agent?" Tom asked harshly, enraged all at once by how simple Pez made it sound. "Catriona killed herself because he was going to divorce her. Because he wants to be with me, Pez. How much deeper can he get?"

There was a beat of stunned quiet, then Pez said, "*Divorce* her?"

"He told me last night." Tom struggled to calm the brutal tremble in his voice. "And he told *her* before he left for Manchester with Jena, and that night she... He said he didn't want me to doubt his commitment." Their eyes met and held in shared horror.

How could Nick have thought he wanted that? If he'd just *talked* to Tom first... But it had been Nick's marriage and Nick's choice. And then, Catriona's choice.

"Okay," Pez said, trying for calm. "But you didn't want him to do it, did you? No. And you can't pretend you feel anything like he feels."

Tom's face twisted involuntarily, emotions rushing in on him at once.

"Pez, leave it!" He sounded desperate. He felt desperate. The weight of inevitability was settling around him like a steel cloak.

Tom's phone, lying on the table beside his right hand, buzzed as if it were marking a time out. He bit his lower lip savagely as he glanced at the display, but he picked it up.

"Hi, Nick," he said. Pez, across the table, let his head fall back in melodramatic despair until he gazed hopelessly at the canopy above them. "How're things going?"

"Where are you?" Nick's voice sounded more urgent than it had since the last call Tom had taken from him.

"At Café Oto," Tom said. "With Pez."

He heard Nick expel a heavy breath. "Right." His voice was uneven. "Tell Pez to go into your Instagram account."

A solid ball of trepidation formed in the middle of Tom's chest. Prescience. His knee began to bounce spastically beneath the table, an old habit he could never quite break. It semaphored his nervousness and he hated that.

"What's wrong?" he demanded. No reply. Tom raised his eyes to meet Pez's unimpressed stare. He snapped, "Nick says you have to look at my Insta."

Pez gave a frowning scowl, but he picked up his own phone and began to tap.

"Tell me why!" Tom burst out.

Nick said quickly, "There's a woman. I don't know her, but she says she's one of Catriona's friends. She emailed me some mad fucking thing... She's saying you bullied Cat to death."

"What?" Tom breathed. He glanced up automatically to Pez to share his disbelief, only to find blank horror on Pez's face as he stared at his phone screen. "Pez?"

"Who the fuck is Jessica Mayhew?" Pez sounded shell-shocked.

Tom's Instagram account was run by Jeremy, Echo's on-the-ball social-media manager who, with Pez's and Tom's input, had crafted and curated a "Tom Gray" fans could latch on to, and obsess over. Given the size of a model's social-media following could increasingly impact chances of getting a top job, 547,000-odd followers on Tom's verified Instagram weren't to be sneezed at.

With obvious reluctance, Pez turned his phone round to allow Tom to see the screen.

At first all Tom registered was the newest photo on his account, posted by Jeremy on Friday. It came from a shoot Tom had done recently for Burberry in South Africa. Tom, pouting moodily into the distance, leaning against a dead tree in a barren landscape, chest bare, wearing an open shirt and long shorts, drenched with a golden filter. It was a lovely image, though it made Tom stand out more than the clothes he should have been selling. Which was probably why Jeremy had chosen it.

The caption from @realtomgray read: *Can't wait for you to see the rest of these. Africa's in my blood now.*

Jeremy's Tom Gray was sweet, enthusiastic, grateful, socially aware and, most importantly, inoffensive. As bland as warm milk.

There were thousands of comments as usual—admiring, gushing, lustful. It didn't take long to find the notable exception.

User jessicamayhew85: *You ugly, filthy fucking bastard. I'm telling the police. She was worth a billion of you.*

Tom's lungs emptied of air and wouldn't fill again.

"Tom?" Pez asked. His eyes looked huge and glassy, appalled.

"Tom?" Nick snapped in his ear. "Speak to me!"

Tom tore his eyes from the screen. He took a gasping breath. "I saw it. The police?"

Pez pulled back the phone. "I'll delete the comment." He began to type, tongue curled up at the side of his mouth in concentration. "But if she tweeted, we're fucked."

He didn't have to say any more. Tom might not be a household name, but half a million social-media followers meant attaching his face to a scandal would be delicious clickbait. If these accusations spread round the internet, Tom's career would be over.

"Tom." Nick sounded very insistent. Tom could hear traffic noise at the other end of the line. On his hands-free probably. "A guy I played squash with a few days ago… He's a criminal solicitor. One of the best. Jena just spoke to him."

Tom nodded, then he remembered Nick couldn't see him.

"Okay," he managed. His knee bounced rhythmically, banging the underside of the table as it jittered. He welcomed the flare of pain. His heart racketed in his chest, guts churning like the drum of a washing machine.

"Simon told her that if there's even a whiff of solid evidence, the police probably won't let a complaint go. They're paranoid about not taking stalking accusations seriously enough right now."

"Stalking?" Tom squawked. Pez's phone rang, but his horrified eyes didn't leave Tom.

"Harassment," Nick said quickly, as if that were better. A car horn blared over the phone line. "Fuck off!" Nick yelled, then took an audible calming breath. "He said, if the police take it up, we'll know that woman must have given them something beyond just…wild accusations. If that happens, he said they'll invite you for a chat—that's what they call it. It's a voluntary interview, so they don't have to arrest you to get you to the station."

"Arrest me?" Tom repeated, stunned. He could hear Pez barking abuse at someone on his phone in the background—probably Jeremy— but the words were incomprehensible. Everything around him seemed to be buzzing and glaring white and green, as if he were very, very drunk, about to be sick.

Nick went on anxiously. "He said to try to put them off for a day or two until you gather some defense. And you mustn't go without a lawyer under any circumstances, though the police may try to persuade you it'll be easier without one. He's going to put one of his best people on to it."

Pez interrupted suddenly. "Jeremy went through all your accounts, Tom. So far it's just Insta."

Tom made himself take a deep, deep gulp of air, as if he were about to launch himself underwater.

"What did the woman say?" He sounded detached even to himself. "In her email?"

Nick answered with obvious reluctance. "She said…that Cat told her you were deliberately driving her to despair."

A hand reached into Tom's chest, to squeeze his heart.

"That's insane," he whispered. "I would never…"

"I *know*," Nick said.

Tom tried to nod again, but it was as if he'd forgotten how.

Nick said, "This guy…the solicitor…said his firm regularly instructs private investigators for their clients, and he advised you to hire one."

"A private eye?" The image flashed into Tom's mind straight from the movies—seediness, squalor, desperation. "But the police'll find out it's not true."

He raised his eyes and met Pez's terrified, pitying stare.

"An investigator can find out whats really going on," Nick said. "Maybe if any of Cat's other friends are likely to back up this woman. The office gave Jena a name. A guy with…" A fumbled pause. "With SFN Investigations in Clerkenwell."

Clerkenwell. Not cheap, or seedy, or desperate. Wasn't that a good sign?

"I'll get Jena," Nick continued urgently. "We'll meet you at your flat, okay? Tell Pez to come. We need to work out how we handle this."

Tom lowered the phone to the table after Nick rang off.

"He wants us to meet him at my flat." Tom's voice sounded thick, dazed. Maybe he was finally in shock.

Pez blinked several times, like a worried bird. "Yeah that's…that's probably best in case she's gone to the press. We don't want any photos."

The irony should have made Tom smile.

3

Tom's flat was in fashionable Shoreditch, on Charlotte Road, just off the hugely desirable Old Street.

Tom had used the proceeds of his first big ad campaign for the deposit, as a symbol of his commitment to his wildly exciting and successful new life, and he'd never regretted it. The flat was his bolthole, his refuge, and he loved it immoderately.

"You have to think about yourself," Pez was saying for the hundredth time as Tom dropped his keys in a dish on the hallway table. "Fuck… Imagine Echo without Catriona. Anyway it's past time we both moved to another agency. There's loyalty and there's stupidity." Pez slammed the door behind him. "You can't let Nick's clusterfuck of a life drag you down with him. Awwww, hello sweetie!" With comical speed, Pez's agitated glower melted to adoration as Tom's cat began to writhe around his legs. "Did you miss Daddy? Did you?"

Tom snorted. "More like a mad old uncle," He trudged along the hall toward his bedroom at the end of the whitewashed entrance hallway.

"I'm just going to change," he called. "Help yourself to tea or vodka or something."

He didn't wait for Pez's reply, but as he began to pull the bedroom door closed, the cat slid in at his heels, regarding Tom with imperial disdain.

"Sorry," Tom murmured, as he always did when he got home after a significant absence. John may have become used to having different people look after him, and was even accustomed to being moved from place to place by cat carrier, but he was never pleased when Tom spent nights away.

John was Tom's sole long-term responsibility, apart from the often surreal demands of his career. In fact sometimes it felt as if his cat and his father were Tom's only remaining investments in real life, where real things lived.

He'd found John in an alleyway skip, near Echo's offices, a couple of years before. He'd been standing, checking his phone, trying to convince himself that the guilt and unhappiness he'd been feeling then were transient. The traffic roar had lulled for just a few seconds, and for those seconds, he'd been in exactly the right position to hear a feeble, squeaking cry coming from behind him.

Something had driven him to sacrifice his Vivienne Westwood sample trousers to clamber into the skip and scrabble through the stinking, decaying rubbish until he'd found a knotted black plastic bag, and inside, a days-old kitten, the last survivor in a ball of tiny tabby corpses.

The kitten had been small enough to rest in the palm of his hand.

Tom's career was just beginning to accelerate at a terrifying rate, which meant being away from home for long periods of time. His work encouraged—demanded—self-obsession and detachment from reality. Keeping the kitten would be a poor choice.

But...he'd just done something cowardly he couldn't let himself think about, and he'd needed something he could cope with loving, to prove to himself he had the capacity to care.

So when Tom wasn't there, John stayed with the couple next door, April and Sonja Gardiner who had a key to come and go, or take John to theirs. Pez stepped in when they couldn't.

Tom leaned down to scratch under John's white chin, then he slowly unbuttoned and pulled off the chocolate suede shirt he'd first donned the morning before. As it dropped to the floor, he wondered if he could ever bear to look at it again without associating it with this disaster. Then he heeled off his boots and slid off his jeans before donning a clinging pair of sweatpants from his chest of drawers.

His heart was beating too fast. He took a deep breath, and then another, trying to calm himself, but dread skittered in his veins, as it had, on and off, since he'd heard about Catriona's death. Worse now.

He looked around at the white and brick walls of his bedroom. His bed, covered with a fluffy white quilt. The big metal-framed, multipaned window. Like a hermit needed his cell, Tom needed this room, the room in which he could be entirely himself. He'd never brought a lover in here. No one got in here, other than Tom and John.

Tom unfastened his watch and walked over to his bedside table to put it down beside the ragged book that lay on top of it—dog-eared and losing pages.

Inorganic Chemistry 5th Edition: Weller, Overton, Rourke and Armstrong

No need for pills. A few pages of that every night cleared Tom's head of bullshit and helped him sleep. It went everywhere with him.

There would be a new edition by now, he thought for the thousandth time. He should get one.

He sighed and turned to the door, ready to go back out to Pez, but as he did, his eye caught his reflection in the full-length mirror hanging on the wall.

He scowled and automatically began to take himself apart, the way clients did right in front of him. Like grading the constituent components of a machine.

His nose was long, and very slightly bent from one too many collisions playing football. His eyes were dark lashed and a light, intense blue under straight dark brows; his skin, smooth and lightly tanned. His upper lip was strongly defined, his mouth full and pale pink, and so sculpted he sometimes seemed to be pouting when he didn't smile. And he didn't smile much anymore, because not many people wanted him to.

His cheekbones were regulation high, but with his strong, narrow jawline his face shape verged more toward oval than male-model-square. Thick, slightly wavy, ash-streaked blond hair brushed the tops of his shoulders. Surfer dude, though he'd never surfed in his life.

Just before he'd hit eighteen, in a surprise late spurt, he'd shot up to an inch and a half over six feet, just above the necessary height for a male model. He had long, muscular legs, a gym-honed chest and shoulders, a narrow waist, smooth well-muscled abdomen and arms, a footballer's lush, curved backside, and a big cock and balls to bulge out the underpants he had to sell.

Check.

When casting directors said they wanted a model to have character though, Tom had come to realize that what they really meant was the absence of it; an expression of near blankness—absent, brooding, almost bewildered. One casting guy told him it was all about the expression he managed to create in his eyes. Except he thought the guy was full of shit.

Nick had said once, hurt, lashing out when Tom had pulled away, that Tom excelled at blankness.

Tom stared at himself a moment longer, gaze almost loathing in the mirror. Then he scooped up John, burying his face for a moment in luxuriant tabby fur, grabbed an old T-shirt and his phone, and strode bare-chested to the living room, where Pez had already made himself at home on Tom's big, comfortable sofa.

The room's decor echoed Tom's bedroom—whitewashed walls and ceiling, exposed brick, huge metal windows, a floor of old wooden parquet. The only living room furniture, apart from the sofa and three chairs, was a big metal-and-wood unit standing against one wall, housing a large flat-screen TV and books. Most of the color in the room came from a bright multihued rug and a huge canvas on one wall.

Tom strode to the sofa and deposited John on Pez's lap, but he didn't sit himself. At any minute he was going to start to pace.

"I should be scything through the D&G sale right now," Pez declared dramatically. Tom could see how hard he was trying to mimic normality. "Thirty per cent *off*, Tommy!" But that cardboard outrage dissolved almost at once into a weak smile. Pez raised his hand and brushed a caress over Tom's taut, waxed skin. "But I will say, your six-pack helps soften the blow."

Tom managed a fair try at a cocky grin in return. His ringtone broke the moment.

He stared at the phone in his hand as if it had done something treacherous. The display showed a withheld number. Tom had to force himself to accept the call.

"Mr. Gray?" The Ballymena burr, ending on an up-tone, was totally, horribly familiar.

Tom's heart began to pound in earnest. His eyes fixed on the pure, white wall across from him. "Yes."

"Mr. Gray," the voice repeated. "This is Detective Sergeant Salt from Southwark and Peckham MIT."

Yes, I fucking know.

Instead, "How can I help you, Detective Sergeant?"

Out of the corner of his eye, Tom saw Pez's hand shoot up to his mouth.

"Well, sir," Salt said cordially. "DCI Lawson was wondering if you could come in for a chat."

It was really happening then.

"A chat." Tom thought his voice probably sounded too casual—he should have tried for surprise. But he was amazed that he managed to hold his tone steady at all. "Will I need a lawyer for this...chat?"

"Well, it'll probably be over sooner without one, sir." Salt sounded amiable, but Tom imagined he could hear strain in his voice. That this was a lie he'd repeated often, but perhaps never before to someone he'd known. To someone who'd once been a friend. "DCI Lawson'd just like a wee word about Mrs. Haining."

Tom swallowed hard. "Well. I suppose I can manage on Wednesday morning."

"But that's three days away," Salt protested.

"Two and a half," Tom countered. "I'm very busy. Things I can't postpone, I'm afraid. You did say it's just a chat. Nothing important?"

He could almost hear the sound of Salt's internal struggle on the other end of the line.

"Right, sir. We'll expect you *and your solicitor* at the station on Wednesday morning then."

It took Tom a second or two to understand the weight of that last sentence. Salt's unsubtle emphasis. That, with colleagues presumably listening on his end, Salt, despite old bitterness, thought Tom was in enough trouble to give that warning: *Bring a lawyer.*

"Thank you," Tom managed, before Salt wordlessly rang off.

Tom clasped the back of his neck with his free hand, blind eyes still fixed ahead, and took a deep breath before turning back to the room.

"Oh, Tommy," Pez muttered, as he rose to his feet, ready to comfort him.

The doorbell rang.

Pez's eyes shot to his, and Tom thought they held an oddly raw expression. It sat strangely on a man who viewed authentic emotion as uncool. Tom didn't like it.

Pez sank slowly back into his seat. "Enter the bereaved husband." And the acid in his tone said everything he no longer bothered to hide about his feelings for Nick.

The bell sounded again as Tom was reaching to open the front door.

Nick stood outside wearing a beautifully cut navy suit, the image of professionalism and control, but Tom could see exhaustion behind the façade. Still, Nick's gaze dropped, as if magnetized, to Tom's bare upper body.

"Come in," Tom said dryly. Perhaps he even felt gratified that Nick's helpless attraction to him never seemed to diminish.

Nick's eyes shot up to his and he flushed slightly, but he moved to pull Tom into a confident hug, the fine wool of his suit prickling Tom's bare skin. Nick smelled of his customary Dior aftershave, heavy and spicy.

"I'm sorry," he murmured. And Tom could hear what he didn't say: *This is all my fault.*

Tom had no patience for it. But he squeezed Nick tight for a second anyway, in reassurance, before easing away.

"Hey, Tommy." Jena, Nick's sister, stood just behind Nick, smiling her gentle, wicked smile.

The navy sleeveless dress she wore flattered her tall, strong, body, and her chin-length, feathery, layered hair, dyed a perennial pale pink, was impeccably fluffy. She had large, dark blue eyes—Nick's eyes—expertly made up, and Tom noted absently that her short nails were painted fuschia.

Pez still lounged on the sofa when they re-entered the sitting room, but his attention was pointedly fixed on the phone in his hand, John lying huffily beside him. Jena made straight for him as she always did, cuddling down beside him—an enduring closeness which puzzled Tom, given Pez's attitude to Nick. But he couldn't deny the friendship was there, and Jena was Tom's friend too, through Pez. They made quite a threesome when they went out on the town.

"Pez," Nick greeted, voice neutral.

"Nick," Pez replied, all stagey disinterest.

And suddenly Tom couldn't be arsed with any of it.

"The police called." His voice was harsh. "They want a chat."

Three identical expressions of apprehension slammed down simultaneously which might have seemed funny to Tom in other circumstances.

But he just wanted *do* something. *Save* himself. Stop feeling like an animal waiting passively for slaughter.

He drew a deep bracing breath through his nose, and let it out again. *Calm. Down.*

"I've held them off till Wednesday," he told Jena. "So that gives two days for your shit-hot private investigator from Clerkenwell to do his stuff."

Jena opened her mouth, closed it again, and her anxiety slid into something else.

"Um…" She bit her lower lip hard. Then she said miserably, "Shit."

Tom's stomach clenched. How the fuck could there be more bad news? "*What*?"

"The solicitor says he really is the best. But." Jena's face twisted into an exaggerated grimace of apology. "The investigator's name's William Foster, Tommy."

Tom stared at her with disbelief.

"Fuck!" Pez exploded beside her. "You have to be fucking *joking*!"

There was a short, shocked pause. Jena put a hand on Pez's arm.

"Foster's a very common name," Tom said numbly. But his heart was galloping again at the simple mention of it, like an exhausted horse trying to keep up. He could feel Nick's curious gaze, sharp on his profile.

Jena let out a heavy breath, all too obviously regretful. "They said he's an ex-policeman."

Pez made another explosive sound of disgust.

"For fuck's sake, Pez," Nick snapped. "What's the big deal?" And Tom thought—Jena really had kept his secrets, even from her brother.

Pez smiled at Nick with poisonous sweetness. "He's Tommy's ex." Then he glared at Tom. "And since when is Captain America a private eye?"

Tom shook his head, dazed, bewildered. Just one more shock—that Will had apparently left the Met, though he'd lived for his job, and been outstandingly good at it.

In Tom's peripheral vision, Pez flopped back in the sofa. "Don't you have enough on your plate, Tommy?" he spat. "Without bringing *him* back from the dead?"

Nick eyed Pez with a mixture of impatience and astonishment, before turning to Tom.

"What *happened* with this guy?"

Tom said, "It just didn't work out." The cliché felt weaker than a cliché had a right to be. "Okay, I dumped him."

"He *is* the best, Tommy," Jena repeated sadly. "The solicitor's office was categoric about it but..."

"He might not agree to do it," Tom said. And could he really blame him? He hated the thrum of tension in his gut.

"Yeah," Jena grimaced again. "Apparently he did say no..."

The dropping sensation in Tom's chest felt like horribly like panic, like hope dashed, and he realized that his old conviction had surged back from its deep, deep grave, that Will Foster could sort out anything. That there were far more important things than a messy failed affair from long ago.

He could almost laugh at the irony. Just the day before, he'd been begging the universe not to inflict Will on him again.

"*But*," Jena paused as if she was about to deliver still more diffi-cult news. "The office said your new solicitor strong-armed him into it, somehow. He's apparently a pretty forceful guy. So I went ahead and arranged a meeting. For tomorrow morning. With Will Foster, I mean. Eleven thirty at Greens." She paused and almost cringed, before rushing on, "I can easily cancel Tommy. It's your choice."

But it was no choice really. "No," he said. "Don't cancel."

Nick's expression remained carefully neutral. Probably because Tom's prickliness had taught him the hard lesson that his take-charge tendencies weren't welcome.

Pez, on the other hand, looked more openly furious than Tom could remember.

"You're making a mistake," he said, and his certainty was terrifying.

4

Tom tapped his agitated foot against the painted metal railings that separated the premises of Greens Club from the pavement of Soho's Dean Street, and looked restlessly to his left, down the long length of the street.

Greens operated from an intentionally unobtrusive Georgian town-house, in an extended Georgian terrace that stretched along Tom's side of the road. There was no obvious sign, and the only clue to the club's identity was the dark green color of the render that fronted the ground floor, below red and brown brick.

It was easy to walk past it, as Tom had done himself repeatedly on his first visit there as Nick's guest, when they'd started seeing each other. That day felt like years ago now, he thought with a flash of surprised insight, not months, as if Nick had been part of his life for a long time.

He leaned back, one knee bent, the sole of his boot flat against the railing, trying to ignore the nauseating smell of burned oil and fried food emanating from the brasserie along the road. He'd insisted he should be the one to wait outside for Will, though he didn't really know why. He supposed...to avoid an audience while he got the worst over with.

It was fucking ridiculous to feel this grinding nervousness though, close to fear.

It had been more than two years, and it wasn't as if they'd been mar-ried. It was ancient history, thank God. And yet the tight knot in Tom's stomach seemed to be growing. Squirming.

The one-way street was relatively narrow and tall buildings flanked it on both sides, so even though Tom could see blue, blue sky up above, everything on the ground all along the road sat in shade.

Dean Street was a media hub, buzzing, usually, with activity—a combination of restaurants, clubs and media offices, for advertising, film and video. But even though it was a Monday morning, unusually, there weren't many people about, so Tom immediately spotted two men—one blond, one dark—emerging from a car parked about a hundred yards away.

They stood closely together for a minute or two, talking, then the blond—handsome, public-school-polished, slightly shorter—leaned up to kiss the other man on the mouth. It was a lover's kiss, clear even from that distance. The blond pulled back, grinning, and walked off, leaving the other man to turn and set off along the pavement toward Greens.

Tom looked sharply away. He found he had to force himself to stay still, in his languid pose, by focusing on his boot. Brown suede, Saint Laurent, new season, straps and buckles.

Hair hiding his down-turned face; heart hammering in a chest as tight as if it were gripped in a vice. Waiting, until he finally felt a solid presence beside him.

It took him a second to look up. He inhaled sharply.

He'd so easily made Will Foster a weak memory of a terrible mistake, escaped. A guilt he'd much rather dodge away from, than wallow in. So he'd managed to forget the full power of Will's attractiveness, and his own old resentment of it. But Will hadn't really changed.

He wore a narrow-cut, no-nonsense, light gray suit, a white shirt and a black tie—to Tom's fashion-immersed eye, all obviously off-the-peg and inexpensive. Just like his no-nonsense haircut.

But the snowy fabric of the shirt set off Will's pale olive skin and big, light-hazel eyes, made still more beautiful by extravagant black lashes and thick, dark, winged brows. The cut of the cheap suit emphasized his broad shoulders and narrow waist. And that basic side-street haircut—short around the sides and back, lengthier than it had been on top—showed off his long, strong neck and impeccable bone structure; his wide lush mouth, his strong angular jaw.

He even smelled the same—the Tom Ford aftershave which Tom could no longer tolerate.

Will's expressionless gaze assessed Tom in turn, and Tom couldn't help a sharp jab of insecurity about the subtle changes Will might see, though Will used to find him beautiful too.

Tom had buffed up his slim frame quite a bit in the past couple of years, though Will was still naturally broader than him. And he was aware he probably looked even…glossier. Waxed and highlighted and tanned and plucked. But he'd chosen his outfit carefully, for non-provocative effect. Worn blue Levis, a loose band T-shirt. Not too scruffy—not quite, *I don't give a fuck what you think anymore.* Not too sexy—no *look what you lost.*

But maybe there had been no need to worry. Will had another lover now. Maybe he was as relieved as Tom to be free of their old mutual obsession.

Maybe, this could work.

"Hi," Tom said at last. "Will." He straightened up. They were exactly the same height.

There was an awkward pause as their gazes locked and held, as if the contact had startled them both. Tom had forgotten that Will's eyes in daylight became some pale shade between green and gold and amber. He'd never seen it on anyone else.

Will raised a cool eyebrow.

Well? His expression said. *What are you waiting for?*

Maybe Tom had been the only one startled. He bristled, and turned to lead the way down the stone steps behind the railing, to Greens' entrance, but he felt oddly deflated.

That was it? The confrontation he'd been so desperate to avoid? No drama. No rage, or accusation, or reproach. No bloody battle. Just—two near strangers meeting. Total anticlimax.

It wasn't until they were at the reception desk, and a man walked by them, dressed in an eccentric tweed suit with plus fours, carrying a beagle, that it struck Tom that he really should have paid more attention to the choice of venue.

Would Will think it was a deliberate *fuck you*? Because there was no way round it, a private-members club like Greens epitomized all Will had once mocked and felt threatened by in Tom's world—elitism, signaled eccentricity, cloaked pretension—all underpinned by casual, essential wealth.

Greens and the more famous Groucho, and Soho House just along the road, were all descendants of the old-style exclusive gentlemen's clubs that used to rule establishment London. But now they were patronized by a new establishment—media executives and talent, successful writers and successful artists of all stripes—to eat, network and do business.

Tom was regularly signed in as Nick's guest at Greens when he was in London, yet—something held him back from seeking membership himself, and it wasn't the steep fees. Maybe it was embarrassment at taking that final self-conscious step into the full embrace of London's media elite. Becoming one of them.

He led the way determinedly up a narrow dark wooden staircase.

Halfway up, they met, first, a respectful black-tied young waiter, then, directly behind him, a slender elderly man carrying a laptop case, sporting a silver man-bun and a goatee. He wore green cargo shorts and a pink, floaty, half-open floral shirt to show off a huge blue butterfly tattoo on his gray-haired chest. He stared at Tom and Will as they sidled past him, as if he couldn't believe his admiring eyes.

Behind him came a small, unsmiling woman in her forties, wearing no makeup, but sporting yoga pants, a nose ring and a piece of bright cloth woven through auburn curly hair. And behind her, in startling contrast, an extraordinarily glamorous tiny-framed Chinese girl teetered on vertiginous heels, with bright-red lipstick, long raven-gloss hair and a very tight red dress, a huge iPad cradled in the crook of her elbow like a clipboard.

As they edged past them, Tom was very sure that Will would be judging all of it—the club, the money, the media people—from his position as "normal". And Tom was furious with himself for feeling hot, defensive embarrassment on their behalf.

One thing though: Will loved old buildings and architecture, and this one had been carefully refurbished and restored to operate pretty much as it had been in the 1700s. Its rooms perched on several narrow floors, all the walls wood-paneled and painted in dark, flat Georgian colors. There were buttoned leather sofas, worn wooden floors, Georgian furniture, and the odd patron's dog.

Tom led Will into a small, cozy room where Nick, Pez and Jena sat waiting at a wooden table by a large multipaned window. They were the room's only occupants. The wainscoting was painted a rich, dark red, and in the veined marble fireplace a modest fire flickered, because even on a sweet July morning, these shadowed rooms would feel chilly without it. Coffee, and a plate of delicate biscuits, sat on the table, beside a small pile of papers.

With a certain inevitability, Tom watched Nick react as he took in Will, his eyes darting to Tom with quick reproach, as if he couldn't quite believe Tom had never explained that Will was this.

Pez simply glowered. Tom was pretty sure he'd hoped Will had run to fat. Started losing his hair perhaps. Grown an ankle-length beard.

But it was Jena who surprised Tom. She'd never met Will through Tom's relationship with him, though she'd been party to the messy aftermath. But Tom knew too well how women tended to react to Will, possibly because Will very much fancied them back. Jena regarded him, though, as if Will were ordinary.

Then again she did work with models.

So did Tom.

Maybe, Tom thought uncomfortably, his own continuing conscious-ness of Will's beauty wasn't necessarily objective.

Tom said quickly, "Will, this is Dominic Haining, co-owner of Echo Models. And Jena Haining, his sister and Echo's office manager." He re-alized with sudden self-consciousness, that it was the first full sentence he'd spoken to Will for two years. They all shook hands. "And you may remember Pez Brownley, my booker."

From when you hated each other's guts?

Pez's lip curled. Will nodded to him and took the remaining chair beside Nick, as Tom slid in behind the table onto a small buttoned-leather banquette, beside Jena.

Further up the banquette, Pez picked up his cup and took a very pointed biscuit.

Will pulled a small black notebook from his inside jacket pocket and clicked open his pen as he looked at Tom with exactly the same profes-sional detachment as he'd shown to Nick. As if they'd just met.

"I understand you're facing accusations of serious harassment." Will's voice was as deep and whisky smooth as ever, and to his own cha-grin, Tom blushed.

"Nick's wife...ex-wife..." Tom began. *Get a grip.* "One of the co-owners of my agency...Catriona Haining. She killed herself, on Fri-day. Her friend is claiming I persecuted her."

Will's mouth pushed out into a considering pout. "There was ani-mosity between you and Mrs. Haining?"

Fuck...how was all of this going to sound to a man Tom had dumped cold for getting too serious?

He threw Nick a sideways glance of appeal. "I've been seeing Nick."

Will's stony expression gave nothing. "So you've been having an af-fair with Mr. Haining. How long did Mrs. Haining know about it?"

"It wasn't..." Tom protested. Then he scowled. It didn't matter what Will thought. "Almost five months," he said defiantly. It was his longest re-lationship by some distance, other than Will. Will had lasted almost seven.

Nick cleared his throat. "Perhaps I can give you a bit of background."

Will looked at him and began to write in his notebook.

"I left Cat eight months ago," Nick said. "We'd been married for nine years. She had long periods of...of depression." He sighed, and seemed to brace himself. "She was a very beautiful woman but she saw herself as...ugly. She self-harmed. She took medication, but...she never really got better. It was…very difficult to live with. Impossible, in the end. No one else knew, except her doctor, and Jena."

"So, you left her because of her mental illness," Will said, still writing.

It sounded so much worse put like that, Tom thought uneasily. Jena shifted in her seat.

"I left her because I fell in love with Tom," Nick corrected, with quiet dignity.

Will glanced up, and somehow Tom found himself, as if by accident, meeting his gaze again. They both looked away at once, but Tom thought he might, for a second, have seen a flare of reluctant emotion in Will's eyes. And he had a horrible suspicion that it could have been resentment.

Despite that pretty, blond boyfriend.

Tom's heart sank. He didn't need Will to be friendly, or to like him, but he did need him to be over their past. To be professional, and do his utmost to help, not nurse grudges.

"I hadn't approached Tom, when I left Catriona," Nick went on. "He had no idea how I felt about him I just…couldn't stay with her anymore. She took it badly."

"How badly?" Will asked.

"*Very* badly," Jena put in flatly. She set down her coffee cup, with a clumsy clatter, onto its saucer. "Cat lived for Nick. She put on a fabulous show at the office, but the moment he left her, she started to sink deeper."

Tom looked at her regretful, determined profile, and he wanted to put his head in his hands. How the fuck had he missed it?

Will nodded thoughtfully at his notebook, then he asked Nick, "Did you have any extramarital affairs before Mr. Gray?"

Nick gave a startled frown. "Well. Just…flirtations. Nothing real, or serious. I wasn't unfaithful. But sometimes the pressure of being in that house…"

"Did your wife find out?"

Nick's mouth twisted. "Yes. Usually."

"How did she find out?"

Nick had all but waved his *flirtations* under Catriona's nose. At least, that's what Pez used to say to Tom, back when Nick and Catriona's marriage had been an idle source of office entertainment. But Pez had always been closer to Catriona than Nick, and he did relentlessly see the worst in people.

"She broke in to his emails." Jena's voice was harsh with old secrets. Tom shot a startled gaze back to her. She looked very pale. "She hacked into his phone, God knows how. She followed him all the time."

"You didn't tell me any of that!" Tom protested to Nick. So much for Pez's malicious gossip.

But Nick looked almost as shocked as Tom felt, as if he hadn't expected Jena to just blurt it all out. "I was…I didn't want to badmouth her," he said. "I was trying to keep things civil."

Pez snorted and picked up another biscuit.

"I was their joint PA," Jena continued doggedly. "I saw…a lot. I didn't even tell Nick all of it. Cat and I used to be very close, even for a while after Nick left her. I felt loyalty…to both of them. But once he started seeing Tom, she just…stopped confiding in me. Maybe, because she knew Tom was my friend too. But she never said a single word to me *or* Nick about Tom harassing her."

Will's eyes had narrowed on Jena as she spoke, as if he were ticking off her qualities from some mental checklist. But he didn't ask her anything else.

He focused instead on Nick. "So. Your wife was depressed. She had a history of self-harm. She was obsessed by you and suspicious of your fidelity." There was no judgment in his tone. It was a dispassionate listing of unfortunate facts. "Then you moved out and began a relationship with Mr. Gray. Was there anything else that might…?"

"I told her I wanted a divorce," Nick blurted. "The day before she killed herself."

There was a short, hard silence. Jena put a comforting hand over Nick's on the table as Will wrote that down too. Inwardly, Tom squirmed with shamed embarrassment, and suppressed it savagely.

Will's expression though, didn't alter from that frowning thoughtfulness. "I understand you found her body?" he asked Nick.

"She wanted me to." Nick swallowed audibly. "She called me, when Jena and I were on our way to Manchester on Friday afternoon, for a business dinner. She asked me to go to the house when I got back the next day because she had something to show me." He cleared his throat. "So when we got back to town, I dropped Jena at her place and went to Clapham about two. And…she was there."

Tom dropped his eyes to the ancient scarred surface of the table. Fixed on it.

Catriona had known what she was going to do that evening then, when she'd passed Tom in the corridor at Echo the day before the shoot —when she'd ignored him for the very last time.

"Did the police give you an estimated time of death?" Will asked.

"They told me…sometime late on Friday evening," Nick said shortly. "She left me a note and…I think she took pills, and…she cut her wrists. She also um…" He pressed his fingers hard against his mouth. "She sliced off her ear."

"Do you have any theories on that?" Will's tone was neutral, as if Nick had merely mentioned something mildly curious. "Why an ear?"

Nick shook his head and closed his eyes. "I have no idea."

Tom said blankly, "I didn't know she left a note."

It seemed to take Nick a few seconds to understand. "Shit." He reached across the table to grab Tom's hand, tight and guilty. "I'm so sorry, baby. The police told me yesterday they found it on her laptop. I was so caught up in this thing with you, I forgot to mention it."

It was understandable, wasn't it? Nick had been preoccupied saving Tom's hide, not to mention trying to come to terms with what Catriona had done to herself. But it was Tom's neck on the line, and he was being blindsided with information that Nick and Jena hadn't seen fit to share with him. Catriona stalking Nick. Catriona's farewell note.

Tom couldn't seem to ease the grind of panicked anger in his head, and somehow it felt worse that it had happened in front of Will.

Nick squeezed his hand tighter his dark blue eyes frowning, worried.

"Can you tell me what the note said?" Will asked.

"Oh. Um…yes, the police emailed it to me." Nick fumbled a sheet of paper from the top of the pile on the table with his free hand, and passed it over. When Will had studied it, he slid it across the table to Tom without being asked, and without looking at him.

Tom freed his hand from under Nick's to pick it up.

It was an unsent email, from Catriona's account, addressed to Nick.

Snap! And as you see my darling, I did, finally, snap. I loved nothing but you. Meet you on the other side. Cat X

Tom's heart was a boulder in his chest.

I loved nothing but you.

"Is there a significance to the word 'snap'?" Will asked. "Mr. Haining?"

"No," Nick said, eyes fixed on Tom, who gazed miserably back. "Maybe it's a play on words."

"What do you know about the individual who's making the accusations against Mr. Gray?" A short silence. "Mr. Haining?" Will's voice sounded sharp.

Nick startled, broke his mesmerized communion with Tom, and looked at Will, almost confused. Then he came back to himself.

"I don't know anything about her. But this is what she sent me." He fished out another piece of paper and handed it to Will. "I don't know what she's told the police."

It occurred to Tom only as he watched Will expressionlessly reading the email, that he was just a spectator at the meeting. That this was all about Nick's life. Nick and Catriona.

He couldn't begin to explain to himself why he hadn't yet asked to read that email.

How passive had he become?

"Can I see that, please?" he asked loudly.

Will glanced up and handed the paper to him, and Tom wondered if he'd registered how much Tom didn't know.

He focused on the email.

It stank of loathing. Outrage. Claims from Jessica Mayhew, one of Catriona's gym friends, that Catriona had given her for safekeeping, examples of offensive and threatening letters and emails, and photographs of objects she knew were from Tom.

As he read, Tom's heartbeat skittered faster—blind fear of something inexplicably real. Because, while he didn't understand why it was happening, he also couldn't believe a woman he'd never met would make accusations like that, unless she thought she could back them up.

Maybe that was why Nick had tried to protect him from the details until now.

"I did something this morning," Jena blurted. All eyes turned to her. "I phoned Cat's best friend. Lily. Lily Adderton. I wanted to ask if she'd speak to you, but she refused point blank. I thought she might know Jessica if anyone did. Lily and Cat were on the same fashion-marketing course at uni, and Cat's godmother to her kids." Jena stopped. Tom thought she looked as if she were bracing herself to go on.

"Ms. Haining?" Will prompted.

"She said doesn't know her...Jessica. But..." She glanced at Tom, stricken. "She said that Cat told *her* that stuff too. That Tom manipulated Nick into leaving her. That he sent her emails, taunting her. Telling her Nick was going to divorce her and demanding she leave Echo."

Tom hands had begun to shake. He shoved them between his thighs.

"Anything else?" Will asked, policeman-calm.

"She said...Cat told her that Tom put things through her letterbox. A rat. Dog shit. That he'd strut round the agency, as if he owned it." Jena sighed. "As if she'd already gone."

"*No!*" Tom pulled his shaking hands up on to the table.

"She said..." Jena looked at Tom, pleading. "That Cat showed her proof."

There was a long, long beat of charged silence. Tom felt utterly lost, as if the whole world had changed when he wasn't looking.

Will said casually to his notebook, "Actually that's all circumstantial and hearsay, unless the police can trace an IP address for the emails back to a specific client. Or find DNA evidence on any of the alleged letters or objects."

Tom's gaze shot to Will's bent dark head, clinging to every word like a float in a drowning pool, until Will raised his eyes to meet his. His expression seemed subtly softer to Tom. Pity.

"Given the fact two of her friends are claiming Mrs. Haining gave them proof of these allegations," Will said to him, "we should assume that evidence has been submitted to the police. If they do charge you, it'll probably be under the Protection From Harassment Act 1997."

Tom's stomach was icy cold, fear surging like floodwater through an open door.

It wasn't going to go away. The police might charge him. "Des let me put the interview off for a couple of days," he told Will desperately. "That's all the time we have to clear my name."

"Des?" Will sounded startled. "Des Salt? He's with Southwark and Peckham MIT, isn't he? *They're* the unit pursuing this?"

"Yes." Tom ran a shaky hand back through his hair. "They were called to Catriona's house. There was a lot of blood."

Will's narrowed eyes glowed amber in the dim light of the room, like a tiger's eyes fixed on Tom, alert with intelligence.

"Hmmm." It was the sound Tom remembered Will used to make when he was puzzling something out, even which angle to cut a piece of wood. He turned to Nick. "The obvious question, Mr. Haining," Will said. "If your wife told her friends that Mr. Gray was harassing her, why didn't she tell you? Or your sister?"

It *was* obvious. Why hadn't it occurred to Tom to ask it?

Nick shifted in his seat. "I suppose…I suppose she…well she probably knew I wouldn't believe her. And neither would Jena." He looked at Tom, then back to Will. "Please understand. She made things up sometimes when she was upset. And she was very upset when I left. For example… when I first told her how I felt about Tom…she…ah…she claimed she knew he was HIV positive."

"*What?*" Pez screeched.

Nick winced and said quickly, "She was just…desperate." Tom found he couldn't even muster outrage.

"You said she knew you wouldn't have believed her." Will again. "Do you believe her now?"

Nick looked agonized. "I don't *know*. There must be evidence, to warrant police interest. How much could she make up? But I *know* it wasn't Tom."

"Why didn't she go to the police?" Will demanded. "Why allow herself to be driven to suicide, instead of reporting the harassment?"

"Because she loved Echo," Jena burst in. "Almost as much as she loved Nick. I've been going over it and over it—*why* didn't she tell the police? And I think that's why. Before Pez found Tom…we were struggling to get any kind of real talent to sign with us. We were too small, we didn't have enough money or contacts. But then we spotted one of the world's top models in a park. Cat used to say Tom put us on the map, and by choosing to stay on our books, he kept us there. And she *totally* believed that, Mr. Foster. If we'd lost him with a huge scandal like that, involving the agency owners…she'd have been convinced it'd finish us as a serious agency. I don't think she could live with that either. No Nick and no Echo."

"Jesus," Tom breathed, stunned. "That's…"

"Was she right?" Will asked. "Does your agency depend on Mr. Gray?"

Jena shook her head. "No. I mean of course he's our biggest name by a distance, but we have a good slate now. We'd be okay even if he left. Models move on. Tommy's actually been incredibly loyal. We'd even survive a scandal—don't they say there's no bad publicity? But I don't know how to explain… His career had become like a…a talisman for Cat." She sighed miserably. "Then with what happened, with how she came to feel about him, I suppose that must have felt more like a curse."

Tom made a stifled sound of distress. Even Pez looked sick at the implications.

Had Catriona really believed that Tom had her over a barrel? Unable to escape her tormentor's malice without destroying her own life's work? Thinking Nick wouldn't believe her or forgive her?

Will said evenly, "Given Mrs. Haining's mental health issues, I'd like to interview her GP. If you could get permission for that, Mr. Haining? When's the postmortem?"

"Today," Nick said. And Tom hadn't known that either. Nick reeled off the doctor's details from his phone as Will scribbled them down.

"Well," Pez drawled into the unhappy, preoccupied quiet. "This is all *very* lovely. But if someone really was harassing Catriona, shouldn't we be talking about who'd frame Tommy?"

Will glanced up at him as if he'd forgotten he was there. Maybe he had.

"The idea hadn't passed me by," he said dryly. Then, to Tom, "Can you think of anyone, apart from Mrs. Haining, who might hate you enough to set you up?"

"Well there's you," Pez said sweetly. There was a frozen silence, but Will's expression showed nothing. Pez made a sound of pure impatience. "He has a stalker," he announced with digust.

And Tom had thought he couldn't feel any more shock that morning.

"A stalker?" Jena repeated. "Tommy! Why didn't you…?"

"I don't have a stalker!" Tom snapped.

"You *know* you do," Pez came back. "Max The Dick."

"Who the *fuck* is that?" Nick demanded.

Pez took yet another biscuit and leaned back—the picture of relaxed malice. But Tom knew it was all front. Pez hated it when they fell out, and he was well aware Tom did not want him to do this; that Tom would be furious with him. Inside, Pez wouldn't be relaxed at all. But he was still doing it, as if he was driven to it.

"I don't know who he is, or what he does," Pez said. "But he's rich. Max Perry. Tommy went to his gym once, and he got totally obsessed. Tom finally went out with him, just to shut him up…and he roofied him. He took photos *and* a video. You said you woke up sore, didn't you, Tommy?"

Tom hid his face in his open palms. At least they weren't shaking with fear anymore. Just outrage.

There was no reason to feel humiliated. They were all adults, who had sex. Yet somehow having Will and Nick hear it made him feel sleazy and gullible, whereas telling the story to Pez had just felt like admitting he'd stumbled over one of the risks of their shared hedonistic world.

"When did it happen?" Will asked.

"It doesn't matter," Tom gritted. "It has nothing to do with this."

"A couple of months ago," Pez replied, as if Tom hadn't made a sound. "Tommy met him first during Men's Fashion Week in London. That was January."

Tom thought he saw Will throw a quick glance at Nick, as if he expected a reaction. And he understood exactly the question behind that look: *Why is he seeing other men, when he's meant to be with you?*

A burst of defensive anger annihilated Tom's humiliation. A welcome reminder of what an insane aberration his relationship with Will had been— that single venture into romantic exclusivity.

"Has he contacted you since?" Will asked him.

"He texted me a couple of pictures," Tom replied with stony unconcern. "He said he'd post them all, and a sex tape, if I didn't agree to fuck him again. I told him to stuff it."

"Why didn't you *tell* me?" Nick breathed, horrified. "Why didn't you tell the *police*?"

Tom rolled his eyes. "Because I'd rather not have the story sold to the press by some copper on the make. They all think models are thick as shit as it is. I told Pez to keep it to himself too, so don't blame him." Pez met his seething glare with defiance.

"But what if he sells them? Or posts them?" Jena looked aghast.

"It doesn't do reality TV people any harm," Pez pointed out with provocative relish.

Nick and Will shared a quick, shocked glance, and that moment of basic connection irritated Tom still further. Sometimes he could barely believe these weirdly puritan moments Nick had, even after so many years in the industry. At least Will had the excuse of coming from a judgmental world.

He glared evilly at both of them, ready to burn the next sign of disapproval to the ground.

"Right." Will rose to his feet, tucking his pen and notebook into his inside jacket pocket. They all stared up at him, and his mouth quirked at one corner, as if their surprise amused him. "Thanks for your time. I'll be in touch to report any progress."

There was a short flurry of startled goodbyes, Will nodded in return, and exited the room in a few long strides. Then the only sound was the fast hollow tap of his shoes on the wooden staircase, as he left to begin the job.

And Tom knew he couldn't let that happen.

The meeting had been more than enough proof that he had to stop just standing by, watching other people make the decisions. He felt as if he'd been doing that since he became a model, more or less. Standing by. Letting events and other people carry him along. Not paying attention. Self-absorption had got him here.

He slid out of the banquette.

"Tom?" Nick asked, as Pez protested, "Tommy!"

"I'll call," he said, and he was off, boots thundering on old wood as he ran down the staircase and burst out the front door and up the stone steps. Will had barely made it a few yards along the pavement, and he turned, surprised, at the sound of his name. When he saw Tom though, it was as if a curtain closed.

"I'm going with you," Tom announced.

For the first time since he'd seen him again, Will's expression was unguarded. He looked appalled. But composure returned quickly.

"I don't take an audience along when I work," he said with implacable decision. *Unlike you*, Tom heard in his own head.

"I'm paying you," Tom countered, though they both knew how close to the wind he was sailing, given Will had been arm-twisted into taking the job. "Did you like the club?" he asked.

It came instinctively—an old tactic with Will. Get him off guard. Attack from the flank.

Will's expression flickered. "The building's beautiful."

"But the people are pretentious tossers?"

Will's brows rose minutely, and that was all the reaction he gave.

Tom smiled. He hoped he made it superior. "You judge everything on appearances, don't you? That's a terrible trait in a detective."

"It is," Will agreed, and he was in on the game now. He cocked his head to one side. "But *being* a detective, I checked it out beforehand. And apart from having the odd half grand lying around, the entry criterion is to be 'fascinating, thought-provoking and exceptional'. Oh, and 'a free spirit.'"

QED, his expression said. *Pretentious tossers.*

Tom flushed hard. "A friend of Samuel Pepys built that house," he snapped. "You don't get these kind of surroundings for free."

"Oh, I don't know." Will's voice had an edge to it. He'd walk off in a minute, Tom thought with a jab of worry. "Look at where we're standing right now. Dean Street. Did you know Nelson spent the night before Trafalgar here?" Will asked. Tom blinked and looked involuntarily at the buildings across the road. "Mozart gave a recital at No. 21, down there, when he was a boy." Will pointed behind Tom, who had to force himself not to turn round to look. "Karl Marx lived there." He pointed again. "Dickens used to do some amateur acting in a theatre five or six doors along. And we can wander about in their footsteps for free. Imagine that. No one to judge how *exceptional* we are."

"I'm coming with you," Tom rapped out. He'd forgotten how fucking smart Will was. How he'd been able to play Tom at his own game sometimes, come out of left field and demolish the ground Tom was standing on. How Tom had once relished that challenge.

But in the end, Tom was sneakier. Getting Will into the argument had undermined his walls. It was the closest thing they'd had to a normal conversation in two years. Mission accomplished.

"Why should I let you?" Will demanded.

"We have almost no time," Tom shot back. "I can tell you anything you need to know on the spot…tell you what might be significant or not true. Maybe I can even shock them just by being there."

Will's expression resolved into a disgusted grimace, but Tom could see the idea made sense to him.

"All right." Will's voice was stained with distaste. "I agree I don't have time to flounder around in the dark on this. But if you're hindering me doing my job, one of us is going home."

Tom beat down an elated grin, stoked that he still knew Will well enough to get his own way. It felt as if he'd won something important.

"Agreed," he said.

5

Will's car was an anonymous dark grey Volkswagen Passat—an economical car, a boring car. Pez would laugh his bollocks off if he could see it.

All through the walk from Greens along Dean Street, and buckling into their seats, Tom had been trying to pluck up the nerve to speak again. Because, while he had no wish to pick at old scabs, unearth old guilt, equally he knew they had to get over this awkwardness if they were to accomplish anything as a kind of…team. They were going to have to at least try to clear the air, even if it required a walk down their particularly unpleasant Memory Lane.

Perhaps Will was thinking the same thing, because rather than switch on the engine, he sat with his hand on the steering wheel, looking thoughtfully out the front window.

Tom looked down at his own nervous fingers and braced himself to make the first move.

"Before we start," Will said neutrally. "It'd be a good idea to tell me how much of this has a basis in reality."

It took Tom a second to understand. He raised his head slowly to glare his utter disbelief. "*What?*"

Will's expression didn't change as he turned his head to look at him. "You heard."

"You know me!" Tom spat. "You *know* I'd never do that!"

Will's eyes looked huge and dark in the shadows of the car interior. His silence lasted too long. Tom didn't know whether to scream or weep. Inevitably, he chose attack.

"I can't believe this! You're meant to be a professional! You're supposed to put aside your personal feelings and make use of the information you have. You fucking *know* I wouldn't do it."

Will's lush mouth thinned. "I have a rough assessment of who you were two years ago. I can't assume some life-changing event hasn't altered you, though deep traits rarely disappear."

"Oh, do go on, Detective Inspector!" Tom seethed.

Something blanked in Will's eyes. He tilted his head in acknowledgment. *If you insist.*

"The subject is charming and manipulative. Capable of targeted, deliberate cruelty to achieve a desired result. Either an emotional coward—" His tone was calm and relentless, a police officer delivering his report. Tom couldn't breathe. There was a stone on his chest, holding his lungs down. "—or emotionally unavailable due to childhood experience, and unable to connect with feelings which aren't centered on self. He's in touch with his conscience, to some degree, and capable of empathy, but motivated almost exclusively by goals which don't demand an emotional return. Fame, adulation, money. Difficult at this stage to know how much that need for material success has grown in the intervening years, and how far the subject would go to realize those aims." Will met Tom's wide, stunned eyes. "Definite narcissistic traits."

There was an awful silence.

Tom knew that after all that had happened—the fear and shame and bewilderment since Catriona's death—it shouldn't matter. Will was twisted by anger and thwarted love. And how could Tom deny that there was enough truth in what Will had said to pull away the rocks and uncover Tom's own self-contempt.

But...some part of him had trusted that Will would believe him. That Will would save him, maybe because he'd loved him.

He welcomed the tsunami of rage that swept over him, consuming the nervous guilt he'd felt around this man for their shared past. Because Tom was fucked if he was going to let Will take advantage of this disaster to punish him for not loving him back.

Things he'd learned: if someone hit him, hit back twice as hard.

They were going to do this after all.

He manufactured a furious, disbelieving laugh. "Seriously?" he sneered. "Is that what you've been telling yourself to get yourself through the nights? Or is that supposed to be a professional assessment? When you're still wanking off to your outrage at being dumped after two whole years! How about...the subject couldn't stand watching you pretend to be straight to your police buddies? How about the subject felt smothered? The subject was bored out of his mind. The *subject* didn't want to spend his life ironing in suburbia." Will eyes were blank-flint when they met his, but Tom thought he knew him well enough to see something flicker there. Pain. Good. "The subject isn't old before his time." *Unlike you.* He might as well have said it. "So how about you grow the fuck up and do your job?"

At last Tom could see real anger. It felt to him like an achievement. The beautiful catharsis of finally taking on all the mess of this old, unresting ghost of a relationship.

But his satisfaction lasted only seconds before reality returned. All that had happened and all that he was facing. And just like that, Tom's storm of rage snuffed out, like a candle deprived of oxygen.

"If you want to pull out," Tom said stiffly. "If you really think I harassed…"

"I didn't say…" Will grimaced, the most extreme facial expression Tom had seen from him since they'd met again. As if Will had been containing himself behind a wall of robotic professional competence, showing himself only in flickers like an old film. "What I asked *originally*," Will went on. "Was if there was any grain of underlying truth which might have been distorted by the fact that Mrs. Haining already believed the worst of you."

His brows had pulled together in a dark frown, and he looked almost as uncomfortable as Tom felt, embarrassed perhaps by the resentment he'd allowed free, just as Tom was now.

It seemed though that they were both going to ignore that quick flurry of mutual destruction.

"For the record," Will said, all stiff dignity, "I don't believe you'd deliberately torment anyone for the fun of it."

Not…just for the fun of it.

Tom nodded miserably and looked down at his hands. He didn't have the life in him for sarcasm. He felt lost and alone in that moment, hoping that he wasn't bleeding out his need for some kindness. Aware that Will was the last person he should ask for it.

•••

The receptionist at Catriona's GP's surgery in Vauxhall looked red-eyed and tearful, but her emotional state so fitted Tom's mood that he simply accepted it.

The girl was tiny, perhaps in her late twenties, with dark brown skin, wearing a yellow dress decorated with tiny blue flowers. She made a brave try at normality as she dealt with the steady stream of patients at her desk, but every so often an audible sniffle would emerge.

The crowded waiting area in which Tom and Will sat was lit harshly by fluorescent bulbs, exposing every tear on every health poster, every skid mark on the rubber floor. The room smelled sterile, unsurprisingly.

Tom shifted nervously in his orange molded plastic chair.

"Are we going to try to find Jessica Mayhew today as well?" he asked Will's profile.

Will blinked very slowly and that was his only reaction, but somehow it looked like a release of tension. Perhaps he'd been dreading Tom would try to clear the air again.

"Nope," Will said. He popped the P for emphasis, but he didn't look at Tom. He spoke to the air in front of him instead. "Since she's made an official police complaint, it could be interpreted as attempting to intimidate a witness if the SIO felt sufficiently pissed off. And Lawson's an officious, conviction-hungry shit, so he wouldn't hesitate to charge you."

"Oh," Tom said. The large elderly women sitting beside him, shifted away minutely.

"Mr. Foster. Room four," the receptionist called.

Will stood and set off down the only corridor, as if he were alone, and Tom trotted nervously behind, until Will stopped at a door and knocked.

Dr. Carys Rolfe rose from her desk to greet them, eyes catching on Will, almost with startlement, then widening even further as Tom introduced himself. "I've heard a lot about you, Mr. Gray," she told him, but still, she smiled.

Dr. Rolfe was quite tall, perhaps five foot nine, and heavier than was fashionable, dressed in a dark trouser suit that looked slightly too small for her. Her hair was dark, thick and short, with a light sprinkling of grey; her eyebrows unplucked; her un-mascaraed eyes weary-brown. Tom placed her in her midforties perhaps, though she could be younger, since vanity appeared to be foreign to her.

Tom thought she looked kind though. Tired, intelligent, and sad. In fact, he thought perhaps she'd been crying too. It felt at odd moments as if normality had blipped out, and the whole world was caught in sorrow.

"Mr. Haining emailed me," Dr. Rolfe said. "So I have a rough idea why you're here." Her accent was distinctively Welsh, a strong musical lilt that hung on some syllables as if they were too delicious to let go. She sat, waving them to the chairs in front of her desk. "So, with his permission, I can answer some questions. I can give you ten minutes. That's a whole appointment." She raised her untidy eyebrows, as if conveying the magnitude of the gift.

"Catriona Haining." Will got straight to it. "Is it the case that she habitually self-harmed and suffered from depression?"

"Yes," Dr. Rolfe said. "To both. Catriona joined this practice maybe… eight months ago, as her marriage ended. Mr. Haining stayed with his old GP. Catriona created a formidable façade, but she was very vulnerable and easily distressed. I referred her to a therapist, but she didn't stick to a routine of appointments. She insisted she didn't need that kind of help. I prescribed antidepressants and some sleeping aids. The bottles were found empty beside her bed, so I expect I'll be testifying if there's an inquest."

Her mouth tipped up in a pale smile, directed at both of them. At least she wasn't treating Tom like a villain, he thought gratefully. She hadn't even questioned his presence.

"Were you surprised by her suicide?" Will asked.

Dr. Rolfe rubbed one reddened eye. "I should say yes, shouldn't I? But honestly?" She shook her head. "She was pathologically fixated on her husband. The way some people fix on a religion, as a kind of answer. Her husband was her religion. I never met him, but I can only imagine how difficult that must have been. When he finally cracked and left, she cracked too. She kept up appearances, but for the last eight months, she was severely depressed and self-loathing."

Tom didn't know what he'd hoped to hear. That Catriona's long-term mental state hadn't really been that bad? That she'd been just as tough as Tom had imagined? But by now her vulnerability, and the extreme depth of her need for Nick, were beginning to feel like truths he'd always known.

"Did she manifest any signs of paranoia?" Will asked.

"Paranoia?" Dr. Rolfe lilted. She sounded surprised. "Well." She tapped her lip with a short fingernail. "She did believe her husband spent his life being enticed into affairs with…pretty much everyone really. She saw the whole world as her rival. But she never blamed him. She always saw him as a victim of his own attractiveness. She tried to be *perfect* for him, to hold on to him as she saw it. The way she dressed… All of that. She tried to be his fantasy woman."

His fantasy woman.

Tom could see Catriona clearly in his mind's eye, and the question was so glaring that he could barely believe it had never occurred to him before. If that super-stylized, obsessively groomed kind of womanhood was Nick's thing, what did he see in Tom? A male equivalent—impeccably plucked and tanned and manicured? The idea made him feel vaguely ill.

"You said she mentioned Mr. Gray?" Will prompted.

Dr. Rolfe eyed Tom apologetically. "Oh. Quite a lot. She showed me photos, which is how I knew you."

"Did she allege to you that Mr. Gray was harassing her?"

"Yes," Dr. Rolfe said regretfully. "She did. Repeatedly."

It took all Tom's strength not to show the despair he felt.

Will asked steadily, "In your opinion was Mrs. Haining a truthful person?"

"Well..." Dr. Rolfe blew out a breath through pursed lips. "I think she convinced herself of what she said, but she was prone to...accusations. She demonized people she thought were tempting her husband, so imagine how much she loathed the person he *actually* fell in love with." She gave Tom a smile of rueful sympathy, and he found himself so grateful for the understanding, for the thread of hope, that he could have climbed over the desk to hug her.

"Did *you* believe her?" Will pressed.

Dr. Rolfe's smile fell. She hesitated, then said very carefully, "It's not for me to judge, Mr. Foster. But if you're asking for a clinical diagnosis, *with* the caveat that I'm not a specialist...I'd say she displayed strong indications of Borderline Personality Disorder. Supported by the fact that she was prone to making and believing accusations which had no basis in reality."

Something painful in Tom's chest began to loosen, a barbed-wire band of tension and fear that had been scrunched up there, all that time. It was what Nick had said, backed up now by Catriona's own doctor. If she really was being harassed, maybe she'd just assumed it was Tom.

There was a short silence, and Dr. Rolfe's gaze remained fixed on Will, almost as if she were memorizing him. Mesmerized. Much as he liked her, Tom felt like rolling his eyes.

Will shifted minutely, and Dr. Rolfe flushed.

"Oh. Sorry," she said. "You seem...familiar somehow."

Tom's lip curled. The old "haven't we met before?" gambit.

"I don't think so," Will said neutrally. He'd missed his line, Tom thought irritably. Wasn't he meant to say, *I'd definitely remember you*?

"It's probably someone in the movies. Or in a magazine." Dr. Rolfe's look of embarrassed realization seemed to hit her at the same time it hit Will. *You look like a movie star.*

Will cleared his throat. "Why did Mrs. Haining join this practice? It's not close to her house in Clapham, or her workplace in Soho."

Dr. Rolfe grabbed the escape wholeheartedly. "Well, she just uh... decided she wanted me as her GP. I actually met her before she joined us, on a train journey up North. We sat across from each other, and...we started chatting. She wanted to find a new GP practice, so she enrolled here. She was generally...well...quite reserved. And obviously troubled but...I liked her." Dr. Rolfe's expression softened. "We went to a few film festivals together, in fact. Scorsese, Hitchcock and Mel Brooks. We had a lovely time." Her accent got even stronger with reminiscent enthusiasm. It was very endearing.

"Your receptionist seems upset," Will said. "Was *she* fond of Mrs. Haining too?"

"Aisha?" Dr. Rolfe's looked momentarily startled, then her animated expression closed—a startling fall to tired regret. "Oh. No, it's... She just heard this morning that her friend died suddenly last night. She refuses to go home, though I'm sure she's worrying the patients." Dr. Rolfe's dark eyes filled with tears, until they looked like two shiny pieces of jet. "Molly was only thirty, and she was pregnant. You see so much death in this profession, it should be routine by now, but..." Her face twisted. "The thing is...my...my husband died quite recently and it all...brings it... Please forgive my unprofessional..." She waved a hand rapidly in front of her face, eyes squeezed shut against emotion, shaking fingers then pressing hard against her nose and mouth to try to contain her grief.

Her rapid disintegration was startling and horrible, and it felt totally wrong to Tom, watching her become, in an eyeblink, a victim of pain, rather than a compassionate observer of it. But he had no idea what to say.

Will took charge. He stood and thanked her, as if nothing were amiss, and Tom followed his lead.

Dr. Rolfe nodded tearfully and regarded them with reddened, damp eyes. "You're very welcome. I hope I helped." She sniffed hard. "And I apologize again. I'm very embarrassed. If I can do anything else..."

Outside in the car park, the air was still and humid, almost muggy, in the cruel afternoon sun. The inside of Will's car felt scorching and stuffy, the seats unpleasantly hot.

Will switched on the engine, but he didn't put the car into gear. He seemed to be waiting.

"What did you think?" Tom ventured, because his need to confirm that there was hope now was stronger than his pride. "Did that help?" He looked nervously at Will's profile, the neat nose and firm chin, the silky dark hair, shaped cleanly around his ears.

"Imagine you're using what she said to put together a defense case in court."

Tom's pulse lurched unpleasantly. He looked ahead, out the front window, as Will was doing.

Tom said slowly, "Catriona's doctor says she probably had a personality disorder that displayed as paranoia and obsession. And...she always directed her anger toward people she imagined were taking Nick away."

Will nodded with restrained approval. "That's your answer."

•••

Will dropped Tom at the nearest Tube station while he went back to his office to start some fast research on Catriona, and any friends he could dig out. So Tom headed for Shoreditch to feed and coddle John. It was just after six when he called in to tell the Gardiners that he'd be away for the night.

He'd called ahead, so he knew Nick was in, but he needed the motorbike journey to Notting Hill to try to process the day. He already felt more like he wanted to be, on the back of the bike. In control. Independent. Free from demands.

He just…didn't think he could stand to be alone for the whole night.

He'd brought tomorrow's clothes, and training gear for his gym session with his personal trainer the following morning, which he daren't miss again. He still had a job to do, after all. But though he was guiltily aware that he couldn't afford to let crucial things like waxing, facials and manicures slide, he couldn't convince himself of their importance—not compared with Catriona's death and the crisis Tom faced.

Durham Terrace, where Nick lived, was built from white limestone and brown brick. Its first-floor windows adorned with cast-iron balconies, and every house had its own pointless, open front gate. It was an unremarkable, expensive London street, but as Tom parked his bike outside Nick's building, the gentle mellow light of the early evening added something almost unfairly idyllic to it. In the shadow of Catriona's mortality, he felt the need to notice beauty and drink it in.

Nick must have been looking out for him, because he had opened the door of his first-floor flat before Tom, juggling his helmet and backpack, could get his key into the lock. And once inside, Tom found himself propelled back against the wall of the windowless hallway, with Nick crowding in on him to kiss him, hands gripping the lapels of Tom's black leather biker's jacket.

Tom allowed it; opened his mouth to Nick's strong, pushy tongue and let him have his fill. He liked the way Nick kissed with a confidence, an arrogance Tom wasn't accustomed to with his casual shags. Usually, it got him in the mood pretty quickly. But today…

Nick was too fine-tuned to him not to notice. He eased off the kiss gradually and pulled back until he could press his forehead against Tom's.

"Sorry," Nick muttered.

"Hey. No need to apologize." Tom's bike helmet and backpack were stuck awkwardly between them, and he shifted them surreptiously.

"I was being ridiculous. Possessive. I know you hate that."

Tom frowned. "Possessive?" Carefully.

Nick sighed. "You were out all day with your ex, Tom. Who looks better than most movie stars. Why haven't we signed him?"

Tom gave a strained laugh. "The operative word is 'ex', Nick. And he thinks modeling's shallow. He doesn't want to look like a movie star. He only ever wanted to look like a detective."

Nick's smile was wry. "Tough luck for him then. If this were a movie, he'd be totally unrealistic casting."

Tom grinned, because actually, it was true. "Like one of those… pouting, supermodel nineteen-year-old nuclear scientists."

"Well," Nick said. "*You* wouldn't exactly be believable as a shit-hot chemist."

They both began to giggle, and Tom felt a grateful surge of affection for this man who stayed by him with barely a reproach, even though he wanted so much more than Tom could give. Nick's integrity was just one of the things about him Tom had come to admire.

Nick led the way into his lounge—a huge, bright living space, made up of two, tall-ceilinged rooms with most of the wall between them removed, and lit by enormous windows at either end. It had polished wooden floors, interior-designer décor and two fireplaces, a common layout in refurbished London townhouses, but one which had always secretly felt wrong to Tom. The room smelled of the air freshener Nick's cleaning lady used lavishly all over the flat. Lavender and something metallic.

Nick's wall shelves displayed books on his main interests—marketing, psychology, and eastern cultures—and some of the beautiful, ruinously expensive bronzes Nick collected with relentless zeal. His stash of DVDs of Old Hollywood films, Nick's other big enthusiasm, had their own shelf. Tom couldn't count the number of Huston, Hitchcock and Wilder movies he'd sat through since he'd started seeing Nick, to the extent that he'd pretty much caught the Film Noir bug himself.

"Drink?" Nick asked. "Sit down! You look knackered."

Tom eyed the two fashionable, boxy, cream sofas, set perpendicular to each other in front of the left-hand fireplace. But he sank instead into the bizarre-looking purple designer chair, which was, despite appearances, weirdly well-moulded to the human body.

When Tom looked up, Nick was hovering, and Tom thought he saw a kind of calculated uncertainty in his expression, as if Nick were rifling through a selection of verbal gambits.

Indecision looked wrong on him, like bad acting.

Tom opened his mouth to ask, but Nick blurted, "You have to have a verifiable alibi for Friday night." Tom froze. "Look, I was the one who made you promise to stay at home that night, because of the shoot the next day. So…I've asked Pez to tell anyone who asks that he went to see you at your flat. He's fine with it, and I'll verify it. He did actually call me early Friday evening, if they check phone records."

"Nick!" Tom felt both horrified and touched. Nick was all set to perjure himself to save him, while Pez had charitably chosen not to lob in a hand-grenade about Friday night, to do damage. Tom was going to have to do that himself. "That's really sweet, but there's no need to lie to the police."

"But…" Nick began.

"I *was* with Pez on Friday night. We went out in Dalston."

There was a tense pause.

"But…you texted me that you were at home." Nick sounded bewildered, as if the idea that Tom might lie to him had never entered his head until that moment.

Tom bit his lip. "Yeah. I know." He felt as if guilt was becoming as reflexive to him as breathing. "I just…fancied a night out, and I didn't want you to fuss."

Worry, he'd meant to say. Not fuss.

But truthfully—he'd wanted to avoid the sense of silent reproach. Avoid Nick wondering if he was going out on the pull. Or if he was going to have sex with Pez.

Nick drew in a deep breath, and Tom couldn't help wondering what upset him more: Tom lying to his boss before a shoot, or deceiving his sort-of boyfriend about going out?

"Look." Tom kept his tone as apologetic and free of irritation as possible. "I'm sorry. I didn't drink much." He shrugged. "I was still a bit out of sync because of jet lag, and I wasn't ready to sleep. But…hey, it's lucky I did go out, isn't it? Lying to the police'd be a sure way to make things worse." Nick's frozen expression seemed to be thawing, so he went on, "Is it okay if I stay tonight? For company?"

Nick regarded him inscrutably for a moment longer, but then he smiled. "You know I'd love it if you did," he said, though he sounded cooler. "I'll order something in. You must be feeling pretty shit."

"Nothing on what you must be feeling," Tom pointed out, because somehow the fact Nick had lost his ex-wife was being overwhelmed by Tom's drama.

Nick sighed. "Yeah. Let's just…eat. We can open a bottle of wine and watch a movie."

Tom nodded, feeling the insane wire-tension of the day begin to loosen at last.

"What was the one I fell asleep on last time?" he asked. "With the mad diva."

"Oh, *Sunset Boulevard*. Billy Wilder."

Tom smiled. "Yeah. Let's watch that."

Tired gratitude began to prickle behind his eyes. This quiet feeling of being understood; this confidence in being adored, whatever he managed to feel in return… He didn't feel threatened by it. In fact, he realized, as he watched Nick retreat from the room, Catriona's death, far from finally tearing them apart, seemed to be pushing Tom the other way.

For all Tom's cemented-in hangups, he'd never felt closer to Nick, who'd tried to protect him and put him first when he really shouldn't have, and now, was providing an undemanding sanctuary for him.

They ate the takeaway Thai food as Tom gave Nick a detailed run-down of the interview with Dr. Rolfe, and then they sat, sipping red wine, packed in together on one of the small sofas, Tom's bare feet on Nick's lap.

Nick ran the movie from the top. It was a flamboyant melodrama, played out in black-and-white glamour. But Tom found that parts of it hit new raw spots. Maybe it was the character of Norma Desmond: mentally ill, manipulative, pathologically possessive. And Joe, her lover and victim. He wondered if Nick saw parallels, but he didn't dare ask.

The story was cranking up to its gothic climax when Tom's phone buzzed on the coffee table, and when he fumbled it into his hand, Will's name on the screen dispatched Tom's tenuous hold on contentment as brutally as if someone had dumped a bucket of cold water over his head.

The contrast between the effect Will and Nick had on him had never felt so stark.

He dug his toes into the muscle of Nick's thigh for reassurance as he pressed *Accept*.

"Hi." He kept his tone cool.

"I've found something interesting," Will said at once. No greeting. "I have to go somewhere tomorrow. I'll brief you when I get back."

The last echoes of Tom's relaxation vanished like snowflakes hitting warm ground. Nick's thighs tensed under his feet.

"If it's to do with my case, I'm coming with you." On the TV screen, Gloria Swanson looked half-mad with outrage. Join the club. "I've a gym session at nine. Then I'm free. Tell me where to meet you."

"Tom?" Nick said. "Has something happened, baby? Is there anything I can do?"

Tom pulled the phone away, to shake his head. "No, it's fine. Just organizing a meeting tomorrow. Will's found something."

"Something?" Nick asked.

His frown of anxious concern was enough to prompt Tom to put the phone back to his ear. "Look," he snapped. "Can't you just *say* what you've..."

"I'll text you the address and the time," Will said curtly, and rang off with no warning or farewell, leaving Tom staring, unseeing, at the TV.

Suddenly he felt wide awake, gut fizzing with anger. So much for contentment.

But whatever happened, at least tomorrow would be the last day he'd have to deal with Will Foster.

6

Tom's favorite travel app told him the journey from his gym in Shoreditch to Barnet should have taken twenty-five minutes by car. But it was almost fifty minutes after he'd straddled his motorbike when he finally defeated the unusually heavy late-morning traffic and pulled into the pub car park in which he'd arranged to meet Will.

The Mason's Arms was not a salubrious building, but Tom could only imagine that its location—just off a major road on a busy junction in Chipping Barnet—was its commercial salvation. It was a single-story, flat-roofed, brown-pebble-dashed monument to architectural disinterest. In fact, the extreme contrast between the ugly, mundane practicality of this meeting place and Greens the morning before—felt almost like social commentary. Almost deliberate on Will's part, if Tom believed he was the type of man to play those games.

Tom switched off the music in his helmet speakers and heard instead the sounds of real life—the roar of traffic passing on the A1000 alongside the pub, the purring of the bike's engine.

He coasted the bike through the car park, half-full of anonymous cars, scanning for Will's equally anonymous Passat. And somehow he zeroed in on it as efficiently as if it had a flashing beacon attached. As he spotted it, the driver's door opened, and Will climbed out.

He was wearing a white collared shirt again, and a dark green tie, with slim-cut dark gray trousers. No suit jacket in the dense city-swelter. Just like the day before, none of it was remarkable in any way; it was all incredibly boring. Tom knew that all Will really bothered with was looking neat and clean. But again what he wore emphasized Will's beautiful coloring and physique—his thighs and bum especially, when he turned to close the car door—as effectively as if a stylist had worked on him for hours.

Tom took him in, from behind his visor, and felt the old tidal pull of Will's resented power in his gut.

The first time Tom had ever seen him—across the room, in a Soho pub—the force of attraction he'd felt had pretty much shut down his rational mind. With unbelievable luck—it had felt like fate—Will had been in with his colleagues, one of whom turned out to be also a friendly acquaintance of Tom's from UCL—Des Salt, working then under Will, as a DC at the Met. Tom had gone in like a guided missile.

Will'd been with a girlfriend that evening, and Tom had believed, with unfamiliar desperation, that he didn't stand a chance. It'd been totally against his own rules on cheating and involvement to try. But he hadn't been able to help himself.

Tom had never experienced anything like that gut punch of lust and fascination…not before or since. Not hanging around with, or sleeping with, some of the most beautiful men in the world. Then, all that had mattered was that he'd wanted, and that level of wanting had been enough to overcome all his instincts, to believe he had to have.

Until he'd come to his senses.

Will stood by his car, waiting for Tom to park his bike, and his expression was as cool and disinterested as if he were watching a school bus pull in. And suddenly, all Tom's hated awareness of Will's beauty seemed to just…coalesce into a need not to be alone in it. To see some reaction back.

It was like slipping into an automatic gear.

Deliberately, Tom pulled his bike into a space across the car park from the Passat, instead of beside it. Because he knew how he looked climbing off a bike. Plenty of people had told him.

Tom's Honda was a practical city machine—a red NC750X—designed to twist and accelerate through traffic rather than cruise on the open road, and the fact it looked good had been incidental. Now he was glad of it.

He turned off the engine and swung his leg smoothly over the seat, knowing his jeans would mold to the sweet, exaggerated curve of his arse. Then he turned toward Will, carefully pulling off his helmet, leaving his shades in place, and ran a hand through his long hair. He wore tight, faded-blue Levis; a short, black leather biker's jacket, and over his shoulders hung a small backpack, holding the gym gear he'd used that morning.

The traffic on the main road beside them sounded unpleasantly loud without the protection of his helmet, but underneath it Tom could still hear the muffled grumble of a cleaning machine, sweeping along the gutter somewhere beyond the car-park entrance. The sky was hot blue, pollution-hazy.

He let his thoughts drift in a kind of guilt-free stasis as he began to cross the car park toward Will with a slow, loping stride, like stalking a catwalk, always aware as he moved, of the effect. And he refused to examine what he was doing.

Will watched his approach impassively, but the burst of restless frustration Tom felt at that began to succumb to the understanding, as he strolled closer, that he was testing Will's reaction simply because he wanted to know, in some part of him, that his power over Will was still there.

Pure ego. That's all it was, without a single rational thought for the consequences.

From behind his shades, he watched Will's expressionless face, and all at once he felt ashamed that he'd surrendered to whatever instinct had driven him. Weren't there enough corpses buried in the aftermath of their relationship, without his digging in the graveyard?

He stopped awkwardly a couple of feet away and, for something to do, shrugged out of his backpack.

"Could I um…put these in there?" He gestured toward the back seat of Will's car and held up the pack and his helmet. "I don't have a secure box."

Will wordlessly opened the closest back door, letting out a gust of cool air, and Tom dropped both items onto the cloth-covered seat. Then he eased off his jacket and threw it in too, because it was far too hot to leave it on. And felt instantly self-conscious again.

He'd fitted all his clothes for the day into his backpack when he'd left Nick's flat that morning, already dressed for the gym. If there was one thing modeling had taught him, it was how to pack efficiently and quickly. But it seemed he'd unconsciously decided, even then, to stop trying to disappear around Will. Maybe when he'd packed the night before, back in Shoreditch.

The black tank he'd chosen was simple and high street. But after years of being drilled in the power of clothing choice, Tom was fully aware of how well—how sinfully—the top showed off his neck and arms and framed his collarbones.

Now meeting Will's cynical eyes, he felt ridiculous and childish, as if he'd breached some unspoken agreement between them. *Don't go there.* And he didn't even want to, that was the thing. Maybe stress was driving him over the edge.

He forced his voice to coolness. "You found out something you wouldn't tell me over the phone."

Will's tone was equally chilly. "I thought you may need time to consider whether you want to upset Mr. Haining."

Consideration for Nick. Why did that irritate him?

"And you couldn't tell me without dragging me to a car park in Barnet?" Tom snapped.

Will raised an eyebrow, and Tom flushed. They were both well aware Tom had demanded to come. He knew he was being petulant. Unreasonable. And it had to stop.

Will said dispassionately, "An anonymous call came in to the office yesterday, which is…interesting in itself. It pointed us in the right direction to do some…extensive new background work on Mrs. Haining. Her maiden name was Telford. But that wasn't the name she was born with."

Tom propped his hands on his hips, and waited.

"She'd covered her tracks pretty well," Will went on. "But Mrs. Haining's birth name was Denise Susan Heath. And *as* Denise Heath, at the age of fifteen, she was sent to a secure unit for three years."

Tom's hands dropped limply to his sides. He stared at Will in disbelief, yet Will looked cool and certain.

"Why?" Tom thought he sounded as stunned as he felt.

"She had a record for persistent theft." Will's detached tone didn't alter. Just reporting the facts. "But she was given the custodial sentence because she committed a serious assault on a girl she claimed was trying to steal her boyfriend."

Tom waited for the punchline. He was totally unable to imagine Catriona doing any of those things. Stealing. Assault. He said flatly, "That can't be true."

Will's dark brows pulled in to a frowning line. "It is, actually. Do you plan to tell Mr. Haining?"

"God. No!" Tom replied, appalled. And he found he believed now, because Will was sure. He ran an agitated palm over his face. "Not unless I have to. He's going through enough."

"I assumed as much," Will said. "Which is why we're here. I can't talk to the staff at Red Moss—that's the unit she was sent to—without Mr. Haining's permission to disclose information about his wife. So—this is Plan B."

Tom's brain felt numb, scrabbling to keep up. But a part of him still managed to feel unnerved that Will had been so certain what Tom would do with the information, that he'd dragged them both out to Barnet. As if it had been a foregone conclusion.

"What's Plan B?" he asked weakly.

"Plan B is in the pub," Will replied. "His name's Brian Glanville, now a lecturer at Barnet and Southgate College. He's an experienced, senior social worker, but community college is the best job he can get."

Tom ran a hand back through his hair, letting the silky strands fall comfortingly around his face. Impatience and that strange resentment were beginning to dispel the fog of shock.

"Why? Stop fucking around, Will!"

Will's mouth tightened. "Because I remembered he wrote a best-seller—which he shouldn't have—about a celebrity murderer being held in the detention center where he worked."

Tom frowned. "A bestseller? Then he shouldn't need to work."

"Focus on the career suicide," Will said. "It was a single nonfiction book, not *Fifty Shades of Grey*. It made him pretty much an outcast as a criminal-justice social worker, because he broke his contract. Not to mention the rules of his profession. But that's lucky for *us*, because his book happens to center on Red Moss at the time Denise was there. He's agreed to talk to me for the price of a coffee and the chance to bend someone's ear."

"But all that's the distant past," Tom protested. "Shouldn't we be trying to find whoever harassed Catriona?"

"Lawson isn't going to look into any of this," Will said. "He's investigating a straightforward accusation of harassment. Though the fact is, he shouldn't be. MITs deal with murder and some kidnappings…not this kind of thing. So. I had a quick chat with Des last night." Tom didn't move a muscle, just in case Will stopped talking. "He said the team've been wondering the same thing, since all available evidence points to suicide. The word is, it's coming from above Lawson."

Tom stared at him, uncomprehending. "Someone above DCI Lawson…is ordering him to investigate me?"

"I think someone above Lawson has told him to investigate why Catriona died," Will corrected.

"But…" Tom felt lost, unmoored. Afraid again. "Maybe we should be investigating that too then. All we're doing here is digging up old dirt."

"What we're doing here," Will countered. "Is casting doubt on the reliability of your accuser."

Tom gripped his hair hard, and tried to calm down.

It made sense, distasteful or not. They had so little time, and Will was doing his new job as brilliantly and ruthlessly as he'd done his old one.

"Okay," Tom said. "Okay." And he tried not to feel as if he were ruining Catriona one last time.

•••

The inside of the Mason's Arms proved to be a perfect match for the depressing utilitarianism of the outside. Faint muzak was playing, and little of the sunny brightness of the day was allowed to creep into the sizable single room.

The carpets were dark red and patterned. To hide stains, Tom assumed. The furniture and the bar were dark too, and the seats had wine-red patterned upholstery. In the far left-hand corner he could see the garish flashing lights of two slot machines. The room smelled vaguely of stale chips, and it looked exactly like every airport pub Tom had ever been in. Atmosphere not included.

A few customers had been drawn in though, seated here and there in the large space, mostly drinking coffee. Will led the way unerringly toward a man sitting alone in a window booth, typing on an open laptop set on the table in front of him. The man was in his late fifties, Tom judged, with short, sparse, graying brown hair and metal-rimmed double-lensed spectacles. He looked as anonymous as the pub.

"Mr. Glanville?" Will asked. The man glanced up and took them both in, his drab-brown eyes widening slightly behind their lenses. "I'm Will Foster. Thanks for agreeing to meet me." Glanville nodded then eyed Tom suspiciously. Will was clearly going to make him introduce himself then.

"Tom Gray." He smiled cordially at Glanville. "Mr. Foster's associate."

Will slid into the bench seat across from Glanville and Tom slid in after him.

"So, how can I help you?" Glanville asked.

Will gave him an easy white-toothed smile, and Tom realized with an unpleasant jolt in his stomach that he hadn't seen that smile—any smile from Will—for over two years.

"I'd like to pick your brains if I may, Mr. Glanville," Will began. "Use your expertise with young offenders."

Glanville's brows rose, and Tom could almost see his parched ego inflating. "Well I'll…do what I can."

Will ordered the coffee he'd promised, along with a pastry for Glanville, and encouraged him to relax and talk for a while, mostly about himself, while Tom sat and observed the masterly softening-up process.

Glanville chatted about his commute. About the college course he taught, preparing students who hadn't achieved direct school qualifications to go on to study social work at university. About his hopes for promotion. But Tom could see that Barking College was not where Glanville had wanted to end up.

Will let the man talk for the best part of fifteen minutes, before he moved in for the kill.

"I really am grateful to have the chance to talk to you, Mr. Glanville. As I mentioned on the phone, it's a very delicate case." Will leaned toward him, across the table; Glanville leaned forward too, eager to participate in the conspiracy. "I'm looking into a past client of yours at Red Moss. A girl called Denise Heath."

Glanville blinked for a second as if he didn't understand. "Denise." His tone was flat and loud with betrayed disappointment. He sat back again. "I thought you wanted to talk about David."

"David?" Tom frowned.

"David Burchill." Glanville made it sound as if there could be no other David. As if they'd both deeply offended him. "I wrote a book!"

"Ah," Will said. "I'm afraid not. The book was excellent though," he hurried on. "I studied that case at university."

"Oh. Well then." Glanville looked slightly mollified.

"Yep." Will smiled winningly. "Criminology."

"Who's David Burchill?" Tom asked, irritated.

Glanville eyed him with disapproval. "*You* haven't read my book, then."

Tom produced a bland smile. "I did Chemistry."

Will looked down at his notebook. Tom suspected he was inwardly rolling his eyes.

"A boy who kidnapped and murdered a couple of toddlers," Will said shortly. He glanced quickly at Glanville. "*Allegedly* murdered. He was big tabloid box office for a while."

"An appalling miscarriage of justice," Glanville intoned.

Will deliberately caught Tom's eye, and the message read loud and clear. *Don't encourage him.*

Tom bit his lip. "Was Denise there at the same time as…David?" he asked. It wasn't subtle, but Glanville seemed appeased.

"Yes, she was." Glanville hesitated, and his drab eyes narrowed to something like cunning. "She might have been mentioned in the book. She *might* have been…Girl X."

"Girl X." Will's tone was sharp, and when Tom darted a glance at him he thought Will looked almost stunned, before surprise vanished beneath careful interest.

Glanville appeared delighted by his reaction. In fact, Tom realized, Will had him in the palm of his hand. He really was good at this.

"Since you read my book," Glanville said archly, "you already know about her." He took off his spectacles and fished in his jacket pocket for a paper hankie to polish the lenses. His eyes looked larger naked. But a thought seemed to strike him, and he frowned. "Though of course I wouldn't be able to *formally* identify Denise as…"

"It's off the record, Mr. Glanville," Will said. "I'm just trying to put together a picture."

"Who's Girl X?" Tom demanded, because he was fucked if he was going to be left on the outside of an insiders' conversation.

This time, Will joined Glanville in eyeing him with impatience.

"Chemistry," Tom reminded them sweetly.

Will looked away, but Tom liked to think he saw the ghost of amusement.

"The identity of all the other inmates had to be concealed," Glanville said primly. "The book was about a miscarriage of justice in *David's* case." He put on his glasses and sighed with resigned impatience. "Is Denise in trouble again?"

"No," Will said. "But I can't breach confidentiality."

Glanville gave a bitter smile. "Very wise."

"Remind me about her?" Will coaxed. "For my associate's sake."

"Well…" Glanville sounded uncertain, but the temptation was obvious and it struck Tom that he was hungry to talk about a time when he'd felt important. "When I knew her, *Girl X*…" he widened his eyes meaningfully, "…was an opportunist. Manipulative. The usual traits of a habitual thief. She certainly used to be very attractive, but also insecure and obsessive in her emotional relationships. She's one of…life's worshippers." Tom looked sharply at him. The echo of Dr. Rolfe was startling. "That said, she seemed to have some awareness of her tendencies. When she arrived she was adamant she didn't want to get involved with anyone, as I remember."

"But she didn't hold out," Will prompted.

Glanville said, "Well, David seemed to fall for her straightaway, but she was quite a challenge. Of course, when she succumbed and they began a relationship, her…shall we say her basic traits, manifested themselves."

"If I remember," Will said slowly. "There was a significant incident with another boy?"

"Oh yes. Boy T. Glassy." Glanville perked up, though he didn't seem to notice he'd broken his own rules on protecting inmates' privacy. "That's what the other kids called him. He was a bit of an acolyte of David's. David looked out for him."

"And…Girl X set him up," Will said. "This Glassy."

"She initiated a situation…just some kissing and petting which Glassy went along with," Glanville agreed. "I don't think he'd ever been in a sexual situation before. Anyway, she made sure Glassy got all the blame from David, so she eliminated a rival for his attention."

Tom absorbed that, trying to accept that this man was describing Catriona Haining. But to him, they were talking about an entirely different person.

"I seem to recall you mentioned her psychiatric diagnosis," Will commented. "In your book."

Glanville looked uneasy again. "Well yes. But that was Girl X. Not necessarily…the person you're investigating."

Will widened his eyes with exaggerated, almost unctuous understanding. Tom thought he might as well have winked and tapped the side of his nose. "Of course. Again—it's entirely off the record."

Glanville hesitated, but he said slowly, "I should say that the lead psychiatrist attached to the unit wasn't exactly what I'd call stellar. He… Dr. Galloway…wasn't slow in throwing diagnoses around. David, for example." His disdain was clear. "In this case though"—*unusually*, his tone said—"he could hardly miss pathological codependency issues and suicidal tendencies."

Tom stilled, as if any tiny movement might stop Glanville talking.

"Suicidal tendencies?" Will's tone was delicate.

"Well…yes. Dr. Galloway put her on antipsychotics, but they made her put on weight. Which in turn fed her insecurity. So she overdosed. Personally, I think it was a cry of rage, more than a cry for help." Girl X clearly did not have Glanville's sympathy. "In any event," Glanville went on, "she was put on antidepressants instead. *But* she overdosed again. Out of jealousy that time."

Tom knew he should feel relief, validation. But he felt sick. He rubbed a hand across his mouth.

"How old was…Girl X when she left?" Will asked.

Glanville shrugged. "Eighteen? Nineteen? She took her A-levels just before she went, as I recall. David was very focused on education, and he drove her on. She actually tried to get her sentence extended by attacking one of the other female inmates, but…well…she forgot all of us soon enough when she was out. She stopped visiting after a few months. I expect she fixated on someone new."

Tom stared at the littered brewery coasters on the table, the empty coffee mugs, the flakes of Glanville's demolished pastry.

I expect she fixated on someone new.

He barely tuned in to the rest of the conversation as Will began to disengage and say their goodbyes. Instead he thought of Nick, who'd unknowingly picked up the baton of responsibility for Denise Heath.

He thought about how hard it must have been to try to live with that. How Nick had tried for nine years to fulfill her emotional needs, until finally he'd cracked and tried for his own happiness. And how Tom had failed to give him the fairytale ending he must crave after Catriona.

Tom didn't really come back to himself until they were back in the car park.

Will pressed the key fob to open his car, and Tom didn't ask permission. He simply pulled open the passenger door and slumped into the seat, feeling like a newly risen zombie.

"I can't use that," Tom muttered. "I can't do that to her, on top of everything else."

Will sighed. "That's useless sentiment. You have substantive evidence now that the woman who accused you was manipulative, unstable, and obsessed with her husband who had fallen in love with you."

He sounded like a machine, Tom thought with an unexpected burst of rage. As if the sympathetic, humane Will Tom had known had been obliterated, and cold practicality was all that remained.

"She could very feasibly have set all of this up for revenge," Will went on, and Tom's anger blinked out.

"Do you think that's what she did?" His voice sounded small. "That she hated me so much she wanted to…to punish me from her own grave?"

Will glanced at him at last. "Incredibly," he said with dry economy, "that seems like the likeliest scenario at this point. Deciding to kill herself, and having the satisfaction of punishing you too."

"But if I tell the police all this," Tom said. Why couldn't Will understand? "It'll reach Nick. It'll break his heart."

"You don't have to tell the police all of it, unless you know you have to." Will still sounded steady, impersonal. "The information we got from the doctor may be enough to cast doubt on the allegations. If Lawson's bothered to talk to her, he may already know the case is dodgy. But if you do have to use Denise's record, threaten Lawson with legal action if it gets out to the press."

Silence fell. Tom stared blindly across the car park, and it struck him then that his temporary teamwork with Will, their bizarrely renewed acquaintanceship, had reached its end.

Will had delivered for him—he really was the best. And it was over.

He didn't plan to blurt out, "Why did you leave the Met?" Will froze, but Tom blundered on. "You really loved it." He hadn't even allowed himself to worry properly that the reason might be to do with him.

But he wouldn't see Will again. And something in his head screamed at him: *last chance for absolution.*

"Not. Your business," Will bit out. His eyes fixed ahead on the car-park wall and the scrubby bed of shrubs that separated it from the busy road beside the pub. Tom could see the muscles bunched white in his jaw, pinkness inching up over his throat and his cheek, staining his clear olive skin.

"I'm sorry," Tom forced out. "I just wanted to say…sorry. I'm sorry for how I ended things." Will flinched minutely. "I was a cunt."

The silence felt eternal. Then at last, Will turned his head to look at Tom straight on. His eyes were dark and liquid in the shadow of the car cockpit, shockingly beautiful.

"Bit of an understatement," Will said.

"Will, I…"

"No honest grown-up conversation for you," Will went on relentlessly. His voice sounded raw. Hoarse. "You time it 'til I'm safely waiting for you in an out-of-town hotel to text me that it's over. Attaching a couple of selfies with your tongue in Pez's mouth and his hand on your crotch. To underline your point."

Tom swallowed the barbed-wire lump in his throat.

He remembered the amount of alcohol and the line of coke it had taken to do it. The horrifying excitement of snapping the photos, and the hand-shaking thrill of sending them, as Pez—wired—giggled and egged him on. Like turning the key to a prison door and darting out from claustrophobia, into the free, fresh air.

The brutal stab-stab of regret and pure panic that had followed, the second he heard the message whishing off into the ether. Too late then.

"I just…I had to make it final. I'm sorry."

Will's cold eyes told him how completely useless that was. "So you keep saying. But it worked. Especially choosing the pub my team used, to do it. Des wasn't the best eyewitness to choose though. He agonized for days before telling me he'd seen you all over your mate. Very big on Presbyterian guilt, is Des. I ended up having to comfort *him*."

Tom stared down at his hands. He could feel his mouth trembling. He deserved this. More than deserved it.

"It was for the best," he pleaded. "We were in too deep."

"No," Will countered ruthlessly. "*I* was in too deep. And the only person you thought about when you did it, was yourself."

The knife slid unerringly home. Because Tom hadn't let himself consider the consequences for Will—in love for the first time in his life. That might have weakened his resolve.

"Well…" Tom said in bitter acknowledgment. "I'm a narcissist, aren't I? Selfish to the core."

Will gave the typically Italian, one-shouldered shrug that Tom had loved once upon a time, and looked out of the windscreen again at the sunny car park. He didn't deny it.

But then, he turned to look at Tom directly and his expression had shifted to determination.

Just one second of prescience had Tom begging in his head, *Don't...*

But Will had never been craven.

"Did you ever give a fuck?" he asked. "Do you really regret doing it?"

Tom held his eyes for a long agonized moment. "I regret hurting you," he said, "but not ending it. You always knew I needed—*I need*—to be free. To follow my career."

And it was true. He didn't regret it, at least...after living through the first shock of what he'd lost. When he'd chosen, he'd promised himself he wouldn't look back. He'd made sure he hadn't.

"So. You never loved me," Will said. It was a statement not a question.

Tom drew a glass-sharp breath. But this time Will was going to make sure it was all nailed down, ready for the ground.

Tom couldn't understand the dread the question created in him, except...perhaps he didn't want to say it to Will's face.

Wasn't that why he'd done it as he had, the last time? Because as brave as Will was, Tom had always been just as much a coward, who hated witnessing the wreckage he left behind.

But there was no option now but honesty.

"No." He forced the word out. "I'm sorry. It wasn't fair to you."

And Tom made himself watch Will's face this time, as he accepted that his love had not been returned.

Pain. A flash of humiliation. Instant acceptance.

Will had wanted to hear the confirmation from Tom's mouth. No mistakes. No miscommunication. *I never loved you.*

"Where should I send your bill?" Will asked. There was no emotion in it.

Tom's mouthed twisted. "To me. Please. Care of Echo."

Will nodded once. He trained stony eyes ahead, out of the driver's window.

Tom swallowed. "Thank you for helping me," he managed.

"It's what I'm paid for," Will told the windscreen. "Remember: don't relax around Lawson. He'll always look for the easy collar. I'd advise you to tell your brief about Mrs. Haining's record, but it's up to you how much information he can use."

"Right. Thanks," Tom whispered. Something was squeezing his throat. "Well. Bye then, Will."

"Goodbye," Will said.

Tom climbed out of the car and fumbled his helmet, his jacket and his bag from the back seat. Then, without another word, he slammed the door shut and strode to his parked bike.

His abdomen felt rigid, braced, waiting for something. He pulled on his jacket and helmet and shouldered his backpack. When he looked back at the car, Will was still staring impassively out of the windscreen, watching him go.

He told himself, as he slammed the bike's engine into life, that this was a thousand times better than their last parting. However painful, the boil had been lanced and now the poison could seep away. Will had needed closure. Tom had needed to sit and take it, and tell the truth. Absolution required penance.

He should feel relief. He didn't understand why he didn't, yet.

He'd driven his bike out of the car park and rejoined the steady traffic onto the A1000 back to town before it occurred to him, that, in all the time since he'd seen him again, Will hadn't called him by his name.

7

The bike helmet made a satisfying thud as Tom slammed it onto Pez's glass desk and collapsed moodily onto the visitor's chair, legs sprawled out in front of him.

Pez, who'd been typing on a large MacBook when Tom barged in, regarded him in silence, but his kohl-lined, dark green eyes were wide.

Tom could tell he thought it had to be bad news.

Pez was worried for him. And Tom was an arsehole. Two constants of the universe.

Tom sighed and let his head drop back on his shoulders until he was staring up at the spotlights set neatly into the white ceiling. He couldn't work out why he still felt as he did, and why he'd felt that way through the whole journey from Barnet to Echo's offices in Soho. Maybe it was the inevitable aftermath of this quick nightmare. The endless shocks about Catriona. The unpleasantness of closure with Will. The anticlimax of imminent back-to-normal. He rubbed his eyes hard.

"So?" Pez demanded imperiously. "Did Officer Dibble find *any-thing*?"

Tom's mouth tightened, but he didn't comment. Pez's nailed-on hostility to Will should have been irrelevant, but somehow it pushed his mood even further out to the edge.

"We found some proof it wasn't me harassing her." Which was what he wished the truth to be, rather than the reality—that they'd found secrets to discredit Catriona. Secrets he now had to carry with him.

"*Some* proof?" Pez persisted. "So who was it, really?"

Tom shrugged. "Who knows? But it had nothing to do with me."

Pez nodded slowly, fingers rubbing his lower lip. "So…it's over."

"I think so." Tom grimaced as his spirits sank lower still. "*After* the police interview tomorrow, of course. That'll be fun. And there's the funeral, once they release the body."

"Yeah." Pez continued to study him narrowly as he'd done since the moment Tom had barged in. Almost taking careful mental notes. But Tom could tell the moment Pez decided to shift tactics, as clearly as if he'd had spoken his intentions aloud.

"Oooh. Change of subject," Pez said, and his wrist flopped dramatically. "You know that big *Elle* spread at the Marshall Street Baths? That super-arty underwater thing? I told you Cheryll was clawing for it? Because she thought it could get her on to the trending list at Models.com?"

Tom nodded, trying to join in Pez's bid for their own insane normality. Tom had never had to go through the stage most models did of fighting and begging their booker for jobs, but he empathized with Cheryll's desperation.

"I let her take it because she *swore* she could swim," Pez pronounced with disgusted precision. "I mean she's from fucking Alaska!"

"She couldn't?" Tom played along.

"She didn't admit it till she was underwater in full McQueen couture," Pez hissed. "She almost drowned. It was one of the most h*umiliating* phone calls of my life."

Tom snorted. Pez appeared genuinely outraged, but Tom knew fake melodrama when he saw it.

"I mean, what did she *think* was going to happen when they fucking submerged her? Oh, by the way, this came for you." Seamlessly, Pez whipped out from behind his desk a large rectangular box covered in brown wrapping paper, stained a shade of muted tomato-red.

Pez raised expectant eyebrows—he loved gifts—so Tom dutifully pulled the package toward him, something he couldn't quite place prodding at his memory. Perhaps it was his own familiar disinterest.

He opened the paper neatly to reveal a white box with black block lettering on the lid. Givenchy. Just a sample then.

When he opened the box though, inside the tissue paper, Tom found for once, something he could really love. It was a black biker's jacket, and he pulled it out at once and held it up, admiring the placement of buckles and zips, the quilting on the shoulders. There was a large, solid silver cross hanging from the tab of the main zip, and the label inside said the jacket was made of buffalo leather.

Pez had begun to paw idly in the debris, looking for documentation, and that was when the memory clarified for Tom.

"I can't find anything," Pez announced. And it was perfect déjà vu. Café Oto. Blue-stained paper, not red.

"It's from the same nutter as the Tiffany cuff," Tom said with disgust. He'd really liked the jacket too. A horrible premonition made him catch the dangling cross and turn it. And yes, sure enough—an inscription: *Than anyone else*

He had to fight to clamp down on his boiling temper as Pez took the jacket out of his limp hands, but it felt as if the last dregs of his patience had just blown to atoms.

"Is that…a quote?" Pez frowned. "'Than anyone else'?"

Tom unclenched his teeth. "The bracelet said 'I want you more'. It's 'I want you more, than anyone else.'"

Pez's eyes widened, then he hooted with loud and delighted scorn. "Fuck me! A true romantic! Sending three-thousand-quid jackets and two-grand jewelry anonymously on the off-chance." Tom suspected that Pez was actually no more amused than Tom was, but still he barrelled on, as if his default mode that afternoon was "cheer Tom up". "It's *totally* sick though. I mean you can still wear it. They obviously have money to piss against the wall."

"*They're* obviously a tosser," Tom spat.

Pez's brows rose. "But a tosser with taste," he reproved.

Tom scowled and looked away.

Why had he come here? Even Pez couldn't chivvy him out of this mood, and he sure as hell didn't deserve to suffer through it with him.

Pez, as always, read his mind. "You should go and get some sleep, Tommy. You have the Mulberry go-see tomorrow." His voice softened. "Look, once the funeral's over…things'll get back to normal."

Which was more or less what Tom had been telling himself just a few minutes before. But somehow that echo fed the restless, suffocating ball of discontent grinding in his guts.

"Normal?" His voice was thick and angry. "Nothing we *do* is *normal*. It's complete fucking *strangers* sending presents that could pay for a small family car. It's *fantasy*."

Pez gaped at him for a hurt second, before his expression resolved into a knowing sneer.

"Oh I *see*," he mocked. "This isn't a job for a *real* man, is that it? I fucking knew it! Two days and you're parroting Captain Suburbia!"

Tom glowered ferociously. "It has nothing to do with Will. It's that for the last two days, I got to use my brain. I'd forgotten I fucking had one!"

"Oh for fuck's *sake!*" Pez rolled his eyes with violent flamboyance. "Now it's 'poor me, no one takes me seriously.'"

"No one does! I'm just a…a vehicle for someone else's fantasy. Like every fucking model out there. Everyone has power over us—photographers, stylists, designers, agents." Pez's eyes narrowed to furious slits, but Tom kept spewing it all out, like sickness. "None of them are interested in what any of us have to say. When I'm on a job, it's a fucking miracle if anyone acknowledges I'm a human being."

Putting it into words at last didn't make Tom feel better. In fact, he felt vaguely shocked by himself. He'd always made sure to cement any doubts or discontent beneath the knowledge that he'd been given chances few people ever got. He'd chosen to do this. And most of all, he'd been careful never to voice any of his restlessness, or periods of self-contempt, to Pez. Because he knew Pez had always suspected he might be less than one-hundred-percent committed to modeling, and that ambivalence in Tom would upset him.

But Pez didn't look upset. "You ungrateful fucking wanker!" He looked incandescent. "If you weren't a model, how could you even touch the world you live in now? The travel? The glamour? The amazing people you've met? The money you've made? You got to go to the Met fucking Gala the last two years! So, you'll always get a quarter of what the girls get—you're still a hell of a lot better off than you'd have been if you'd… spent your life sawing away at *dead* things!"

"It's called forensic science, Pez." But Tom's appetite for confronting any more truth had vanished. It was pointless and too late, and he felt too aimlessly sad, too weighed down, for aggression.

"I don't care what it's fucking called. I saved you from it!"

Tom huffed a false laugh. "I'm not blaming you," he said, appeasing. "I made all the choices. But…fuck, Pez…why am I so easily led?"

"*What?*" Pez's short bark of laughter rang with disbelief and scorn.

"I just…go with the flow, don't I? I take the line of least resistance and…"

"Oh, I fucking knew it!" Pez seethed. "You do blame me! Because I lured a nice little scientist into all this shallowness."

"Pez. I don't." And he didn't think he did.

"*You* are the most stubborn arsehole I know, Tom," Pez said with quiet, furious vehemence. "And it doesn't matter how much my advice makes sense, if you didn't want to listen, you wouldn't. You wouldn't have put your career first. You wouldn't have chased the top rankings, if you hadn't wanted to deep down. Because in the end, no one makes you do *anything* you don't want to do."

The stared at each other in painful, fractious silence. Tom's mind whirred.

A knock sounded at the door.

Pez's mouth twisted. "Yes!" he barked. His defiant eyes never left Tom's.

"Pez?" A woman's voice.

Rachel, Echo's main receptionist, hovered just inside the office, uncharacteristically subdued. Almost embarrassed.

"I'm sorry to interrupt, but there are two men at Reception looking for Tom." She glanced at him with nervous apology. "They say they're police officers."

Shock caused Tom's stomach to lurch violently. Des had warned him Lawson may not be willing to wait, but Tom hadn't taken that warning seriously enough.

He rose to his feet, caught between horror and fury that they'd come here to the office just to try to intimidate him, and in the process, they'd made him the subject of the kind of gossip and speculation the place fed on.

"It's all right, Rach," he said, with as much unimpressed languor as he could manufacture. "It's no big deal. I know what it's about."

Pez stood too, and the moment Tom moved toward the door, he followed. Even at loggerheads, his loyalty never faded. Tom had no idea what he'd done to deserve such a friend.

In the bright light of the reception area, he spotted at once the copper-wire glow of Des Salt's hair. The man standing beside him at the desk was shorter, heavier-set and sported a haircut of skinhead severity. Tom could see his eyes were fixed hungrily on Cheryll, the American model from the Marshall Street Baths. Cheryll, in turn, chatted to Echo's other receptionist behind the desk, pretending she wasn't hanging around for the drama.

Both officers seemed to notice Tom and Pez coming toward them at the same time, but while Des's expression remained neutral, his companion's gaze skidded over Tom in his biker's jacket and fixed on Pez, and his reaction said everything.

Tom was used to the assumption that all male models must be gay. Like ballet dancers. Neither of which was true. But Tom himself didn't seem to register on most people's gaydar, and as his fanbase had grown, Pez had pushed that ambiguity to set up a couple of minor pap walks, where Tom was "spotted" spending time with a female model, to be published on celebrity gossip sites. It was just normal showbiz procedure, to build a wide fanbase.

But when it came to himself, Pez never compromised, and Tom saw the policeman's disgust as clear as glass as he took in Pez's painted fingernails and his eye makeup, and his tight black mesh tank and PVC trousers.

Pez clearly saw it too. When he came to a halt, he deliberately cocked his hip.

Despite himself, Tom took a protective step in front of him. "Detective Sergeant Salt," he said. "I thought I was seeing you tomorrow."

"Mr. Gray." Des gestured with a quick nod toward his companion. "This is DC Barraclough. We'd like you to accompany us to the station, sir." His demeanor was grim, but Tom thought that his eyes seemed to be almost pleading for cooperation. Des never had been a man for open conflict.

Still. "I'm afraid it's not exactly convenient right now, Sergeant," Tom said, as if his stomach wasn't threatening to turn to liquid on the spot. "The appointment was tomorrow morning. As I told you, I'm very busy."

"Sir, I'm afraid if you don't come voluntarily, I'm going to have to place you under arrest."

Absolute silence fell. Cheryll and the receptionist stopped pretending not to eavesdrop and turned to gape.

"*Arrest?*" All of Tom's defenseless shock was in his tone.

"If you agree to come in to help us with our enquiries, it won't be necessary," Des hurried on.

Pez's comforting hand pressed hard against the small of Tom's back, and he felt pathetically grateful for that gesture of solidarity. Then rage struck, hard.

He was almost tempted in that moment to dare Des to just do it... but he couldn't risk it hitting the gossip sites.

As if on cue, Cheryll lifted her phone to take a photo.

"Cheryll!" Pez pushed between Tom and the camera. "Sweetie! I know you just want a record of a *disgusting abuse of power*." He glared venomously at Salt, then at Cheryll. "But you're terrible at taking pictures."

Cheryll reluctantly lowered the phone.

"All right, Detective Sergeant," Tom said with poisonous courtesy. "If DCI Lawson wants to play hardball, he's going to be sorry. Shall we?"

He stared Salt down a moment longer, then set off for the exit, leaving Salt and his colleague to scurry after him.

They were all outside on the pavement before Tom realized Pez had followed them.

A white, unmarked Astra saloon sat shamelessly on the double yellow lines directly outside Echo's offices. The police in pursuit of their duty.

Salt opened the nearest back door—on the passenger side—and waited for Tom to climb inside. But as he did, Pez trotted round the back of the car and pulled open the other back door.

"I'm coming too," he announced.

Barraclough's expression spoke of a man who'd lifted up a rock and now regarded the slimy thing he'd found underneath.

"This is a police vehicle, *sir*." His accent was solidly Midlands, and his tone made sir an insult. "It's not a taxi."

"Well." Pez smirked at him across the roof of the car. "Arrest me then, *honeybunch*." He slid into the car, pulled the door shut behind him, and began to fasten his seatbelt.

Tom didn't think he'd ever loved him more. He'd never stand alone, as long as Pez was breathing.

Barraclough was forced to crouch down, to speak through the open front-passenger door. "If you don't get out of the car, sir, I'll have to physically remove you."

Tom could almost feel his need to spit out what he wanted to say… *You fag…you poof…*

Tom had never understood how anyone could believe flamboyant men were soft when every day they faced the potential of situations like this, and still refused to conform or hide.

"Oh, do *try*, Constable," Pez camped as if to prove it, all provocation. "I fancy a bit of a wrestle. Have I mentioned, I love your look?" He waved a majestic, fey hand. "Nothing says twenty-first-century policing better than 'bullet-headed thug', does it?"

It took Barraclough a couple of seconds to understand, then his face distorted, suffused with rage.

"All right!" Salt snapped. "We don't have time for this. Let's just go. The DCI's waiting."

Tom began to climb into the car. But as he crouched, halfway in, he felt Des's palm on the crown of his head, pushing down slightly, until he'd cleared the door.

He'd seen it happen multiple times on TV and in movies, but he'd never imagined what it would feel like. Will had once told him it was to ensure the suspect didn't bang their head and claim police brutality. It was procedure—an automatic thing for Salt to do, because Tom wasn't just an ordinary man getting into a car. He was a suspect.

When he sat down, his knee began to bounce spastically.

Barraclough got in behind the wheel, Salt beside him, and the car pulled out into the traffic.

At once, Pez pulled out his phone and placed a hand on Tom's knee to still it.

"Who are you calling, sir?" Des turned in his seat, the better to try to intimidate Pez. He needn't have bothered.

"Our office manager. To get Tom's lawyer."

"A lawyer could slow things down for you," Barraclough put in from the driver's seat. Tom, from where he sat, could just see his profile. "It's already midafternoon. Quicker for everyone without a brief dragging things out."

He made it sound as if Tom would be doing them all a solid by not bothering. As if they were all in it together and just trying to finish and get off to the pub.

Pez had only reached the message service. "Fuck! Look. Jena. It's me. The *Filth*," he enunciated like a theatrical grande dame, "turned up at the office and made a *terrible* scene to *demand* Tom go in for that interview. Couldn't wait until tomorrow. Maybe they had other *plans*." Obviously the message was aimed as much at the officers in the front of the car as at Jena. "When you get this...we need that lawyer, and he'd better be a *bastard*. Send him to..." He clicked his fingers demandingly at Salt.

Des seemed almost dazed when he said, "Southwark."

"To Southwark police station," Pez told the answer machine. "*Now*."

The car quietened after that, the two men in the front murmuring to each other so softly, Tom couldn't decipher anything they said.

After a few silent minutes, Pez nudged Tom with his elbow and nodded at the back of Barraclough's shaven head.

"I wonder if *he* came up against Captain America," he said darkly. "DC Barraclough does not like poofs. Mind you," he sniffed, "the Cap wasn't exactly out and proud was he?"

Rhetorical question. Tom slid his fingers along the fake leather of the seat to clasp Pez's hand. It was trembling, and that was the only outward sign Pez would ever show of fear.

"Why d'you call Will that? Captain America?" Tom asked. He'd never dared before.

"Oh, come on, Tommy! Truth, justice and the American way?"

"That was Superman," Tom said. It felt like wisecracking on the way to the gallows, but at least Pez's hand had stopped shaking.

"*Sweetie*. Muscles. Leotards. Huge bulges of...morality. Who can tell them apart?"

Tom snorted and squeezed Pez's hand tighter. And they were still clinging on when the police car finally pulled to a halt in the car park of Southwark police station.

Salt got out at once and pulled open Tom's door, as if he thought he might make a run for it. Procedure, Tom reminded himself. But Salt's eyes zeroed in at once on Tom's hand in Pez's. Slowly, Tom let go and climbed out.

A woman was sitting in reception as their little procession entered, and Tom took too long to realize that it was Jena, head in hands. She looked up when she heard her name, an expression of horrified alarm on her face. "Tom!"

And Tom began to understand then that much more was going on than he'd believed.

"Jena? What the fuck's happening?" He tried to stop to talk to her, but Barraclough's hard hand on his biceps propelled him forwards until he had to move past Jena toward an internal door. He could hear Pez and Jena protesting loudly behind him. But Barraclough, still grasping Tom's arm, keyed in a code on a security keyboard with his other hand and pulled open the door to reveal a maw of beige corridor.

"What's happening?" Tom yelled again as he was pulled inside. But the door closed behind them, and he was alone with Barraclough and Salt.

Apprehension throbbed inside him like a pulse.

"Let go of my arm," Tom snapped, because fear only made him more pissed off.

Barraclough dropped his grip as if he was loosing toxic waste. Tom could see he was barely containing his contempt.

It didn't feel at all like a chat.

•••

The name beside the door read *Meeting Room 2*, and inside the decor was heroically generic, with a long lightwood-veneered table and pale pink padded chairs round it. It looked like every other budget meeting room Tom had ever been in.

But he forgot everything when he spotted the man seated at the far end of the table, like the chairman of the board.

He was young, well-scrubbed and very good-looking, with neat, symmetrical features and bright, sharp, periwinkle-blue eyes. He wore a smart, dark suit and a neatly knotted striped tie, his blond hair combed to ruthless tidiness. He was also the man Tom had seen kissing Will in the street.

"Tom." The man rose to his feet and smiled with extravagant charm. "I'm your solicitor." His accent was public school to the core. Tom shook his proffered hand automatically. "My name's Mark Nimmo. Call me Mark." And Tom, despite everything, felt an irrational burst of humiliation that Will's boyfriend of all people had to be the one to rescue him. "Did they arrest you?" Mark asked. "Where did they pick you up?"

Tom said numbly, "At the agency." *Concentrate!* "They threatened arrest, but it's still a chat."

Mark's megawatt smile dipped to reassurance. "Okay. That means you can still leave at any time then. But I wouldn't test it out. Why don't you take a seat?" Mark gestured to a chair across the corner of the table from his and slid a business card into the space in front of it. "Mr. Haining's been in for a while."

Tom felt his legs gave out, more than voluntarily sitting down. "Nick? Why's Nick being interviewed?" Tom's knee immediately began a violent bounce. "I don't understand."

Mark regarded him carefully. "Right. I've had very limited disclosure. I did try to get as much as I could, but Lawson always plays dirty." He paused. "So. Initial postmortem results indicate Mrs. Haining may have been murdered."

Tom stopped breathing and waited for the full shock of it to hit. But he found that he'd known deep down, that he'd been bracing for it after the way Salt and Barraclough had behaved.

Everything he'd believed about Catriona's death, all the evidence he and Will had gathered in his defense, had just become irrelevant.

His lungs opened again with a loud gasp for air.

"But there was a suicide note," he protested. His voice was weak with horror.

Mark grimaced apologetically. "The postmortem found fresh injection sites on the backs of Mrs. Haining's thighs, beneath her buttocks. Awkwardly placed, extremely unlikely to have been self-inflicted. The angle of the slash wounds on her wrists and ear were questionable too. They're still waiting for the toxicology report, of course. That could take anywhere between days and weeks."

"*Weeks?*"

"It's not like it is on the telly, I'm afraid. It takes time. But for now, Tom, you're here because the police want to question you in connection with Mrs. Haining's possible murder."

Tom had been staring at Mark with blank disbelief, and he found himself unable to change that expression to something more engaged.

Mark raised his brows and ploughed on. "So. They'll use the existing harassment accusations, because that's the reason you're a suspect. They'll caution you, but don't panic! It's not an arrest. A caution's used just in case a suspect ends up in court. It makes anything they say in an interview admissible. Plus it intimidates the fuck out of interviewees who're not used to it."

"Am I their prime suspect?" Tom asked, appalled. Then, as he caught Nimmo's expression, "Am I their *only* suspect?"

Mark gave a diplomatic moue. "At this stage you're a person of interest. You're helping them with their enquiries."

The jargon no longer seemed comical or clichéd; it felt terrifying.

"I've been told...this guy Lawson is lazy," Tom said, shakily. "He goes for the easy result every time."

And Will's warning now felt horribly important. It seemed more than possible that Tom could be targeted and disbelieved and charged, even convicted, because it helped maintain Lawson's statistics.

Christ, could Catriona's posthumous accusations convict him? How ironic would it be, if she'd planned for a vindictive conviction for harassment that she could enjoy watching play out, and got him walled up alive for her murder instead?

Mark gave an unexpectedly wicked grin. It made him look like a well-brought-up shark.

"Well," he said smugly. "We'll make sure it's *not* an easy result, won't we? We'll make him wish he'd never brought you in. I don't sit by buffing my nails while my clients talk themselves into court." His smile widened to gleeful spite. "And that's why the police hate my guts." Tom nodded, unedifyingly grateful for Mark's cockiness. "Now, tell me anything you think I should know."

All doubts Tom had ever had about revealing Catriona's secrets vanished.

"I don't know how much you've been told but...Catriona told her friends and her doctor I'd been harassing her. After she died, one of her friends told the police that...that I'd driven her to suicide."

Mark, who'd started writing on a large notepad, looked up, frowning. "So...Mrs. Haining herself accused you of harassment?"

Tom said quickly, "Yes but...Will and I found out something." He hesitated, then said awkwardly, "Will Foster. You hired him for me." *Strong-armed him. Your boyfriend.* Tom could entirely understand now why his office had described Mark to Jena as "pretty forceful".

Mark's expression was inscrutable.

Tom hurried on anyway and gabbled out all they'd learned from Dr. Rolfe and Brian Glanville, all about Denise Heath and her personality disorder. By the time he'd finished Mark was smiling at his notes.

"Will always delivers," Mark said fondly. He looked up. "When the police took you in, were there witnesses at your agency who understood what was happening?"

Tom frowned painfully. "The worst kind of witnesses."

Cheryll would probably be on the phone to *The Sun* right now. Unless Rachel got there first.

"Excellent." Mark glanced up and winked. "You have no idea how lucky we are to have a plod like Lawson to use this stuff on. We could have the South Kensington unit. They're shit hot." He blinked and gave an oddly distant little scoff of a laugh. "In so many ways."

It took Tom a second or two to get the implication.

Mark had just told him they were lucky to have a less talented detective on his case. Which meant even his own lawyer thought he was so likely to be guilty that his best chance was stupid policemen.

"I didn't actually *do* anything, you know!" Indignation sharpened and raised his voice. "I didn't even harass her, far less murder her!"

Mark pulled his expression into instant solemnity. "Of course you didn't." It sounded like a verbal pat on the head. "I couldn't represent you if you admitted you were guilty."

And Tom understood then that it wasn't a question of Mark doubting his innocence, it was that he didn't care either way.

"Anyway." Mark flashed his charming smile again. "That alibi should get them off your back for the murder for the moment. Your friend will back you up?"

Tom glared at him.

Mark put up both hands. "Just checking. They'll ask around the bar you went to as well," he warned. "The historic stuff about the victim is gold though. If I know Lawson, he won't have a scooby about it. He'll have focused everything on you." He tapped his pen on his notepad, then his expression sobered and he leaned forward slightly.

"Okay, Tom. Listen to me very carefully," Mark said, and it was like suddenly meeting a different man. "We don't know what evidence they think they have against you. Bear in mind, they don't have full forensic results yet either, so they're feeling their way too. They're hoping you're going to trip up and do their work for them. And they know that if you say something wrong, or just…make a simple mistake that's countered later by DNA or IT evidence…that'll look like a lie in court, when a good prosecutor gets on it. It's a dangerous thing to allow the police to control the interview by trying to answer everything they decide to ask."

"But…they'll think I have something to hide if I don't answer their questions," Tom said uncertainly.

Mark leaned back, as if Tom had proved his case. "That's the basic mistake they hope everyone'll make. We think Mrs. Haining's criminal record will be news to them, but *they're* going to try to blindside you too at some point, with things Lawson didn't disclose to me. If there's even a grain of truth in any of the accusations you already know about, I'm advising you now to refuse to comment. Because it's very likely you'll make a mistake that could convict you in court."

"Court? But it won't go to court," Tom said, and even to himself it sounded like a plea for reassurance.

"On the other hand," Mark went on as if Tom hadn't spoken. "Listen to the caution. It'll say 'remaining silent may harm your defense'. That's because a jury may decide you made the story up in the meantime, because why wouldn't you tell the police the truth the first chance you get?"

Tom reached up and gripped his hair, pulling it hard, trying to focus on the pain. "Then—I'm fucked either way!"

Mark sighed. "It's my duty to tell you all possible consequences. If you have a defense that you're sure won't incriminate you, you can use it. But as I said, they may unleash things we don't know about yet, in the interview. They'll want your computer equipment too. Do you want to give it to them?"

"What? No! It's got all my information on it!"

"Good." Mark grinned widely. "I always advise my clients to make them go for a warrant. Never help them if you can avoid it."

"God…" Tom moaned. He covered his eyes with his hand.

"Look. Tom. If you want my advice, the safest thing to do is refuse to answer anything you're not a hundred percent, cast-iron sure won't get countered by new evidence. Offer a prepared statement. Leave it all to me."

How could Mark have known that "stick to looking pretty", was the worst button to press?

"I didn't do any of it," Tom bit out. "My DNA was in her house for a good reason, which they already know. I have an alibi. She had serious mental-health issues. And I didn't harass her. I'm totally innocent. I want to answer."

Nimmo eyed him neutrally, then gave an on-your-own-head-be-it kind of shrug.

"Well, not even Lawson can ignore the fact she was a raving nutcase with a record of violence. There could be all kinds of thugs in her past."

Tom stared at him and ran guilty fingers through his hair. "Fuck. I didn't want to expose her like this. I didn't want Nick to know."

"There isn't room for being *nice*, Tom." Mark began to tuck his notes into his briefcase. "In a murder case, you throw anyone you need to under the bus."

Tom watched him packing everything away, fear building under his breastbone, diving and battering like a brace of moths against a lit window.

But Mark looked full of anticipation, like an athlete before a game. He checked his watch and stood up, stretching lithely.

"It's a pantomime. Just take my cues. Don't let them rattle you into saying anything, if I tell you not to. Don't try to be friendly. Don't try to be *honest*. They'll hang you if they can."

8

Des Salt was waiting for them outside, leaning on a beige wall in the corridor, and without a word, without eye contact, he led them toward a door bearing the legend *Interview Room 2*.

He opened the door and ushered them in. "DCI Lawson will be with you in a few minutes," he said, and left.

The gloomy featureless grey-blue room felt almost offensively like a cliché, like a drama set. Like every police interview room Tom had ever seen on TV.

Four chairs, two on each side, were set around a basic table, which was apparently bolted to the floor. Another narrow table sat perpendicular to it, against a wall, beneath a high rectangular window, and that table bore a recording device. There was even a large mirror on the other wall, which Tom was sure, from police dramas, had to be two-way.

The awful familiarity of the setting, the reality of officially "being of interest to the police", of how wrong this could go, just about took Tom's legs again. He sank into one of the chairs on the far side of the table as a uniformed officer he hadn't noticed until then asked if they wanted a cup of tea. Tom had never needed anything more.

He and Mark didn't speak as they sipped, and it felt like a long time before the door opened, and Salt walked in, followed by a bulky, unhealthy-looking middle-aged man in a bad suit.

The man wore a moustache that had been clipped to curve down around the sides of his mouth, and he was mainly bald, but what was left of his graying dark hair was close-cut around the sides of his head. He had a long, narrow nose, a wide, thin mouth, and his eyes, behind incongruously trendy wire-rimmed spectacles, were dark, baggy and cold.

He gave Mark a cursory nod of familiarity as he took a seat across from Tom, and Salt sat beside the man, grim-faced, before reaching over to switch on the recorder.

They all stated their full names for the tape, a ritual which seemed as bizarrely familiar as the room.

"Tom." The man's voice was deep, with flat, salt-of-the-earth Lancashire vowels. "As you've 'eard I'm Detective Chief Inspector Derek Lawson. Thank you for comin' in."

Before Tom could open his mouth, Mark began to earn his fee.

"Mr. Gray hardly had choice, Chief Inspector. He volunteered to talk to you tomorrow, but you had him publicly *dragged* out of his company's offices by two police officers! Mr. Gray's a public figure! I hope you realize that if any of this reaches the press or social media, there will be serious legal repercussions."

Lawson opened and closed his mouth. Tom noticed a dull flush creeping up from underneath his shirt collar. His own skin felt hot.

"He wasn't dragged," Lawson protested with disgust.

"He was threatened with arrest in front of witnesses," Mark countered with melodramatic outrage. His delivery sounded almost comically plummy and upper-class beside Lawson's matter-of-fact accent. "This heavy-handedness doesn't look good, Chief Inspector, when my client has always indicated he was happy to help you with any questions or uncertainties you may have."

Which made Tom sound like an expert the police could call in when they were stuck.

Lawson's narrow nostrils flared. He looked angry, off-balance, and Tom relaxed minutely until Lawson fixed his eyes on him. They held all the emotion of a scientist about to dissect a laboratory rat.

Tom noticed sickly that the buttons of Lawson's pale blue shirt strained and gaped over his plump stomach. He could see slivers of white skin, thickly covered with coarse dark hair. It made Lawson seem both more, and less, human.

"Thomas Sebastian Gray. I 'ave grounds to suspect you of an offense," Lawson intoned.

And here it was. Tom's stomach turned violently once, twice. He wondered what they'd do if he threw up on the table.

"You do not 'ave to say anything, but it may 'arm your defense if you do not mention when questioned somethin' you may rely on later in court. Anythin' you do say may be given in evidence," Lawson finished.

"My client was told this was to be a chat!" Mark protested. "You didn't state that this would be an interview under caution." He sounded like a Victorian lady, shocked and disappointed by modern manners. "What is Mr. Gray being cautioned for?"

"I want to talk to him with regard to incidents surroundin' the death of Catriona 'Aining."

Mark gave a showy sigh, followed by an oh-all-right-get-on-with-it-then sniff. A muscle in Lawson's cheek twitched. He took a second to gather himself.

"So. Tom. You're a…*model*, is that correct?" The tone was intended to undermine.

Tom raised his chin, but before he could say a word, Mark snapped, "You're well aware of Mr. Gray's occupation, Chief Inspector. He's a very busy man. Can we cut the games?"

Tom almost loosed a shocked snort of amusement at his sheer cheek. The thunderous scowl Lawson directed Mark's way was met with studied unconcern in return, and Tom thought suddenly that it was like watching an improvised drama. Mark clearly relished his role, and Tom wasn't sure whether to feel grateful or resentful about that.

Lawson's expression was glacial as he turned his focus back on Tom. "Can you tell me your whereabouts between seven and twelve o'clock on Friday the thirteenth of July?"

Friday the thirteenth. Tom hadn't made that connection before.

Tom glanced quickly at Mark, but Mark's carefully bored expression didn't change. So he replied, "For most of the evening, I was with Pez Brownley. He's my booker."

"Booker," Lawson repeated as if Tom had said *pimp*.

"It's like an agent," Tom said with dignity. "He's also a friend."

"So what were you doing with your…friend?" The implication was obvious.

"I went to meet him in Dalston. That's where he lives. We went to a pub and had a bite to eat and a few drinks, then went on to a club." He gave both names.

"And when did you leave the club, Tom?"

The repetition of his Christian name was starting to get to him. He felt like a schoolboy, diminished in front of authority. But he didn't react.

"Around midnight. I got a cab home to Shoreditch. I had a shoot the next day in Greenwich."

Lawson smirked unpleasantly. Des Salt didn't take his eyes from the notes in front of him. Mark worked to radiate superciliousness.

"What was your relationship with Mrs. 'Aining, Tom?" Lawson's vowels sounded flatter than ever on that word. *Relationship.* Dragging it out to sound meaty and salacious.

"She was the co-owner of the agency I work for," Tom said.

"So your relationship was purely business?"

"Yes." Tom forced himself not to embellish.

"An' 'ow did she feel about you stealin' her 'usband?"

Tom goggled at him. "I didn't...*steal* anyone! Nick left Catriona before we got together."

The light from the overhead window shone opaquely on the lenses of Lawson's spectacles. Tom couldn't see his eyes, but his moustache lifted in a sneer of disbelief.

"*She* believed you did. An' Mr. 'Aining's admitted to us that he left her for you. That doesn't happen with no encouragement."

"Surely you aren't implying that there is no such thing as unsolicited romantic or sexual attention, Chief Inspector," Mark put in silkily. "Perhaps your diversity training has slipped your mind."

Lawson's complexion darkened and his jaw clenched.

"Do you recognize these?"

He shoved a small pile of papers individually, encased in plastic bags, across the desk to Tom. On the top he could see a printout of an email, from an email address: *narcissus1190.* He picked it up.

The title was: *You lose.* And below, a slew of insults, threats, demands, boasts about the writer's insanely good sex life with *Our Daddy.*

You may as well fuck off for good you insane sow, because he'll never go back to you. Our Daddy says I'm the sweetest fuck he's ever had. But do you know what he loves best of all, you sad old bitch? He loves wriggling and moaning on my cock. My big, fat, bare cock.

Tom stared at the words in front of him, trying to believe he wasn't reading them. He felt ready to hyperventilate.

"No!" he managed. It was close to a gasp. "I've never seen this before."

"They were all sent through a Virtual Private Network. Foxy. Do you use a VPN service called Foxy?"

Lawson's accent made the word sound ridiculous, but nothing was funny.

"My agency here does," Tom replied. "Echo. But so do thousands of..."

"Narcissus. That's an in-joke is it? Being a model an' all? And November 1990...your month and year of birth."

Tom could see the gleam of victory in Lawson's eyes. He thought he'd rattled him. That he was about to crack. Well *fuck* him.

Tom took a deep breath and said with as much calm as he could fake, "The first I heard about any of this was when a woman posted abuse on my social media, and then *you* asked for an interview. So I decided to find out more."

Lawson's eyes narrowed. "Find out more?"

"I hired a private investigator."

There was a long pause. "Well. Tom." Lawson's voice sounded dangerously soft. "Most people would have gone to the police."

Tom gave a cool smile. "I thought you'd have enough on your plate, as a *murder* team, without chasing harassment allegations. So I decided to find out where all this was coming from. Since you…wouldn't have the time."

Lawson's glare darkened, but Tom was on a roll.

"And it's as well I did, Chief Inspector. I found out that Mrs. Haining was actually born Denise Susan Heath. And when she was fifteen, she seriously assaulted someone *she* believed was trying to steal her boyfriend. When she was in custody, she had a habit of making hysterical, manipulative accusations about the same thing. She also attempted suicide. Her GP says she had a serious personality disorder. I can send you the details if you like," he finished innocently.

Lawson glare seemed to be stuck on his face, and Salt had stopped writing to look up at Tom in disbelief. Everyone in the room knew he'd just given the police information they should have searched out for themselves. On tape, and for the record. And as he watched Lawson's skin redden, Tom had a horrible suspicion that what had been a lazy cop's wish to grab a nice straightforward collar had just become personal.

Lawson rapped out, "Do you use G, Tom?"

Tom blinked. "G? GHB?"

"You know the terminology. It's big on the *gay* scene, isn't it? Chemsex."

"It's not my thing, Chief Inspector," Tom gritted, refusing the provocation. But his chest had begun to tighten again.

Lawson smiled nastily. "But you'll have 'eard of it. Seen it used?"

"I've heard of it," Tom said.

And he began understand then, too late, what Mark had tried to warn him about. How very easy it could be to say the wrong thing, to entrap himself, when he had no idea of the other person's agenda. He could sense Mark's tension beside him, waiting.

"Do you have access to insulin, Tom?" Lawson's tone was extravagantly mild, as if it were a matter of vague interest, like asking the time.

Tom blinked. "*Insulin? No.*"

"Do you know any diabetics?"

"I...I suppose Pez. He's diabetic."

Lawson's expression sharpened. "Is he? How does he take his insulin?"

Tom glanced sideways at Mark who reminded him, all at once, of a dog being held back by its collar. But he hadn't told Tom to stop answering.

"He uses those pens," he said. "Epipens."

Lawson's expression shifted, and Tom thought perhaps he'd just given him a disappointing answer.

"But *you* know about it," Lawson persisted. "Insulin."

Tom said cautiously, "A little bit."

"You did a degree in chemistry, Tom," Lawson said. "You were very good at it too. Got First Class Honors." Any small release in tension Tom had felt evaporated. They'd poked into his past, but not Catriona's? "More than that," Lawson went on with relish. "One of your lecturers told us you did a project on insulin, specifically."

Mark sat forward, as if someone had poked him in the back.

"I did a summer placement in my last year," Tom said tightly. "On insulin receptor interactors."

Lawson sat forward slightly too. "So, you actually know quite a bit about it then," he said with gotcha satisfaction, as if Tom had just been caught in a fatal lie.

"I know a bit about its chemical structure," Tom countered. He had no idea how he managed to sound so calm.

"Actually, Chief Inspector," Mark drawled with pointed ennui. "This interview is becoming increasingly obscure. You had your men *haul* Mr. Gray from his agent's offices to question him about nonexistent experiences with party drugs and what he studied at university. Perhaps you could get to the point?"

Lawson's gimlet eyes didn't move from Tom. "An empty bottle of gamma-hydroxybutyrate and four empty bottles of insulin were found in Mrs. Haining's room, along with a recently used needle. We have reason to believe she may have been murdered."

"She was killed using insulin?" Tom's pulse hammered in his temples like a blood-pressure headache. Agony. He flashed back on those four small purple-labeled bottles on Catriona's dressing table. "But..."

"But what, Tom?" Lawson was a cat, watching a bird.

"It wouldn't be a reliable murder method, that's all. Someone who's taken an insulin overdose would fall into a coma, but a healthy person would be likely to survive unless they were left for a long time. That's what my lecturer told us."

"Did he? And why would he tell you that, Tom?" Lawson asked, all silky insinuation.

Tom regarded him with loathing. "Because some of us wanted to become forensic scientists."

"And how many ended up on billboards, poncin' around in their skivvies?"

"Chief Inspector!" Mark exclaimed in faux outrage. But Tom thought he knew what Lawson was trying to do. A man who lost his temper could blurt out anything.

Lawson surged on. "Mrs. 'Aining was left for dead with her wrists cut. There was little to no prospect of anyone finding her 'til it was too late. So tell us, *Tom*, in your *expert* opinion, would a shot of GHB and four vials of insulin, injected into the body of a nondiabetic adult, cause a subject to be sufficiently incapacitated to allow their wrists to be cut?"

Tom had never imagined it could be possible to feel such outrage while simultaneously gripped by absolute terror. "I...yes. The GHB would incapacitate if given with alcohol. The insulin...like I said. But why bother? Anyone who knew anything..."

"But whoever did it, *did* know. Because she's dead. Quite a series of coincidences, isn't it, Tom? You 'ate Mrs. 'Aining. She dies with injection marks on her body, and empty bottles of insulin and GHB in her room. And here *you* are, our resident authority on insulin used as a murder weapon. Not to mention you party on the gay scene, *and* you know all about G."

He should have listened to Mark. Refused to comment. He wondered how many people incriminated themselves just through fear and a man like Lawson across the table from them, laying traps. But fear—adrenaline—was what cut through his panic.

"I did not hate Mrs. Haining. I did not harass her. I'm *not* an authority on insulin... I studied its chemical structure for eight weeks as a student. Perhaps you should be looking into Mrs. Haining's past for answers, Chief Inspector."

"Imagine the many undesirables she must have known," Mark added swiftly. "Mr. Gray's done your job for you, Chief Inspector. You should be thanking him. The potential for blackmail alone, with her old identity, should keep your happy little team ferreting for weeks, *without* any more harassment of my client. He's been more than helpful. Now, if you're finished?"

Lawson gave him a glare of vicious disgust before his full attention swung back at once to Tom.

"We'd like to access all your computer devices, Tom. Just to exclude you from our enquiries, of course." He didn't even try to make that believable.

"Oh, I think we should see a warrant before we get to that stage, DCI Lawson?" Mark interrupted again, and that deftly took responsibility away from Tom for refusing to cooperate.

Lawson scowled at Mark balefully. Mark smiled and raised his eyebrows.

"We'll want to speak with you again, Tom," Lawson said. It sounded like a threat. He stood up so suddenly that his chair screeched backwards on the hard floor. "See them out," he snapped at Salt. Then, snatching up his papers, he swept from the room.

Tom stared at the partly open door, his heartbeat hammering in his throat, as Des Salt and Mark climbed to their feet. Mark's expression was extravagantly smug and satisfied, calculated to annoy. And Tom understood, now, how effective a tactical mask that could be.

"Thanks," he said numbly to Mark, as they followed Salt through anonymous corridors. "I should have listened to you…refused to comment."

"You did very well, actually," Mark returned. "That insulin thing was a bear-trap. Not to mention the G. But we knew he'd spring something on us. That's the thing about Lawson. He does his research when he focuses on a target, but he can't see beyond it. Confirmation bias. He forces the evidence to fit his theory. He should have been put out to grass years ago, not given an MIT."

Salt, who was only a yard or two ahead, pretended he didn't hear.

Reception seemed almost blindingly bright after the gloom of the interview room and the artificial strip lighting of the corridor. Surreal and summery.

As Tom and Mark emerged, Nick, Jena and Pez, wearing identical expressions of apprehension, leaped anxiously to their feet from their plastic chairs in perfect unison, as if someone had set off a spring. Jena raced straight at Tom and hugged him.

"Hey. It's fine!" he said and forced a smile, because he couldn't afford to show how shaken and afraid he really felt. And he realized in that instant how much he played a role for all of them—strong and self-sufficient. Absolutely independent. Needing no one.

"Mr. Brownley," Salt said loudly to Pez. "Perhaps you wouldn't mind answering a few questions. Since you're here." Checking Tom's alibi already.

Pez met Tom's eyes with startled horror, and Tom could only imagine how DC Barraclough would gloat that Pez had saved them a trip. Insisted on it, in fact.

Mark checked his watch and stepped forward. "Would you happen to need a lawyer by any chance, Mr. Brownley?"

Pez looked him wildly up and down. "*Darling!*" he said.

Mark grinned. "After you."

Salt sighed and led them both back into the bowels of the station.

"Dear God," Tom breathed.

"N," Nick said to Jena. "Would you hang on to see Pez is okay? I need to get Tom home. He's had a shock. And he has the Mulberry meet tomorrow."

Tom stared at him. "*I've* had a shock? Nick! Catriona was murdered!"

Nick's face twisted into an expression of pure agony. Then it was gone.

Because Nick was playing a role for him too, and for Jena, and everyone at the office—keeping going when his pain must be beyond measure. Nine years of companionship and love and guilt, to end like that. Imagining Catriona's fear. Imagining her at the mercy of someone who would do those things to her.

Tom felt disgusted by his own self-pity, choked by too much knowledge.

"Look after each other," Jena said. Her eyes looked sad and worried as she kissed Nick's cheek.

Nick gave her a feeble smile in return. "Peck peck," he said softly.

It was one of their many private things, that saying; part of the enviable sibling bubble they sank into. Nick called Jena *Birdie* sometimes. And *N*. She called him *DM*. Tom had asked about it once, and Nick told him it was just a stupid childhood thing. Tom had guessed Danger Mouse and Nero the evil caterpillar but, though Nick had laughed hard, he'd never quite admitted that Tom was right.

Tom waited until he and Nick were out on the street to say, "There's something I need to tell you."

Nick looked indescribably weary, and Tom wanted more than anything to insist that it could wait. But it wouldn't wait. He had to tell Nick what he'd found out, before Lawson went blundering in.

"Okay." Nick smiled. "There's something I need to tell you too, actually. And you know I never turn down your company."

Tom waited until they were sitting side-by-side on Nick's uncomfortable sofa in his flat, stiff drinks in hand, to begin.

He kept his eyes fixed on Nick's stash of DVDs, breathing in the familiar scent of lavender and metal as he talked, knee bouncing. And he told Nick, as delicately as he could, about Brian Glanville, and Red Moss, and Denise Heath.

"I'm so sorry, Nick," Tom said when he finished.

He felt the weight of Nick's hand on his jerking knee, stilling it.

"Thanks," Nick said. He looked ashen. "Thanks for telling me so gently. But, I already knew." He lifted his hand.

When the sense of that hit, Tom felt muscles he didn't know he'd tensed begin to loosen as relief demolished some of the rock weight of responsibility.

"I'm David Burchill," Nick said.

9

"Tom?"

Tom couldn't wrench his stunned gaze away from the anxiety twisting Nick's mouth, his frowning eyes. From the familiar, neat perfection of his swept-back brown hair.

"Is this some kind of…?" Tom managed. "Do you think that's funny?"

Nick drew a deep breath. "No. It's true."

And Tom couldn't stop staring at him, as if he were some Victorian-manufactured freak of nature. Knowing he should look decently away, and yet…mesmerized by the horror of it.

David Burchill.

A celebrity killer. A killer of babies.

"I had to tell you once I discovered Cat was murdered…that way. I'm so…so sorry." It sounded desperate.

"I don't understand," Tom said. His voice sounded distant and hollow, coming from the end of a long tunnel. Maybe he'd fallen asleep on the sofa, and this was his psyche wreaking some kind of gruesome punishment. A really, *really* bad dream.

Nick swallowed. "When I got out, I got a new identity. Lifetime anonymity. It's only given to…well…to people who have a high profile. Who become the subject of serious hate campaigns."

"Criminals who have a high profile," Tom corrected viciously, and from nowhere anger rushed to the rescue, fully formed, crowding out shock and repulsion.

Nick flinched, but Tom barely noticed.

He'd been played all along.

Nick was an imposter. Like a bad movie.

"Yeah." Nick looked like a kicked dog, as if he'd expected nothing else. "Criminals."

Nick and Catriona. David and Denise, who'd once ruled over Red Moss secure unit. And they'd fooled everyone, burying their violent pasts beneath a cloak of glamour and success.

"The tabloids called me the Babes in Arms killer," Nick went on stolidly. His head was bowed, eyes fixed on the glass he held. "Because that's how the…the victims were found."

Tom felt a new rush of panic, pure and fast like heroin to the vein. *Murderer.*

"I was still a minor." Nick didn't raise his head. "It was after the Bulger case, and the twins were just two years old. My mug shot was splashed on every tabloid front cover the day I was convicted. 'The Face of Evil.' There were tabloid columns demanding I should die in jail. Preferably not of old age." His gaze remained on the whisky in his glass.

Allegedly! Glanville's indignant retort burst into Tom's brain. *An appalling miscarriage of justice!*

Tom choked out somehow, "Did you do it?"

Nick looked up. He seemed amazed to be asked.

"I was thirteen," he said. "Bethany was my first girlfriend…older than me. The first time I had sex. I thought we'd get married and be together forever." He gave a dead smile. "She was babysitting her brothers and I went over to see her. We smoked some of her pot." A bitter huff. "I didn't inhale. She passed out and I went home and cried, because she'd been distracted and bored and I'd heard rumors she was seeing another boy. I thought it was the end of the world. But I went to school the next morning, and then the police came to take me out of my class and ask me questions, because the twins had disappeared overnight. They were found by their father, under a bridge, in each other's arms. The police could tell they'd wandered around a bit in the dark, scared, crying, but they'd been fed an overdose of ground-up sleeping pills in milk, and…injected with massive amounts of insulin, and eventually they must have…given up and laid down together to die." He drew a shaky breath. "That was the worst bit. That it was obvious how afraid they'd been. Of course… my DNA was all over the house. And Beth and her friends told the police she was seeing someone else but she was terrified to break up with me, because I was creepily intense, and controlling, and violent."

"Were you?" Tom demanded.

Nick regarded him with no visible emotion. "Intense? Yeah. Like a thirteen-year-old being led by his dick. Controlling...I suppose I tried, mainly through insecurity. Violent? That was her dad."

"Her *dad*?"

"Beth was fucked-up even at fourteen. Drinking, dope, flirting with smack, sex, skipping school. She used to say her dad tried to get into bed with her, but...maybe she lied. I'm pretty sure he hit her. She used to wind him up almost to see how far she could go before he snapped."

"Didn't you tell the police that?" Tom asked, aghast.

Nick's laugh was bitter. "Oh yeah. I threw him to the wolves, first chance I got. I thought, maybe, Beth drove him too far, and he killed the twins in a fit of madness, because...perhaps they saw him having sex with her or something. But Beth denied everything. And he was a police inspector."

Christ. "So...you think it was him?" Tom ventured.

"They said he had 'a solid alibi'. And the crime scene showed premeditation. I was the suspect they thought had enough of a grudge, because she was cheating on me. But looking back now...they didn't have anything. Hearsay. Circumstantial evidence. A jury wouldn't convict a kid on that. I'd probably have been fine. But then Ava decided to try to save the day and gave a statement saying she'd done it because Beth had been about to break up with me, and she wanted to punish her, and that meant..."

"Hang on. Who's Ava?"

Nick blinked. "Oh. My younger sister."

"Your..." Revelation struck. "Oh, God."

Nick studied his hands. "Yeah."

His friend. His friend, and his lover, and his boss. He hadn't known any of them.

"But Jena's older!" he said, pleading for Nick to scoff, *Oh, it wasn't her.* But of course, it had to be.

Nick gave a tiny shrug. What was one more lie?

"The police believed her," Nick went on doggedly. "Or they made me believe they did. I didn't have a proper lawyer or an experienced social worker...just some out-of-her depth kid. They entrapped me really. But I thought I had to confess to save Ava. My mum was diabetic, so I said I used her insulin. And that was that. My life was over at fourteen. I thought."

"Your *mum*!" Tom repeated. His sense of betrayal was so huge. "Of course! Let me guess. She's Maureen in Accounts."

Nick looked away. "Mum's dead. She and dad had one of those... fairytale romances, you know? But happy-ever-after's not such a good idea in real life, as it turns out. Ava and I were born in India. On a commune, in Goa. That's where we lived for the first part of our lives. But they focused totally on each other, not us. Then Dad died suddenly, a few years after we came back to London, and—Mum checked out on us after that. There, but not present, you know? Ava and me: we were all each other had." His voice drifted. "Mum really loved birds. We had loads of them in the house, in cages. Parakeets and budgies…canaries… That's what Ava means. It's Latin, for bird. And Jena means the same thing. In Hindi."

Peck peck.

Dear God.

"So do I call you David now?" Tom choked out. "And Ava?"

"No! Tom…I'm still me. I'm *Nick*. David's gone! So's Ava. Neither of us thinks about them."

Nick's dark blue irises were shiny with tears as he looked at Tom, begging for a reprieve. Tom felt close to crying himself.

Still Nick.

Still his lover. Who could be lying again. Who could be a murderer of children.

Or a man who'd sacrificed his youth to try to protect his sister.

"Glanville believes in you." Tom said, just to avoid answering Nick's tacit question: *Can you accept me?*

"Yeah." Nick sighed, subdued. "Brian's a decent guy. He was so outraged for me. I really wish he hadn't screwed his career to write that book though. If only because it made me news again, when I was trying to hide."

"But how did you…*become* someone else? If you were so well known?"

Nick shrugged. "Maybe because it wasn't my adult face that most people recognized. It was…the Babes in Arms killer. I did my A-levels at Red Moss, then a degree in Wandsworth, and I was twenty-three when they released me with a shiny false CV, some money to start a business, and a new identity. I had a nose job, and I didn't look much like the thirteen-year-old kid in that mug shot. You'd have to have known me before. Denny'd already become Catriona Telford, shaken off her old life…gone on to uni, the way we'd planned in Red Moss. She'd waited for me…incredibly. And I tried to pay her back. For nine years."

"Did…Ava have to go with you?"

"She wanted to come. We both got official protection. Cat didn't, but…no one was looking for Denise Heath. Well. Until you."

"But…" It was really beginning to sink in. Tom shook his head. "Why am I still Lawson's prime suspect when you have a record like that?"

Nick sighed again. "Because he doesn't know, Tom. That's why I told you the truth now. My handlers aren't happy about letting someone else in, but I can't let you suffer to keep me safe."

"Your *handlers*? And *why* don't the police know?"

"It's how it's done. There are only four other people in the whole country notorious enough to need lifetime anonymity. And apart from Jena and Cat—and you, now—only three people know who I am. An official in the Public Protection Unit at the Ministry of Justice, a very senior police officer, and my probation officer. No one else."

"Then…why are you telling *me*?"

"Because…I really believed Catriona'd done it to herself and invited me there to find it. The insulin bottles. What the note said. Echoes to punish me. But now…I think she may have asked me there to finally try to tell me about the harassment."

Tom had to consciously force himself not to recoil. "*Snap*. What the note said. Insulin. That's what you thought she meant. Like before."

Nick looked sick. "Yeah. That's what I thought. I blamed her for trying to make it hurt as much as she possibly could. And all the time, she was the victim."

"So…" Tom said. "Her killer must be someone who knows your identity, if they used insulin."

Nick nodded miserably. "Seems so."

"Then what are you going to do?"

"Whatever's necessary." Nick looked down at his empty glass, smeared with the sweat of his fingertips. "If I have to, I'll blow my cover to get the police off your back. It has to be something to do with us. Cat and me. Denise and me."

"But if you say who you are…" Tom protested. "You'd lose everything you've built."

And he realized in that moment of alarm that he believed David Burchill had been innocent.

"It may not come to that. I hope not. But I'd do anything for you, Tom." Nick regarded him with exhaustion. "Don't you understand how much I love you?"

Tom made a sound as if he'd been punched. Just one more blow that day.

Nick had never put it into words before because he'd known it was against the rules. That nothing would propel Tom out the door faster. But maybe now he felt he had nothing to lose.

"It was just after lunchtime," Nick said softly, relentlessly. "On a Monday, and I was in the lift. And you came in on the first floor. You were wearing a biker's jacket." Tom stared at him, with mesmerized horror. The sad curve of Nick's smile. "I mean, obviously I'd seen you around before but… I don't know why it was then. You looked tired and depressed, as close to terrible as you can look. But somehow…it made you even more astounding. Jena told me later you'd dumped some guy you'd been seeing. My mouth was so dry I could barely say hello but you were… polite. I don't think you really noticed I was there. You were away in your own head. And I knew right then that I needed to get to know you, to see if you could be anything like as beautiful on the inside. I pined for more than a year before I did anything about it."

When he finished, he regarded Tom steadily with a touching defiance, underlaid with uncertainty and misery. Tom looked sharply away. But the damage was done.

He'd always prided himself on his detachment, but since Catriona had died strong emotion seemed to hover close to the surface all the time.

He hadn't wanted to know that Nick had loved him for so long. He still wished desperately that he didn't know. But witnessing Nick's pain piled on top of pain, he could only feel compassion.

"So you have some kind of martyr complex then," he managed.

Tears tracked down Nick's cheeks though he seemed unaware of them. "Maybe. I just want to try to keep the people I love in my life."

He bowed his head, and Tom knew he was waiting for his verdict. And Tom was well aware that he hadn't had enough time to process any of what he'd heard.

The fact was that so much he'd believed about Nick and Jena had been an enormous lie. But in the end, who knew anyone else really?

All Tom could do in that moment was go with his gut instinct, and for once, it wasn't telling him to run when someone else laid their heart at his feet. It was telling him to show some kindness.

He took Nick's glass from his hand and pulled him into a hug, staring out blindly over his bent head, chin resting on its crown as Nick sobbed in his arms. And when Nick finally looked up blearily and tentatively sought out his mouth, Tom allowed it.

They hadn't had sex since a couple of days before Catriona died, but Tom didn't have the heart to stop Nick as he unzipped Tom's jeans and dropped to the floor between his spread thighs to pull out his half-hard cock.

Tom couldn't understand how he'd managed even that much arousal. Adrenaline maybe. Drama. He didn't feel anything he recognized as desire.

He slid down in the sofa to allow his head to rest against the back and closed his eyes to try to focus on the feeling of Nick's hungry, anxious, pulling mouth, but it was a struggle. Sympathy brought his hand down to stroke Nick's hair in reassurance, and he tried to blank out everything but sensation and physical pleasure.

Will's angry, hurt eyes flashed into his mind. Will's beautiful mouth, turned down in disgust.

Tom's eyes sprang open, heart racing, and just as suddenly Nick came up for oxygen.

Tom's erection felt wet and naked, cooling in the air. The reminder was shocking.

"Shit." He fumbled for his leather jacket, draped over the back of the sofa near his head. "I need a rubber."

Nick sat back on his haunches, watching Tom extract a foil packet from his wallet.

"It's okay," he said. "I don't mind."

Tom glanced at him him, at his swollen mouth, chin wet with spit, his dark hungry eyes, his erection jutting up from his fly, obscenely red.

It had always amazed and sometimes unnerved Tom how quickly Nick got turned on just by touching him.

Tom absently tore the packet open and rolled the condom onto his hard wet upright cock. At least he was holding on to his erection. "Always best to be safe," he muttered.

"We don't have to," Nick said. "I mean, if we both got tested and…"

Became exclusive.

Tom froze, condom-covered dick in hand, and whatever showed on his face, it must have been clear enough.

Nick's expression darkened. "Never mind. I don't mind sucking rubber, if your cock's inside it."

His leaned forward again to grasp the base of Tom's penis, pushing Tom's hand away and guided the latex-covered head back to his mouth.

It took too long for Tom to get back into the act, but eventually Nick's demanding suck took him to a place where the day's horrible events—the final fight with Will, the terror of Lawson's accusations, Tom's unwanted awful new knowledge, Nick's reckless admission of all he felt and wanted from Tom—all of that worry blew away into the mind-wiping sensation of desperately needed tension-relief, sex tingling and thrumming through every molecule of his body.

He released his seed hard into the condom, and Nick finally eased off to a gentle mouthing of his satisfied cock.

Tom's eyes were still shut, muscles trembling faintly in the afterglow when he heard a long, hard moan, and he cracked open his lids in time to see Nick unload his spunk all over the hem of Tom's jeans and his biker boots.

Marking him maybe, Tom thought with distant exhausted distaste.

Tom's thought his own cock, lying, deflating on his thigh, still clad in its semen-filled condom, looked undignified and ridiculous and sad. But nothing could dent the enervating tiredness that snapped in all at once, to encase him. The blow job had sucked all the anxiety and adrenaline-wire tension out of him, and it seemed to have taken all the activity in his brain with it.

Tom had planned to go back to his own flat that evening, because, although Tom had left his timer-bowl full that morning, John would be alone, unless Sonja or April looked in.

But instead, he allowed himself to be led, stumbling and docile, to Nick's bedroom. Undressed, groin wiped clean, and put, naked, to bed. Sliding to oblivion was by far the best part of the day.

10

Thank God.

Tom's first, dazed thought when he woke the next morning from a deep, deep sleep.

He didn't open his eyes but stretched his long body luxuriously, naked skin slipping against silky sheets. He smelled lavender and metal. And memory started to gnaw like a toothache as his reluctant brain and speeding heartbeat told him to accept where he was. He forced his eyes open.

He was in Nick's bed, alone. But he still felt sufficiently disorientated by the depth of his sleep to wonder how much of the previous day's horror had actually happened, and how much was a product of his own disturbed unconscious.

He stared at his clothes, folded neatly on the back of a chair, then rolled out of bed, pulled on yesterday's underpants and jeans, and went into Nick's ensuite.

Don't you understand how I love you?
If we both got tested…
If I have to, I'll blow my cover…

He flinched as memories began to hit, splatting like flies against a windscreen.

Murder. Accusation. Secret identities. The lover whose semen stained Tom's jeans—a notorious child killer. A stranger.

Tom clenched his teeth and forced himself to assess his reflection as he always did. Just that. Just how he looked.

He had a go-see that day. A career to think about.

His light-blue eyes were as translucent and colorless as glass in the artificial light. The shadows underneath them were going to have to disappear, along with the light stubble on his chin. It could wait till he reached home.

He splashed water on his face and blotted ineffectually at the splotch of dried spunk on the hem of his jeans before going back into the bedroom, hovering by the rumpled bed.

He was stalling—he might as well admit it to himself—praying that Nick had already left to start his day.

But even as the thought formed, he heard the doorbell ring and, seconds after that, the sound of voices. There was to be no reprieve then.

He stomach ached with nerves, but he firmed his jaw, grabbed yesterday's black tank off the chair and hauled the door open. Directly opposite, at the other end of the short hallway, Nick and his visitor looked round, startled, at Tom's emergence.

Tom stared back.

He could hardly deny, in that instant of shocked vulnerability, that his instinctive reaction to the sight of Will Foster standing on Nick's doorstep was pure, exhilarated relief. He didn't want to analyze it. He just let himself feel it, drinking in Will's steady, sane presence like a rescue.

Will was wearing a black suit, a white shirt and a thin black tie, his dark hair attractively tousled. But the raw, startled expression in his eyes shuttered quickly, and Tom found himself wishing desperately that he'd at least dressed and shaved, rather than emerging disheveled and half-naked from Nick's bedroom after a very obvious night spent there. The gut punch of guilt shouldn't be there, but it was. He wondered if Will could see it.

"Baby! You're awake," Nick said happily. "Did you sleep okay?"

Tom found he had to force his gaze away from Will to look at Nick, but the obligation of what he now knew tied him in. There was a pause—just too long, as they eyed at each other, and Tom could see the apprehension beneath Nick's bright, determined smile, as if Nick fully expected rejection now, in the cold light of day. But Tom found, to his vast relief, that his mind couldn't process David Burchill. All his new understanding felt...flimsy. He was still Nick.

"Yeah." Tom managed a reassuring smile. "Like I took a pill or something."

He didn't realize how closely he'd been watching Nick's reactions until he saw a minute flinch in his smile. Which gave the game away.

Nick had given him something to make him sleep. Without being asked.

Resentment rose like a fast tide, drowning any wish to tiptoe round Nick's obvious insecurities.

Because, yes, Nick might have meant well, knowing Tom had that go-see meeting, just as Tom knew he wouldn't have slept without an artificial aid, exhaustion or not. But—Nick had taken the decision for him.

"What's going on, Nick?" he snapped.

Nick's smile thinned. "Come on," he said, and Tom thought he sounded oddly resigned.

He ushered them into the lounge—Will in the lead. But when Tom got through the door, he saw Nick already had company.

A woman Tom had never seen before stood, idly examining the collection of bronzes on Nick's wall unit. As they entered, she turned to face them.

She looked to be to be in her late forties perhaps, with attractive, even features and tanned lightly lined skin. She wore her hair in a peroxide-blonde crop, and her makeup was discreet, her lips a pale, frosted shell-pink.

She wore a short-sleeved open-necked white blouse, a black knee-length skirt, with black tights and high-heeled black shoes. It was only when he'd taken in all those details that Tom allowed himself to accept that, though the shoes were wrong, and the checked neckcloth was missing, the epaulettes on the shoulders of the woman's blouse belonged to a Metropolitan police officer.

Shrewd gray eyes took in Will, then narrowed on Tom standing a foot or two behind him, returning his assessing stare in full. Tom realized he was becoming used to the feeling of swooping alarm in his stomach.

"Fuck," Will muttered. Tom looked at him anxiously, but he couldn't see his face.

"DI Foster," the woman returned.

"*Former* DI." Will sounded hostile, and Tom moved forward an instinctive step, to stand beside him.

The corners of the woman's mouth twitched up. "Yes. Not the smartest decision. On either side."

Tom glanced anxiously at Will's profile. But strangely, after a moment, Will smiled, in what looked like reluctant amusement. The woman smiled too.

"This is Assistant Commissioner Christine Hansen," Nick announced as he moved forward to stand in Tom's eyeline too. "She's my designated officer."

Will's smile slipped. His confused gaze swung to Nick.

And Nick told him everything. Everything he'd insisted to Tom could not be told.

Will's usually excellent poker face crumbled like stale cake before his astonishment.

"*David Burchill?*" he breathed, as he gazed at Nick, wide eyed. He sounded and looked like Tom imagined a stamp collector would confronted by a Penny Black. It completed the process of fraying Tom's nerves.

"You told me your identity's top secret!" he snapped at Nick. "If you're telling Will, why not Lawson? He can't investigate Catriona's murder properly if he doesn't know about you. The only lead he has right now is me!"

"That's the problem," Hansen put in. "It's an impossible fucking mess."

Tom eyed her with a surprise he knew he shouldn't feel. Will, and Des, and all the officers he'd known had sworn constantly.

Hansen gave a gusty sigh. "I was alerted by the Police National Computer—when the Southwark and Peckham unit entered Nick's name after Catriona died. I've…had charge of Nick's case since I was a commander. So, if his name were to pop up on the PNC in connection with *any* police involvement, it'd be flagged to me. No one else in the force. I have to decide if he's broken his terms of release. But as it happens, Nick has a better than cast-iron alibi…since he and his sister were in Manchester having dinner with his probation officer at the time Catriona died."

Nick had told Tom it was a business meeting. They'd each lied to the other. It didn't feel amusing.

"The fact is DCI Lawson may look into Catriona's past," Hansen continued. "But there's no real reason to question her life after she changed her name and went to college. So unless there's a handy suspect from before, we can expect he *is* going to focus on you, Tom."

"Then tell him the truth!" Tom said furiously. "The connection with…the Babes in Arms."

"It's not that simple," Hansen retorted. "Once that information's thrown into an active investigation, it's inevitable it's going to leak, and Nick's new life goes up in smoke. And that's *not* justice. He's one of our success stories, and we'd all prefer to keep it that way. Apart from anything else, it's millions of pounds of taxpayers' money."

"Lawson's team would stay quiet if they were ordered to," Tom argued.

Hansen shot him a look of pitying skepticism. "We can't seal leaks on ordinary murder inquiries, Tom. Even if he weren't famous, David Burchill's alleged victims were also the children of a serving Met officer. You can imagine how popular *that* makes him in the force."

Tom slid a hand in his hair and gripped tight. He'd never felt so confused and conflicted and disgusted in his life. Because knowing why didn't make it better.

Ultimately Hansen had just told him he was collateral damage in their bureaucratic games. Nick's anonymity was paramount. Except— Nick had insisted on handing Tom the power to blow up his life.

"We're not hanging you out to dry, Tom," Hansen said, as if she could read his mind. She sounded almost jovial. "DI Foster's going to save the day."

Will didn't look particularly surprised to suddenly have the spotlight, more as if he'd been cynically waiting his turn. Then again, he'd be well aware he hadn't been invited out of sentiment.

"Your involvement's actually the only stroke of luck we've had in this shit-show, DI Foster," Hansen went on. "And my counterpart at the Justice Ministry agrees. We need you to find out who killed Catriona and whether Nick's identity *has* been compromised. We'll reimburse you for your time, of course."

Will gave a bark of humorless laughter. "Of course. *With* respect. You can't expect one man to carry out a full murder investigation without police resources. It's impossible. Ma'am."

And, like pulling on a pair of old, perfectly fitting gloves, Will had fallen into the respectful address to a superior.

"It had better not be, DI Foster," Hansen said. "Because I can't assign active police officers to investigate a live case, in parallel to the official team. And I can't take the case away from DCI Lawson without explaining why to his superiors. As it is, I'm having to fight to make sure he doesn't get the press involved on more than a routine basis. You're our only option. You have your company's backup. And I've arranged a contact who can access any information you need from HOLMES and the PNC. He's a DI on an MIT." Will's brows rose. Hansen answered the unspoken question. "Obviously he doesn't know *why* he's been asked to help you, but he's more than smart enough to realize there's a good reason."

"It's a lot harder to get information from people when you don't have the authority of a warrant card," Will said.

"A PI will always be more discreet," Hansen countered. "And if Lawson hears you're nosing about, he'll think you're working for Tom."

"I haven't said I'll do it yet," Will said. But he sounded unconvincing, and Tom could already see a spark of anticipation in his eyes.

It seemed almost as if Hansen's trust in Will's ability and discretion had…reanimated him. Stripped off that layer of robotic apartness that had grown over him like a carapace, since Tom had known him as a lover.

It was obvious to Tom that Will had never left the Met in his own mind.

Hansen went on briskly, "First information—Tom's accuser may not exist. Fake details and a fake ID for a Jessica Mayhew were used to set up both email and Instagram accounts. Lawson's chasing the VPN that was used to mask the ISP address."

"What? You mean Lawson went after me because of an anonymous accusation?" Tom said disbelievingly. "They didn't even *speak* to her?"

Hansen gave an apologetic moue. "That may have been me. I asked him to keep me informed of developments, given the self-harm involved in Catriona's death seemed so extreme. At least that was the excuse. But my interest made him decide to cover his arse by showing he'd investigated all possibilities. And he came up with you."

Tom shook his head, but there was nothing to say really. Because in the end, Catriona had been his accuser. He sat on one of Nick's sofas, and after a moment, Nick sank down beside Tom, while Hansen took the other sofa and Will the purple chair. Tom stared at the fireplace in front of him, and he registered oddly for the first time that there was a proper grate in it, with pieces of coal that would never burn.

"With no other information at this stage," Will said, "I'd say there are three possibilities. It centers on you," he said to Nick. "Because of the insulin link and your past. The fact the victim was your wife. Or it was about Mrs. Haining, for obvious reasons. Or, it could be about you"—he glanced up at Tom—"because you're the person the killer took the time to set up."

Hansen gave a slow nod. "And the likeliest?"

Will gave a quick, frustrated shake of his head. "If I had a team, I'd be looking at all of then. As it is, the only thing we can safely assume is that the killer knows who Mr. Haining used to be."

"Please." Nick sounded exhausted. "Call me Nick."

Will threw him a wary glance. "Even if the killer's motivation orbits round one of the other two possibilities, Mr…*Nick's* past is where I'd start."

Hansen nodded, her lower lip caught hard in thought between her teeth. "Who and where?"

No one spoke for a second or two. It took those seconds for Tom to work up to it.

"Something that struck me," he blurted. "The killer deliberately flagged up the use of insulin. At uni, our lecturer said one of the attractions of insulin for a murderer is the fact it's incredibly hard to prove as a means of homicide. It's like…a perfect murder weapon…*except* it's not that effective at killing. But if it works, it dissipates really quickly, and low blood sugar can be attributed to anything…kidney trouble…heart disease…an infection. But Catriona's killer used unlikely injection sites… He left the insulin bottles and the needle. He didn't *want* the insulin to go unnoticed. He didn't want the murder mistaken for suicide. So why choose insulin, if it's not to try to conceal a murder?"

When he finished he more than half-expected to be patted on the head, and ignored. But Will was looking at him oddly, with a kind of reluctant recognition.

Hansen's grin was approving. "I read you had plans for Forensic Science."

"The Morton twins," Will said to Nick, "What was different from your wife's murder?"

Nick looked startled. "Well…the kids were given an overdose of sleeping pills then injected with huge doses of insulin. But their wrists weren't slashed. And their ears were left intact."

"As were their tongues," Hansen added. There was a bewildered pause. "Ah," she said. "So DCI Lawson's held that back. Right. The postmortem notes say Catriona's tongue was slit antemortem. It was subtle, there wasn't much blood in her mouth but it turned up in the PM."

"Ante…?" Tom tasted bile. "She was alive?"

Hansen hesitated. "According to the pathologist, yes. For that and… the amputation of her ear." Nick made a sound of agonized distress. She hurried on. "Though it's very possible she wasn't conscious with the amount of GHB in her system."

Or perhaps, Tom thought, unwilling to say it aloud, she was just too doped to stop what was being done to her. Maybe she felt every moment of her mutilation.

Will glanced up from his notes, imperturbable. "So…not the same MO, but similar enough to seem like…a shout-out to the Babes in Arms case? A copycat? A tribute killer? Or, the original killer back for attention, with a few additions?"

"Fuck." Hansen shut her eyes. "Cheer me up some more."

Nick shook his head dazedly. "I can't believe this. I really thought it was over."

"I need a search on recent sudden deaths involving insulin," Will went on, as if none one else had spoken. Hansen nodded, took a notebook from her handbag and began to write. And Tom thought, resenting their calm, that notetaking when in doubt must be in their DNA.

He still felt sick to his stomach. Trying not to think about Catriona's terror; praying she'd already been gone.

Will tapped his pen against his lower lip. "From what I recall of the original case…" His eyes were intent on Hansen. "In 1995, when it happened, no one doubted the conviction. Glanville's book came out of the blue, the year before I graduated. 2009. The press paid it a lot of attention, but there was no try at re-examining the case?"

"Ah." Hansen looked uncomfortable. "There was an internal enquiry into the conduct of the investigation. At the end there were a few… sudden retirements. One officer who was criticized, but not sanctioned, was embarrassingly senior by then. The case notes were sealed. Only the Commissioner has the power to reopen them."

Tom gaped at her, then at Will, then back to her. "Wait. Are you saying the Met *knows* Nick wasn't guilty? That none of this is necessary? He shouldn't have to hide!"

Nick put his hand on Tom's thigh. "The inquiry was into how the police ran the investigation, Tom, not the conclusions they reached. Yeah, I could have appealed on those grounds, but…I didn't want another public court case either. I was set up for a new life by then. I didn't *want* to be David Burchill anymore. You can't rehabilitate a name like that. Even if an appeal court did find my conviction unsafe, there wasn't another suspect to charge. It'd always be 'no smoke without fire'. By then there was no point."

"But David Burchill's grant of lifetime anonymity wasn't a secret," Will pointed out. "You'll always be looking over your shoulder."

Nick gave a sour laugh. "Oh, I know. There were outraged articles about it when it leaked. Questions in the House. Journalists were looking for me, the way they looked for Venables and Thompson, and Mary Bell. But they never found me, and it's been eleven years. The sensible thing would've been to choose somewhere far away, but…I wanted to stay in London." He sighed. "Anyway, they gave me a super-powered and probably illegal—stun device to hold off the lynch mobs."

"Who were you close to in Red Moss?" Will asked, and Tom realized then that the investigation was underway.

Nick seemed to understand the same thing. He straightened in his seat. "No one really, after Denny left. People came and went. The only constants were the staff and the visiting psychiatrists. There were two I saw over the years. Dr. Galloway—he was a cold bastard. And Dr. Wykeham. He was all right. And there was Brian Glanville of course."

"Glanville mentioned a boy who got into trouble, because Denise set him up. He called him Glassy?"

Nick gaze shifted to the past. "God. *Glassy.*" He looked far away. "Yeah. Martin…that was his name I think. I don't remember his second name."

"Maybe"—Hansen's tone was thoughtful—"it comes down to solving the Babes in Arms killings."

Will stared at her. "So all I have to do is solve a twenty-two-year-old cold case. On my own. With no access to the original findings." He shook his head in wonder. "Piece of cake."

"Well the thing is…" Hansen smiled sweetly. "I remember what you can do, DI Foster. Which is why I'm even considering this as a viable plan."

There was a startled silence. Will's skin suffused with color, and Tom, watching his attempts to conceal his flustered pleasure, felt stupidly gratified for him. Proud of him even.

"I suppose if the original notes are sealed," Will said gruffly, "that means HOLMES won't flag up a link between the Haining case and the Babes in Arms through insulin. Lawson's completely in the dark."

Hansen appeared uneasy, which was understandable, considering the fact that she was plotting to undermine a police investigation.

"If Dr. Galloway and Dr. Wykeham are still practicing," Will went on as Hansen began to make more notes, "I need to talk to them. Plus, any witnesses from the night of the killings."

"The twins' older sister is dead," Hansen said as she wrote. "Bethany Morton. She ODed."

Tom turned shocked eyes to Nick, but Nick didn't seem surprised. Of course he'd have been told.

Hansen looked up. "The father is ex-Superintendent Keith Morton. He retired last year. The mother's also alive."

Will chewed his lip. "The problem would be explaining why we're interviewing him about it now. He's a copper. If we give any hint of a link to Mrs. Haining's murder, it'd take him ten minutes to find Nick and recognize him off the back of that." Will was getting better at the *Nick* thing, Tom noticed absently.

"I can't risk Nick's identity getting out to anyone else," Hansen said. "Especially not someone personally involved with his original conviction. So stay away from Morton."

"What about a cover story?" All eyes turned to Tom again. "How about…I'm making a TV documentary? Famous crimes that may have been wrongly solved. This is research. I mean if *he* killed Catriona, he'll already know who I am *and* who Nick is, so no harm done except he'll know we're on to him. But if he doesn't know about it, it could cover us."

Will studied Tom from under his brows. "What if he saw me when we were both serving in the Met? It's possible."

"You're the expert I hired to give advice."

Will frowned. "That's…"

"Actually pretty good," Hansen said. "I'll get someone to make a couple of preliminary calls to him. Set up the façade of a production company for you. Webpage and so on. We can frame it as a kind of vanity project… He's going to research who you are. I'll let you know if he takes the bait."

Tom regarded her with startled admiration—the speed with which she'd assessed, accepted and begun to implement an out-of-the-box idea. She was quite something.

As she rose to her feet, Hansen pushed a card and an envelope across the table to Will. "That has my private number and the number of your contact. In extremis, this is a letter confirming that you're working for me. Use it *only* in extremis."

Will eyed the envelope, then looked back up at Hansen. His eyes had widened, and they appeared almost pale gold in the morning light, framed by those lush dark lashes. And Tom suspected that Will probably hadn't expected Hansen to put her neck so far on the line. Perhaps, he'd expected to be left swinging in the breeze if things went wrong. Yet he'd still agreed to it.

Hansen pulled on a light beige raincoat, and with heels rather than regulation flat shoes, her uniform disappeared and she melded into office-drone anonymity.

She put a hand on Nick's arm before she left. "Try not to worry too much."

Nick returned a tight smile. "You know if Lawson charges Tom, I'll have to…"

"Then DI Foster will have to move fast," Hansen said.

Nick caught Tom's unnerved stare.

"Former DI," Will said again.

Hansen's laugh sounded genuine. But Tom could feel the responsibility of the emotion in Nick's eyes weighing down on him like lead.

11

"Our target reach is a little younger than our previous campaigns." The woman sitting on the tan buttoned-leather sofa across from Tom leafed through his open portfolio, laid out on a low black-glass coffee table. "These are fabulous." She stopped on a catwalk shot from the Parke and Ronen show he'd walked in New York earlier that year. Swimwear. And not a lot of it.

"I'm twenty-seven," Tom heard himself pointing out—an old crock. Pez would have his balls for earrings. But at that moment, he couldn't give much of a fuck.

Wrenched directly from murder and secrets and agony to hugging and air kissing and this.

Tom caught the thought with furious impatience.

This is your fucking job, not playing detective!

This was the life he'd clawed to succeed in. It had only been four days since he'd been on the Greenwich shoot for fuck's sake—posing without a single qualm.

But however hard he tried to get back in the zone, that last day at work felt like years ago. Or never. As if he—an imposter—had taken over the body of Tom Gray, top model. As if that life had been someone else's dream.

"I know," the woman said absently, eyes still scanning the glossy photographs sliding under her hands. The woman—*call me Marina*—was in her early-botoxed-forties, Tom guessed, with long tightly curled brown hair, filler in her cheeks and lips, and the superficially friendly distance of a casting director.

In this case, they were in the initial stages of casting for a magazine- and digital-ad campaign for an upmarket British fashion house, which had made its name mainly on luxury handbags and luggage. The office space screamed success and discreet good taste—wood and stone flooring, rolled steel, white concrete and glass walls—looking out over the expanse of Hyde Park. Everything was open plan, which meant the meeting was taking place in a little gathering of leather and glass furniture by a window-wall, in full view of everyone else in the office. But that was normal.

At least it wasn't an underwear casting, Tom thought idly. Then again, he'd long since become used to getting his kit off on demand. He'd ridden a horse, stark naked, beside a busy riding school for a magazine spread in his first year. Showing his tackle to thirty or forty fashionistas in an office would be nothing.

It could be a lucrative series of adverts if Tom landed the contract. There could be potential for much more work with the company if Tom showed them how easy he could be to deal with. He just needed to focus.

As if mocking him, his phone beeped in his hand. He glanced down at it.

Will.

Meeting set up with Morton 3 p.m. Tom's pulse leaped.

I'll be finished in 15, he typed quickly. Then, in for a penny... *Can u pick me up?*

"But we aren't talking Insolvent Young," Marina mused, still scanning, and almost managing an absent frown. "More...Available Liquid Asset Young."

Tom raised a brow. He appreciated anyone in the business who skipped the bullshit. "It's nice luggage," he said.

Marina glanced up at that, eyes assessing. "We were considering the usual sportsman or celebrity but...we're looking for someone who'll appeal to that younger demographic but looks...together enough to afford the product." She studied him, and Tom attempted, somehow, to project togetherness. "Someone relatable but...out of reach. It's an aspirational campaign of course, but not alienating."

Tom faked an approving expression, wearily disappointed in Marina after all.

"We still want someone who's got a bit of a fan base to attach the brand to that buzz." Marina closed the cover of his portfolio on one of the most recent South African shots. "So you tick that box, of course. But also someone our target base would know they couldn't actually get a date with in real life, but...who doesn't look as if they'd be a 24-carat arse if they got the nerve to sidle up and ask."

Tom's smile twisted and widened to something lopsided and close to genuine. Maybe Marina had redeemed herself.

"There." She leaned back on her sofa, smirking with satisfaction. "That's what I mean."

"I like to think I'm no more than a 22-carat arse," Tom said.

Marina laughed at last, and Tom caught a glimpse of who she'd been before too much cosmetic enhancement got the better of her.

"How about standing over there by the window." Marina rose and picked up a camera from the table. "I'd like to take a quick shot." She handed Tom a beautiful brown leather carryall as a prop.

Casting directors always wanted "a quick shot", as if the model's portfolio might have been doctored to hide that they were actually hideously unphotogenic.

Tom strolled obediently to the wall-sized window, ignoring the interested office eyes on him, and arranged himself by muscle memory into a pose which would best use the bright light shining in on him from one side. One hand casually rested in the pocket of his light-blue linen trousers, the other held the bag as he looked out into the room at a shallow angle to light his cheekbone and the pale blue of his eyes. He rifled through his repertoire of expressions to find Warm Blank and threw in a shade of Self-Satisfied Blank on top, to suggest success and wealth.

And he found himself thinking idly as he posed that it was just as well Nick had drugged him to sleep, otherwise these shots would be horrible.

Then the implication of that thought hit him straight on, and with it came horrified shame.

How the fuck had he come to feeling grateful to have decisions about his own well-being taken away from him? He was grateful for being controlled?

"Gorgeous," Marina cooed. "Yes…I think you have it."

•••

Tom slid into the now-familiar passenger seat of Will's car, still clad in his slouchy Boss suit and white T-shirt and feeling suddenly highly aware of it. Inside the office, it had been a perfect outfit for the meeting. Now, it felt mildly ridiculous, like a costume. As if the simple act of passing through the huge black doors of the fashion company's offices had landed him in a different world—a world where top-to-toe pale-blue linen wasn't a regular thing for an adult man to wear.

Or perhaps it was the realization that Will, eyes safely hidden behind his sunglasses, might be judging, inwardly laughing, as he watched his approach.

Self-consciousness made him ask at once, as he pulled down his seatbelt, "Do I need to change?" No other greeting, because he understood pleasantries wouldn't be welcome.

Will switched on the engine and threw him a quick glance, before pulling the car out into the empty road.

"Nah," he said. "He'll definitely believe you work in the media."

Tom glowered at his profile, then looked away. "It's based on a vintage design," he said loftily.

"Yeah?" Then, as if Will were forcing himself to make conversation, "Please God it doesn't make a comeback. You could get a family of four in the trousers."

Tom laughed, and suddenly, suddenly they were talking. As if they were just colleagues facing a joint challenge. Tom didn't want to work out what was motivating Will, or himself. He didn't care, as long as the détente lasted.

"This is a fucking ridiculous plan," Tom said. "Whoever came up with it should be sectioned. Oh wait…"

Will threw him a long-suffering sideways glance. "Yeah, well, luckily you're doing most of the talking. There's an envelope in the seat-well from AC Hansen. She's got a ghost company up and running, with a website and an email. Phone numbers. 'End to End Productions.'"

Tom picked up the envelope and fished inside to find elegant business cards in the name of *Tom Gray, Production Executive* and a short typed note informing him that he'd helped set up the company with a friend to explore TV and Film opportunities beyond modeling.

His heart began to race with the challenge to come, and it reminded him of how he felt waiting to walk in his first big show. Except—this was life or death. But he liked the adrenaline buzz of it—the feeling, at last, of doing something undeniably important.

"You're sure you never encountered Morton?" Tom asked.

Will shook his head. "He was with CO19. Firearms Command. I did some firearms training as a DS, but he was too senior for me to come across. He may have seen me around sometime though. It's impossible to tell."

"Firearms," Tom repeated. "Fuck."

"They have to be calmer than most people, you know. Under pressure."

Something felt wrong about that. "Nick told me Bethany's dad hit her…that he may've been abusing her. Nick thought at the time Morton may have lost it and killed the kids himself."

Will chewed his lip. "Well. I suppose it's possible his alibi wasn't examined that closely since they had someone else in custody. And…Morton was one of ours."

The sat-nav kept talking as they drove for a quarter of an hour, past the V&A, through Fulham, across the river, and then southwest, past Putney Heath.

"I haven't been in Wimbledon since last summer," Tom remarked idly as they drove along the edge of Wimbledon Common.

"Let me guess," Will deadpanned. "Centre Court."

Tom almost denied it. Then he realized what he was doing.

"Yep. Men's Singles Final." And a man who'd invited him in the vain hope of getting up his arse.

Will gave a cool smile. "Well, it's more plebeian this time." The Passat turned right into a suburban street lined with large, mainly red-brick houses, with red-brick garden walls. "Calonne Road," he announced.

"This isn't far from the All England Club," Tom pointed out. "It must be worth a fortune."

Will slowed the car, scanning the houses on his side for a number. "Morton's father bought it, back when ordinary people could live here."

"How do you know?" Tom asked.

"Pixie," Will said absently, still scanning.

"Is that some special computer program?"

Will glanced over at him and grinned. "She'd love that."

Tom looked away and refused to ask.

There was nothing unusual about the street. Some houses were bigger and set further back from the pavement, with long drives and gardens— features hard to come by in central London. But others were more modest, built close to the road.

Will maneuvered the car into a space by the pavement and pulled on the handbrake.

"Here we are," he said. "The scene of the crime."

Tom stared at him, then out of his own window at the house bedside them. It was large, with multipaned windows, red brick to the first floor and white-painted harling above. 1930s perhaps.

"I can't believe he hasn't moved," Tom said softly. "This is where the kids were killed?"

"On the Common." Will climbed out of the car. Tom scrambled to follow. "And the Burchills lived…" Will scoped around, past a huge house set well back from the road and a set of three garages. "Just there."

He pointed to a low, small bungalow of red brick with a tiled roof, a short paved driveway, and a tiny, lavishly planted front garden beside it.

"They were neighbors?"

Will raised a dark brow. "It's not like you not to do your research."

Tom almost claimed a lack of time. But the truth was he'd avoided reading the gory details of what David Burchill was supposed to have done. Stupid. Weak.

"The Burchills moved into that house a few years before the killings," Will said. "David's mother walked under a train soon after he was sentenced. So someone else lives there now."

Tom stared at the unassuming little house.

Nick's mother had killed herself violently? And Tom had made that crack to him. *Fuck.*

"You ready?" Will sounded careful, as if he half-expected Tom to freak and back out. But though Tom's guts began to writhe faster with apprehension, he found the tension just made him feel more awake.

There was no gate to No. 15, and an immaculately clean navy-blue saloon sat in the driveway. The back door was set in a porch at the side of the house, and it opened before Will could put a finger on the bell.

Former Superintendent Keith Morton looked like a casting director's idea of a headmaster in Tom's opinion, or a senior businessman perhaps.

He was tall and very upright and he looked fit. The skin of his face and forearms was tanned and ruddy, and his hair receded far off his forehead. What was left was short and gray. He was dressed for golf, but he could just as easily have been about to take a board meeting. Tom found himself relieved they'd been precisely on time for their appointment.

After perfunctory introductions, Morton led them into a living room that didn't suit him—full of ornaments and too many patterns, smelling strongly of furniture polish. It looked out, through a shallow bay window, to the quiet of Calonne Road.

Tom and Will sat together on a long beige velour sofa, while Morton took a matching adjacent armchair. They declined tea or coffee. Tom's linen-clad knee wanted very badly to bounce.

Showtime.

"So, as my associates will have mentioned, Mr. Morton…" Tom was amazed by the ease in his own voice. "If we can get it off the ground, our production company is scoping out a new documentary series to pitch to BBC 4, or possibly the main streaming channels."

Morton's expression remained unreadable.

"It's revisiting famous potential miscarriages of justice," Tom went on. Morton's mouth thinned. "I'd be producing it and fronting it. And Mr. Foster is advising, as a former police officer."

All of Morton's attention turned to Will, as if he'd just identified him as the most important person in the room.

"Where did you work?" he asked. "The Met? What was your rank?"

"Yeah. An MIT latterly." Will's tone was relaxed. "I was a DI. I studied the Burchill case at university."

For a few beats of silence Morton considered him as if he could peel away his skull and read his thoughts. Then he returned his attention to Tom.

"All right," he said. "How do you think I can help you?"

Tom braced himself. "Do *you* believe David Burchill was guilty?"

Morton didn't hesitate. "Of course he was," he snapped. "Even after that whitewash of a book came out, he didn't contest his sentence. And if there'd been a chance at overthrowing the conviction, believe me he'd have taken it. Of course the author said it was because Burchill didn't want us to suffer any more distress." He made a bitter, vicious sound. "David always did cast himself as the hero in whichever play he was running in his own head."

Tom pulled in a shallow breath and tried to strategize. Morton's loathing of Nick was so obvious it was almost impossible to find a way in to suggest an alternative theory.

But he tried, "He had a very difficult childhood though, didn't he?"

Morton glared at him with disbelief.

"*Difficult?* They weren't *starving.* They weren't *beaten.* So their parents weren't…practical people. They were hippies. Barely seemed to notice their children were there. But that meant David and Ava did what they wanted. My wife felt sorry for them. Mothered them. Tried to give them structure. She'll never forgive herself for that."

"It must have been hard for David, then?" Tom ventured. "Having to look after his sister alone?"

Morton gave a sour laugh. "She looked after him, more like. She was…" One hand gestured impatiently. "Ava was a nice enough girl. She loved the twins and they loved her. *David* used to come here because he was obsessed with Bethany. My wife and I used to laugh about it. His crush on an older woman." He grimaced painfully, eyes unfocused as if he was watching the memories. "Then he hit thirteen, and it was as if… overnight he looked and acted older than his age. Weirdly…confident. So Beth let him take her out a few times. But *he* acted as if they were in a full-scale adult relationship, heading for marriage. He was just a little boy to Beth. She got fed up quickly."

Tom asked, too carefully, "Did *you* have a good relationship with Beth?"

Morton stilled and raised his eyes to Tom's, and they reminded Tom of the blue-glazed ice-eyes of a dead fish. He found himself quite ready to accept that violence wasn't beyond Morton.

"I see you've heard what Burchill alleged to investigating officers to try to save his own skin." Morton sounded as if he was barely restraining himself, and Tom was well aware the interview was on a knife-edge.

"It's a matter of understanding *why* Burchill insinuated you were abusing Bethany, Mr. Morton," Will put in quickly. "Obviously no one believes it."

Morton's gaze snapped back to him. "Why do you *think* he said it? If I hadn't had the alibi I had, who knows what could have happened."

"So you and Bethany did have a good relationship," Will said, and Tom could see again how good he was at his job, refusing distraction. Nailing everything down.

"Yes," Morton said, sharp with impatience. "We did. She was immature and she acted out sometimes… She didn't like my laying down the law. But that's what parents are meant to do. She was a lovely girl at heart."

"She'd started seeing another boy while she was with David," Will said. "If David wanted revenge against Bethany, why wouldn't he kill him? Or…her? Why her brothers?"

"Because he's a twisted little bastard," Morton burst out. "He knew how much Beth loved Josh and Kieran. She was supposed to be looking after them, while we were out. But she got stoned and drunk instead and let them get taken away. We never blamed her, but after the twins died she was on self-destruct, and nothing we could say or do could stop her. It just took him longer to kill her."

No one broke the thick silence, until Tom forced himself to venture, "Am I right that, apart from the confession, the only evidence against David was circumstantial? It...could be argued that he confessed to murder as a child under duress."

Morton's gaze on Tom was narrow and very hard. Without warning he rose to his feet.

"Come with me." He set off out of the room, and Tom and Will, after a startled second, followed—across the small hallway and up the flowery-carpeted stairs. At the top, Morton opened a door.

Inside, stood two white wooden single beds, neatly made, with blue covers. Soft toys sat like little soldiers against the pillows. Shelves were filled with Tellytubbies and Thomas the Tank Engine trains. Two small pairs of pyjamas were laid out, ready. Tom's throat closed.

"They were woken up and taken from here," Morton said. "My wife insisted on leaving the front door unlatched because Bethany's friends were in and out. Whoever took Josh and Kieran knew Beth was unconscious, or else they were prepared to kill her too if they had to. How would a stranger know they were here? That the door was unlocked? How would a stranger be able to give the twins tablets, ground up in milk, in their own sip cups? Then walk them in their dressing gowns and slippers down those stairs and along to the end of the road?"

Morton gave them a hard, challenging look and led the way back down the stairs. But he didn't turn off into the lounge; instead he headed for the front door and out, down the path, and then right, along Calonne Road.

It took less than five minutes to walk to the end of the street and then cross a perpendicular road onto Wimbledon Common. Grass and scrubland and trees. Tom could imagine it painfully easily. The darkness lit by the orange sodium glow of streetlights... The two little kids tottering trustingly on, believing perhaps that it was an adventure.

He and Will followed Morton, trudging over the uneven ground, for a few minutes more, the loose trousers of Tom's suit catching awkwardly on the undergrowth, until Morton stopped dead in the first thicket of trees, like a toy that had run out of batteries.

It was sunny, and the birds were singing heartily in the branches above them, but to Tom it still felt eerie; the path the children had taken to their lonely deaths.

"He took them far out into the trees." Morton spoke at last. "So no one could hear them crying, and he injected them both with insulin from his mother's supplies. Over and over again. And then he left them to die, frightened and alone. Because *he* couldn't get his own way." Morton's face twisted violently. His voice shook. "People keep calling them the Babes in Arms, like they're…like they're fairytale characters. But they were *real*. Keiran…was the leader. He was only older by a couple of minutes but…Josh was timid. Keiran would have tried to be brave for him."

The picture was vivid in Tom's mind. He said, choked, "I'm so sorry."

Morton shook his head. Tom saw then that his cheeks were wet.

"No one spotted the twins being walked or carried along the road," Will said, quietly. It was a statement.

"All it would have taken was one nosy neighbor," Morton said. "But that night no one looked."

"We just want to go over the case again with a fresh eye." Tom was aware he was apologizing, almost pleading. "Make sure the police got it right and the real murderer isn't still out there."

Morton laughed, no humor in it.

"But the real murderer *is* still out there," he said. "David Burchill killed all three of our children. My wife and I are dead too. All we're doing is…clinging to each other in the wreckage. That's what David Burchill did to us." His voice dipped so low that Tom could barely hear it over the sound of summer birdsong. "And he's definitely *out there*. Living the life my children should have had. *Mister Gray*."

12

"Are you all right?"

Tom sat, eyes closed, head back against the seat headrest, as Will drove. Hardly a position that would reassure anyone he was *all right*. Actually, he wanted to sit with his head in his hands, surrendering to his confusion and incipient despair.

"I thought…" When he opened his eyes the car was already back in Fulham. "Fuck, I don't know what I thought. Maybe I thought Morton would be obviously guilty."

"It's very possible the original murderer isn't behind Mrs. Haining's death, you know," Will said. "So going over the historic case may be a waste of time. Rationally, it'd be insane for a murderer who got away with it for twenty-two years to deliberately draw attention to himself again. What happened to Mrs. Haining…that feels like revenge to me or… some kind of obsessive emotion. It was more than just dispatching her. It was a message. It was showing off."

Tom turned his head to look at the beautiful profile he still couldn't quite take for granted.

"Morton has to be the main suspect, then?" he ventured. "If it's revenge?"

"Perhaps. At this point…if he's found out who Nick is, Morton's a man with nothing left to lose. We need to find out if he has an alibi for Mrs. Haining's death. But we couldn't exactly ask."

Tom smiled wanly. "Yeah. Bet you miss the warrant card."

One corner of Will's mouth curled up. "Not at all. I prefer conducting complex investigations with my hands tied behind my back."

Tom huffed a laugh. "Kinky. So what now?"

The car slowed at a pedestrian crossing, beside a long row of red Boris bikes.

"I'm meeting AC Hansen's Met contact in his local on the Kings Road. Where would you like me to drop you?"

Tom thought briefly about the string of anxious unanswered texts on his phone from Pez—still trying to talk to him about his own interview with Lawson the day before. And the realization that he'd basically ignored Pez since he'd found out about Nick startled him into messaging quickly suggesting they meet up that evening.

But nothing could stop him announcing, "I want to go along." Then he catalogued their surroundings. Red-brick buildings and canopied shops. "Which you assumed I was going to say because this is the New Kings Road."

Will's profile looked quietly amused as their queue of cars merged onto the Kings Road itself.

"I might have decided I didn't want to come," Tom sniffed.

Will raised his eyebrows. "Yeah. You might."

Tom looked away to hide his smile.

Will finally found a parking space on a side street, and they both walked the short distance back to the Kings Road.

The street was iconic in its own way—a huge part of 60s youth culture—wide and long and straight, flanked by red-brick and white-render

Georgian, Victorian and Edwardian buildings, with shops set into the ground floors. The pavements were already filling up with early after-work drinkers, jackets off, arms bare.

Tom followed Will, darting through the traffic to the other side and on to a red and yellow brick building with its ground-floor render painted deep blue. It was a pub called the Trafalgar.

Inside, it was cool, shady and half-empty. The room had wooden and black-and-white-tiled floors, raw brick walls and an eclectic mix of antique furniture, and painted built-in booths.

Will scanned quickly around, then headed toward a table set in a back corner with a black-and-white patterned padded bench behind it and purple and blue velvet cubes set in front of it to act as stools. A man sat there, looking at his phone.

If Tom had expected a world-weary copper, balding and portly, as Will's contact, he could hardly have been more wrong. The man was startlingly good looking, with broad, strong shoulders in what looked to Tom like an Armani suit—short thick blond hair and fine chiselled features. He gave them a lopsided, almost ironic, smile.

"The swans are flying high tonight," he said to Will. His eyes were large and a remarkable silver-grey, his mouth beautifully shaped. "I wasn't given code names. So…hello, DI Foster." His accent floated at the upper end of posh, but his voice was warm and attractive and he radiated an easy confidence.

"DI Henderson," Will said with a charming grin. "And it's just Will."

Tom frowned as he looked from one to the other. "I'm Tom Gray," he said loudly. "I'm working with Will."

Henderson took in Tom properly then, eyes widening slightly. "Nice to meet you both. Please call me James. Do you want to take a cube?"

Will sat at once, still smiling, but Tom found he felt weirdly unsettled by Henderson. "I'll get a round in," he said, to give himself time, took orders for two pints of lager, and retreated to the blue-painted bar.

He got served at once and ordered a beer for himself too and screw the empty calories. But as the pints were pulled, he couldn't help but turn round to survey their table. He didn't want to put a name to the feeling in his stomach as he watched Will and James Henderson in the corner, grinning at each other as they talked.

Will hadn't smiled like that at Tom for two years.

Tom felt suspicious of DI Henderson. It was an instinct.

He got back to the table as quickly as he could and put his tray down with a decisive clang. There was a large framed picture behind Henderson, Tom noticed—a Renaissance winged god and goddess. He was unnerved to realize Henderson was prettier than either of them.

"Well, they're begging her to take it but she's holding them off," Henderson was saying as Tom sat on the blue cube beside Will's. "She wants to stay in the field."

"Ingham's far too good to end up sitting behind a desk," Will said. "Too smart and too honest."

"Yeah, but it's more money." James sounded resigned. "And prestige. They won't accept she's turning it down. I suppose…at least if she were in charge of the whole area things would change."

Tom took a pointed sip of lager.

"Sorry," Henderson said, with charming grin. "Will used to work with my boss."

Henderson was intuitive, Tom noted sourly. He could tell Tom felt left out. And his manners were impeccable.

"You know each other then?" Tom asked.

Will gave him a surprised glance. "No." His glanced at Henderson and gave a wicked smirk. "Though I've seen him on *Crimewatch*."

Henderson froze with his glass halfway to his mouth, and a charming blush flooded his fine skin. "Yeah, thanks," he muttered. Tom's obvious incomprehension seemed to prod him to add, "I've had to do some…telly appeals." And then, with dogged politeness he answered Tom's initial question. "I was in business before I joined the Met so I came in late, so— no, we never worked together. But…I did see Will around." Henderson's blush, which had been fading, deepened again, and it felt very clear to Tom why Henderson had noticed Will. They'd have made quite a pair, if Will had noticed Henderson back.

Tom looked down at his pint.

"I…er…heard what happened," Henderson said. "Got to say, if ever a man deserved a haymaker it was Archer."

Tom's raised stunned eyes just in time to see Will's barriers slam down.

Because Archer…Archer had been Will's DCI.

Henderson though, obviously caught on at once that Will didn't want Tom to know.

He swept on smoothly, "Anyway, the HOLMES legwork you wanted." He pulled a small police notebook from his inside jacket pocket, Will relaxed minutely—and just like that, the subject disappeared as if it had never been raised. Tom found himself torn between admiration at Henderson's social adroitness, and a powerful resentment at being the one on the outside.

"So—a search of insulin-related deaths in London over a six-month period," Henderson said. "The only three recent unexpected deaths I could find in the insulin search tag were a possible murder a few days ago, and two suicides. Both the suicides took an insulin overdose with antidepressants. Not as rare as you'd like to think."

Will wrote it down. It occurred to Tom as he watched that the note-taking might sometimes be a delay to allow Will to think, as much as taking a record.

"I'll give you the details anyway, yeah?" Henderson said. "The suspected murder was the thirteenth of July. A thirty-three-year-old woman…"

Will solemnly took notes through Henderson's recounting of the official basics of Catriona's case, as if he didn't already know every detail. Then Henderson moved on to the insulin suicides.

"Both straightforward. A female, twenty-nine. Discovered in her bath with her wrists slashed and a stomach full of sleeping pills, wearing only a bracelet and necklace. She had a documented history of self-harm, and she left a note for her parents. And a forty-three-year-old male, found in his bed with insulin syringes and an empty bottle of prescription medication beside him. He was also naked, apart from his watch, a red string round his wrist, a neck chain, and his wedding ring. His wife was abroad on holiday when he did it. She's a doctor. He'd been getting treatment for depression, and he also cut himself before he died. No note."

Henderson finished and regarded them patiently. But Tom's stunned mind was circling one sentence.

"What was the male suicide's name?" he asked.

Henderson checked his notebook. "Michael Gregory Rolfe. 5 Courtenay Square, Kennington."

She's a doctor…

"Will…" Tom breathed.

"He died March second," Henderson said, as if someone had asked the question. His expression made it clear he knew something was up.

"Coincidence?" Tom asked Will.

Will glanced at him, and one side of his mouth quirked up suddenly in a wry grin of such charm that Tom felt winded.

"My old DCI used to say there's no such thing as a coincidence in a murder case," Will said. "You find a crumb, you pay attention. Who knows if it's going to turn into a trail."

"Sounds weirdly familiar," Henderson deadpanned, and Will at once turned that smile to him.

"Strange that," Will said. Tom looked down at his pint again. "Look, James. You've been a huge help already but I'm going to ask for something a bit more…um…delicate." He tore a page from his notebook and slid it across the table to Henderson with a smile that was now sheepish.

"I need to discreetly establish the whereabouts of this individual on July thirteenth between eight p.m. and say…one a.m."

James raised a sardonic eyebrow. "The thirteenth. And I assume you don't want me to to mention the Haining murder to this…individual?"

Will grinned at him, obviously impressed. "Nope. *And* he's an ex-copper."

Slowly James responded with an unwilling grin of his own. "Wonderful."

Fuck, he was gorgeous. But Tom couldn't think of a thing to say to break the connection between the two men beside him. He didn't even know why he wanted to.

As if on cue, James's phone beeped. He picked it up with an impatient frown but his expression softened the moment he read the screen.

"Ah. Got to go home. Sorry." He didn't look sorry. When Henderson stood, Tom could see that he was tall enough to carry off those shoulders, and he looked sensational in the suit. "It was nice to meet you properly at last," he said to Will, and blushed that pretty pale pink again. "And you, Tom. I'll call you when I get something, Will."

He winked and turned to thread his way to the door, through now-numerous knots of drinkers. A number of people watched him go.

Tom stamped hard on his irritation. "Fancy another pint?" he asked.

But Will rose to his feet as Tom had known he would. "I should get going."

Tom stood too, because he had no option, and followed Will through the crowd and out onto the pavement. And he seethed.

Will didn't want to spend any more time with him than absolutely necessary however hard Tom hoped for simple peace between them.

How could he blame Will for that though, after everything? Necessity had compelled them to work together, and Will was behaving like a good colleague,

But. But Tom was jealous.

Simple as that.

Or not simple at all. He'd resented watching Will interact with a man he obviously liked. Exactly the way he used to feel insecure watching Will talking to attractive women. Treacherously afraid on a gut level that Will might find something in one of them he wanted, something Tom couldn't give. And Tom had always hated that. Hated the turmoil of need and dependence and apprehension. The lack of control.

Outside, more groups of drinkers had gathered on the pavement. The oppressive heat of the day had lowered to a more pleasant level.

"Where would you like me to drop you?" Will asked. The afternoon sunlight flattered him unbearably, lightening his tiger eyes, painting a sheen of gold on his olive skin. "Nick's place?"

The absolute absence of jealousy in Will's tone made Tom's turmoil all the more humiliating. It recalled too clearly a similar moment of desperate resentment in the car park of that Barnet pub.

He needed to remind himself of reality—as opposed to fairytales. Give himself a dose of antidote. He needed to see his father.

"No," Tom said. "I'm fine from here."

•••

Tom called Nick as he got into a taxi outside Kew Gardens tube station, to update him on Mulberry and Morton. He could hear the disappointment in Nick's voice when he refused an invitation to go round to his flat and told him he'd promised to go to Pez's instead. But Tom couldn't do much about that.

It took just ten minutes to reach the front gate of his childhood home—a narrow yellow-brick house on Gloucester Road with a three-windowed brick-and-glass extension at the front, one of the many appeasements his father had made which he couldn't afford.

Tom rang the doorbell and waited. His key was back at the flat.

When his father opened the door, his delight and surprise were immediately evident. "Tom! Come in. I'm just home from work. I have the kettle on!"

Alistair Gray was tall and handsome, with thick dark-blond hair, cut respectably short and now mainly gray. His eyes were a darker shade of blue than Tom's and gentle. Sad. Waiting for life to once again do its worst. He wore his work uniform of soft light-brown corduroy trousers and an off-white check buttondown, and he looked, Tom thought, like any suburban drone. Tired. Older than he should.

Tom followed Alistair into the house, and the true point of the visit immediately began to make itself felt.

There were the beige-carpeted stairs he'd thundered up so often in rage and despair, as his parents lived out their pathetic dramas in front of him. The fancy wooden flooring his father had installed the third-last time his mother had come home after another affair fizzled out. The fashionable furniture he'd bought at the same time, now already off-trend, stretching his research scientist's salary to breaking point. And his mother's restless, charming voice in Tom's head: *"Oh, Ally! If we're going to have people round, we need the house to look half-decent!"*

Tom and his father settled with their mugs of tea in the big lounge,

Tom on the sofa and Alistair in his armchair. Their usual seats. The room was ruthlessly neat and clean, because Alistair kept the whole house like a show home, waiting to be lived in again.

Tom babbled aimlessly about work, about the potential of the Armani fragrance contract for his future career, though usually he didn't talk much about modeling to his father. Alistair had never overtly shown his disappointment, but Tom knew he'd been proud that his only child had followed in his footsteps into science. On the other hand, Tom had never been as interesting to his mother as when he became a model.

But eventually Tom couldn't postpone it any longer; he had to tell his father something about the crisis in his life. He gave as little information as he could: really just the fact Catriona had been murdered, but leaving out his own troubles with the police and everything he'd learned about Nick and Catriona—because he didn't want his dad to worry. And because, when Tom had understood how Catriona had lived to love Nick, he'd seen at once the uncomfortable parallels. He'd known where all his father's sympathies would lie. Tom could all too easily imagine his disappointment. *How could you?*

But Alistair grilled him about it until Tom came so close to lying outright that he found himself wading head-on into incendiary territory he'd long avoided.

"I've kept an eye on property prices round here, Dad, and you could easily get a million for the house. You could move somewhere a bit livelier, yeah?" Though of course Tom knew it was hopeless. "You're rattling round here. It's all old memories."

Alistair regarded him with surprise, as if he'd believed Tom had outgrown this stage. "You know I can't sell, Tom. This is our family home."

"But there isn't a family anymore, Dad!" Tom snapped.

Alistair flinched, as if he'd said something unexpectedly cruel.

When he'd left for university, Tom had stopped fighting to save his father from himself and became instead what Alistair wanted him to be—a passive observer. An enabler.

But today, something was making Tom want to try again. To change the story.

"You're depressed," he said. Pleaded.

Alistair studied his mug of tea, but he could hardly deny it. In fact, Tom was sure his father forced himself to ration his calls to him so as not to appear needy.

"You hardly see any friends," Tom went on. "You need a new start."

"I don't want a new start."

Tom pressed his lips together hard.

"Are you looking forward to visiting Bernie and Joan?" he asked, desperate.

But the silence that fell was enough to tell Tom what was coming. *Here we go.* Somehow, Tom still managed a burst of reflexive, guilty contempt. Well. He'd come for the full experience.

"I decided not to bother," his father said. "I can't face two days of happy couples. Pity."

"You're a good-looking man, Dad," Tom said for the millionth time. His tone was begging. "You could easily find someone."

But Alistair looked at Tom, eyes swimming with inchoate distress, and he might as well have said the words aloud: *I just want Angela.*

He was living in suspended animation, waiting for his wife to come back and start the cycle over again. A few weeks of happiness then a plunge back into jealousy and paranoia, waiting for the next blow to fall. A life sentence.

Once, Alistair had said, exhausted, to a teenage Tom, who'd been ranting at him to stop being a doormat: *You're a child. You haven't been truly in love. You can't understand.*

But Tom had known he never, ever wanted to. His father was a flesh-and-blood cautionary tale.

Tom sipped his tea, and changed the subject.

Job done.

• • •

The noise of a television was loudly audible through the front door of Pez's flat as Tom let himself in. He'd gone straight there from his dad's house, because he didn't have the energy to go home and go out again. The Gardiners were looking after John.

Someone shouted and swore, a female voice screeching at batlike levels. Reality TV then. Pez loved that.

"Tommy?" Pez called.

The flat door led straight into Pez's main room but a wall directly in front of the door created a kind of alcove, which allowed Tom a moment of privacy to try to gather himself.

So much was happening, so many things crawling into the light... He couldn't pinpoint the exact reason he felt so low.

He rubbed his eyes, squared his shoulders and walked into the main part of the lounge.

Pez sat on a large scarlet velvet sofa, holding a wine glass, and dressed for seduction in his Alexander McQueen best black sleeveless top, and black skinny jeans, hair gelled and eyes dark with kohl.

"I thought we weren't going out." Tom moaned and slumped onto the sofa beside him.

Pez's flat was smaller than Tom's—in fact, it was tiny, with a little kitchen stuck on to one side of a single reception room, and its only bathroom off the single bedroom. But it was in a good location—Dalston Square—in a brick-and-glass tower block, among other tower blocks.

"We're not. This"—Pez swept a hand in demonstration down the length of his body—"is all for you."

His delivery was almost perfect—Pez could hold his alcohol pretty well—but a small slurring of his words told Tom that the wine was beginning to affect him. Tom smiled gamely but he realized it hadn't been a very good effort when Pez's sexy grin melted into a frown.

"How did you get on with Lawson?" Tom asked quickly. Distraction. His own interview at the station felt like years ago. How could so much have happened in just twenty-four hours?

"I've been trying to call you to tell you! He's an absolute cunt! He did everything he could to make me say you hadn't been with me that night. That lawyer's a total arsehole when he gets going though, isn't he? Hot as fuck too."

"He's Will's boyfriend," Tom said tiredly, though he had no idea why. Or why he then went on to tell Pez about the kiss outside Greens.

"Well, we'll have to put a stop to that," Pez said finally, after some satisfying screeching and gasps of horror. "Mark's far too good for Captain Suburbia."

Tom didn't rise to the bait.

"Anyway, how was the go-see at Mulberry?" Pez demanded. Then, "Great choice on the Boss suit. You look amazing."

Tom had totally forgotten he was still wearing the pale blue linen. No wonder James Henderson had looked at him so oddly when they met. Compared with the suits Henderson and Will'd been wearing, Tom might as well have come from the circus.

He shook his head, trying to burrow desperately back inside Pez's world. His old world.

"It went okay. I think," he said. "You know what it's like." Marina was one of those casting directors who liked to make everyone feel they'd won. "Nice office though," Tom said, to try to dampen the sudden suspicion in Pez's pretty eyes. "Nice luggage." *Fuck.*

Pez looked even more wary. "So where did you go after Mulberry? I thought you'd come to the office. I texted." There had, in fact, been eight missed texts, before Tom'd bothered to check his phone.

"I did some more investigating," Tom admitted.

Pez rolled his eyes with furious disgust. "You *could* leave it to the professionals, you know," he said, without much hope. "Such as they are."

Tom managed a pacifying smile, but he was all too aware he could tell Pez almost nothing of what was really happening. In the space of a single day, an unbridgeable chasm of secrets and lies had been created between himself and Pez. And that realization propelled him to lean forward and press his mouth to Pez's, to try to reaffirm…something. Their connection, perhaps…

Pez began at once to kiss back hungrily.

"Thank fuck," he moaned, when they each pulled back for air. His tone was pure relief.

But Tom realized his mistake quickly. This was…the sensation of soft mouth on soft mouth. This was full awareness, all the time, of what it was. Nice. Arousing—if they went at it long enough. But nowhere near enough to make him forget anything. It was fantastic when that was what he needed—affectionate, recreational sex. But he didn't have the concentration or focus left to make it work that evening.

He pulled back when he could and slid restlessly back to his original place on the sofa.

Pez looked dazed, bewildered, then he scowled accusingly. "You were with him today, weren't you? Will fucking Foster. That's why you look as if someone's been slapping you for hours with a wet fish."

Tom didn't even bother to argue. "It was fine."

Pez's expression grew still sourer. "And?" He sounded betrayed.

Tom closed his eyes. "And. I'm glad it was fine. Maybe he's on the road to forgiving me."

"*Forgiving you?*" Pez sounded beyond outraged.

Tom pinched the bridge of his nose between thumb and forefinger, headache looming. He sighed. "You know I hurt him."

"Oh boo fucking hoo," Pez snapped. "Shit happens! He's a grownup. Or he claims to be."

"Fucking hell, Pez. Why're you being such a dick about this?"

But Tom's bewilderment felt false. Was he really going to pretend surprise that Pez reacted badly to the idea of Tom and Will coming to terms? And he didn't even know why he was pushing the point anyway, when it seemed more than likely Will would never want to see him again after the case ended. "It'd be good if Will and I can be friends," he finished weakly.

"Friends," Pez sneered. "Like we're *friends*?"

"No! Pez!" Tom stared at him, stunned. He grabbed Pez's hand, which lay, twisted with its fellow, on Pez's lap. Pez's knuckles were strained and white. "Look, I know you worry about me and I appreciate it. Let's stop talking about Will. Why don't we go out? Or have another drink here and go to bed. Forget about things. Have some fun."

"Fun?" Pez voice sounded strange. Thick. Dangerous. "You think it's fun to lie there while you pretend you're dicking *him?*"

It took a couple of seconds to fully accept what Pez had said, then panic swept everything else away.

Pez had never said anything like that before. Pez defined easygoing. Yes, when Tom had dumped Will, it'd taken a fair bit of therapeutic fuck-ing-around to work the last hooks out of his system—in which Pez had taken part enthusiastically. But it had never meant anything.

"You know that's not... You've had too much to drink and—"

"I love you, you blind fucking cunt!" Pez yelled.

Tom drew a ragged breath. His chest felt iron-band tight. How long before he succumbed to an actual panic attack? How many things could fall apart, all at once?

"I love you too," Tom tried. "You know that."

Pez's face was flushed, distorted by alcohol-driven fury, but still Tom was entirely unprepared when Pez twisted up onto his knees on the sofa cushion, and shot a hand out to yank Tom's head backwards by his long hair.

Tom made a sound of shock and pain, staring up into Pez's wild eyes. Then Pez pressed a fierce, tongue-filled kiss to his open mouth.

It was over in seconds, but it had made its point.

Pez went ahead anyway, and said the words.

"I'm in love with you, you arse! Since the day I met you playing that fucking game in the park. So beautiful I couldn't understand why everyone wasn't standing and staring." His thin face twisted with grief. And Tom's world moved brutally sideways once again—another foundation kicked away.

Pez and he were meant to understand each other. Pez was his partner in crime. Neither was meant to demand too much. But Pez's truths were out there now and flying, incinerating the one relationship Tom had re-lied on.

An unwanted memory hit out of the blue—the night Will suggested, after a bout of particularly mind-blowing sex, that Tom move in with him to his house in Leyton, when he'd finished renovating it—despite all he knew about Tom's attitude to anything permanent. Will had let down the cool, amused mask he'd used to protect himself and said those words. *I love you.*

And all that Tom had been able to stave off till then by self-deception, had been right there on Will's face. As if he'd expected Tom to surrender himself too, the way he'd just handed himself over to Tom. He'd had to end it then.

"I can do friend with benefits, Tommy," Pez said, all but sobbing, and Tom couldn't tell if it was grief, rage, or just alcohol. "I've lived on it for years. But I'm losing even that now. Because *he's* back. I see how you look at him!"

"What…? No!"

"Then why are you pulling away?" Pez yelled. His eyes were red. Black-stained tears coursed down his pink cheeks. He looked nothing like Tom's cool, cynical Pez.

"Jesus!" he blurted. "I'm a murder suspect! I'm thinking about other things!"

Pez searched his face for a few more seconds, but whatever he sought, he obviously didn't find it. He slid back on his knees to the edge of the sofa and stood up. He looked devastated.

"It's more than that," he said, voice shaking. "I know it is. I want to help. But you're hiding from me now."

For a second Tom was tempted to just spew it all out—all of Nick's secrets—but he couldn't. He'd waited too long though, to reply.

Pez moved a step back from the sofa. "You should go, Tommy," he said distantly. His pale skin had lost the flush of emotion, and his eyes looked like ragged black holes in his narrow face. He didn't seem drunk anymore.

Tom tried to strategize, but he could find only one option.

He couldn't lose Pez. Not him as well.

He reached up and grabbed Pez's thin hand. Squeezed it with desperate ardor.

"I don't want to," he said. "Please. I want to stay."

Though he didn't know at all if that was true.

13

The day began with disaster. At least, it felt like that to Tom when he woke in Pez's bed to the beep of a text message and the realization that, in the emotional upheaval of the previous night, he'd forgotten to set his phone alarm to get himself home in time to be picked up by Will.

The message informed him that Will was outside his flat, ready to go. And then, Tom had no choice but to text him Pez's address. Pez woke only as Tom fought his way out of the bedding to get to the ensuite bathroom, frantic to shower the stink of sex off his skin.

Even with rush-hour traffic, Tom knew it wouldn't take long to get from Shoreditch to Dalston, yet he still jerked with shock when the street door buzzer sounded as he was pulling on spare underpants he kept in Pez's drawer.

Pez, sitting sleepily naked on the side of the bed, watched him with dopey, replete eyes. Black makeup was smeared over his face. They hadn't exactly had time for bedtime routines.

Tom ignored the bell and pulled on the yesterday's crumpled linen trousers. As if things weren't bad enough, he was going to have to wear that fucking suit again.

A peremptory knock sounded at Pez's flat door. Tom stared at the bedroom wall in front of him as if it had betrayed him.

Someone had let Will into the building, when Tom had been counting on him waiting outside.

Pez yawned and stood up.

"No!" Tom protested. "It's for me." The knock sounded again. Tom's pulse rate elevated another notch. "I'm getting picked up."

And that was when Tom remembered it didn't matter.

He forced his panicked movements to calmness. Because he had no reason to feel this absurd guilt around Will. Or Pez, for that matter.

It was his life. No one owned him. Why was he behaving as if he'd been caught in flagrante?

He zipped his trousers and headed into the main room to open the flat door.

There was no miraculous reprieve. Will stood outside, dressed in a black button-up, sleeves rolled up over his forearms, and tight black jeans. He must have decided that he should try to match Tom's casual dress if they were supposed to be a team. He looked effortlessly sexy.

They gazed at each other for a long moment, Will expressionless, Tom silenced by awkwardness he shouldn't feel, as Will's gaze fixed on his damp hair, his bare chest—a perfect echo of the morning before at Nick's.

Well, Tom had obviously stayed overnight. What did it matter if he wasn't fully dressed yet?

"*Well*," a languorous voice drawled behind Tom. "Morning, Cap. Don't you look...bushy tailed?"

Something in Will's expression told Tom what he was going to find, even before he turned round.

Pez was standing at Tom's shoulder, naked, his hair standing on end. His makeup was still smeared liberally over his face, his smirking mouth red and swollen. The only other color on his tall slender body was a small, ruthlessly trimmed patch of inky pubic hair, his dark pink cock, and the lurid red and blue marks Tom had left scattered all over his torso in passion. Contrition. Appeasement.

Tom drew in a long breath through his nose. His stomach had dropped to his boots; embarrassment clawed at his nerves. But he didn't protest or move away when Pez slid up beside him and slung a possessive arm round his waist.

Pez was feeling vulnerable and threatened, and he was marking his territory. Tom shouldn't feel compromised. Or ambushed. It didn't matter if Will was having his nose rubbed in the fact that he'd had wild sex with Pez.

But God, Tom felt…beyond mortified.

"I'm parked at the side," Will said. His voice sounded further away, and when Tom swung round, he saw Will's broad back disappearing down the flight of stairs at the corner of the lobby.

Tom clenched his jaw until his teeth ground together. He slammed the door.

When he turned back into the flat, Pez was standing in the same spot, arms folded, expression defiant. But Tom knew Pez well enough to see his uncertainty now that the moment of crazed impulse had passed. That was how Pez worked. Tom should be kind.

Rocketing outrage smothered the impulse.

"You forgot to piss on me," Tom spat. He stalked off to the bedroom, snatching up his white T-shirt from the ground where Pez had thrown it after he'd ripped it off the night before. He pulled it on and hunted for his socks and shoes. It shouldn't be hard to find them.

The room was tiny, womblike, dark red, with one feature wall behind the bed of expensive dark-gray patterned wallpaper. Tom had hung it.

Pez appeared in the bedroom doorway as Tom spotted the first sock, half under the bed on the side he'd slept in. Handily, both shoes were under there with it.

"If he doesn't matter, what do you care?" Pez demanded.

An excellent fucking question.

The second sock winked at Tom from underneath a long silky-red curtain. He grabbed it and sat on the bed to pull it on.

"I'm not a bone to be fought over." Tom's tone was savage, all his resentment in it. He yanked on the other sock, aware of Pez moving to stand near him. "You think you have to warn him off as if I don't have any agency of my own? What the fuck do you think I am?"

A shoe. Hauled on.

"His *bitch*! That's what you are! He looks at you, and you start panting!"

The second shoe dangled in Tom's hand, frozen in midair. Pez looked almost as shocked as Tom felt, until defiance came back to push out regret. He was shivering, scowling with rage, and he reminded Tom in his trembling nakedness of an angry chihuahua he'd once seen go for someone's leg.

It didn't make him smile. He pulled on the second shoe and picked up his suit jacket.

His bare arm brushed Pez's cold, naked belly as he strode out of the bedroom.

"Tommy!" Called behind him, desperate.

"I'll text you," Tom shouted back.

He slammed out of the flat, ignoring the lift and racing down the stairs three flights to the ground. When he burst out of the glass street door onto the concrete concourse, pushing his arms into the sleeves of his suit jacket, he felt as if he'd already been awake for days.

He'd stomped round the corner of the building, heading to the back, before he spotted Will fifty yards along, leaning against the wall, waiting. His arms were folded, head down.

He looked absorbed in his own thoughts, but he glanced up at the sound of Tom's shoes on the pavement.

"You don't know where I'm parked," Will said calmly, as if he hadn't essentially fled before he could give Tom that information. But there was no other indication from Will that the scene with Pez had involved him, or that Tom was intending to spend another day working with him dressed in look-at-me, pale blue linen.

Tom's raging indignation began to flicker and fail.

The night before, he'd used sex to distract and exhaust Pez—and himself. But distraction was over.

How long had Pez felt like that while Tom had ignored it? Tom's affairs, like his relationship with Nick... How much did they hurt Pez? The old affair with Will had obviously hurt him badly. Still *was* hurting him. How must Pez be feeling, now that he'd confessed his feelings and Tom hadn't said it back? Because Tom hadn't been able to lie that much.

"Right," he said, briskly. "Let's go."

He could ignore what had happened just as well as Will could. They had no time for this shit anyway.

Will's expression remained unreadable as he straightened from the wall and strode away. Tom, taken aback, ran a little until he caught up with him and they were walking side by side.

"So where to?" he asked.

Will didn't look at him as he said, "Bedlam."

•••

It took them an hour and a half to drive down to the southernmost part of London—just past Beckenham, a pretty suburb of Bromley, which looked to Tom like an old Kent village with an identity crisis.

Tom spent the first part of the journey silently brooding out the passenger window in horror at Pez's confession on top of Nick's, and his own mishandling of everything. And he felt as if he could never trust his own judgment again. Nick, Pez, even Jena. None of them were the people he'd thought they were.

More than that, he was constantly aware of Will.

He kept telling himself he had nothing to be ashamed of. But Will had encountered Tom twice in the space of two days, in the aftermath of having sex with two different men. It was…awkward, that was all.

Will behaved the same way as he had the day before though—as a pleasant distant colleague, and as the journey progressed, Tom tried to mirror that. They discussed the case, and Will told him that they really were going to Bedlam.

The Royal Bethlem in Monks Orchard was the direct successor of the original thirteenth-century foundation, now Europe's oldest operating psychiatric hospital. The location had moved, but the institution remained the same.

The hospital grounds, which they entered through huge gates, were extensive and beautifully kept—acres of parkland around a grand red-brick, 1930s mansion that housed the *Institute of Psychiatry, Psychology and Neuroscience*. River House Medium Security Unit adjoined it—white-washed, with a reception block of dark blue—crouching, industrial-park ugly behind a massive fence and very obviously monitored by cameras.

Will had explained the definition of medium-security units on the way. They were intended to house inmates with mental health issues who posed "a serious but less immediate threat to others" and weren't at high risk of absconding. Still a prison in all but name.

Dr. Paul Wykeham came to collect Tom and Will from behind reception, though reception at River House involved handheld scanners, multiple locking doors and fingerprint ID.

Wykeham didn't disappoint as a psychiatrist.

He looked like a cookie-cutter TV version, with an impressive head of swept-back silver hair, a long craggy face with bushy eyebrows, and an air of unending patience and wisdom. The sense that he could outwait anyone until they blurted out all their secrets. He didn't blink at Tom's suit.

He took a seat behind a cheap beech-veneered desk, positioned in front of a huge window, through which the security fence was very visible.

"I'm sorry to have to bring you into this place," Wykeham remarked as Tom and Will sat on the other side of the desk. "But at such short notice, it was the only way I could fit you in. I never have been able to refuse Christine Hansen anything."

Will gave a hard half-smile. "You're not alone."

"So?" Dr. Wykeham raised his generous eyebrows and waited.

"I understand you used to visit Red Moss, Doctor," Will began, "as a forensic psychiatrist."

Wykeham's eyebrows rose higher. "Some time ago. I've been here as a consultant for…twelve years now."

"This concerns your time at Red Moss," Will said. They'd discussed in the car how much they could get away with asking, without alerting Wykeham to the real story. "Do you recall a inmate about 2000 to 2003? Her name was Denise Heath."

Wykeham pursed his mouth in thought, then he suddenly brightened. "Oh—David's girlfriend!" Tom's stomach tensed. "David Burchill. He was a bit of a celebrity in there. Yes. She was an absolutely classic BPD—that's Borderline Personality Disorder," Wykeham added, for the plebs. "Paranoid fear of abandonment and abnormal efforts to avoid it, depression, manipulative tendencies, distorted self-image, codependency, self-harm…"

Will broke in, "The information we're going on came from an incident described in a book written about Red Moss."

Wykeham sighed with gusty ennui. "Brian Glanville."

Will pushed past it. "It's about a boy he said Denise set up. A friend of David Burchill's who was…"

"Glassy," Wykeham cut in with revelation in his tone. "You're here about Glassy."

"Yes." Will pulled out his notebook hopefully.

"Well." Wykeham tapped manicured fingers on beech veneer. "I'm not sure how much detail I can uh… This *is* a police matter, isn't it? You don't have warrant cards."

"We're under AC Hansen's orders, sir." Will spoke with the blank confidence of an Official with Authority.

Wykeham didn't appear entirely convinced, but he went with it. "Well. Glanville *was* correct about that incident. Glassy was sexually naïve. Denise set him up and claimed Glassy had forced himself on her. All very consistent with her particular form of BPD. Glassy couldn't process dishonesty very well, so he was confused. Devastated. Then David cut him loose, which meant open season on Glassy, I'm afraid."

"Open season?" Will didn't look up from his notebook.

"David was…the king of the unit, one might say. In David's eyes, Glassy had betrayed him. Glassy wasn't going to come out of that well."

Tom frowned, almost offended. That sounded nothing like Nick. But he'd still have been a teenager then, seething with hormones and emotion.

"So, Glassy would have cause to hate Denise?" Will asked.

"Oh, yes. Once he understood what she'd done, he certainly hated her."

Tom asked quickly, "Can you say what he was in for?"

"Murder," Wykeham said, as if it were as routine as stealing a mobile phone. "He killed his friend's sister."

"Do you know how he killed her?"

Wykeham raised his eyebrows and looked almost amused, as if they were playing a game. "He drugged her and slashed her wrists. He also cut out her tongue, of course. Textbook stuff."

Tom's stunned reaction was so intense that Wykeham couldn't fail to notice it.

But Will's voice remained merely curious. "Why textbook?"

"Because," Wykeham answered cautiously, glancing at Tom, "he thought the girl was going to tell tales about him. Ergo…the tongue was removed."

Tom's knee began to bounce. Excitement and wild relief boiled in his veins.

"Was insulin involved?" he asked.

Wykeham blinked. "Not that I know of."

"Can you tell us anything else?" Will put in. "Glassy's real name?"

"Martin Holmes," Wykeham said at once. "But Glassy's what he goes by. He didn't understand it was a derogatory nickname when he was given it."

Martin Holmes. Catriona's murderer.

Wykeham went on, "I always thought he had bipolar disorder with psychotic features, but Dr. Galloway wouldn't agree while Glassy was in Red Moss. When it might have helped. Before he was moved to an adult institution. We didn't agree on a number of diagnoses, David Burchill's included. *But*…Galloway was the senior colleague."

"David Burchill's?" Tom's tone was too sharp, but Wykeham was immersed in old grudges.

"Oh yes. Galloway went blindly along with the pretrial diagnosis of NPD…that's Narcissistic Personality Disorder. When *I* saw him, I realized David was just…unusually focused for his age. Charismatic one might say."

Will asked, "Do you remember where Glassy was moved at eighteen? After Red Moss?"

Wykeham frowned. He looked almost puzzled. "Wandsworth."

Another part that fitted. Nick had been sent to Wandsworth too. So Glassy would have known what Nick looked like as a young adult when he was released, subsequent nose job or not.

Will glanced up from his notebook. "I don't suppose you have any idea when Glassy got out?"

Wykeham frowned and pulled back his chin, the universal gesture of impatient disbelief.

"He didn't get out," he said.

There was a startled moment of mutual reassessment. The sudden feeling of emptiness in Tom's chest could have been anticlimax, or panic.

"But David Burchill's been out for twelve years," Will pointed out.

"Yes." Wykeham dragged out the word as if he were talking to idiots. "But David wasn't a denier."

In Tom's peripheral vision, Will's expression changed abruptly to revelation.

"What's a denier?" Tom asked impatiently.

Wykeham frowned at him. "A prisoner who refuses to admit their guilt." He sighed and muttered, "I'll try to explain. Anyone who's found guilty of committing murder gets a statutory life sentence. If they're under eighteen at the time, as Glassy and David were, they're Detained At Her Majesty's Pleasure. There's a minimum tariff...a number of years they have to serve...then the Parole Board decides if and when they can be released on a life license." His tone was pedantic, delivering a child's version, but Tom was grateful for it. "So they're bound by the specific terms of that license until they die—that's the life sentence. If they breach those terms, back to prison they go. But to get that license the Parole Board must decide an inmate no longer poses a risk to the public. And one of the main ways of gauging *that*, is if the inmate has taken part in behavior-modification programs during their sentence." He paused and studied Tom expectantly.

"Okay," Tom said.

"Unfortunately," Wykeham went on. "A key part of these programs is admitting guilt and examining why the crime was committed. So...deniers can't take part in the programs. They can't prove they're a reduced risk, so they can be inside indefinitely. All rather unjust on people who're genuinely innocent, of course."

"But," Tom said desperately, "Glassy must have eventually admitted his guilt. He must have got out."

Everything about Glassy fitted. He was the answer that made sense.

Wykeham let loose a gusty sigh. "Mr. Gray. Mr. Foster." Wykeham sounded like a man who had finally lost patience. "I *had* been under the impression you came here because you knew this and were dancing round it for reasons best known to yourselves. Glassy's condition deteriorated sharply in Wandsworth...stress is a trigger. His episodes became rapid-cycling...severe aggression and self-harm. Attempted suicide. Because of *that*, he was sent to a secure unit, where he was diagnosed correctly at last. This. Unit." Wykeham looked between them severely, like a headmaster badly let down by hitherto promising students. "So, no. I can promise you. He isn't *out*."

Will recovered first. "Can we talk to him?"

Wykeham gave him a charming smile, as if Will had finally met expectations.

"Absolutely not. We're trying to get him back on an even keel now he's on effective medication. He's been incarcerated for twenty years with no hope of getting out, and that takes a toll. He should have been in a secure unit years ago, not a training prison."

"Does he really believe he's innocent?" Tom asked. "Is it possible he could be?"

Wykeham raised a patient eyebrow. "Glassy's friend saw him cutting out her sister's tongue. Someone else saw it too."

Tom drew a sharp breath. His stomach lurched. "All right."

"And there was overwhelming circumstantial and forensic evidence. His friend—the one who saw it—actually used to visit him in the unit and in prison, which is very...Christian. But his own family disowned him. As to whether he believes he's innocent... He convinced himself of it before the trial. I suspect he may have entered a psychotic episode when it happened; certainly he suffered from hallucinations. He accused his own sister, his friend, his father..."

Tom let out a tired breath. "Right."

"An incident that violent... For some people it can be too much to ever process or accept," Wykeham said. "In fact, I heard one of the two witnesses killed herself up in Sunderland last year, because she never got over it. Glassy simply doesn't want to believe he did something so unforgivable." Wykeham raised his eyebrows and stood up. "So. Is that all I can help you with?"

The three of them walked back to reception along an institutional corridor, dotted with doors. No one spoke. But as they passed one open doorway, Wykeham's pace slowed and then stopped. He showed a second of uncertainty before his expression firmed, and he gestured Tom and Will inside.

There was no one in the room, but Wykeham strode across to the window that dominated its far wall.

He said quietly, "He likes the garden."

Outside the window, a man stood alone near the tall fine-meshed fence. Sunflowers grew with incongruous joy against it. He was dressed in brown trousers and a short-sleeved collared shirt in a purple check; tall and skeletally thin, with cropped mouse-brown hair and stooping shoulders.

Glassy.

Tom could only see part of his profile…a long, large nose dominating a hollowed face. But then the man turned right around—180 degrees—until his other side was in view, and where his ear should have been, there was only a hole and a white gnarl of old scar tissue.

Tom breathed, "He did *that* to himself?"

"No," Wykeham said. "That's a legacy of Red Moss. When I said it was open season, that's what I meant. Courtesy of Denise, I suppose."

14

"It doesn't make any fucking sense!" Tom barely kept his frustration in check as they said their farewells to Wykeham and left River House. And as Will pulled the car onto the route back to central London, he stopped trying. "It *has* to be him! Everything fits! But he's fucking…in there! Is there any way…?"

"No," Will said. "There is no way someone let him out of a secure unit to murder Mrs. Haining."

Tom scowled at him. "But it's the same method! The ear as well! *And* he has a motive."

"Not exactly the same," Will reminded him. "No insulin."

"One detail, which ties to Nick! And he has reason to hate Nick *and* Catriona." Will's silence told him what he didn't want to hear. Not close enough. "Maybe it was someone who'd get his revenge for him, then? Someone angry *for* him."

"Dr. Wykeham said his family disowned him. And the friend who visits him isn't likely to help him, is he? Given the victim was his sister."

"Fuck." Tom scowled out the passenger window. He felt like punching his fist through it.

"That's the Chinese Garage." Will nodded toward a building on the right-hand side of the road as they left Beckenham. Tom stared at it through his window, bewildered. It looked like a car dealership, housed in a Chinese pagoda. "It was built in the 1930s."

Tom eyed it with perplexity for a second or two longer before he understood.

"You don't have to distract to me," he spat. "I'm perfectly calm."

Will threw him a quick side-eyed glance and his mouth twitched, and just like that Tom felt ridiculous. Deflated.

This wasn't him. Or…maybe it was. Maybe it was the Tom that Will remembered, raging with frustration over anything he couldn't control.

"We learned this much," Will said. "Whoever killed Mrs. Haining seems to have known how Martin killed his victim, as well as how the Morton twins died. *And* they know what happened to Martin in Red Moss."

"It has to be Morton then," Tom blurted.

"Why?" Will asked.

"There's no one else left."

There was a beat of startled silence and then Will laughed, and his amusement transformed his face from darkness to light. Tom had forgotten how young he looked when he laughed.

"Last known suspect standing," Will said with a grin. "Sadly—that's not how it works."

"But he did read Glanville's book," Tom argued, trying not to smile too. "So he knows about Glassy."

"He knows about Boy T," Will corrected. "Anyway, how about we wait till James finds out Morton's movements on the night Mrs. Haining died. He'll probably fake a door to door."

The casual admiration in Will's tone rubbed at Tom like sand against sunburned skin. But he didn't argue.

Will's phone rang as the car was easing along Shoreditch High Street, nearing Tom's flat, though Tom wasn't really ready to go home. He felt too restless, too aware of time running out.

Will glanced at the number and his eyes widened. Then he pressed his forefinger against his mouth before he put it on hands-free. *Ssssh.*

"How's about ye, Guv?" The voice was loud and cheerful.

Tom sat up straighter.

Will rolled his eyes. "Des, I'm not your…"

"So are ye still working for You Know Who?" Des Salt asked.

Tom stared—appalled—at Will. Lawson had sent Des Salt to try to milk Will for information?

"He's not Voldemort, Des," Will returned, though his attempt at cool disdain was ruined by a smirk. It took all Tom's self-control not to react. Why was Will behaving as if it was all a joke?

"Ya think?" Des returned. "Anyway...I'm sitting in the car park... I told everyone I'm having trouble with Hannah, so I need privacy." He was still with Hannah then, Tom noted absently. Tom used to really like her sarcasm. Des sighed showily. "I hope to fuck no one mentions it to her. Anyway, just a heads-up. The person behind the accusations of stalking was a wee girl called Lily Adderton. She's not taking back the claims though, so..."

Tom stared at the microphone on the dashboard.

Des was *giving* Will information, not trying to get it?

"Also, it's now officially a murder case," Des swept on. "The presence of significant quantities of insulin's been confirmed in the tissue round the injection marks at the back of the victim's thighs. Still waiting on the final toxicology report though."

"Okay," Will said. "Thanks, Des, but...look...be careful. I don't want you to put yourself in..."

"Ah, ye wouldn't be working for him if he was guilty, Guv," Des said. "He may be a dickhead, but he's no more a homicidal maniac than Hannah is. Though, actually..." He trailed off.

Tom didn't take his eyes of the dash. They were stinging anyway with emotion. Gratitude. Regret.

Des ended the call just as the car pulled off Old Street into Tom's road.

"Here we are." Will inched the car to a halt.

"Will Des get into trouble?" Tom asked.

Will grimaced. "Only if someone finds out. He shouldn't have done that. But really...he didn't give us anything that'd compromise Lawson's investigation."

"Okay," Tom said, subdued. Immediately awkwardness descended. Anyone else, Tom would have asked if they wanted to come in for a cup of tea.

"Nice area," Will commented with deliberate ease. "You been here long?"

Tom had been living with his father to save money when Will had known him, just starting out, really, as a model. His dad had loved Will, of course.

"About twenty months." Then, though he didn't know why, "I have a cat now too." Will's expression slid from polite interest to surprise, and Tom could only imagine what he was thinking—that Tom was far too self-centered to be in charge of a helpless creature. "I found him in a skip."

Will nodded gravely. "You must have help looking after him," he said. "Since you're away a lot."

"My neighbors are great." Tom heard his own defensiveness and, perversely, it made him add, "And Pez helps when I'm away on long trips."

He wondered if he imagined Will's expression closing slightly. "Of course."

"So would you like to come in and meet him?" Tom blurted though he hadn't meant to. "He's called John."

Will gave one of his lopsided half smiles, powerfully attractive. "A cat called John. Barely better than Alan." He hesitated for a beat. Tom held his breath. "I can't, sorry. I've been invited somewhere."

Tom let the breath go. "Right. That's okay." Part of him was relieved. "So what're we doing tomorrow? I have a shoot late morning, but after that I'm good."

Will frowned but didn't challenge Tom's assumption he'd be included. "I'm going to get Pixie to access everything available on Red Moss and Martin Holmes. Lily Adderton too. We can reassess tomorrow after you've finished work."

Pixie again. In Tom's head she was blonde, fluffy, deeply irritating and five feet tall.

Tom didn't look back as he let himself in through the front door of his building.

But all the way upstairs, he railed at his own stupidity, because he couldn't work out what the fuck he was doing. Wanting to hold Will away, annoyed when he wouldn't come any closer. Maybe, he acknowledged, it was just that he'd never felt as much for anyone as he'd once felt for Will. Because the end of that was still there, like a scar he'd got so used to that he didn't really see it.

He could hear John behind the flat door as he got close; Sonja and April must have put him back. John always seemed to sense when Tom was coming, though he shouldn't be able to hear footsteps on the stair carpet, and the meowing rose to deafening levels as Tom opened the door and bent to pet him. But even John's outraged, avid welcome couldn't distract Tom from his nagging discontent.

He trudged toward his bedroom, John at his heels.

It was only early evening, but his big bed looked wildly inviting, covered with the fluffy white duvet he'd pulled into place the last time he'd slept there. The morning of the day he heard about Catriona. He was tired. Tired after the night before, and then the morning, with Pez. Tired after the trip to Bedlam. Tired of himself and his own fucked-up head.

He didn't bother to close the bedroom door. He just pulled off his suit jacket, walked forward and collapsed, prone, onto the duvet, shoes still on. John hopped up beside him.

He closed his eyes tight against the hungry churn of worry and self-reproach swirling round his mind and souring his gut.

A stray thought needled in: the police would get their warrant to take his laptop soon. He should get up and erase his porn. But he didn't have enough energy left to bother. Let them get an eyeful of *Packed Raw* and *Straight Boys in Distress*.

He rolled onto his back, wriggled up the bed until his head rested on his pillow and groped by feel for the old textbook on his bedside table, his emotional comfort blanket. He pulled it down onto his chest with his right hand.

It took him a few seconds of exhausted puzzlement to realize that the book he held wasn't his tattered university copy. There was a different image on the cover.

Inorganic Chemistry 6th Edition; Weller, Overton, Rourke and Armstrong. The edition he never had got round to buying. Yet here it was. Brand new.

In his room.

In his hand.

15

Tom's lungs felt solid, like iron.

He turned his head very, very slowly on the pillow to peer at the bedside table from which he'd pulled the book, as if the person who'd put it there might be sitting behind it, waiting. Watching.

A square of neatly folded wrapping paper lay on the tabletop. The book must have sat on top of it. Ordinary brown paper, stained green this time. Tom took a loud gulp of air and sat up.

His hand shook as he pulled open the book's cover.

Fear hit. Pure fear, liquefying his bones.

Someone had come into his flat. Into his bedroom. His sanctuary.

He fumbled his phone from the bedside table and scrolled frantically until he found the number he needed. The phone picked up on the second ring.

"Will!" he gasped.

A startled pause. "What's wrong?"

"Someone was here. In the flat! I can't…I don't know…" He sounded unhinged, he realized with a gush of shame. Like an hysterical old lady.

"Is the flat clear now?" Will asked sharply.

Tom's breath caught again. "I don't know." His voice sounded calmer at least. "I'll go and look."

"No!"

"I can't just…"

Tom heard the sound of the front door clicking shut.

For one merciful second he thought he'd imagined it—it had been discreet, barely a noise. But he couldn't pretend he hadn't heard.

Instinct drove him to his feet, out the open bedroom door and down the hall. He could hear feet thundering down the outside stairs, and he wrenched open the flat door moments before the heavy door into the street slammed shut.

He heard tinny shouting from the phone he still held in his hand but nothing could stop him leaping down the stairs too and fumbling open the front door. He exploded out onto the pavement just in time to see a figure dressed in dark clothing, with a hood pulled up, darting round the corner of the narrow road into Shoreditch High Street.

He knew it was pointless, but Tom raced after the figure all the same, skittering round the corner at top speed, narrowly avoiding a full-tilt collision with a bald man in a suit. He muttered apologies, straining and stretching to his full height to try to see over the crowds of milling pedestrians on the pavement. But no one was running now. The intruder had been smart enough to slow and blend in.

Tom jammed his hand into his hair and tried to steady his breathing, though his pulse pounded like a trip-hammer.

Fuck! Get a grip!

There was no room for pretending. It hadn't been a thief or a burglar. It had been more sinister than that.

He turned round and began to trudge miserably back to his flat, but out of the corner of his eye, he caught a figure moving too fast, running across the High Street, dodging through traffic, barrelling toward him like some hero in a movie.

Tom's body seemed to recognize the man before his brain did, because his limbs weakened with relief.

"Is he gone? Did you see him?" Will panted. "I left the car a couple of streets away."

Anxiety was etched into his brow, and his expression looked almost bizarrely animated after the unemotional stillness he'd shown Tom since he'd come back into his life.

Tom stepped blindly forward and snaked his arms around Will's torso to squeeze him tight in pure gratitude. And after a moment, he felt Will's arms creep up to comfort him in turn. They stood like that, hugging, for a few still seconds. It was the first time Tom had touched Will for two years.

As the thought registered, he dropped his arms and stepped back. A self-conscious hand pushed back his hair. "Come on," he said softly.

He led the way back along Charlotte Road to his front door, describing the little he'd seen of the intruder—dark trousers and hoodie, trainers, he thought. Medium height or maybe a bit taller; it was hard to tell for sure from a distance. Fit anyway. Agile.

It was only when Tom found the street door of his building wide open that he remembered he'd left his flat door open too. And what that meant.

He ran inside with an inarticulate cry of alarm, taking the stairs three at a time, but though he called for John in the lounge as he passed it, ran to the bedroom and scrabbled under the bed, and then rushed back out into the hall, there was no sign of him. And that really was the last straw.

He stood in the hallway, his back to the front door, hands gripping his hair, eyes squeezed tight shut, and fought the urge to bawl.

"John, I assume," Will said behind him. "He was poised to make a break for it at the bottom of the stairs."

Tom dropped his hands and swung round.

Just inside the doorway, Will was holding an unusually amenable John against his chest with one large hand. He raised an eyebrow, pushed the flat door closed behind him with the sole of his shoe and held John out to Tom.

Tom's hands shook as he lifted the cat into his arms and buried his face in its soft fur, trying to calm his pounding heart.

"Thank you," he said fervently. "Thanks, Will."

Will cleared his throat. "Well, your door looks intact. No sign of tampering, but it's just a rim lock. A pro could have bumped it or picked it pretty easily." When Tom looked up, Will was chewing his bottom lip in thought. "The outside door lock's a decent five-lever mortice though—that'd take some time to get past in daylight." It seemed to Tom that Will had begun to talk to an imaginary sergeant, taking notes beside him. "It's possible one of the neighbors buzzed him in, of course, or he had keys."

"*Keys?*" The snakes writhing in Tom's abdomen twisted faster.

Will glanced up. "Probably not keys," he said quickly. "How much was taken?"

Tom swallowed convulsively. "Not...taken," he managed. "I don't think. He...*left* something."

Will's eyes narrowed. "Show me."

Tom's bedroom looked the same as it always had, yet it had changed entirely in Tom's eyes. The book lay like a stain on the white duvet.

"I had an beaten-up uni copy of that chemistry book. I've been meaning to get a new edition but…I didn't look at it properly 'til I picked it up and opened it."

Will slipped purple nitrile gloves from his pocket and snapped them on, then he opened the front page of the book. He frowned down at the inscription neatly pasted there.

"*Ever can?*" He looked up.

Tom sniffed hard. "I think… I'm certain it's from the same person that sent me this." He went to his chest of drawers and extracted the Tiffany box Pez had given him at Café Oto. "And…he sent a leather jacket. It's the same wrapping paper every time, just a different colored stain." He opened the box and took out the bracelet. "This and the jacket… they both have inscriptions too." Tom had to concentrate to keep his voice even. "Put together with the book, they make a message: I want you more…than anyone else ever can."

Will's poker face held steady but his mouth pushed out into a considering pout as he took the leather cuff and cupped it in a purple palm. "It looks expensive." His matter-of-fact acceptance steadied Tom as nothing else could.

He said, "Tiffany's Paloma Picasso range. Apparently. Two-thousand quid according to Pez. The jacket's expensive too. The two together? Maybe five thousand pounds."

Will made an impressed face. "So there's money behind it. And all three objects are connected to your interests. Fashion. Bikes. Chemistry."

"Oh God," Tom breathed. And the steadiness was gone. Because he hadn't thought in those terms. But—yes. The gifts were from someone who'd studied him.

He felt hollow and shivery. The tipping point approaching, when finally he'd had all the shock and stress and unwanted change he could withstand. But Will didn't seem to see Tom's rising panic; he was focused on the puzzle.

He strode over to study the big metal-framed window.

"No signs of entry. I wish I had SOCO to set on this." He sounded frustrated suddenly. "I'd bet he didn't leave prints, but…there could be other traces. At least we'd know for sure how he got in."

"He's stalking me." Tom fought to steady his voice but it sounded thin. "The killer. I don't understand. How do I fit into revenge for Glassy?"

"You're making assumptions," Will said. His tone was professionally mild. "It's very possible this is unrelated to the case. It could be…someone in your own life. An ex-lover, maybe? If it *is* related, it could be that frightening you's another way to get to Nick."

"Or the murderer could just kill me too." Tom's voice shook. "That should do it."

Will stared at him as if he'd only just seen him.

"Okay. Go and sit down. You need a drink." He frowned, and Tom finally saw a moment of indecision, the first since Will had raced to the rescue. "I'd better call AC Hansen. Though God knows I should be calling 101…"

"What's…?"

"It's the police number for incidents that aren't ongoing. This is…" He shook his head.

The net of secrets covering them felt more and more like a trap.

Tom firmed his jaw. "I'll get drinks. The lounge is down the hall."

He went to the kitchen and poured two hefty vodka and slimline tonics— the only alcohol he had—and took them to the living room.

He found Will already ensconced on the big sofa, talking on his phone, with John sitting imperturbably on his knee like, Tom thought suddenly—like some Bond villain's cat, waiting for blood to flow.

Just one more surreal moment to handle. Will Foster in his flat.

Will said to his phone, "No signs of forced entry I could see, windows or doors. We should call it in, ma'am." A pause as he listened. "It may not even be related to the Haining investigation. It could be personal." He listened again, frown deepening to a glower. "Right. We'll be here."

Tom handed Will his drink when he rang off, then sat on the other end of the sofa, a cushion's width between them. John settled deeper into Will's lap.

"Still vodka," Will remarked, as he took a sip. Once upon a time, he'd teased Tom mercilessly about the dietary quirks imposed by Melanie, his agent in New York: Goja berries. Mung beans. Coconut water. Kale. Only vodka.

"I need to keep my girlish figure," Tom said and took a huge steadying gulp of his drink. "Tell me."

Will grimaced. "She doesn't want us to call it in. But she's sending someone round in case the intruder left something useful. A Crime Scene Investigator. God knows how many officers she has in her private army."

Tom eyed him uneasily. "You think it's dodgy then? You think Hansen's dodgy?"

"That's not what I mean." Will scowled down at his drink. "She's conducting a covert operation. And she has the authority to do it. I just…it's uncomfortable not doing things by the book."

Tom necked most of the contents of his glass in one desperate gulp.

Will looked up at him. "Do you want to ask Nick to come over?"

Did he? He probably should want to—but…Will had always made him feel safe in a way no one else ever had. Which'd perversely made Tom feel ever more threatened.

Tom shook his head. "Is it okay if you wait with me?" He gestured to Will's glass nervously. "I forgot you have to drive. You don't have to go yet, do you? You were invited somewhere."

"I told my friend I have to work."

Work.

"Thanks," Tom managed.

After a few seconds, Will said, "It's a nice place." The admiration in his voice sounded genuine. "The windows and the brick. The light. Really nice. You must be doing pretty well to stay here." There was no edge to it. One person, pleased for another.

Tom said honestly, "I spend as much time here as I can."

Will threw him a quick glance, but he didn't comment. When he'd been with Will, Tom had fought hard against any suggestion that staying in—without having sex —was a reasonable thing for any young guy to do. Even though, secretly, he'd really liked helping renovate Will's house.

"Shove him off if he's bothering you." Tom nodded toward John as Will petted him. "He usually hates strangers." He clicked his tongue. "You've got cat hair all over your clothes."

"It's fine." John's eyes had closed, ears flexed to the side, purring in cat-ecstasy under Will's gentle fingers. Tom looked away, trying not to notice. "I've this theory that cats target dog people like me," Will went on. "To make them pay, you know? Except…John didn't realize I'm a cat person too, did you, mate?"

Tom managed a weak smile. Will's lashes curled up at the ends, and they were so thick they cast little shadows on his cheekbones as he looked down at the cat on his lap.

"I'll get refills." Tom grabbed Will's glass out of his hand without asking if he wanted one, and safely in the kitchen, he necked another drink on his own, just to try to get a grip. The adrenaline in his system would neutralize the alcohol anyway.

When he arrived back in the living room, somehow Will had managed to move John to the sofa beside him without John stalking off in a huff. Will's notebook was out.

Back to work then, now he judged Tom sufficiently calmed.

The doorbell rang.

Tom stared at Will, wide eyed, but Will's small smile was wry and kind. "That was quick. It'll be Hansen's CSI. I'll handle it."

He rose and went out to the hall, and seconds later Tom heard low male voices, moving along the hall toward his bedroom. He tried to sit and wait, but after a few minutes he couldn't stand his own company anymore.

In the bedroom, he found a man with a long, lugubrious face and fluffy receding brown hair, kneeling by Tom's bedside table, rubbing the top of it with a small brush. Will leaned, arms folded, against one wall, watching him. The book and the folded wrapping paper, already smeared with dark dust, were lying on the carpet in transparent evidence bags.

Will glanced at him. "Hey. Larry's looked for bootprints and DNA traces. He's just doing fingerprints." Larry glanced up and nodded to Tom, then went back to work. No introductions beyond that. Will straightened. "Let's leave him to it."

He led Tom back to the lounge and sat down beside John again. "I've told him to concentrate on the bedroom and two front doors. But I doubt we'll get anything even if Hansen can access any available CCTV. The guy had a hood up... Probably gloves. But just in case, they have your fingerprints and mine for comparison. I'll need to ask you some questions though. Starting with everyone you can remember who may have left prints in the bedroom."

"No one else," Tom said. "Unless my neighbors go in when I'm away." Will's doubtful frown prompted him to snap, "I don't take people here for sex."

Will blinked, but he wrote it down. Then he drew precise details from Tom about the presents he'd received—timing, packaging, print used, ink, precedents of other people who sent him gifts. And, humiliatingly, everyone he'd gone out with, or had sex with, in the previous twelve months.

It took a while. Will patiently wrote it all down.

"The man who roofied you," Will said suddenly, flipping through his notebook. "Max Perry. Pez called him your stalker. Does Perry have the same build as your intruder?"

It took a second to sink in. " I don't know." Then Tom said defensively, "Look, the roofie thing is Pez's mad theory. The boring truth is I got really drunk. Paralytic." He shrugged. "Max Perry's just a big-headed twat."

"Rohypnol has the same symptoms as GHB," Will pointed out mildly.

Outside in the hall, Tom heard the sound of the front door opening and the muffled thud of an object dropping on the floor. Larry's bag presumably, as he readied to dust the lock. The distraction worked only for a moment.

"You can't be serious," he said.

Will raised an eyebrow. "It doesn't always follow that someone who rapes will stalk," he replied. "Or that either one will escalate to murder. But this man has already committed several serious crimes. And if he was reckless and driven enough to try drugging and blackmail to get close to you, it shows a pattern of fixation."

Rape.

Tom stared at Will. The word was all he heard.

He'd very carefully refused to allow himself to frame it that way in his own mind. Refused to let either himself or Pez, view it like that. Just brushing against the concept in connection with what happened…he felt dirty. The way he'd felt when he woke up, naked, exhausted and covered in come, in Max Perry's bed, in Max Perry's greedy arms, with no recollection of anything he'd done to get there. Until Max had texted to tell him, in smug detail.

A tentative knock sounded at the lounge door. They both stared as it swung open, and Larry stood there, shouldering into an anorak to cover a black uniform jacket, emblazoned on the chest with the letters *CSI*.

"I'll do the downstairs door on the way out." He sounded tired. End of a long day, presumably. "I'll send everything on to AC Hansen."

Will stood to see him out, and Tom listened distractedly again to the sounds of their voices at the door. His mind seethed.

"He didn't rape me," he said, the moment Will appeared in the lounge doorway. "That's fucking ridiculous!"

Will looked startled but he waited until he'd sat down again and picked up his notebook to ask neutrally, "Did you agree to have sex with Perry?"

Tom glared at him. "I don't remember anything after the club," he said, with dignity.

"Did you want to have sex with him?"

Tom's glower deepened. "Not sober. But I have to take responsibility for…"

"For what? For trusting him to behave decently?"

Tom sprang to his feet, maddened. "Decently? For fuck's sake, it's the scene! I got bladdered, and he took advantage. It's not fucking…playschool!"

"Rape is rape," Will said with ruthless certainty. "On the scene, or off it."

"Oh. Well, there speaks the right-on copper! What's next, Officer? No always means no? Never talk to strangers?"

Will looked careful. He knew better than to argue. And after a few more impotent seconds without pushback, Tom's flimsy defensive rage fell from him like beggar's rags.

He hung his head. "I'm sorry." He began to rub his forehead with shaking fingertips, trying to hold on. "That was obnoxious."

Will slowly rose to his feet. "No. You've had a lot of shocks. Stresses." His voice was soft. "You're doing incredibly well to keep functioning."

"Don't treat me like a victim. Please don't." Tom held Will's eyes until Will nodded in acknowledgment. "I don't remember any of it. Literally. Nothing. To me it's like…it happened to someone else in a story. I didn't live it. I mean objectively the photos tell me he may not be…making some of it up. But deep inside I don't believe any of the things he says I did, or he did."

Will's said gently, "Suppression's a survival mechanism. Not many male victims come forward. I mean not many…"

"It's okay I know what you mean." And Tom did. How many men would admit out loud to any of it, first to the police, then possibly to a court?

"Even if you choose not to pursue as a police matter, you could talk to someone privately."

They were standing too close, Tom realized, but the moment was too sensitive to break by pulling away.

"Maybe," he conceded. Maybe there was a wound in his psyche somewhere he didn't know of. Maybe, more than one.

"It might help, Tom," Will said.

Tom gave a shaky laugh. He felt lightheaded. Well. Three vodkas. "That's the first time you've said my name. Since we met again."

Will's expression of concern flipped with almost comic speed to a kind of startled defenselessness, as if he'd been tricked into a terrible error. And Tom couldn't stand to see that look on his face. Or the idea that Will had only unbent enough to use his name out of pity.

"Will you tell me what happened with Archer?" Tom asked, perhaps because…one secret for another. Or because this bubble of intimacy they'd created might allow it.

The distress on Will's face changed Tom's mind immediately.

"Never mind," he said at once. "I shouldn't have asked. I just…I'm not myself…" He swallowed hard against the lump in his throat. "At the moment."

"I punched him. In the face."

Tom stared at him. "Why?"

"Why?" Will grimaced. "An operation I'd set up. To bring in a suspect in a gang murder. I'd requested armed backup, but…I came into the office...later than I should have. Archer took over, decided to go in early and canceled the backup. He said it was an unnecessary expense for a straightforward arrest. And he sent my DS and two DCs to the address in plain clothes. No body armor. Not even stab vests, because Archer said it'd remove the element of surprise. Des was one of them. They'd already been dispatched when I got in." He gazed blindly over Tom's shoulder as he spoke. "Des got a knife in his side. My DS...Sanjay...Sanjay Anand was shot twice in the chest and he died at the scene." Will bowed his head. "Archer, being Archer, bawled me out in front of the unit, said I came in drunk, that it was my fault. So I laid him out in the middle of the office."

Tom couldn't look away. "They *sacked* you?"

Will gave a bitter laugh. "Nah. Suspended. And exonerated, eventually. My recommendations for the raid were all on record. And other officers testified I came in sober. Archer was retired early. Full pension, of course. I resigned."

"But why?" Tom asked. "Hansen... They all knew it wasn't your fault."

Will looked at him. "I *was* drunk. The night before. A lot of nights before. I was drinking far too much to deal properly with shifts. That morning I slept in later than I planned because I had a hangover. Archer was right...it would still have been affecting me."

"A hangover isn't the same," Tom protested. But he felt a cold, prescient instinct. Still he said tentatively, "You didn't drink that much. When I...knew you?"

Will's mouth worked as if he couldn't quite make himself say the words. "I didn't deal with it...very well," he said. "What happened. With you."

All Tom managed was a flat, "Oh."

"It's all on me," Will said immediately. "I should have taken it like an adult, but I got pissed the night you sent the texts and I kept going. Until that day. I stopped then." His expression twisted. "Too late for Sanjay, though."

"Archer was an incompetent cunt," Tom said fiercely. "Even if you'd been there he could have overruled you."

Will looked away. "That's what Des said. But I'd have fought what he did if I'd been there on time."

"Des still calls you Guv," Tom said stubbornly.

Will's mouth twitched into a reluctant smile. "His head'd explode if he called me Will."

"Or maybe...you're still his Guv."

After a moment, Will looked at him again. His eyes were stricken whisky-gold in the early-evening light that flooded the room.

"That's why you left?" Tom asked. "Penance?"

Will shrugged one shoulder and frowned. "Maybe." Tom thought in that moment of rare vulnerability, he looked like a small boy.

"And it's why you still hate my guts." And Jesus, Tom could absolutely understand.

Will sighed and shook his head, but Tom was very aware he wasn't denying it.

Will said, "Let's...not. It's old news."

Except, Will had made himself live with the consequences every day.

"Blaming yourself's the easy way out, you know," Tom blurted. "Because it makes sense of things. It's much harder to accept that something can be so random. So out of your control."

Will's eyes locked on his, frowning, as if he'd said something shocking, but he didn't reply.

They regarded each other in exhausted silence, until Tom couldn't resist any longer.

He lifted his right hand and pressed the palm against Will's chest. The fabric of Will's black shirt felt warm, slightly damp, real.

Will froze, like prey. *Second touch*, Tom's conscience warned. His lungs felt too heavy to breathe, as he waited for Will to step back.

But they both stood still, as if they were balancing on a landmine, ready to go off. Tension roared in Tom's ears, an overfilled balloon, straining for relief.

He recognized only then that his cock was already straining in his trousers, full of needy blood and readier than he could remember. And once he registered that, the steady, aching want in his groin and thighs felt overwhelming.

It was totally insane Tom thought—obscene—to feel such lust given what they'd just been confronting. Assault. Death. Betrayal.

He had to step back. Or, Will should step back. One of them had to do the right thing.

But Will pushed minutely closer, eyes still locked, mesmerized, on Tom's. And Tom echoed the movement until there was no space between them, chest tight with the hugeness of his excitement, heart pounding and pounding.

Tom smelled the faint echo of...Tom Ford as he leaned forward and felt the prickle of evening stubble, and he could almost taste Will's shame and want.

The press of Will's mouth was as soft and lush as he remembered, though he'd told himself his memories were idealized, treacherous. The sweet smell of Will's skin, as his nose pressed close to it—it felt like euphoria and guilt. Like he imagined a long-dry alcoholic might feel, tasting that first disastrous, lusted-for drop on his tongue after years on the wagon.

He had to stop, and he couldn't. Wouldn't. Didn't want to. God he didn't want to.

Just a kiss.

He opened his mouth to coax Will's lips apart, to slide his tongue between them, courting response, tasting molten liquid velvet and alcohol. Addictive. Then their tongues began to move against each other, gaining desperation quickly—licking, probing, devouring, and Tom's hands rose to grip Will's head and hold it in place for his kiss.

Will's arm slid round Tom's waist and jolted him hard against his body, and they both groaned. It was like kindling that had been waiting too long in the heat—shrivelling, parched for this spark. And the power of that feeling was entirely familiar. Tom didn't know if he was drunk or not.

The kiss went on and on as they ate at each other like starved animals until at last they had to give in to the need for air. Tom, gulping in oxygen, stared into Will's half-closed eyes, the irises almost eaten by black pupils until only an edge of hazel showed, and he just wanted to kiss him again.

It had to stop before they both sank again into the swamp of their impossible relationship. But the pull was swamp-strong.

Will's Adam's apple bobbed in his throat as he swallowed hard, and Tom could see a huge bulge at the groin of his jeans. His own cock felt ready to burst, leaking in his underwear. It was time to step back.

Last chance.

But Tom leaned forward instead and pressed his lips against Will's neck. And he realized that, somewhere inside, he'd craved the sensation of Will's throat under his mouth since he'd looked up and seen Will standing beside him that first morning.

Suppression's a survival mechanism.

Will's head fell back with a long groan that sounded almost like relief—or despair, Tom's conscience prodded him—and gave himself up to it.

He allowed Tom to manhandle him out of the lounge and down the hallway, kissing voraciously and fumbling at buttons as they went, until they stumbled into Tom's bedroom. The doorknob dug a bruise into the curve of Tom's backside as they went, but it was just one more high sensation.

Larry had left the lamps on because the evening sun didn't reach this side of the flat, so Tom could see everything as he wrenched the last of Will's shirt buttons out of their buttonholes to expose tanned skin.

They staggered together closer to the bed, Tom fumbling at the opening of Will's jeans. And Will helped, by pulling the shirt off his own arms, heeling off his boots, stepping blindly out of his jeans and socks. Before he could start work on Tom's clothes though, Tom shoved him backwards with a palm on his chest, flat onto the bed, greedily watching his big erection bounce with the impact.

Will didn't look very shocked, perhaps because they'd often mock-fought in bed for control, for who'd end up on top. Slowly, eyes locked on Tom's he wriggled on his back up the mattress, until his head rested on Tom's pillow. And the thought of touching him…of touching that body again, threatened to turn Tom's bones to water.

He stripped off his T-shirt, toed off his shoes and pulled off his socks. Then, he unfastened those model's trousers, feeling the silky lining slide down his legs as they dropped to bunch at his ankles. He hauled down his underpants with clumsy, eager hands, then stepped naked out of the mess of material and crawled onto the mattress to crouch over Will.

Tom's blood-tight cock hung beneath his tense stomach, the weight pulling on his aching balls as he tortured himself with just looking. Because Will was just as beautiful naked as Tom remembered. Had worked not to remember.

The hair on his body was sparse, despite his part-Italian heritage… thick only on his head and at his groin, sprinkled lightly on his broad chest and his forearms and the trail on his taut stomach. The rest of his body was olive-smooth, all beautifully muscled and strong, his cock a dusky rose-gold, long, thick and uncut. Tom had loved to worship that cock.

His arousal flicked up another impossible notch.

He felt almost on the edge already from anticipation. From the terrifying chemistry between them. Will letting him take the lead this time.

He had always loved dominating Will—perhaps in part because Will's attraction to women as well as men had rooted and fed Tom's jealousy, his insecurity. But he couldn't remember when he'd last been so ruled by the desperate need for sex.

"You're so gorgeous," Tom murmured.

Will reached up and touched Tom's pectoral muscle. "You've worked at this," he said with a small smile, watching the nipple react and tighten. "You're really buff now."

"Still not as buff as you." Tom's throat felt tight. "You're still the prettiest."

Will's eyes looked sad suddenly, and the moment of connection felt more intimate somehow than their nakedness. Tom couldn't stand it.

He used his knees to push Will's thighs impatiently apart so that he could lie between them as he lowered most of his weight on to Will's body, propped on his forearms—and it was skin against skin at long last. Their swollen genitals rubbed and kissed. Emotion wiped out under sex.

Will arched his back and pressed his hips up into the movement, head back against the pillow, throat open and vulnerable. And Tom's spine was ready to melt.

Tom was so close just from this—a minute or two of frottage. He could barely believe the strength of his desire, as if he'd been sexually asleep for two long years. This was always what it had been between them. Like being in love might be.

"I don't have rubbers," he muttered. But neither of them stopped. Tom knew he couldn't. Not a chance in hell.

"I'm safe," Will panted. Their lips met again.

Tom wrenched away to slur out, "Got tested. After Max." He felt sick with desire, his ears buzzing with it, his body pumping with it.

He had no coordination to resist when Will pushed up and twisted, and the tables were turned—Tom on his back blinking at the ceiling. When he focused again, Will was already in position, his engorged cock dangling over Tom's face, his own head bending to hover over Tom's groin.

Sixty-nine.

Tom gulped in air and stared up at Will's swaying erection.

"Just as well," Will said and sucked the helmet of Tom's prick inside his mouth.

Tom howled, and thought whited out.

Somehow he found enough coordination to guide Will's cock down between his own lips, and then they were off, sucking and licking until they were both writhing and moaning and choking on each other cocks. It was primitive, uncompromising, ungentle—driven by greed and lust and need, and it didn't take Tom long to hit the stage of desperation—making muffled incoherent noises, body shaking. But he didn't beg to come, because he didn't want it to end.

He didn't know what inflamed him most, the feel of Will's hot, wet, hungry mouth, or the heavy weight of Will's cock on his tongue, the prickle of his silky pubic hair against his nose, the smell of him. All Tom wanted was for the sensations never, ever to stop. They were caught in the between-world of ecstasy together, and as long as they stayed there…

But when Will began to bob his head, pulling hard with his mouth, using his hand to stroke and pump the base of Tom's erection, the game was up. And Will knew it. He dragged his own erection out of Tom's clinging mouth, and began to suck on Tom's cock as if it were the only source of nourishment in the world.

He didn't pull off, as he should for safety, so Tom's bare prick was resting on his tongue when it finally swelled and squirted, and the wicked knowledge that he was shooting into Will's mouth, down Will's throat, made Tom come even harder, body locked in an exaggerated arc of ecstasy. It felt as if every last drop of semen in his body was pouring out of him, tension and suppression and fear and denial and pure desire—releasing. Gushing and spurting out of him like poison, as if his balls were turning inside out, a pleasure so glorious it could have been pain.

Will's body crouched above his as he took in Tom's orgasm, his own erection dangling wet and red, parallel to his body. And Tom thought hazily, that it looked obscene in its desperation.

"'s all right," he crooned but he had to regain control of his spaghetti limbs before he could bring it down to his eager mouth. It took less than two minutes' work before Will spent his seed copiously inside.

Tom didn't care what it tasted like. It could have tasted of anything. It was Will, and for these moments he could allow himself to accept that he'd missed everything about him—the taste of him, the feel of his cock in his mouth, the smell of his skin, the knowledge that for those minutes he'd been the center of Will's world.

Will somehow held himself upright long enough to pull himself sideways rather then collapsing onto Tom, hauling himself round and up, until they lay side by side in gasping enervated silence, the punishing sexual tension between them finally sated.

And then, reality began to slither back in. The price for the high.

There was no point trying to deny it had been the best sex Tom had experienced for two long years. He hadn't come close with anyone else to the level of lust and heart-clenching excitement he'd reached just waiting for that first kiss with Will. His bones now felt liquid and light, as if Will really had managed to drain days and months of stress and unhappiness from him, in those short moments of joy.

And that was exactly why Tom had ended it the last time.

He didn't dare look at Will's face, afraid of what he might see there.

Regret? His own insecurities mirrored back to him? Hope? He couldn't bear any of them.

But when he slid his gaze furtively sideways, Will's eyes were closed, those extravagant lashes laying dark smudges on his cheekbones. His breathing was deep and slow, and he looked at peace—young and innocent, when he wasn't guarding himself. Nothing like the sternly beautiful DI Foster.

Tom didn't know how long he watched him, letting himself feel so much that he'd suppressed, like a dry sponge soaking up water, until he had to turn his head away because he wanted to cry. Just sob his fucking heart out.

He forced himself to focus on a network of cracks in the corner of the ceiling he looked at every morning when he woke, and the realization seeped in that the room wasn't just his any more.

He'd had sex with three different men over the last three nights: for pity, for appeasement, and now...

He rolled his head restlessly again and watched Will sleep. And there was nowhere to hide from it. Two years, and Will's power over him hadn't died as Tom had convinced himself it had. It had just been lying dormant under the surface like a seed, waiting for its moment to grow. If anything, it felt even deeper rooted than before, as if now Tom knew what it was to be without, it felt more desperately unique than ever.

The acceptance of that truth felt exactly like panic.

A single beep broke the solid quiet: Tom's phone, still in his trouser pocket on the floor near the bed. He grabbed at the diversion, though he knew it would most likely be Pez or Nick, and he'd be far better not looking. He moved carefully, so as not to wake Will, hooking in the pile of pale blue cloth and extracting his phone.

It was Melanie, in New York: *Ready for a Times Sq billboard choochie? You got it!!! Booked you Heathrow-NY 8.25, July 30.*

He stared at the text—a message from another universe.

He'd got the fragrance campaign then, against the top three ranked models in the world. He'd reached the rarified air at the very top. Global magazines. TV ads. Prime billboards. The best campaigns—

He squeezed his eyes closed, scrabbling to grasp the triumph he'd have felt just a few days before. It was everything he'd been working for—the last door he'd needed to force his way through to enter the biggest league—the top few earners, the male supermodels.

If he'd begged for a sign it couldn't have come to him any more clearly, at exactly the right moment.

Something to remind him: you can have this, all you've worked for—all the money and security and independence and self-respect. Or you can have the man who can make you lose yourself.

When a person loved too much, they became the victim eventually, the corpse left behind. He'd known that all his life. And two years ago he'd understood that if he didn't run, that corpse would be him—losing his purpose, his aloofness, his freedom from need—leaving himself at Will's mercy. At Will's whim. Becoming his father.

The pain was horrible after the emptiness and indifference of the past two years. He hadn't noticed his slide into emotional apathy; he'd just kept going. And now that he'd allowed himself a last feast on his drug of choice, he had to climb back on the wagon.

He rolled onto his side to look at Will. He didn't want it to be over yet. But this had been wrong in so many ways. And it was all his fault.

"Will," he said. Then louder, "Will."

Will blinked open sleepy eyes. Tom's heart clenched to a pebble of agony.

First things first. "I'm sorry," he said softly. "I didn't even consider Mark."

Will's eyes focused, but Tom didn't want to decipher the expression in them.

Will frowned, then revelation. "How did you know...? Mark and I are... It's not a serious thing. We're friends, mainly."

Tom allowed himself to feel relief. He hadn't wanted to cheat on top of everything else he'd done, or put Will in a role they both despised. But to his own disgust, he realized that he also hadn't wanted Mark to be that important to Will.

Dog in the manger to the fucking end.

He took a deep breath to center himself.

"You know this was a mistake. Will." He watched with masochistic attention as Will's cautious expression began to close to blankness. "I'm still...what I am."

"And what's that?" Will asked without emotion. "A model at the top of his game? That's it?"

Tom swallowed.

"Yeah," he said. "That's it." Will waited. His fucking interrogation technique. But even knowing that, Tom blurted, "We've been here before. Your life and mine...they're too different. I can't give you someone settled. I can't give you commitment. I can't even look after a cat without a fucking support network. I can't give you what you want."

"That's crap!" Will pulled himself up on one elbow and looked down into Tom's startled eyes. "There are married models. Models with kids. Models who don't fuck around. Don't use that as an excuse." He raised his free hand and cupped the side of Tom's face. It felt almost tender, but his eyes were terrible, bleeding pain and bitterness. "You're just afraid. So you always do the hurting first. I'll sleep on the sofa."

He was still thinking of Tom's peace of mind, in the aftermath of the break-in. Even then. And Tom couldn't bear it.

"No. I'll be fine. I need you to go, Will. Please go."

Will's mouth twisted. He rubbed his thumb gently over Tom's lower lip, and it felt like a gesture of finality. Then he slid out of Tom's bed, scooped up his clothes and disappeared into the en-suite bathroom, closing the door behind him.

And Tom lay where Will had left him, trying to calm his breathing, trying not to cry.

16

After the flat foor closed behind Will, Tom got up, shoved the crumpled blue linen of his trousers into the laundry basket where he wouldn't see it and determinedly washed the sex from his skin. Then he went right back to bed, John beside him, though it was still early.

He tried to focus on positive things. New plans. The opportunities the Armani contract had just opened up, the elevated attention it was going to bring, the suddenly attractive idea of moving to New York, as Mel always insisted a top model must.

But his thoughts refused to be ordered; it was like trying to catch eels in his hands. Because Will's musk was still on the sheets, and Tom's body was still singing. So after a while he just lay there, and let himself worry and regret, mentally stumbling through the wreckage of the closest thing to a love affair he'd ever had.

The sound of his mobile woke him from the shallow sleep he'd finally managed to court around three a.m. It took a few seconds to fumble the phone from the bedside table to his ear.

"Tom." Nick's tone was pure relief, and Tom's first bleary response to it was a vicious blast of irritation with himself for failing to screen the call. Then, hard on its heels, reflexive guilt.

Because that raw, unedited reaction told him far too much of what he'd been trying to hide from himself, as well as everyone else. That though he forced himself to see Nick still as the man he'd come to care for, something uncivilized inside him now bridled around him, as if all their previous intimacy had been an illusion, and Nick was a pushy stranger, taking liberties.

Tom couldn't even judge how much of that was because of David Burchill, and how much his feelings for Will.

"Are you there?" Nick sounded less relieved, and more impatient. In fact, he sounded frantic.

"Yeah. Sorry," Tom muttered. "Just woke up." He looked at the clock on his beside table. 6:43 a.m.

"Where were you last night?" Nick demanded.

Tom pulled the phone away from his ear and stared at it, as if he could convey his dazed disbelief. Nick knew better than to ask that, and especially not in that tone, like a cartoon wife waiting by the door with the rolling pin raised. And to wake him up to ask? "That's not…"

"Were you with anyone?" Nick shouted. "Where *were* you?"

Outrage swamped bewilderment. *Fuck* Nick's feelings, then.

"I was with Will. We were here." He closed his eyes, memories and emotions swirling around inside him like clothes in a dryer, flying around, out of his control. He couldn't think about Will.

There was a short pause. "When did he leave?" Nick's tone was curt, almost wounded, but still demanding.

Tom scowled at the wall. "About nine," he said. Clipped. Resentful. Unsure why he was even replying. "Maybe nine thirty…" His doorbell rang. Escape. "And I have to go," Tom said, with no regret. "There's someone at the door."

"Tom! Listen!" The bell sounded again, longer and more persistent. Tom's heart rate began to accelerate. "You went to my place immediately after he left! Jena was there too."

The bell again. And then, knocking on the flat door. Fast and demanding. John jumped off the bed and stalked out into the hall, curious rather than afraid.

"What are you talking…?"

"You left at…three a.m. Something like that…"

"Nick…" Tom said weakly. The knocking became banging. The bell sounded, imperious and threatening. "I have to…"

Nick said, "It's going to be all right."

Tom stood and fumbled on some sweat pants and a T-shirt then walked down the hall to pull open the door.

He found he wasn't surprised to see Des Salt there, doing his best to appear inscrutable. But this time, he was the sidekick. DCI Lawson stood next to him. Fear began to flutter frantically in the middle of Tom's chest, like moths in a jar, just at the sight of Lawson's hostile, satisfied face.

Behind them, he could see the Gardiners' door had cracked open and April's frowning face, asking silently if he needed help.

He squared his shoulders. *Get a grip!* He couldn't afford to show a second of weakness to this man, who saw Tom as the easy answer to his problems.

"It's all right, April," he called. Then he turned to Lawson. "It's half past six in the morning," he said curtly. "You could have waited a couple of minutes to let me get up, without trying to wake the dead."

He turned and headed along the hall and into the lounge, without inviting them inside. They would follow anyway.

"Interesting turn of phrase," Lawson said. He and Salt stood just inside the living room, when Tom turned, Salt was looking around, stone-faced. His freckles stood out vividly against his chalk-white skin. He looked drained.

"Just get on with it, Chief Inspector," Tom said wearily. "Why are you here?"

But his tone belied the full awareness of threat in his mind. Something else had happened, something Nick knew about.

"Can you account for your whereabouts last night between the hours of ten and one a.m.?" Lawson rapped out.

Tom tried to look surprised to be asked, but it occurred to him that he might not have succeeded very well. Nick's call had taken away his natural reaction to that question, and Lawson would put one more mark under Guilty.

Then he had seconds to choose. The truth—admit he had no alibi? Or trust Nick?

"I went to Nick's flat. His sister Jena was there too. I stayed till maybe... three a.m."

The lie sent his pulse skyrocketing, but he put all he had into model-blankness. Who knew it would be such a vital life skill?

Lawson's eyes narrowed to dark slits. "'ow did you get back 'ere? Taxi?"

Tom's mind raced around the lie. He'd consumed enough detective dramas to know taxis could be traced.

"My bike." He forced himself not to embellish further, and not to fret about the weaknesses of the story. "Can you *please* tell me what this is about?"

Lawson's mouth curled into a sneer. Obviously, he believed Tom already knew, alibi or not. Tom's phone rang in the bedroom. He could hear its desperation through the open lounge door.

"We're investigating the murder of a woman, last night. Her body was found in an 'otel room in Paddington."

Tom didn't say anything. Didn't breathe. Waited. A woman?

"She was found with insulin bottles beside her," Lawson went on relentlessly with those flat Northern vowels, watching Tom like a cat at a mousehole. "Her tongue and her fingers 'ad been amputated."

At least Tom's reaction this time was unfeigned. Pure horror.

"Who?" he breathed. "Do I know her?"

"You tell me, Tom. Her name was Lily Adderton."

Tom's tongue was thick and huge in his mouth.

He couldn't admit he'd known Lily sent the anonymous messages, because Des had told Will. Christ…he was even keeping secrets for Des now.

Should he say anything about the gifts he'd been receiving? The break-in? But he hadn't reported it. Lawson would never believe him.

He should just tell them everything he knew. But how would David Burchill tie in to Lily Adderton? Lily Adderton only tied in to Tom. His mind blithered with panic.

They're hoping you'll trip up and do the work for them. It's a dangerous thing to allow the police to control the interview by trying to answer anything they decide to ask.

Mark's advice careened around his brain—but there was so much now to hide.

Then, as if someone had whispered in his ear: *You have to pull yourself together.* Calm descended.

He'd deliberately lived his life to rely only on himself. And he was meant to be smart, wasn't he? Maybe it was time to channel Mark Nimmo.

"I've heard her name, as Catriona's friend, but I never met her." That at least was true.

Lawson's eyes were jet beads.

"Detective Inspector," Tom went on. "Forgive me but I've answered your basic questions. My lawyer emphasized to me the danger of talking to you freely, given…your theories." He made it sound like alien lizards or the Illuminati. Full Nimmoesque disdain.

Lawson's mouth thinned under his moustache, and in his peripheral vision, Tom could see Des Salt begin to examine his shoes.

"If you have any more questions," Tom went on. "I'd feel…safer if Mr. Nimmo's present."

Lawson didn't say anything for a few seconds. After all, Tom had just implied he expected Lawson to try to frame him. But then Lawson smiled unpleasantly. His cold eyes glared righteous loathing.

Tom met that stare, and there was no doubt left in him that Lawson saw him as a killer, who had to be outwitted and brought down. A brutal double-murderer of women. Lawson really believed it now. It wasn't convenience.

He could almost walk through Lawson's thought processes at that moment—whether to arrest him and take him in to be cautioned and questioned. Or wait. Pick holes in his story first.

After all, Tom thought, with a jolt of terror, this time his alibi was a lie. But he kept his neutral mask in place.

For a few seconds he thought he'd won. But Lawson didn't have the discipline to hold off in the face of Tom's cool defiance.

"I'd like you to come to the station with us then, Tom," Lawson said, unpleasantly pleasant. "You can do it voluntarily. Or I can arrest you. DS Salt has a warrant to seize your computer equipment."

Tom refused to show any emotion as Des handed over the paper.

"All I've got's a laptop," he said. "I'll get it for you."

Lawson's false smile widened. "We'll be wanting to look at your phone too. But you're not under arrest," he said. *Yet* rang loudly in the silence.

Tom went into the bedroom to get dressed, collected the laptop and phone for Des, and then he had no reason to delay other than to ask April, who was lurking loyally by her open doorway when they left, to keep an eye on John. She gave Lawson and Salt—very obviously policemen—a formidable glare. April and Sonja had never been much for authority.

It was the same routine as before, except Tom was alone—head pushed down as he entered the back of the illegally parked police saloon, a silent, horrible journey, and the entrance to the station through the reception area deserted this time.

Salt didn't speak as he led Tom to the same meeting room as before, but this time, it was empty. Tom hadn't had the chance to use Mark's business card to try to get him to come to help—he had to rely on the police to do that—but it barely took ten terrifying, lonely minutes before the door opened and Mark swept in, freshly scrubbed and impeccably suited. Nick must have called him, Tom realized. And all Tom's ambivalent feelings toward Mark—guilt, envy—were easily swamped by relief.

"We must stop meeting like this," Mark said with a small grin as he sat and pulled open his briefcase. "I've just had the usual *minimal* disclosure from DCI Lawson. Still being a complete arse, of course. You know the victim's name and the murder method?"

"I think so," Tom said tentatively. "I'm not exactly sure."

"A similar method to Mrs. Haining." Mark pulled out a clipboard-sized iPad. "Do you have anything I need to know? *Not* whether you did it," he added slyly.

Tom managed a facsimile of a smile. But he was acutely aware that, this time, his militant innocence had gone, and he was seriously tempted just to blurt it all out. Tell Mark and Lawson about the edifice of secrets and lies he'd stumbled into, and let them make of it what they would. But he was no longer sure it could save him.

So, he gave Mark his false alibi—part of the evening spent in Will's company and the rest with Nick.

Mark glanced at him quickly as he spoke, frowning slightly, before going back to typing on the screen, and it occurred to Tom only then that Mark may have been the friend Will was meant to meet.

"Right," Mark said when he finished. "This time I'm strongly advising you to say nothing other than to clarify your alibi. Maybe we can walk the wire that way."

Tom remembered how sanctimoniously he'd rejected that suggestion last time, when he'd been telling only the truth.

"All right," he said.

Mark's expression gave nothing away. Did he seem sterner? Maybe, Tom thought with a rush of alarm, Will had got it as wrong about Mark as Tom had about Pez.

"It's going to be harder than you think," Mark warned. "You're going to need serious discipline not to blurt something out. Because Lawson will provoke you all he can. Follow my lead." He waited until Tom nodded his understanding. "And do exactly as I say."

Tom's guts writhed, but he followed Mark obediently to the door, to be escorted to the interview room.

Again it was familiar, waiting in the same seat with Mark beside him, as Lawson and Des Salt arrived and went through the same pre-interview routine.

Then Lawson began. No thanks. No niceties. A murderer's interview.

"Have you ever met Lily Adderton?" he asked.

Tom swallowed. "No." His mouth felt like dry straw.

"Are you still employing William Foster as a private investigator?"

"Yes," Tom said cautiously. Lawson had checked who Tom had hired? Or had Des told him?

Lawson's lip curled into something unpleasant. "A disgraced police officer," he sneered, as if he were grandstanding to a jury already.

"He's not disgraced!" Tom snapped. "He chose to leave. *And* he's a brilliant investigator."

Mark moved in his chair, and Tom suddenly wished he'd sounded a little less evangelical. He glanced at Des and held his brooding gaze for a fraction of a second before Des looked away.

The difference from Tom's last interview, fired up by his own righteousness, was agonizing.

"So. Tom." Lawson's tone sounded suddenly almost conversational. "Did your *investigator* tell you that Lily Adderton was the individual who made the original complaints about you, behind the pseudonym Jessica Mayhew?"

Tom thought he might have seen Des's hand clench on the desk. How compromised must he feel? God, did Des think he'd handed Lily over to her murderer?

Mark leaned over the short space between them and murmured urgently against Tom's ear, "No comment."

Tom pulled back and stared at him, appalled, but Mark glared at him with fierce meaning. *Do as I say.*

Tom made himself obey. His reply would have been close to a lie anyway.

"No comment," he said, voice shaking. And to him it felt exactly as if he'd said, *Guilty.*

Lawson's thin nostrils flared. "You found out this woman was threatening to expose what you did to her friend on social media…to your big *Instagram* following, with all your *fans. And* the press." Lawson's tone was silky. Satisfied. "Lily could have ruined you anytime she felt like it."

Tom choked out, "No comment."

How could that not incriminate him? All his instincts screamed at him to defend himself.

"Have you ever been to the Park Grand 'otel in Paddington, Tom?"

Tom turned with desperate appeal at Mark. Mark shook his head minutely.

Tom closed his eyes. "No comment."

"Were you there last night, between the hours of ten p.m. and one a.m.?"

Surely he could answer that? He'd already given an alibi. But Mark shook his head again.

"No comment," Tom managed. His pulse was pounding in his ears.

Lawson sniffed and leaned forward in his seat, forearms on the table, hands clasped. The backs of his hands were liberally sprinkled with coarse black hair. It made the nausea at the back of Tom's throat swell and thicken. He swallowed again, hard.

"It's where Lily Adderton was found. Mutilated," Lawson went on. "Like Mrs. 'Aining. Only…Lily's fingers were gone—as well as her tongue. I'm sure you get the implications of that, a clever lad like you." Tom clenched his jaw so hard his teeth ground together. "Thing is, she 'ated your guts, Tom. So how did you trick her into meetin' you there?"

"No comment." His voice sounded thick, as if he were going to cry. He cleared his throat aggressively.

"You'd do anything to silence her and protect your big reputation, wouldn't you, Tom? Or is there someone else sick enough to do all that to make you 'appy? So you don't have to break a nail."

Tom glared loathing at him; Lawson smirked triumphantly back, as if he thought he was winning. And something Will had said flashed through his mind—that whatever else Lawson was, he'd been trained in this. That he mustn't underestimate him.

He forced himself to lean back in his chair and fold his arms. "No comment."

"A narcissist like you, who'd kill one woman to stop his lover going back to her," Lawson said almost nonchalantly. "He'd remove a threat like Lily without a second's thought."

Narcissist… Will had said…

"No comment." He saw the excitement of the hunt on Lawson's face. It repelled him.

"Lily left two little children, Tom. Nessa…and Georgie. Aren't you *disgusted* with yourself? Or did that add to the thrill? Murdering a *mum*? I bet you 'ate mothers, Tom. Since your own runs off with any man that can pay for 'er."

And that was it. Tom was halfway to his feet, chairlegs scraping and screeching on the rubber floor, ready to knock the arsehole's teeth down his throat, when strong hands grabbed his arms, wrestling against his momentum. Dragged him back down into his chair.

"My client declines to comment," Mark half-shouted.

Tom, seated again, turned to him wildly. "But that's…!"

Mark ignored him. "Mr. Gray has provided you with a full alibi for the time you requested, Detective Chief Inspector. He'll also provide you with a written statement explaining all he knows about recent events, but he'll make no further comment in this interview, until matters become clearer. Now, do you intend to detain him any longer?"

Mark and Lawson locked gazes, Mark steely and impassive, Lawson glaring at him as if he could fry him on the spot. Just like Tom's first interview—a battle of wills between Lawson and Mark. Let Tom go, or charge him before Lawson's case was ready.

"We'll want to see you again, Tom," Lawson snapped. "Very soon. An' get that statement to us."

For a second time, he barged from the room in a huff, Des scuttling along behind. But Tom didn't feel like thanking Mark. He felt instead as if Mark's advice had just confirmed all Lawson's beliefs about his guilt. Cemented Lawson's course, locked on, like a guided missile.

"Don't. Bother," Mark warned, before he could get a word out. "You want to get them to prove what they believe you did. You don't have a duty to help them do it, whatever they want you to think."

Tom ran a shaking hand back through his hair just to feel the familiar fall around his face. Mark's unexpected aggression had shocked the panic out of him. "I'm sorry," he said meekly.

"Let's go." Mark seemed guarded and tense, and there was no playfulness left in him. When they reached the locked door to reception, he collared a passing police constable to let them out with her security pass. And just like last time, Nick was waiting, with Jena now, and Pez.

God—Nick and Jena were actively lying to the police for him, Tom realized sickly. He wanted to scream with frustration, but instead he pasted on his game face.

He nodded to them but he kept walking until they all followed him out the sliding door onto the pavement. There was no hint of a breeze. It was still early, but the air felt solid already. It smelled of exhaust fumes and rubber. Stale. A woman passed them pushing a child in a buggy, two thin white plastic bags bouncing on its handles as she walked.

Tom was vaguely aware that behind him, Nick and Jena were grilling Mark, but the words sounded almost burbled, as if the conversation were taking place underwater. Everything felt artificial and distant.

A hand clutched his arm. Black nail polish.

"God, Tommy." Pez's face was anxious-white, his black-lined eyes filled with apprehension. He looked like a poor copy of Pez, his energy and joy and confidence muted to low. "You look gruesome."

Tom snorted but he had enough presence of mind left not to tell Pez that he looked gruesome too.

"Look," Pez said urgently. "Can we just…forget everything about the other night? And the morning? I didn't mean *any* of it. I was just…drunk and angry. Let's go back to how we were, ay?"

But somehow, instead of grabbing on to it, as Tom knew he should, the plea for even less honesty upset him.

"It doesn't work like that," he said. Too harsh. Pez's obvious dismay softened his tone. "It doesn't have to change things, but I can't just pretend I don't know."

Pez laughed, though it sounded closer to a sob. "God, Tommy. You can pretend better than anyone I've ever known."

Their eyes met and locked, sick with feeling. And it felt significant somehow, to Tom. As if Pez had just told him some vital and unwelcome truth.

17

After Mark left, Nick led Tom, Jena and Pez to a café further along Borough High Street from Southwark police station. The rush hour was underway, but the café was almost empty.

Tom sat next to Pez on a long wooden bench behind their pale green formica table. Jena took a chair across from them and gave Nick a watery smile as he sat down next to her, sliding a tray with four mugs onto the tabletop.

They all sat in dazed silence for a few seconds, then Jena seemed to rouse herself to fish in her shoulder bag until she produced a brand-new mobile phone, which she handed to Tom.

"Nick told me the police were going to confiscate your devices, so I organized this yesterday. I passed the number…and the news about…about Lily to…" Her hesitation was noticeable. "A couple of people." Hansen, Tom supposed. Will?

"Thanks, Jen," Tom said quietly, "You think of everything." He laid the phone on the table. But the fresh reminder that they had to censor themselves because Pez was there prompted him to to take Pez's hand in his, under the table—almost an apology. Pez's startled pleasure was anything but discreet.

Nick glanced at them, then he looked away.

Whatever he did, Tom thought numbly, he hurt someone. He should have a warning sign around his neck.

"So what did the police say?" Nick's tone was cool and he didn't look at Tom.

Tom sighed, but he didn't let go of Pez's hand as he began to talk—laying out all the details he'd learned from Lawson. As he went on, Jena began to cry quietly, running agitated hands through her hair until bits of it stood up in little airy tufts, like pale pink feathers.

When Tom ground to a halt, Nick said, "Piers called me early this morning. Lily's husband. That's how I knew. He was distraught…making wild accusations that you killed Lily to silence her, like Lily thought you killed Cat. But he didn't know why she was in that hotel."

Tom nodded, lips pressed together hard, to contain everything. His brand-new phone gave a loud beep.

He glanced down at the screen in surprise, and the wave of pure, blind relief he felt when he saw the message told him how badly he'd needed to hear from Will. He could have kissed Jena.

Got some info. Come to the office: SFN Investigations, 33 Farringdon Street EC4

Tom knew he should have expected the curt matter-of-factness of the text. Fuck, Tom couldn't blame Will if he threw him to the wolves now. But still, he couldn't stop fretting over its lack of concern.

"Who would have *access* to that much insulin?" Nick asked suddenly. "A diabetic?"

"I'm diabetic," Pez said quietly.

Tom squeezed his hand tighter, and Pez smiled wanly and leaned closer.

"I didn't mean…" Nick stopped. He looked tired and sad.

Tom felt almost brutal as he said, "There's something else." And he told them about the break-in and the presents and the message, as dispassionately as he could.

He barely made it past the description of the package and the inscription, when Pez exclaimed, "Oh my God! Another one came to reception!"

He yanked his hand free and rummaged frantically in his messenger bag, to pull out a small, square package. It was wrapped in brown paper, tinted gold.

"We should we give it to the police." Pez sounded small and frightened as he placed it on the table. "But it's already covered in my fingerprints."

Tom was very sure there would be no more useful forensic evidence on it than had been left in his flat. Whoever was behind it was prepared and aware. So he picked up the box and ripped off the wrapping paper, ignoring Pez's weak sounds of protest.

Inside he found a tan-colored box with black lettering on the top: Louis Vuitton. And inside that—brown monogrammed canvas on soft white leather.

"I didn't know they did pets," Pez said stupidly.

A small silver plate on the collar was engraved JOHN. And underneath, in tiny italics, *So you will.*

"So you will, *what?*" Pez looked close to tears. Tom didn't feel far behind.

"He knows John's name," Nick observed.

Tom swallowed down the nausea in his throat. "Maybe…when he was in the flat—"

"He's stalking you!" Jena burst out. "He's trying to push his way in. To include himself. Right down to your cat."

"You can't go home, Tom," Nick sounded appalled. "Come to mine."

"Oh my God!" Pez pressed his hand with stunned theatricality to his chest. "It must be Max Perry!"

"Who's...?" Nick's eyes narrowed, then to Tom— "The man who raped you?"

And that was enough. Tom slid out from the wooden bench.

"I can't just sit here," he said. "I'm going to Will's office. He said he has information."

"I'll drive you," Nick said at once.

Tom didn't bother to argue.

•••

Farringdon Street was long and narrow, flanked by ugly three-story box buildings of brown, red or grey brick, concrete and glass. It was brutally utilitarian, a street for offices.

Tom climbed out of Nick's Porsche, his new gift clutched in his left hand. The slow, inevitable ebbing of adrenaline had left him feeling shaky and stiff.

But still, some instinct made him register a woman emerging from a hairdresser's salon across the street, several doors along to his left, before she began to walk away from them along the pavement.

Blind impulse sent Tom darting across the road after her.

"Dr. Rolfe!" He sounded anxious. The woman stopped and turned.

"Mr. Gray." Dr. Rolfe gave Tom one of her wide, sweet, dimpled smiles.

Tom couldn't help but smile back. "Getting your hair done," he said.

Dr. Rolfe patted her head self-consciously. "Oh. Well, it's a lost cause to be honest, but I have to put in a bit of effort or no one believes I'm a doctor."

Tom's smile widened, and he wondered if he was going to have the guts to do this. It felt like gearing up to kick a puppy.

"Tom?" Nick sounded confused when he arrived beside them, and Dr. Rolfe's politely blank expression reminded Tom that she and Nick had actually not met. He introduced them quickly.

Dr. Rolfe's smile faded into startled sympathy. "Oh. Mr. Haining. I meant to call you. I saw the pathology findings. I'm so sorry." The final word lilted to silence.

Nick cleared his throat. "Well. Thank you, and thanks for all you did for Cat, Doctor. I know you meant a lot to her."

Dr. Rolfe's acknowledging smile was sad. "I wish I could have done so much more."

She and Nick subsided into mournful silence, and Tom's doubts about what he was about to do ballooned. But Will wouldn't be squeamish.

"Dr. Rolfe…" he began.

"Oh. Call me Carys. If I can call you Tom?"

Tom managed another smile. "Carys. Look…I know this is intrusive." Carys's solemn brown eyes fixed on him. "It's just…Catriona's murder. Can I…?" He forced himself on. "Your husband. I'm sorry to ask but…he killed himself with insulin. Is that correct?"

Carys expression switched in an eyeblink from concerned interest to total disbelief, like lights turning off.

"It's just…" Tom hurried on. "Insulin and…and self-harm? There are parallels."

Carys dropped her shocked gaze from Tom's face, to the pavement.

"Tom…" Nick cautioned.

Carys's gaze snapped up. "No. No. It's all right," she said. Her voice shook and her eyes filled. Tom had made her cry. "It's all right. I'm sorry. I understand what you're saying. Catriona hadn't been a patient for long…when it happened. She was very kind when I came back. But Mike wasn't murdered. He killed himself using his insulin, and his antidepressants. I can't even say it was a cry for help. He meant to die." She drew a wet breath and her face distorted. "He couldn't adapt, you see? To being a late-onset diabetic…he thought he'd get every side-effect a diabetic could get. Go blind." She sighed shakily and rubbed her forehead. "He'd actually become impotent, though it was probably psychosomatic. But it drove his depression. He was just…angry with life. I tried everything I could. But I failed him."

"I'm sorry," Tom said again, because, whatever her husband had been like, he was very sure Carys Rolfe would have tried her best. But he wouldn't stop now. "He cut himself too."

Carys pressed her lips together hard.

"You have been doing your homework." She nodded. "Yes. He mutilated his…his ah…his penis." Her voice trembled violently. "He used to say the diabetes had unmanned him. I suppose he just decided to finish the job."

Shit. "I'm…"

Carys stared over his shoulder. "I found him, you know. Me and my friend had been in Tenerife, see? But I'd missed him…even as difficult as he'd been. I always missed him. And there he was on our bed, two days dead. Like he'd set the scene for me to walk in on. I wonder if he was punishing me."

All Tom's instincts told him to back off. He was blundering around in delicate things.

But he had to complete this as as precisely as Will would have.

"The police report said he was naked," he said. "Apart from jewellery and a red string. Was that a Kabbalah string?" The thought had struck him in passing when he'd heard James Henderson mention it. A few models and celebrities he knew wore them all the time.

Carys looked startled, perhaps at this latest proof that he had access to a detailed report on her husband's death, but she didn't challenge him on it.

Instead she shrugged weakly. "I think so. He worked his way through all the religions after he was diagnosed. Hinduism, Buddhism. That Kabbalah thing, like Madonna. I didn't really pay attention since it helped him. I remember he said the string was meant to…ward off misfortune." Her face twisted.

"Thank you, Carys," Tom said softly, sincerely.

Carys shook her head.

"Was that really necessary, Tom?" Nick hissed, as they watched her walk away, looking significantly more subdued than she had when Tom had hailed her.

"Yes," Tom snapped back. "Since we can't involve the police, we have to do their job, don't we?"

"*We?*" Nick sounded upset, but Tom didn't try to coax him out of it.

Part of his mind was still fixed on Carys's pain and the information she'd given him nonetheless. The rest raced around his wildly conflicted feelings about his imminent meeting with Will. He wasn't close to ready to face him after the night before, but he was also desperate to see him. To feel safer, somehow.

They took a lift in the overly air-conditioned lobby of SFN's building, and when they emerged on the brightly lit fourth floor, Will's nameplate was one of the first Tom saw. The office door lay wide open.

Will was leaning, braced, over his desk, when they entered his doorway, frowning down at a computer monitor. The sleeves of his white shirt had been rolled up over his strong, tanned forearms, and gravity pulled his maroon tie to dangle over the desk. The longer hair on the top of his head was wildly tousled, and Tom felt the disastrous urge to walk over and just…touch him. But Will didn't look up.

The woman who stood beside him, also looking at the monitor and talking quietly, was leaning far too close. She was partly in profile to Tom, so he could see the curve of her spectacular arse, shown to blatant advantage by a fitted black dress in the same 50s style as Catriona had worn, so tight it forced a kind of a hobbled, geisha walk. Old-season Victoria Beckham, Tom catalogued automatically, before biting off the thought with a burst of irritated self-contempt.

The woman's skin was clear brown, her dark hair was worn in thin braids, brushing a long, graceful neck. She wore fashionable black-rimmed spectacles, and she looked, Tom thought spitefully, like a perfect cartoon secretary, coming on to her boss. His hostility to the girl was instant and implacable.

Will glanced up and took in Tom and Nick with a quick nod, but his focus returned at once to the screen, glowering at it, listening to the woman murmur on. He looked unsettled, Tom recognized with a pang of alarm, as if anger rippled under the surface.

Finally the woman finished talking and Will straightened up.

"Sorry," he said. He gestured to the chairs set in front of the desk.

Tom chose one and sprawled deliberately in it, posing, and he couldn't seem to help himself.

He announced, "You said you had information." It sounded more imperious than he intended.

"Yeah," Will replied, distractedly. "Pixie's been working on some background info on Max Perry." So. This was *Pixie*. Tom curled his lip. She was even more ridiculous than he'd imagined. "She's very good with computers," Will went on. "And when I say very good, I mean she's a genius."

"I have no idea why I'm slumming it here," Pixie chimed in, and her accent was as posh as James Henderson's. Large dark confident eyes swept over Nick, then fixed on Tom's glowering expression.

They eyed each other for a long challenging moment, then Pixie very deliberately rolled her gaze over Tom—from head to toe and back again, stopping for effect on his crotch, bulging in tight blue denim, and ending on his flushed, hostile face.

"I'm *very* user-friendly though..." she purred seriously. "If you ever need anyone to...unzip your files." She waggled her perfectly groomed eyebrows, in a semaphore of lechery. "Press...*any* key to continue."

It took a moment, but Tom laughed.

Pixie grinned too. She was beautiful. Unfortunately.

"I had to get that look off your face somehow," she said to Tom. Tom glanced guiltily at Will, but Will in turn was gazing at Pixie with something close to despair.

"These are our *clients*," he reproved, then sighed. "Tom Gray, Dominic Haining. My colleague, Tiana Braithwaite. Otherwise known as Pixie."

Pixie bowed her head to them graciously. "I've been doing a bit of digging for you, where maybe just possibly I shouldn't."

"You didn't hear that," Will said. Pixie smirked.

Tom looked at Will quickly, then at Pixie, and back to Will, hating the ease and familiarity between them. Will was behaving to Tom as if the night before hadn't happened.

Exactly as Tom should want him to behave.

He needed to catch a fucking grip.

Pixie went on, unperturbed. "Maximillian George Perry." She sat down on the other side of the desk from Tom and Nick. Will sat beside her.

"Very regal," Tom muttered.

"His parents had definite ideas that way," Pixie agreed. "His brother's Edward Theodore. But their birth name isn't Perry. It's Butts."

"Butts?" Tom grinned, diverted. "Max *Butts*?" It felt like a kind of justice.

"Yeah," Will said. "I don't think many people were smiling when Eddie Butts was taking off their kneecaps."

Tom stared at him.

"Gangster family," Will said. "Ron Butts was their dad, the brains beside Joey Clarkson and *his* dad before him. Ronnie died a couple of years ago, and now Eddie's in the family business. He's not bright enough to do what Ronnie did, but he's a vicious little bastard, so he fits right in. He's Joey's chief enforcer now."

"Who the hell is Joey Clarkson?" Nick asked.

"A *businessman*. With very expensive lawyers." Will sounded beyond bitter. Disgusted. "He runs a swathe of nightclubs and bars. Massage parlors. They front for gunrunning, drugs, prostitution, people trafficking… but we can't pin a thing on him."

We, Tom noted with a stab of sadness.

Pixie chipped in. "Max took all the brains and went off and got a degree in computer science. Changed his name—legally—and started his own firm. He's nowhere near as good as me, of course."

"Of course," Tom said.

"He's far too rich for what he does though," Pixie went on. "So I made some enquiries and found he didn't leave the family business after all. He's doing all the IT stuff for Joey Clarkson. Hacking. Encrypting. Countering surveillance. Wiping files…"

"Most criminals don't have the patience to implement encryption software." Will's voice was tight. "Not on a continued use anyway. Or they use partial encryption. Sloppy. If they only encrypt a few files on hard drive, then our…then police investigators can analyze unencrypted copies on the same drive, to find what they want." His dark brows pulled harder into a furious frown. "But our mate Max is making sure it's all nice and watertight for Joey."

"Which is why Max is seriously loaded," Pixie finished. "And I *mean* loaded. His bank accounts are embarrassing."

Tom was pretty sure that breaking in to someone's bank account was illegal, but he focused instead on a mounting sense of certainty that pieces were falling into place.

Max had the computer skills to frame him—to leave the suicide note on Catriona's laptop. And he apparently had the crime links to get people killed to order.

"Incidentally," Will went on. "Eddie did some time in Red Moss. Two and a half years."

Pixie frowned at him curiously, as if he'd just thrown in an obscure and pointless fact, like *Chelsea didn't win the League.*

But it was just another puzzle piece that fitted.

It hadn't been about David Burchill after all. It had all been about Tom. And his insane, murderous stalker.

Will was clearly on the same wavelength. "He's pointed the police at you," he said to Tom. "And the reason you haven't been charged is because he hasn't given them anything definitive. He's playing."

Tom found he didn't have the emotional energy left to conjure up any more fear.

"So...he wants Tom's attention," Pixie said to Will. "I mean...he is *spectacularly* lush." She threw first Will, then Tom, an evil little smile, and Tom had a sinking feeling, close to certainty, that Will confided in her. "Maybe...Max thinks he's killing in tribute," she went on. "Or marking his territory? Making sure Tom knows Max is in control of his life. His freedom. Plus, the gifts are expensive...showing his status."

It made a kind of sense. Then Tom remembered what was held, un-thinking, in his hand.

He rose and put the box containing the cat collar and the wrapping paper onto Will's desk.

"Another one came. It went to Echo."

Will eyed the package as if Tom had put a turd in front of him, but he picked it up and scrutinized the paper and the box, then turned the collar in his hand until he'd absorbed every detail.

He said matter-of-factly, "He wants you to know—to be *certain* he's watching you. And he wants to dominate your thoughts. You're meant to be waiting for the next part of the message. 'So you will'...what? He wants you to be scared."

"Well he's doing a stellar job," Tom said.

No one spoke for a few moments. The only sound came from Pixie's long, pale green fingernails tapping idly against the desk. Then she said brightly, "We could do a sting."

Will, who'd been examining the collar, stared at her with extravagant incredulity.

"A sting," Tom repeated flatly.

"Yeah," Pixie went on, ignoring Will's forbidding expression. "Will says, for some reason, we have to operate totally apart from the police. So…we can give you a GSM-bugged phone. You meet Max, find out all you can. We record it."

Nick exploded. "What…? *No!*" He'd sat and allowed them to talk around him. But now his face looked flushed, distorted with outrage. "You're seriously suggesting Tom goes to meet a deranged murderer?"

"It'd be in a public place," Pixie said, unperturbed. "He'd be safe."

"Safe?" Nick countered venomously. "Like my *wife* was safe? Like her *friend* was safe?"

Will said, "It's far too dangerous. If it's Max, Tom's the focus."

Tom stood up. "Show me," he said to Pixie.

He wasn't going to be babied. He needed all of this to stop.

"Do ya ting," Pixie drawled approvingly, accent abruptly pure Caribbean. She smiled at him. Somehow, he smiled back.

•••

"*Please*, Tom. Look, maybe it's time to tell the police everything."

Tom let his head fall back against the tall, purple-cushioned back of Nick's designer chair, clutching a tall glass of vodka and soda, and seriously questioning his own judgment in coming here. But he couldn't stay at his own place, and he couldn't let John stay there now either, since John had received his own present. So Nick had driven Tom to Shoreditch to pick up his cat and pack a bag. Then Tom had followed Nick's car, on his bike, back to Notting Hill.

Before Nick and he left Will's office, they'd all composed a text on Tom's new phone to send to Max Perry, proposing they meet the next day. The reply had been almost instant, as if Max had been waiting: *I'll be at the gym till 10. After that?*

Nick, though, still hadn't stopped trying to talk him out of it.

"We have no proof against Max to take to the police," Tom said, for what felt like the hundredth time. "I'm not pretending I'm not shitting myself, but I have to do it. And I'm not helpless. I've done boxing…some self-defense."

Will had consulted Hansen by phone and she'd agreed. Get her solid evidence quickly, and she'd get Lawson to redirect his focus. As it was, Lily's murder had forced her to consult her contact in the Public Protection Unit at the Justice Ministry. The decision could very soon be made above Hansen's head to pull the plug on Nick's deal, even though he'd done nothing wrong—ending his life, and Jena's, as they knew it now.

"You have a shoot tomorrow," Nick burst out, as if that was the unanswerable argument he should have used all along. "You have a responsibility to your clients."

It was a Saturday booking—the second day of a bread-and-butter job for Marks and Spencer. As it happened, the first day had been in Greenwich—the day everything went to hell.

"I'll go there after," Tom said steadily. "There'll be plenty of time."

"Have you even been getting ready?" Nick demanded.

Tom eyed him with impatience. He understood why Nick was pushing it. Reminding him of his priorities. But he really didn't need this… superficiality in the face of huge things.

"I'll have a good sleep tonight," he said shortly. "Use a peeling cream in the shower. Some exfoliator."

"When did you wax last?"

"Fucking hell, Nick!" Anger bubbled very close to the surface, but he had to try to accept that Nick was his boss too. And part of being a model was being treated like a child. "Just before the first shoot last Friday. Yes," he snapped, as Nick opened his mouth. "Eyebrows too. Anyway, tomorrow's not underwear."

"*Tom.* Just think about it. When you should be making sure everything's on point for the client, that you're calm and centered—you're planning to confront a murderer!"

"And isn't that a bit more impor…" Tom made himself to stop. He was aware that Nick was desperately trying to manipulate him, but also that Nick was right. Then again, Tom was right too.

"Tell me about Glassy," he demanded and he didn't know what had driven him to ask that now, other than a lingering unease he'd felt since the interview with Wykeham.

In David's eyes, Glassy had betrayed him. Glassy wasn't going to come out of that well.

Nick looked stunned and then hurt. Possibly, Tom realized too late, because he'd totally avoided talking to Nick about his past since he'd been told about it.

The light flooding through the windows at both sides of the room made Nick's smooth brown hair shine like the shell of a hazelnut.

Tom should probably have sat on the sofa beside him. But he hadn't.

"We got on well," Nick said stiffly. "He followed me about really. But he made a pass at Denny… I mean Brian said she set it up and I believe him now. But at the time I wouldn't listen. I just…stopped speaking to him."

Tom said, "Dr. Wykeham said your friends cut his ear off."

Nick grimaced but to Tom's relief, he didn't try to deny it. "Maybe they thought they were avenging me. I didn't… I tried to talk to Glassy afterwards, but…he thought I'd had it done to him. He was just…immature. I should have been kinder."

"He's bipolar. Actually," Tom said. Perhaps Glassy deserved that Nick should hear it.

Nick certainly heard Tom's censure. He said, anguished, "It was like living in a jungle, Tom. You had to try to look like one of the big beasts to survive."

After a moment, Tom nodded. "Do you remember Eddie Butts?"

"There were always new people," Nick said distantly. "Coming in. Leaving. And the last year before Wandsworth, I disengaged anyway. I was terrified of adult prison."

"Your dates overlapped," Tom persisted. "If Max involved Eddie in stalking me, and Eddie saw you… Maybe he recognized you. That would explain why they echoed the Babes in Arms."

"I don't know!" Nick said desperately. "It fits! Everything about Max fits. That's why you shouldn't go!"

Tom sighed. He should show a little mercy. Nick was as confused as he was, maybe as scared.

He focused on a few of Nick's gorgeous bronzes: a rearing horse, an elephant god, a slender male dancer.

"I forgot to tell you," Tom said. "I got the Armani campaign."

He didn't know why he'd chosen that moment, other than the growing urge to get on the next flight out of the country.

"Baby!" When Tom looked back at him, Nick wore a beaming smile. "That's fucking…incredible! I'm so proud of you. Fuck, I don't have champagne in!"

Tom grinned, but he didn't try to mimic an excitement he couldn't feel at that moment. He should be able to show Nick at least that much truth.

"What's the matter?" Nick asked, still smiling. "Look, I know everything's shit at the moment but…this is… It's what we've been working toward!"

We.

How to say he was toying with leaving for good? He'd been that honest with Will.

That gouging stab of memory made him blurt, "I've been thinking maybe Mel's right. Once all this crap's settled, it's probably time for me to spend more time in the States." He met Nick's eyes. "Maybe I'll rent a place in New York to take advantage of the Armani contract. I've been stubborn about it, but…"

He trailed off. Nick's frozen expression silenced him. His customary tan seemed to have faded over the past days. Now his skin seemed milky-pale, almost sallow.

Nick said calmly, "Well. I can't blame you for running away."

"Nick, come on! I'm not moving from Echo. I'll still do jobs here for you. It's just maybe time to move. For my career," he reasoned. "I'm not running away."

Except he would be. Running from too many feelings, returned and unreturned—all unwanted. Pez's pain, which he seemed to add to day by day. Nick, who wasn't Nick anymore and loved him too much. And Will...

"Funny," Nick said with a bitter bark of laughter. "I thought the person I should be worried about was Will Foster." Tom's mouth opened with shock. "I didn't reckon on you leaving me for Melanie."

Tom blinked. "Look... It's not a plan. I love London. I love my flat..." And the next line, he recognized too late, should have been, *And I love you.*

The silence stretched too long. Nick stood up.

"Nick," Tom sprang to his feet too. "Please don't worry about it. Please. You have so much more to..."

"It's all right," Nick broke in. But he sounded awful. And the drowning guilt Tom felt around him flooded in again.

Here was a man who tried to give him everything, who'd laid his heart and future at his feet, who never let him down—who lied to the police for him for fuck's sake. Christ...that was the benchmark of loving him these days.

Nick was ready to blow his whole life out of the water to help him, and what could be more noble than that?

Saving his sister. Trying to save Catriona. Begging to save Tom. All Nick wanted was to give him a haven.

Tom could hardly deny, at that moment of vulnerability, that his glorious career seemed to stretch ahead of him less a shining road of excitement than a life sentence of emptiness.

But with Nick, Tom would never have to worry about being the one who loved more. Tom would never love Nick enough to feel threatened by it. He'd never *need* him. But he wouldn't be alone.

On blind instinct, he tugged Nick toward him, getting some resistance at first, but then Nick gave in and allowed himself to be hugged. He didn't resist when Tom kissed him, and he let himself be led to the bedroom silently (other than John's chorus of protesting mews behind them).

And then Tom did everything Nick wanted, except allowing him fuck him, of course. He even let Nick bruise his neck, though he usually refused, especially with a shoot the next day. Knowing how much the sense of possession seemed to mean to Nick. Knowing the possession was illusory. Aware Nick knew it too.

18

It was Saturday and Nick was free, but Tom asked him to look after John as a thin excuse to stop him coming along to the SFN offices with him.

Tom took the bike, using the solitude of the trip to center himself.

The night before he'd done to Nick again what he'd done to Pez—he'd used sex to try to avoid truth and loss. In the cold light of day, his own cowardice disgusted him.

When he arrived at Will's office, Will and Pixie were sitting close together at Will's monitor. Tom did his best not to care. But a part of his mind worried at the idea compulsively. Had they slept together? Were they still doing it? Like Will and Mark? Or maybe, it'd become more.

Beyond hypocritical, Tom knew, but he couldn't seem to help it.

Will had dressed casually in a close-fitting black shirt, sleeves rolled up, and light blue jeans, and he leaned against a wall and watched, arms folded, while Pixie, wearing an unlikely white jumpsuit and vertiginous heels, explained to Tom the workings of the GSM phone.

And it felt to Tom, every time his eyes fell on him, as if the sex they'd had only increased Will's power. As if Tom had allowed a vital wall to fall, and his defenses were thinned.

He was taken aback when Will said without expression: "That might wind him up. I'm not sure if that's a good thing or not. Maybe Pix should give you some covering makeup."

It took a moment to realize that Will, still leaning with his arms folded, had been eyeing the spectacular bruise Nick had left on his neck the previous the night before Tom fucked him. Which Tom, in his passive, fatalistic mood, had accepted. Like a fucking moron.

He met Will's shuttered eyes, and he wished he'd resisted, because he felt again that irrational, maddening guilt, as if he'd cheated. And around Will the feeling wouldn't go away.

Unless he made it.

They drove to the gym in silence.

Max was alone in the gym room when Tom found him, focused entirely on himself.

Narcissist.

The word Lawson and Will had thrown at Tom circled his mind as he stood in the open doorway and watched Max exercise. As Max watched himself exercise.

Every flex of muscle as he used the weights machine on which he sat, every trickle of sweat, every flare of his nostril—Max watched it all in the wall-sized mirror.

Tom had rarely seen such self-focus, and he worked in a career built on it. In fact Max was so fixed on himself that he didn't notice Tom reflected behind him inside the doorway.

Some stalker, Tom thought with contempt.

He made himself saunter across the room until he stood in Max's direct eyeline. Looking at him made Tom feel almost physically sick.

"Tommy!" Max exclaimed.

Tom tried to place the unmistakeable emotion in those opaque eyes. Surprise first, of course. Hunger was part of it. Pleasure. Triumph. None of the madness that must be fueling him.

But what Tom stuck on was his hatred that Max called him "Tommy". Only Pez and Jena got away with that. Tom had called time on it for the rest of the world when he was thirteen.

"Max."

The last time Tom had seen him, Tom had been leaving his flat feeling disorientated and confused, and very sure for some reason he couldn't define, that he didn't ever want to go back.

"You've been pestering me to talk. I'll be in Artisan Coffee for twenty minutes." Which was a café a few doors down from the gym.

Max groped for a towel to wipe his face, eyes still riveted on Tom as he rose to his feet. His shoulders were wide with muscle and his chest and arm muscles bulged with it, but he was a few inches shorter than Tom and his worked-at bulk made him look stocky.

"What changed your mind?" Max asked. His accent was smoothed-out South London.

Tom shrugged. "Curiosity." He kept his tone offhand.

"You look good." Max grinned. He had startlingly white teeth, bleached too often probably. "Unreal."

"I'll see you in the café." Tom turned and strolled out, all bravado, feeling Max's gaze locked to his back and arse as he went. Feeling soiled.

The moment Tom stepped out onto the pavement, his gaze shot to Will's Passat, parked fifty yards along from the café. And he was beyond relieved that of all people, Will was with him.

He chose a table by the window with two bench seats, ordered a coffee, and had to wait only a flattering fourteen minutes before Max strode into the café as if he paid everyone's salary. Tom swallowed down his revulsion and waved him over.

His phone rang, on cue. He picked it up and answered as Max neared the table.

"Is it on?" Will asked.

Tom pulled the phone back from his ear until his peripheral vision registered the tiny green light on the front. "Yeah, yeah. Fine," he said. "See you then."

He put the device on the table in front of him.

A waitress arrived immediately to take Max's order, which gave Tom time to study him surreptitiously.

It wasn't that he was ugly. Objectively Max was quite attractive. His features were even, his skin tone was a light browny-orange—a sunbed tan—and his hair cropped, very short, was mid-brown. His eyes were large and some indeterminate shade that wasn't brown, blue or green. Mud, Tom decided, vindictively. He wore beige chinos and a white Henley, hair damp from the shower, and he looked well. Healthy. He made Tom's skin crawl.

The waitress left, and Tom piled in. His mind felt clearer and sharper than he could remember, since facing big exams at university. Adrenaline, fear, and everything at stake.

"You've been messaging me. I told you I didn't want to see you."

Max smiled broadly. "Yet here you are."

"Yeah, isn't that a surprise?" Tom asked. "Given the fact you raped me." And he hadn't known he was going to say that himself.

Max's smile slid away. He looked around quickly.

His voice was low and outraged. "It was consensual."

"Come on, Max," Tom scoffed. "What was it? Roofies? G?"

Max's eyes narrowed. "I can't be responsible for the stuff you take, Tommy."

Tom easily produced a narrow-eyed, disgusted moue. He'd more than half-expected Max to gloat, rather than deny. "I wanted to clear the air, but there's no point if you're just gonna lie through your *fucking* teeth. We both know what happened."

Max eyed him warily.

Tom gave a heavy sigh and shrugged. "Have it your way."

He began to rise to his feet, reaching for the phone device as he went.

Max's broad, tanned hand slapped down on top of his. "All right. Calm your tits! We can talk."

Tom looked down. The back and fingers of Max's hand were liberally dusted with crinkly brown hair and a thick ring of braided gold banded his middle finger. Those fingers had been all over him, maybe inside him.

Tom swallowed the gorge in his throat and sank down into his seat, pulse pounding. He pulled his hand away.

"So?" he demanded obnoxiously.

"So I may have given you a bit of G to loosen you up." Suddenly, Max grinned. It made him look disarmingly young. "And baby, did you get loose!" Or maybe not. "You like playing *daddy*, don't ya?" His voice lowered to intimate syrup. "You loved sucking my dick, Tommy. An' you fuckin' worshipped my arse. Loved using that big cock. I have it all on tape, how much you loved it."

Tom fought with everything he had not to show rage or shame. He focused on one thing.

Daddy. That vile message to Catriona.

He glared into Max's gloating face until somehow his outrage seemed to get through, and Max wrestled his smirk down to a more neutral expression. But glee still sparkled in his eyes.

"Sorry, baby. It was the night of a lifetime, that's all."

Tom needed to get a grip on this. Put on the persona he was used to showing men like Max, who just wanted to fuck a model. Tickets for Centre Court were the least of it.

He felt neutral non-expression fix on to his features like a paper mask.

"I want you to stop sending me crap things," he announced imperiously.

Max's eyes narrowed again. "Crap…things?" He leaned back against the upright of his padded bench seat and folded his beefy arms.

"I don't care how expensive they are," Tom said. "You're not going to impress me. Not with *your* taste."

Max rubbed his mouth slowly, eyes never leaving Tom. Assessing. Clever. Tom had to remind himself that Max was far, far more clever than he'd allowed Tom to see.

"If I was gonna send you things…" Max said slowly. "It'd only be the best."

"*If.* Come on, *Max*," Tom mocked. "You drugged me to have sex with me. I don't know why you're playing coy about sending me presents."

"I don't know what you mean." Max grinned obnoxiously.

Too confident. Tom needed to shake him somehow. He should have worked out a script, but he'd known in his heart he was going to have to wing it.

And then as if someone had prodded him, he flashed on an image—Will's empty eyes as he saw the bitemark on Tom's skin, just that morning.

Okay.

In a casual movement Tom pushed his hair behind his ear and rubbed at his neck, making sure to edge back his collar. On cue, Max's eyes locked there. His expression changed from ease to suspicion to fury.

"What the *fuck* is that?" Max hissed. "It looks like a *fucking* animal's been at you."

Tom pretended to take a few seconds to understand.

"*God!*" he drawled. "Don't be boring. It's none of your business."

"You won't even take my calls." Max's voice was low, dangerous, and just like that, the mood had switched to ugly. "But you *fuck* no-names. An' that poof agent of yours. An' your beige boss."

"You've been stalking me!" Tom said. He tried for surprised outrage.

"I've been keeping tabs. Why wouldn't I?"

"Because I'm nothing to do with you," Tom retorted and rolled his eyes with diva-ish disdain. "Don't be *creepy*."

Max scowled. "I want you. So you're everythin' to do with me."

Tom stared at him, intimidated for a moment despite himself, by that unwavering entitlement.

"You're very lucky I didn't set the cops on you for breaking into my flat," Tom said. "You're small time, Max."

Max's eyes narrowed to slits. "I don't know what the *fuck* you're talking about."

"Oh, come on!" Tom jeered.

Max leaned slowly forward until he was half over the table, intimidatingly close. His jaw had bunched, eyes bright, like a predator on the hunt.

He looks like a gangster, Tom thought. *Like a murderer.*

"Maybe you're right," Max breathed. "I know everything about you, Tommy. In fact, I probably know more than you do."

Tom's breath suddenly felt so shallow that he understood how people could begin to pant from fear. But somehow he forced himself to hold the façade of blankness. He ran his fingers back through his hair for courage and made it look careless.

"The thing is," he said. "I like powerful men, Max. Men with *balls*… who'll do anything for me. Like my boss. Not little men who send poison pen messages and pathetic little love tokens. Not…*stalkers* like you."

"*Powerful?*" Max looked as shocked and offended, as if Tom had spat in his face. "You think that muppet is powerful?"

Tom leaned forward too, until their faces were close across the table.

"Well he didn't piss about sending anonymous presents, did he? Since you've been *spying*, you'll know all about his wife and her friend. I mean it's…cheaper than divorce." He sat back, stretching slightly, showing off.

"Kinda sexy being wanted that much." He grinned. "Which is *exactly* why he deserved last night."

Max's mouth pursed, nostrils flaring. "Don't ever underestimate me, Tommy. That'd be a mistake."

Tom leaned away despite himself. He tried to make it look relaxed. Max didn't move. He was still leaning forward over the table.

"Underestimate you?" Tom scoffed.

"I can see it's time I laid down the law. Can't be bothered messing around anymore. I've lost my taste for it. Tell Haining if he touches you again, my brother'll take him on a nice walk down Memory Lane. You get yourself away from that twat an'—hey presto. The police'll lose steam. Just like magic. And if your agent wants to keep his looks, he'll stay away too."

Tom must have shown reaction, because Max settled into the beginnings of grim satisfaction. And Tom couldn't understand how he'd ever allowed himself to believe Max Perry was just another spoiled brat.

"Settled then." Max's expression slid into hard joviality. "An' shed that cunt of a copper before I do." Absolute proof that Max had been watching everything he did. "Did you know he tried to bring down someone close to me once." He grinned maliciously. "Didn't turn out so well for him."

"So...it was you?" Tom asked, with just enough bewilderment. "You killed Catriona and Lily? Why?"

Max gave a wolf's grin. "You wouldn't answer my calls. What else could I do?" He chewed his lip, thinking. "What'd you do to reward me, if I told you all about it?"

"Buy you a bun?" Tom said.

Max's expression hardened. "I deserve a thank-you, don't I? An' my dick's so hard right now just looking at that blowjob mouth. You were born to suck cock."

"Come on, Max..." Tom sounded too nervous.

Max heard it. His smile widened; Tom could see the excitement in his eyes.

"There's a loo in the back." Max lowered his voice to a whisper. "The door locks. You can suck me off in there."

Tom didn't know what his face was showing. He hoped it was boredom, but he was very worried it was terror. "I don't do blow jobs in café toilets," he said with all the arrogance he could muster.

Max's expression barely changed. "You'll do it for me. Now you've seen what I'd do for you. No rubbers."

Fucking hell. Tom tried for playful resistance. This felt like a game he was losing badly. "I definitely don't do anything without condoms."

Max's sudden grin was elated. He looked like a man who'd won everything he wanted to win. "But you're gonna dump the others Tommy. It's just me now, so we don't need rubbers. Gonna take you home an' dick you bare after this. Show you who you belong to." Tom's panic began to push to nausea. "Go on." Max nodded quickly toward a door, which Tom assumed must be the café toilet. "You first. I'll wait forty seconds."

"I didn't say…"

The phone began to buzz on the table. Tom stared at it stupidly before picking it up.

"Hi, Jen," he said.

"Get out of there," Will ordered.

"Already? But I thought…"

"Go!"

Tom closed the call and tried to think past the pounding in his ears. Max's eyes were fixed on him avidly, like a thing he'd bought and was impatient to use.

Tom slid out from his bench seat and stood. His legs shook.

"That's a good boy," Max breathed. "Maybe I'll let you play daddy later, if you give me a good hungry suck now."

The greed on his face was repellent. Bestial.

Tom walked away from the table, but not toward the toilet. To the café door. He had the advantage of surprise, because he'd managed to pull it open and get outside onto the pavement before Max came barrelling after him.

"What the *fuck*?" he yelled. His flush of lust had turned to rage again though Tom, looking down instinctively, could see a huge excited bulge in his chinos.

There were other people on the street, thank God.

"Sorry," Tom said with no apology. "I just realized I have an appointment."

"What the fuck are you playing at?"

"Bye, Max."

Tom began to walk away, but he was half-expecting the rough hand that grabbed his arm. Tom tugged at it sharply. The hand gripped harder.

"You don't fucking wind me up and walk away!"

Tom tried to tug his arm free, and they scuffled back and forth for a few seconds, pedestrians moving back, staring at them like a sideshow. But then Max began to haul at Tom in earnest, dragging him, despite all his resistance, a few yards along the pavement, away from the café and toward what Tom feared had to be his car.

At any second, Will would break cover and that couldn't happen. Max couldn't know yet that this had been any kind of setup.

He said sweetly, "Baby! Don't!" And relaxed his resistance. Max hesitated for one crucial moment, and Tom swung his whole body round to face him, using that momentum to knee him brutally in the balls.

Max doubled over with a howling gasp of agony, and as he did, Tom karate-chopped him viciously hard on the back of his neck. Max crumpled to the pavement like a dropped handkerchief. Self-defense classes, courtesy of UCL students' union.

Across the road, a couple of teenage boys gave a faint mocking cheer, and Tom bent down over Max's huddled body.

He steadied his voice to smoothness. "You should know I don't take well to threats, Max."

He strode away, crossing the street and stalking along the pavement, forcing himself not to break into a run.

The Passat was parked facing away from the café, engine running, and Tom wasn't sure if he should walk past it in case Max was watching. But as he neared the car, the passenger door was pushed open from inside and Tom dived in. Will pulled the car out into the road immediately and began to cruise away.

"He's surrounded by people." Will was focused on the driver's mirror. "But they're thinning out. He's trying to get up. Hey—crouch down in the footwell. He might spot your hair." Tom immediately folded his long body down in front of the passenger seat. "What did you do?" Will sounded amused.

"Kneed him in his hard-on."

"Ooof."

"And chopped the back of his neck."

"Good lad."

Tom rubbed his forehead. His ears were still buzzing. He peered up from his crouch. "Did we get enough?"

Will caught his lower lip between his teeth and chewed absently. He drove at a stately pace. Nothing to draw attention. He flicked an indicator, and the car began to turn the corner.

"He was trying to impress you, but—I think you got enough for Hansen to set Lawson on him." Will sounded satisfied. "You played him brilliantly."

"He *knows* about Nick," Tom said with shaky urgency. "He's the one." Then after a second or two, "He knows you too. He said you tried to bring down someone close to him."

A muscle in Will's jaw flexed. "It's okay to get up now."

Tom obediently wriggled his way onto the passenger seat and fastened his seat belt.

Will didn't say anything for a few moments, then he sighed, as if he'd made a decision. "That last op I told you about... It was to arrest one of Eddie Butts's boys." Tom turned his head to stare at his profile. "He'd murdered an undercover officer inside one of Joey's businesses. We had an eyewitness. But Joey has people too. Deep in the Met."

Tom's eyes widened. "In the *Met*?"

"Easy. He buys them. Or sends in his own as recruits, then they work their way up..."

"Fuck."

"Yeah. Only essential personnel knew about that op. Then I played right into their hands by getting pissed and sleeping in, and...Archer sprayed the details all over the place that morning. So...one of Joey's narks warned them our unit was coming. Eddie's boys got there to clean up, remove the weak link, just before Sanjay and the others arrived. The guy we were going to arrest got conveniently shot in the head, the rest got away. Joey sent me a bunch of flowers when I left. And a wreath to Sanjay's funeral, signed from him and Eddie."

Tom swallowed. He felt totally out of his depth. "I'm sorry."

Will shrugged. "It was my fault."

"No!" Tom said, "By that logic, it's my fault for making you so unhappy you drank too much."

Will didn't acknowledge it. "It's not my job to worry about Joey anymore. But Max Butts?" He looked grim. "Him, I can happily bring down."

Tom stared at his profile a moment longer, then out the passenger window, seeing nothing. He still felt sick, not least because of the violence of which he'd just been a part. But the discovery that this was personal to Will, that he had an investment in Max's guilt... It made him uneasy.

A thought hit and Tom checked his watch. "Oh, *fuck*." He made a distressed sound. *Ten forty-two.* "I've got a shoot in Brixton at eleven fifteen."

Will threw him a quick glance. "That's okay. I can get you there."

Tom looked at him hopefully then hauled down the sun visor and pulled the cover off the small mirror. Desperate light-blue eyes stared back at him. He rubbed at the shadows under them with his forefingers as if they were smudges of ink. Then he pulled the mirror lower to peer at the bruise on his neck.

"God, I'm a fucking mess," he moaned.

"You look fine."

"Fine doesn't cut it, Will!"

"Okay. You look like a top model who just cut down a muscle-bound thug in the street."

Tom threw him a startled glance. His gut felt stupidly warmer. "Will that sell trousers?" he asked.

Will threw him that lethal lopsided grin. "It would to me."

19

"Right elbow…out a tiny bit, Tom. Right at me, both of you. Yeah. Nice. That's great."

Tom stared into the lens as instructed, posed in a slim dark-checked three-piece suit and tie, feet together, legs straight, trying to "look sophisticated", as ordered.

"Beautiful, Meg. Look at Tom. A bit more upper-class lust. Uh-huh. Tom can you dial down from homicidal to just moody?"

Tom blinked and tried to channel the music blasting round the loft being used for the shoot. To become "cool, successful man in a suit", taking totally for granted the beautiful woman draped over his left shoulder.

The camera clicked spastically then the photographer said, "Okay. That's it for that one, thanks. Great work. Break for fifteen minutes."

Tom and the girl relaxed from their poses and walked off in different directions without a word. More often than not models barely spoke to each other on a shoot, which had worried Tom at first that there was something wrong with him. Now he barely noticed.

He headed for the menswear stylist and was handed another shirt and tie and a suit—plain, dark and double breasted this time. Then he made for the makeshift changing area he'd been assigned.

Behind the curtain barrier, he assessed his reflection in the mirror— the contrast of his shoulder-length pale blond hair against the severity of the suit he'd just modeled. He could see the potential of the image. And at least his under-eye shadows had been vanished by concealer, and his hickeys were covered by the shirt collar.

The jacket slid off his arms, and he sat down on the only stool in the small curtained space.

He wasn't doing his best work, he was well aware of that. But at least he had one of the decent photographers on; the same guy, in fact, who'd watched him take the call about Catriona.

When Will pulled up outside the Brixton address Tom had been given, the photographer had been sitting on the outside step with his female assistant, taking in the sun, and Tom had been struck again by his beauty: the palest gold skin, long silky dark curls, big dark-fringed eyes. Ben Morgan.

Tom had heard enough gossip about him to know that the guy would happily fuck models and clients he fancied, if it didn't get in the way of a job—and he was notoriously good at talking people into bed. Not—looking at him—that he'd have to do much talking.

So. No ties. No complications. The way Tom liked it best. He should give it a go. Why wasn't he even trying?

The curtain rustled, and Tom swung round with a jolt of fear. How safe could he be now, from Max Perry and his brother?

"Tom? Are you decent?" Ben. Tom closed his eyes, feeling ridiculous.

"I'm a model," he replied.

"Good point." The curtain was pulled open, and Ben stood there smiling good-naturedly, holding one steaming mug and picking another off the floor. "Coffee?"

Quite apart from his beauty, Ben really was a nice guy. It wouldn't occur to most of the photographers Tom worked with to worry about a model's modesty or to bring them coffee. Ben edged forward into the small space, balancing the full mugs, letting the curtain swish closed behind him. It created a false kind of intimacy.

"I just wanted to check you're all right," Ben said. "You seem a little…out of it?"

Tom flushed hot and cold. Because, yes, he'd known he was off form, but he'd thought he could get away with it. Just one bad shoot could hit his reputation for professionalism, for always bringing it, depending on how malicious the gossip became.

"I'm sorry," he said. "I'm not feeling that good."

Ben's eyes widened. Even in the dim light of the makeshift cubicle, they were a remarkable shade of dark glowing blue, framed by thick dark lashes and black brows. Like Will's.

"Hey. No. You still photograph better like this than most of them on peak form." Ben pulled open the curtain, hooked in a wheeled stool from outside the changing area with his foot, and sat as the curtain fell into place behind him. The whole movement had been effortlessly smooth and graceful. He could easily model, Tom thought. He even had the build for it.

"There's just something you do," Ben went on. "It's like…disdain."

"Disdain?" Tom repeated, horrified anew.

"Yeah… Not the right word. I mean—it's the modeling Holy Grail, that expression." Ben winked and handed Tom one of the mugs. "You look engaged…but above it all. People want to get past that look."

And that must be one of the famed Ben Morgan pickup lines. Tom's line would be: *So how do* you *fancy…getting past that look?*

He swigged his coffee.

"So. Is it a girl?" Ben asked, with sympathy. "A guy?"

Tom shot him a surprised glare.

Two murders and an insane gangland stalker. Mainly.

"Then again." Ben took a sip of coffee and peered at Tom over the rim of his mug. "If it was Beautiful Car Guy who dropped you off, I totally see your point. He's well worth pining over."

Somehow, the knowledge that Ben had noticed Will…like *that* soured Tom's mood still further. And the fact that it affected him, at all, made it even worse.

"I don't *pine*," Tom said defensively. "And word is, you don't either."

Ben gave an odd smile. "You'd be surprised."

"His name's Will," Tom said. "I can give you his number." It sounded like a dare.

Ben grinned, unfazed. "Once upon a time, I'd have had your arm off. But I'm all settled down now."

It sounded to Tom like another flirty game. "Yeah? That's not what *I* heard," he flirted back.

To his surprise, Ben's smile faded as if Tom had just been unpleasantly rude.

"Don't you know not to listen to industry gossip?" Ben said cooly. "It's always well behind the curve. I'm with someone."

Tom raised his eyebrows. "But you still play away," he clarified, because he'd definitely been told that just before the Greenwich shoot.

Ben smiled again but it was subtly more strained. "Nope. Though no one seems to believe me." It didn't sound as amused as Ben probably intended.

"Sorry," Tom offered. Ben shrugged and took another sip of coffee. "I just…maybe people don't get it. Settling down and…things…monogamy… In our business. So they don't think you mean it. I mean…*I* don't get it."

Ben grinned suddenly, all mischief. "You don't?" And he was right back to his engaging self. "You didn't like that I noticed Beautiful Car Guy."

Tom's expression froze, his every instinct poised to deny. But since Ben had seen his stupid moments of possessiveness, there wasn't much point.

Instead he said, "That doesn't mean anything." And he didn't know why he couldn't just let it go then. Why he seemed to need to find the words to challenge Ben's choices, as if that could ease his own sense of restless discontent. "I can see the point of having people in your life you care about," he went on stiffly. "But not, you know... *needing* them to love you. So much you cling on when they stop."

Ben cocked his head, considering him with intense interest. "I always believed I'd never need anyone...and I really, *really* didn't want to. But then I met this...this one person, who just...got past everything. Every rule. Every wall. Every evasion. I had to lose him to realize it was pointless to keep denying I'd do anything to hold on to him."

Tom grimaced. It sounded like disaster to him. Obsession and surrender.

"I dumped Will two years ago," he said flatly. "It hasn't made me realize anything, except I'm not built for commitment."

Ben studied him with inscrutable attention. Then finally he said, "Maybe...he's not the one you feel safe with then." Tom blinked at him and Ben went on. "Sometimes...something comes along and...it's so right, eventually—you can't deny it anymore." He grinned. "Or maybe, you're just more determined than me."

"You fancy Will," Tom accused. He sounded defensive even to himself.

"Of course I do," Ben agreed sunnily. "I have eyes. I fancy you! But..." His grin faded to a strange, almost sad little smile. "I don't want anyone but Jamie. I never thought I'd find someone I wanted to be good for."

The phrase struck Tom as oddly childlike. Touching, in a way. And it got through to Tom as nothing else had. Why was he being such a dickhead? Trying to piss all over Ben's starry-eyed romance?

"What does he do?" Tom asked and it felt like an apology. "Your boyfriend."

Ben's smile widened to glee. "This is when people freak out. He's a Detective Inspector in the Met. That's why everyone's stopped asking me where they can score some blow."

Tom laughed, relieved Ben hadn't taken offense. "Will used to be in the Met too," he volunteered.

"Wooh!" Ben whooped. "I thought Jamie had the market cornered in blazingly hot coppers."

And finally, the sense of what Ben had said sank in.

How many blazingly hot gay coppers called Jamie could there be in the Met?

"James...Henderson?" he asked, with a kind of dread.

Ben stilled. Perhaps it was Tom's tone. "Yes."

"It's nothing. Just…I met him," Tom said quickly. Why did he have to sound so guilty? "A couple of nights ago. With Will." Ben's eyes narrowed. And all at once Tom could see something else behind Ben's carapace of surety. "They met when Will was on the force." It was almost true. Then, to wipe away that look of frozen suspicion, "He got a text from you and went home."

Ben searched his expression for a long second, then he looked away and down with an embarrassed little huff.

"Yeah." He made an unamused sound. "Well. You can see I talk the talk better than I walk the walk."

And yes, Tom could see exactly that. Ben's gut insecurity over James Henderson. His blind fear of losing him. Unaccountably, it infuriated him on Ben's behalf.

Ben read his expression perfectly.

"No," he protested. "It's not like that. Jamie's… He's the only person who knows me." His smile returned then, sweet and sad. "I know he wouldn't hurt me. Jamie's one of the good guys."

The pride in his voice touched Tom unbearably.

"He looked really happy when he got your message," he offered, full of remorse.

The corners of Ben's mouth twitched. "Okay. Don't overdo it."

"No, honestly! He had hearteyes."

Ben threw his head back and laughed. "There was a day I'd have had you stay behind after school to show me some respect."

Tom grinned back. "Just as well those days are gone, Headmaster."

"Yeah," Ben said softly. "Just as well."

•••

At the end of the shoot, Ben produced champagne for everyone, but he left fifteen minutes before Tom to go home to his beautiful policeman.

Tom, when he climbed into his cab, felt more restless than ever, because he found that the conversation with Ben kept playing in his mind, unsettling him. He couldn't even go back to Shoreditch to brood in peace.

He wasn't expecting to hear non-TV voices in Nick's lounge when he let himself into the flat with his key. And it took him a second to understand, as he pushed open the lounge door to let Nick know he was there, that the voice he heard coming from inside was actually his own.

Then he recognized the sound of Max Perry, and he understood.

Christine Hansen and Nick sat in profile to Tom on the cream sofa perpendicular to the doorway, attention fixed to an open laptop on the low table. Will, Tom saw with a jolt of elated shock, sat in the purple designer chair, with John perched, all proprietary smugness, on his lap.

Jena was on the other sofa with her back to the door, but she must have heard a noise because she turned, spotted Tom and sprang to her feet to go to him and pull him into a hug.

"Will brought the recording!" She slid an arm round his waist and turned to face the others. Tom could still only see Hansen's profile as she took notes. Nick was expressionless. "He told us you had to fight him off."

Tom cleared his throat. "Well, that's kind of exaggerating…"

"Nah," Will said. "Max went down like a sack of potatoes."

"He tripped," Tom said, skin heating like a schoolgirl addressed by her crush. His throat felt parched and his chest was tight.

"Sell any trousers?" Will grinned.

"Think I might have shifted a few pairs," Tom managed. He sounded almost shy, which was fucking ridiculous. But he and Will smiled at each other, sharing their private joke, for another moment or two.

Jena's hand tightened on Tom's waist, a warning.

He looked away from Will at once. He had to stop this.

"Is the recording enough?" he asked quickly. He took a seat on Jena's sofa.

Hansen glanced at him. "It's not admissible in court, given it was recorded without Perry's permission *or* knowledge. Plus it's entrapment. But it should be enough to point Lawson in the right direction. I'll let my colleague in the Public Protection Unit know." She looked satisfied, but still concerned. Tom thought he knew why.

"Max'll expose Nick, won't he? If he's cornered."

Hansen closed her notebook. "We may be able to make some sort of plea bargain in exchange for his silence."

"Give him a shorter sentence?" Nick spoke for the first time, and he sounded horrified. "He killed Cat! *And* Lily."

Hansen pulled a memory stick from the laptop. "I'm talking maybe a minimum tariff of twenty-five years rather than thirty. The odd privilege in jail. He's not going to get out a young man."

Jena said suddenly, "He must have been watching Cat and Lily for a while, as well as Tom. Or had people do it for him. Do we know where he lives?"

Tom said bitterly, "Lennox Gardens, unless he's moved." Hansen scribbled it down in her notebook. "Basement flat…I think it's No. 38."

"Knightsbridge," Will said. "On Joey Clarkson's blood money." Tom could hear his hatred.

"Do you think he used a hitman?" Jena asked.

Will shook his head. "From the details I read, I think the murders were too personal for a professional hit. I mean…it's possible Max gave precise instructions, and one of Joey's men did it. But only with Joey's say-so. He's had plenty people terminated in his time, but…okaying the murder of two wealthy, connected women to help his employee stalk a love interest? Joey wouldn't risk bringing that trouble to his own door."

Hansen listened to his reasoning with approval. "So you think Max and Eddie went rogue on Joey? So Max has had to get his own hands dirty. Or maybe Eddie did." She rose to her feet and slid the memory stick into her shoulder bag. "I'll get this to my colleague in the PPU. If he agrees, we'll give it to Lawson with the bones of the story, excluding Nick. And play it by ear from there."

"What'll happen to me?" Tom asked. Beside him, Jena had started to tap on her mobile phone.

Hansen raised her thinly plucked eyebrows. "DCI Lawson'll want to interview you as a witness, I expect."

Will had risen too, putting a disgruntled John on the floor. But as he began to follow Hansen to the door, he hesitated beside Tom's seat.

"Do you have somewhere safe to stay tonight?" he asked him.

Tom stared up at him, mouth dry as dust.

Nick didn't *know* he'd come to stay over. If Tom said the right thing, Will might offer protection at his place. Was it still the house in Leyton? Unless…he was only asking to make sure Tom had thought about it. But—Tom could allow himself one more night, couldn't he? No harm in that. There was nowhere on earth he'd feel more secure.

Maybe he's not the one you feel safe with.

And Tom knew that he couldn't. It would be an exercise in masochistic self-indulgence that could hurt Will most of all. He couldn't encourage him to believe anything had changed. And he couldn't do in front of Nick.

It hit Tom only then, with a rush of panic, that this was most probably goodbye. When the police went after Max, Will's job would be over. Tom hadn't even considered that when he and Will had parted at Ben's studio. That he might not have seen him again. And now…he couldn't say anything he wanted to.

His chest was held in a vise. It felt as if every time he did this—let Will go—it got harder and harder. As if, each time, the intellectual and emotional scaffolding that propped up his life choices was being rattled close to disintegration.

All the more reason to hold the line.

"John's here," he blurted, and again that little spurt of wild panic at what he was doing. He said it anyway. "I'll just stay."

Will's expression closed. Perhaps he hadn't just asked out of consideration. Perhaps he'd hoped Tom would choose to go with him. Or perhaps Tom was flattering himself. Why would Will want that anyway, after so many rejections and wounds?

Will nodded, and turned to go.

"Thanks." Nick stood and faced Will. "Thanks for keeping Tom safe." Nick might as well have added...*for me.*

Tom couldn't help himself. He said loudly, desperately, "I'll call you." Will hesitated for a split second, but he didn't acknowledge it, probably because he didn't believe it. Tom could hardly blame him.

Tom sat numbly after the flat door shut behind Will and Hansen and tortured himself with imagining how things might have gone if he'd allowed himself to make a different choice. He and Will would be getting into the Passat now, setting off for Leyton. To the house Tom would never see finished.

"I'll make dinner," Nick said. Tom turned round. Nick stood near the lounge door, still dressed in his trendy suit from work. He looked more like his old self, but tense and stressed.

"You'll stay, N?" Nick asked Jena.

Jena stood and walked over to hug him. "I'd love to. Please don't worry, DM. It'll all be sorted soon."

Tom turned away to face front. He knew he'd done the right thing for himself and for Will but...he felt hollow. Bereft. Wishing fiercely he'd taken that last, selfish night. It was ridiculous and counter-productive. But his stomach felt tight with misery.

The sofa cushion next to him dipped as Jena sat down. "All right, Tommy?"

"You should have held out for Penfold," Tom said gamely. "I mean if he got to be Danger Mouse... You're just...not a Nero."

Jena laughed. She seemed relieved in a way neither Tom nor Nick could manage, as if the evening marked the end of an ordeal.

"So you keep saying." She beamed. "Just give it up. We're never going to tell you the real meaning. It's a secret."

Tom raised a bitter eyebrow.

Jena flinched. "Okay," she said with a wry quirk of the lips. "Another secret."

Tom smiled dutifully but he realized in that second that he couldn't genuinely relax with Jena anymore either. Any more than he could with Nick, or Pez. His own little mini family at Echo. He'd lost them all.

Jena looked totally familiar but…how could he feel he knew her? A girl who'd tried to sacrifice herself for her brother and instead handed him to his enemies. How Shakespearian was that? How much of a burden must that be? What had it done to her?

"Congratulations on the Armani contract." Jena elbowed him lightly. "Pez practically lapped the building."

Oh. Fuck.

Tom remembered with appalled horror that he'd forgotten to tell Pez about Armani. *What* must he be thinking, hearing that news secondhand?

"Nick said you're planning to move to New York," Jena went on.

Tom shook his head, still caught in a backwash of shame at disregarding Pez on something so vital to him. "I may not have a career if Lawson charges me."

Jena looked down at her hands tangled on her lap. "Are you really okay with knowing about us, Tommy?" The directness of her attack froze Tom with self-conscious guilt. It felt now as if guilt was his primary emotion. "I know it must be so hard for you. Christine wasn't keen on bringing anyone else in but…Nick and I agreed you had to be told."

Tom didn't know why that particular revelation should come as a blow, but it did. Hansen had wanted to leave Tom to Lawson's nonexistent mercy?

Jena looked worried, with none of the diva pizazz she donned for her nights out with Pez and Tom. On form, she could do outdo Queen Pez for theatrics. But at that moment, with her pink hair and anxious earnestness, she looked like a student behind with her work.

He said stiffly, "I appreciate that you both trusted me."

"It's just…" Jena touched his hand. "Nick's had such an unfair life, Tommy. He sacrificed his…his youth to save me. And then Cat smothered him until he couldn't breathe. She wouldn't even have kids because they might take his attention."

Tom tried to hold his neutral expression, but he just wanted Jena to stop talking. He didn't want to know.

"We were—we *are* both willing to sacrifice all this…" She waved a hand to encompass the flat. "Echo. To save you. But Tom…don't stay with him out of pity. Or obligation."

It was strange that the words Jena said had exactly the opposite effect. It felt as if she were lowering chains around him. She watched him, head tilted, as if she were cataloguing every minute reaction, like a curious bird.

Peck, peck.

"Well, let's hope he doesn't have to sacrifice anything," Tom said, all too aware how inadequate that response was to the emotional appeal she'd made.

She gave a slow, grave nod of understanding. "You're still in love with Will."

It felt like a hard slap, out of the blue.

"No!" he exclaimed. "What the hell... That's long over!"

Jena looked graver still, as if she didn't believe him. "You're my friend, Tommy. Nick and I both love you. But you don't have to love us back."

Sadness seemed to surround her like a shell, a girl more than a woman. One who'd come to expect bad things. He didn't know what to say. Guilt was an anvil on his back.

Then out of nowhere Jena asked, "You didn't tell Pez about Nick, did you?"

Tom stared at her again. He felt as if she was constantly wrong-footing him, as if he couldn't keep up with her anymore. "No! Of course not. Why?"

"Because, Armani celebration apart, he was acting like someone shot his dog yesterday and he's wasn't any better today. He won't talk about it, not even to me." Jena's mouth twisted into a sad little smile. "So I knew it had to be about you."

"Why me?" Tom asked, offended. He'd made sure to text Pez a few times that day to mimic normality. He'd just been unable to say anything important.

Jena sighed. "If we're finally all being honest, Tommy, because Pez has been in love with you for years."

Tom took a deep breath, toying instinctively with denial. But what was the point?

"So I'm the only one who didn't know." His tone was harsh.

Jena snorted. "He wasn't exactly subtle."

"Well, that's where you're wrong," Tom snapped. "Because it felt subtle to me. I believed everything he said."

"That's because you didn't want to see it," Jena returned. "It's been obvious since he first brought you in to the agency. Which made going to work pretty fucking hellish once you and Nick started to see each other. With Pez and Cat both gutted."

"Pez actually *told* you how he felt?"

"He's my best friend," Jena said simply. "He trusts me. And I had to mop him up all through the Will Foster fiasco. He was a better about Nick at first, but the longer it went on..."

Tom sat a little straighter. "He confided in you about Will?"

"God, yes. Of course he did. Pez thought you were going to settle down with him." She gave him a side-eyed glance. "He's still telling you you shouldn't have a serious relationship, isn't he?" She sighed. "That way he holds on to you, I suppose."

Tom looked blindly over her shoulder. Why hadn't he properly considered how self-interested Pez's urgings to get away from Will must have been? And his advice on Nick, for that matter.

But he couldn't blame Pez for the end with Will—it had all been there in Tom's own head already. All Pez had done was reinforce Tom's instinct to end it while he still could.

"Tom? Are you okay?" Jena asked tentatively.

Apart from the fact that he wanted to cry?

"Yeah. " He smiled. "I'm great."

20

Tom sat at Nick's breakfast bar the next morning—fully dressed and sipping excellent coffee. His third cup in fact.

The room was flooded with early sunlight, muted by white muslin, and it smelled of ground coffee beans and bleach. After his poor night's sleep, Tom didn't appreciate any of it.

His mood was better suited to grey and rain, and an end to the relentless July heatwave they'd been having.

As he'd tried to slink into sleep the night before, his mind had felt almost physically jammed full of things to worry at. And he'd added one more, when he'd had to awkwardly turn down Nick's attempts at love-making, when Nick was already well into the swing of it. Tom had lain there and let it happen, and then he just...couldn't. He didn't want it. But Nick hadn't commented when Tom pushed him off with the excuse of tiredness, just kissed him gently on the mouth and rolled over to lie beside him.

Because Nick was a good guy. Unlike Tom, who couldn't seem to feel enough for anyone to overcome his own survival instincts. His own self-interest.

"Tom," Nick said from the doorway. "Something's happened."

Tom put down his cup and turned round. At once his pulse began to flutter, a Pavlovian reaction now. It could be something good though. For once?

"Tell me," Tom said.

"Will Foster rang." Tom stilled. "Some guy in Lawson's team told him that Dr. Rolfe, Cat's GP, was attacked late last night."

Tom stood up. "*Attacked? Carys?* Is she…?"

Nick said quickly, "She's not dead. Someone partly knocked her out. They're guessing chloroform. She was outside her house, back from walking her dog, and she was dragged inside and…he pumped her full of insulin." Tom sat down again, legs like jelly. "Will said she must have remained partly conscious. She called 999 when he left and…they think she managed to get to her bag to inject glucose or something. She's in hospital."

"But she's all right?" Tom asked anxiously.

"Well Will said she's still not conscious, probably in a coma. And there's always a risk of brain damage… Thank God she knew what to do with a hypo though. A least she stands a chance."

Hypoglycemia. Too much insulin in the bloodstream, leading to dangerously low levels of glucose. Of course Nick would know. His mother had been diabetic.

"But why would Max attack her?" Then, "Because she's connected to Catriona…because I interviewed her twice. To build the case against me."

"Maybe," Nick agreed slowly. "Maybe it *was* to punish you."

"Punish me? Then why not go for people close to me?"

Nick looked exhausted. "From what I remember from my time living among people like him, watching psychiatrists examining the criminal mind… Whatever condition they'd say he has…Narcissistic Personality Disorder, Psychopathic Disorder…whatever… He might leave the people closest to you—maybe people like your dad—to use as bargaining chips when he's established power over you. All these attacks would be lessons. Fall into line, or he'll keep driving you closer to arrest."

Tom stared unseeing at the wall. Lovely, kind, brilliant Carys—in hospital, possibly brain damaged. Catriona dead. Lily's children left without a mother. All because Max Perry wouldn't take no for an answer.

Nick said reluctantly, "Will said…Lawson is going to take you in for an interview."

Of course. Because Max had framed Tom so nicely that probably only he could clear away the web he'd caught Tom in. Max Perry had him by the throat.

"What's keeping Hansen?" Tom asked desperately.

"She has to go through official channels," Nick said. "But I'm sure she'll see Lawson today if she can."

Tom rubbed his forehead hard, but the pressure building behind his eyes wouldn't ease. He felt like an animal in a trap, locked away already.

"I have to go." He stood and headed for the kitchen door.

"Where? Tom! You're safe here!"

"I just want to ride my bike. Clear the cobwebs. Okay?"

Nick opened his mouth, but he perhaps he saw the desperation on Tom's face. He nodded reluctantly.

Tom grabbed his black leather jacket off a peg and shouldered into it. All he wanted was to climb on to the bike and go. Regain some sense of control and autonomy. And maybe when he came back, the process would have begun to try to bring Max down.

"I won't be long."

He surged out of the flat door, his momemtum causing him to stumble over a large soft object lying directly outside on the doormat. He looked down at it with a mixture of startlement and impatience. Looked again. But he couldn't process what he saw.

Fur.

Luxuriant tabby fur. Blood. A lot of blood. Something pale-whitish-pink and wet, spooling out from the pathetic lump of it. Intestines.

Tom's vision blurred, his head buzzed. He dropped to his knees.

John.

The cat had been disembowelled, innards spilling out on the cold concrete. Its head was so mangled and bloody that it was impossible to recognize markings, but Tom could see that its mouth was wide open. That it had died screaming.

"No…" Tom moaned. Tears stung his eyes, soaked his cheeks. "No. John."

Because Tom had defied Max Perry and made him look foolish. John had suffered…this. Another brutal lesson to teach Tom his place.

John would have been easy to catch, because he trusted people. Please God, Max had killed him first.

He let out a loud hopeless sob and touched John's cold, limp body. His fur still felt thick and soft in the spots that weren't soaked with drying blood.

"Tom?" he heard Nick's voice from a long distance. "Oh Christ. What's that?"

Tom sobbed again.

"A cat? Tom?" A hand on his shoulder, comforting. Then realization, "Tom, you think it's John. I just fed him. He's inside!"

It took Tom long seconds to process what Nick had said.

He didn't try to rise. He remained on his knees beside the sad little corpse, but he twisted his head round to look up at Nick, desperate to believe.

"I'll go and get him," Nick said. "Dear God, who would do that to an animal?"

He shot back into the house, and Tom sat back on his heels, torn between disbelieving relief and persistent horror. The cruelty of Max's game.

But what was a cat to Max after he'd killed two women, and tried to kill a third? Who else would suffer, the longer Tom held him off?

Tom's head fell forward, hair covering his wet face, hopeless hands on his thighs. His jeans were stained and smeared with blood. He looked away and registered at last that there was a package, neatly propped against the wall—in the shadows, away from the carnage directly outside the flat door.

It was a chunky square box wrapped in brown paper, stained violet; Tom's name printed on a tag. He leaned forward and grabbed it, still balanced on his knees. With huge, terrified rage, he ripped the paper open. He wanted to see.

It was a white box with the legend in silver—Cîroc—and a circle cut out in the middle to display a circular bottle of royal-blue glass inside. There was a cross in silver in the center of the bottle, with the word *Ten* written through it. And underneath that, two words engraved on the glass, in silver italic script: *always be.*

So you will...always be...

"Tom?" He twisted round quickly. John blinked enigmatically at him from Nick's arms. "Christ, is that from him?" Nick asked, voice hushed. "That's three-hundred-quid vodka."

A tide of red-blood-rage surged up inside Tom's head, drowning reason.

He put down the box, levered himself to his feet, and ran down the stairs to the street door, ignoring Nick's shouts behind him. His bike was parked just along the curb, safe enough in an area like this. He straddled the seat.

He wasn't thinking of anything but his hatred as he gunned the engine and roared off toward Knightsbridge.

•••

He took the shortest possible route, blind to everything around him save the thick traffic he wove through. And all the way he was stoking his rage, his detestation of his own fear, his disgust at Max Perry and his unhinged, relentless entitlement.

It took him less than thirty minutes from Nick's flat to turn onto Beauchamp Place, which merged onto Pont Street and then the junction into Lennox Gardens.

It was a long street with a central garden along one side. Most of the buildings were four stories high—five with the basement—sporting huge, multipaned windows. Rich. Tom knew even a basement flat here would have set Max back a couple of million.

Tom slowed the Honda to a crawl, gliding along the road, and when he finally saw the number "38", his sense of repelled familiarity told him he was in the right place. His fear-fueled rage hadn't diminished at all.

He parked the bike in a space across the road from the gate, and marched across to it, plunging down the steps to the basement door. He pressed the bell. Hard. One, two, three times. Demanded an answer.

Fury pounded in his head. He didn't care if this was sensible or not. Dangerous or not. He'd had enough of being played with, hunted and stalked like an animal, of watching other living things taken down to try to herd him here. Well—here he was.

Max was just a little man, and Tom was no one's fucking victim. No one's *prize*.

He pressed the bell again, and again. A woman walked past walking two terriers and glanced down at him, taking in his agitation. Her wariness of him was obvious, and Tom realized how he must look to her—a tall angry man masked by a motorcycle helmet.

Tom didn't give a fuck. He rang. Again. And again. Tried to peer through the window perpendicular to the door, but muslin blinds ensured he couldn't see anything.

No one came to answer the bell, and gradually the anticlimax of thwarted rage forced an unwanted conclusion.

Max was out. Stalking Tom probably. Maybe—he was even watching him now.

Tom hit the door hard with the flat of his palm. Kicked it once. Then furiously rattled the doorknob. The door opened.

Tom's breath stopped. And he knew—he knew—this was danger now. Max wasn't watching him from outside after all; he was inside, waiting as he had been all along. Because he'd just pushed Tom's buttons again with precision.

Max had always been steps ahead, and Tom had walked right up to his lair. He turned to go, but his reason for coming here still stood. He could remain a victim, an impotent pawn—or he could take his fate into his own hands.

He was certain now that whatever Hansen said, Lawson would find no evidence against Max, because Max had planned precisely. He'd made a fool of them all, using their desperation to protect Nick and Jena, the red herring of the Babes in Arms to waste their time, to help sink Tom deeper and deeper into his web. Tom would remain in the firing line until he surrendered and gave himself up to Max.

Tom's loathing was a solid jagged lump beneath his breastbone, hard and dark. He finally understood the term "homicidal rage".

He pushed open the door and walked in.

The hallway was long and unlit; the front door through which he'd entered was in the middle of it.

"Max!" he yelled. Nothing moved; the spider waiting for the fly. Waiting for Tom to give in and beg for it all to stop.

Fuck. Him.

Tom turned right. Three doors lay ajar. He pushed open the first one on the right and peered in. A bathroom, expensively tiled in brown marble. He moved to the next one. A bedroom with a large bed covered with red fabric and an ostentatious fur throw. The last door: a study filled with computer equipment and papers.

Tom swung round, heart seizing, half-expecting to find Max standing smirking behind him, but the hallway was empty. He strode back along it, past the front door and to another open door on the left. A kitchen, in white and grey.

And that left the living room—the door at the end and the only one that was closed.

Tom pulled off his helmet and took out his phone. He typed quickly: *At Max's flat. 38 Lennox Gdns. Bsmnt. I'll call in 15 mins.* He scrolled instinctively to Will's number, but he made himself stop and send the text to Nick instead.

His pushed open the door.

The room was empty.

No Max, sitting there, smug and vengeful. No one at all.

The room was bright for a basement, with all the light coming through the concealing white muslin at the street window. Mellow parquet wood covered the floor, and a stone fireplace dominated the wall opposite the door, flanked by two extra-long black-leather sofas with wooden legs. A massive television hung on the wall above the fireplace, and there was a large fluffy white rug in front of the fireplace with a red circular pattern at the side. A low table sat in the center, bearing an open bottle of wine and two glasses.

Tom's shoulders slumped with a nauseating rush of frustration and relief.

His enraged imagination had got the better of him. Max hadn't lured him here, to bring his plans to fruition. He'd just forgotten to lock his door. But Tom was inside now, and there was no fucking way he wasn't going to search for solid evidence.

He strode over to the sofa near the window and dropped his helmet on it.

Immediately it rolled onto the floor, and at the same moment, his phone rang.

The sound made him flinch. He bent to pick up the helmet as he fumbled with the phone, and as he did he spotted a light-colored glove under the sofa. It held his gaze because it seemed plumper than a glove, until he realized it was a clever model of a hand.

His phone stopped ringing before he could answer it, and with a huff of impatience he knelt and used his free left hand to grope blindly under the sofa for it. The material felt cold under his reaching fingertips and the texture malleable like putty, the rough, accurate whirl of finger pads brushing against his own. Impressive. He pulled it out into the light.

It lay on the floor in front of him for long, ticking seconds before he could bring himself to accept what it was.

"Oh *Jesus.*"

He dropped the phone and scrabbled back on his knees, horror clawing at his throat, and his mind babbled at him, flapping in appalled, terrified circles.

Max had lured him here and left him this to find. The mauled cat had just been the invitation.

He tried to think, though he didn't want to. Whose hand? He didn't want to know but…

Too big and square to have belonged to a woman. It *had* to be someone connected to the investigation. Or maybe, at last, something to hit closer to home. Someone Max thought had got between him and Tom? Tom tried to force himself to assess it calmly. Too big and square for Pez. Not Nick.

Will then.

No.

No.

But at once horrified belief took hold. Max had warned him. Get rid of Will or he would.

Anyone but him.

Not Will.

Tom made a sound he wouldn't have believed he could make. An animal moan of agony, shocking in the absolute silence of the room.

Not. Will. But already his heart was bursting with grief.

He tried to keep analysing the repulsive object in front of him, but his mind was retreating into despair.

The hand looked as if it could just be…glued back onto a human body and it would work.

Somehow, slowly, he forced focus again, noting the tiny details about it that made it real and human. And all the time begging and bargaining in his head, *Not Will. Not Will. Not Will. Anyone. Not Will.*

The lines on knuckles and joints. Dark hair on tanned skin. Tears coursed down Tom's cheeks. His breath sobbed. Neatly manicured fingernails. Tom's gorge rose violently but he wouldn't look away. The fingers weren't as long as Will's, were they? But the perspective was different without a body attached. It was hairier than Will's hand, wasn't it?

Please. Please.

A thick gold ring on the middle finger.

Tom pushed up to his feet, breath still shuddering, wide eyes riveted to the cleanly amputated hand lying on the parquet floor, as if looking away might change what was there. His eyes held on the ring.

Then he made himself back away to the end of the sofa, nearest to the window. He forced himself to look around the back.

Max Perry lay sprawled on the floor, eyes closed, trousers and underpants clumped around his shins, shiny black shoes still on. And Tom felt only a flash of ferocious, gut-true relief… *Not Will.* Until he had to absorb what was in front of him.

Max still wore a tie, neatly knotted, but his white shirtsleeves had been unfastened, flopping around the stumps of his arms. His groin was a black-clotted wound where his genitals had been.

Tom stared at Max's body and somehow—somehow—he compelled himself to drop to his knees beside it to try for pulse in the neck. There was nothing. Of course there wasn't.

And Tom saw, from his new perspective, that the red pattern on the rug had seeped into the fabric from the objects lying at its edge—until then, concealed from Tom by the arm of the sofa. Max's other hand sat beside a pile of bloody flesh that resolved into a testicular sac with a severed penis draped limply and neatly on top.

Tom's stomach heaved, and he ran out of the room and down the hall, wrenching the front door wide open, breathing deep gulps of city air. Somehow he managed to swallow down the desperate urge to vomit, but his vision blurred green around the edges. And he realized what this meant for him.

Max had been his answer. The murderer who—if he could just outwit and expose him—would turn Lawson away from his mission to bring Tom down. But Max hadn't been the answer at all. And Tom had no more idea now than he'd ever had who was killing people and framing him.

There was no one left for the police but Tom, who'd had a public brawl with Max the day before, who'd conveniently discovered Max's body and left his DNA all over his flat.

He fought against the gibbering panic threatening to devour his reason. He ran back into the lounge and picked up his phone.

Will answered on the third ring. He sounded wary, but after he listened, he began to bark questions. Instructions.

Don't touch anything. Don't call the police yet. Wait outside for me.

So Tom sank down on the pavement in front of the black metal railings beside the open gate to Max's flat. And waited.

•••

It felt like hours before the Passat screeched up in front of him, but when Tom checked his phone, he realized Will had made record time. As he hauled himself wearily upright, Will pulled the car into a parking space in front of the gardens, then burst out of it, crossing the street in a few strides, his dark red tie and grey suit jacket flapping as he walked.

"Will." Tom's voice sounded thin and reedy. "The police... Lawson'll throw away the key."

"It could be gang-related," Will said firmly. "Remember his connections."

But Tom didn't believe it. And when Will examined the murder scene, any last grain of hope vanished. Will spotted what Tom hadn't...a pile of small glass bottles with purple labels, discarded by the window. Insulin.

Tom stood in the living room doorway and buried his face in his hands.

The same killer. Framing him subtly every time. Never anything conclusive. Just a picture building to an inevitable conclusion.

Somehow he'd known Tom would snap and come here to confront Max. Someone had studied him well enough to anticipate his reactions... That fear and pressure and outrage made him defiant and reckless. The cat had been a masterful move. Tom felt like a lab rat in a maze. Whichever way he ran, someone more clever was there, expecting it. Using it.

"Tom." Will had crouched down, purple nitrile gloves on, peering at the mutilated remains of Max Perry. "Look." Tom watched his calmness and detached interest with numb envy. "Look!" Will insisted.

Tom straightened his spine and tried to obey. Will pointed at the body, but Tom fixed instead on Will's gloved finger, remembering his own terror as he'd tried to work out if the amputated hand was that hand. The hand that had once touched him so beautifully.

"You can barely see it because of the blood," Will was saying. "Have you ever noticed him wearing that before?"

Tom forced his eyes to the body on the floor, face twisted with repulsion. He couldn't begin to match Will's detachment.

He stared, and red on red resolved at last into a thin string knotted round what remained of Max's wrist.

Tom's gaze rose to Will's. "No. I don't remember seeing him wearing that."

Will chewed his lip as he stood. "Okay. We need to call this in now. I think he's been here a while. Where were you yesterday evening?" Tom stared at him, stunned. "You need an alibi, Tom."

Tom ran his hand nervously through his hair, and a sudden sense-memory hit—the feeling of Max's cold rubbery ridges of fingertips against his palm as he pulled the hand out into the light.

He took a desperate breath. "With Nick and Jena. Jena left about... ten. I stayed at Nick's all night."

"Right." Will pulled out his phone and tapped in 999.

They sat side-by-side then on the pavement where Tom had waited, backs against the metal railings, and within ten minutes they heard the distant wail of a squad car.

Will showed the first uniformed officers the body then came back bearing Tom's forgotten helmet. He sat down again and put a comforting arm round Tom, and Tom, with desperate gratitude, let his head fall against Will's broad shoulder.

The dark grey cloth of his suit felt scratchy. But it was the safest refuge in the world.

As they sat unspeaking, more cars arrived—the HAT team, then the first murder-squad detectives. Blue-and-white tape was stretched around the area on three sides to close it off, and more and more people tramped past them through the open gate and down the stairs into Max's flat.

"Tom! My *God*, Tom. What happened?"

Tom raised his head reluctantly from Will shoulder to find Nick looking down at them, eyes frantic, and he couldn't understand how Nick had known he was here, until he remembered he'd sent a text to be safe.

He let his head fall back to Will's shoulder and half-listened to Will telling Nick everything he knew. He watched Nick through his lashes as he tried to absorb it all, fixating stupidly on his suit, tightly cut in a light green, large-checked uber-fashionable cloth. Will's was an off-the-peg traditional dark gray. One man, trendy and polished; the other, pragmatic, free from vanity. The contrast felt very stark.

"But why did you come here, baby?" Nick asked with anguish.

Tom jerked back to attention. His past motivation seemed insane now, but at the time all his suppressed, jammed-up fear and rage, his need to take back control—had just…erupted. Unstoppable, like lava.

"I wanted to confront him," he said weakly.

Nick's mouth worked with frustration but he said nothing. Instead he slid down onto the pavement on Tom's other side, fancy suit and all, and took hold of Tom's right hand. Will made as if to remove his arm, but Tom shook his head urgently against his shoulder and Will relaxed the arm back in to place.

"I have to call Chris," Nick said after a few minutes and pushed himself back to his feet. "Let her know. This changes everything. There are things to be set in motion."

Tom didn't respond. He had no more answers. He'd fucked everything up it seemed.

Nick stepped away to duck under the crime-scene tape and began to talk into his phone.

Tom didn't know how long he sat there, eyes closed, shocked silent and miserable—a near-fugue state—before he began to tune in to a conversation Will was having with someone. Someone standing beside them.

It was a young Indian woman with strong, attractive features, hair invisible underneath the pulled-up drawstring hood of a white forensic suit. She was writing in a notebook as Will gave her a rough sketch of the story they'd agreed upon, and she gave no indication of knowing him.

The interview had just finished when she glanced behind her at a black car, which had just double-parked further along the road.

"That's the DI," she said. "He'll probably want to talk to you both."

Tom closed his eyes again.

"Will?" It was a cultured voice—male and startled. "Tom?"

Tom knew the voice, but it was still a jolt, when he opened his eyes, to find James Henderson crouched down on his haunches in front of them, dressed in another of those white forensic suits, with the hood down to reveal his thick, ruffled fair hair.

He looked both surprised and wary. Tom felt only blinding relief it wasn't Lawson.

"Sameera said you found the body, Tom," Henderson said carefully. "Is that correct?"

Tom nodded against Will's shoulder, like a child.

"Can you tell me when you arrived at Mr. Perry's flat?"

Tom sat upright. He had to pull himself together. He thought perhaps he could trust James Henderson. But at the same time, Henderson knew too much and nowhere near enough.

"About half an hour ago," Tom said. "I didn't check my watch."

Henderson took his little notebook out.

"You knew Mr. Perry?" Henderson asked.

"Sort of," Tom said. Then, bitterly, "He was stalking me."

Henderson's eyes widened. They looked pale silver in the sunlight with a dark ring around the iris. Beautiful eyes.

"So you came here to…confront him?" Henderson asked.

Tom nodded again. At least Henderson didn't seem to think it was as insane as it had proved to be.

Tom described finding the door unlocked and finding the body, and Henderson, frowning with concentration, wrote it all down. Tom marvelled absently at the solid strength of his thigh muscles, because his crouch still seemed rock solid as he finished Tom's statement and took a brief statement from Will.

Across the street, outside the blue-and-white crime-scene tape, a large black limousine with darkened windows had parked side-on, and a small crowd of people had gathered in front of the metal railings protecting the garden. They were just rubberneckers, but Tom felt distantly embarrassed to be a part of the spectacle they were gawking at and snapping on their phones.

"So…" Henderson said finally to Tom. "I'll say it's a coincidence that my MIT was on call for this, and you found the victim. But…" He looked stern. "As you know, I'm not big on coincidences. Does this link to the case you're working on for AC Hansen?"

Tom resisted glancing over at Nick, who was still speaking urgently into his phone.

"This is…was my own…" Tom hated that his voice trembled. "Personal problem. He's been sending me gifts, he broke in to my flat. Soon after I met him, he drugged me and…and assaulted me."

Henderson wrote it down in his notebook, and when he finished, he looked up, clicked his pen meaningfully and slid it inside the opening of his forensic suit.

"DC Kaur says there's a pile of insulin bottles beside the body," Henderson remarked. Tom felt Will shift minutely beside him.

"Maybe…" Tom began, with no idea how he would end the sentence. He trailed off helplessly.

"Ben told me he worked with you the other day," Henderson told him. The conversational tone of his voice somehow emphasized his impatience. *Cut the crap.* "I should have known you were a model. So once I got that info…just a little research and I found your agency is Echo, whose chief executive was murdered a few days ago." He glanced over at Nick. "And that looks very like the husband and co-owner."

Tom could barely believe he'd been stupid and reckless enough to tell Ben he'd met Henderson; just casually left such a hostage to fortune and barely gave it a thought, too preoccupied with his own *feelings.*

"You didn't mention you were intimately involved in the case when I told you about it the other evening," Henderson said. "Big red flag, that. Then a bit of asking round Southwark and Peckham MIT, and I find DCI Lawson has a Tom Gray lined up as prime suspect for that *and* another insulin-related murder—just waiting for conclusive evidence to go ahead with a formal arrest."

Tom gazed at him in useless silence. He'd totally underestimated Henderson, and they'd all underestimated how much they could hide, like trying to hold a crumbling dam together with their hands against the ever-building force pushing at it.

"It's a sensitive case…" Will cut in. "And you know AC Hansen wants discretion."

Henderson's gaze darted between Tom and Will, before settling on Will. He chewed his full lower lip. His eyes looked like slits of molten silver through his narrowed lids.

"There have been three killings related to insulin in the space of nine days," Henderson said, unimpressed. "The link appears to be Tom."

And Tom totally understood his conclusion—that was the thing. In the absence of the full facts about Nick—hell, even *with* the full facts— Tom was the only suspect. Henderson would have no choice but to slap on handcuffs. They'd tried so hard—but there was nowhere left to run. "But," Henderson went on to Will, still worrying his lower lip with white teeth. "Since AC Hansen placed you on the investigation *and* trusted Tom to go with you, I'm assuming there's a lot more here than meets the eye."

Tom stared at him, stunned, struck by a dull sort of relief that might have been anticlimax.

"Lawson will be on this once we enter insulin as a term," Henderson warned. "Not to mention Tom's name so…"

"Well. Well," Will said softly as if he hadn't heard a word. "Look who's come to supervise proceedings." There was a puzzled pause, then Tom and Henderson followed his gaze.

Across the street, the driver of the black limousine had opened the closest passenger door to allow a tall silver-haired man to step out.

"Fuck," Henderson cursed softly. He levered himself effortlessly to his feet.

The newcomer was elegantly dressed in a navy suit, very clearly made to measure, and his silver hair was brushed neatly back from a tanned, handsome face. He looked like a wealthy and successful man, and all his attention was fixed on Henderson. Yet for all his obvious affluence, Tom got an odd feeling from the man of masked awkwardness, almost discomfort as he approached them.

"Detective Sergeant," he greeted Henderson. He quickly skimmed over Tom and settled, just a moment too long, on Will.

"Detective Inspector. Actually," Henderson corrected with steely cordiality. The man's gaze shot back to him. "And what brings you here, Mr. Priestly?"

The man—Priestly—frowned. "My employer was told that one of our regular contractors may have been injured. Max Perry. I take it from the activity…?" He trailed off significantly.

"That your paid narks gave you the right information." Will's smile was dangerous. "Again."

Priestly blinked down at him.

"I'm sure you're not implying that members of the Metropolitan police force would take bribes," he said with practised disdain. "That would be ridiculous."

Will returned pleasantly, "Not implying. Saying. Joey has coppers on his payroll, bought and paid for."

Priestly stared down his nose at him, and Tom got the distinct impression that they knew each other.

Henderson said, "You can confirm to Mr. Clarkson that Max Perry has been murdered. We can conclusively say it's not suicide."

"And you'll want to make sure there's nothing sharp around when you tell Eddie," Will added snidely.

Priestly didn't deign to answer. He turned and swept back to the limousine where the driver was waiting to open the door on cue. He disappeared into the darkness inside.

Will breathed, "Come on out, you bastard."

His attention was riveted on the car, and though nothing could be seen through the blackened windows to prove anyone else was in there, Tom felt as if he were watching a battle of wills. Seconds passed before the car peeled slowly away from the curb, and glided along the curve of Lennox Gardens to disappear from view.

"Fuck," Henderson muttered again, watching it go. Then he looked down at Tom and Will, chewing his lip again, before visibly coming to a decision. "All right, you gave your witness statements. You can go." They both stared up at him uncertainly. "I don't know anything about you apart from what you just told me. If I were you I'd use the time before Lawson takes Tom in. Until then, fuck off." It sounded oddly pleasant, in his accent. "Sameera!" he shouted and trotted down the steps to Max's open front door, DC Kaur at his heels. Tom, stunned, looked at his retreating back almost able to understand why Ben Morgan was so besotted.

Will was already on his feet. "You heard him. Come on!" He was already ducking under the tape and heading for his car.

Tom clambered to his feet too and looked uncertainly at Nick, still standing, talking on his phone, but he didn't wait to say goodbye. Instead, he pulled on his helmet and ran to his bike.

21

Tom wove through the traffic with aggressive determination, sticking to the Passat's tail, so they arrived outside Will's offices at the same time. He followed the car under the raised barrier into SFN's car park, then they dashed into the building and into the lift, together.

Tom asked anxiously. "Will. What's…?"

"The red string." Will watched the floor numbers impatiently.

The lift dinged open, and Will shot out and into an office a couple of doors along the corridor from his own. "Pix, I need info."

Pixie glanced up from her monitor as if Will's dramatic entrance were an everyday occurrence. "And that's why I'm here working on a Sunday, honey," she said dryly. Her hair had been pulled up into a bun, and she wore a fitted white blouse. She looked more than ever like Miss Moneypenny.

Will searched quickly through his notebook. "Michael Rolfe. 5 Courtenay Square, Kennington. Recent suicide. *Anything* on him. Close family. Anything at all you can get."

Pixie was already typing with effortless speed.

Tom slumped down in one of the chairs in front of her desk. "I don't understand," he said.

Will paced a couple of steps, then turned and paced, and turned again.

"Somehow," he said. "The Rolfes are connected. *He* was first to die by insulin. He had a red string round his wrist. Dr. Rolfe's also been attacked *with* insulin. It has to be something about them, beyond *her* connection to Catriona."

"But the string could be nothing," Tom said. "Lots of people wear them. Catriona didn't have a string round her wrist."

Will's eyes were fierce under dark brows. "You were at the crime scene. *Think.* There would have been a lot of blood if her wrists were slashed. It hid the string round Max's wrist. Could there have been a string round hers?"

Tom shook his head, but he squeezed his eyes tight shut, forcing the images he'd tried so hard to forget to the front of his mind, though they were dominated now by still more gruesome ones.

Catriona's pristine, white bedroom. The huge crimson stain on the quilt. The few other splashes of color. Tiffany blue. Purple underwear. A baby blue dress. "I don't remember," he said hopelessly. "I didn't look at her long enough to see that kind of detail. There was a pile of letters, though, tied by...a thin red sort of...cord? It could have been string. Would that count?"

Will's tight nod told him that perhaps it did.

"Rolfe's mother and sister," Pixie announced. "They live pretty much beside each other. Sister's married with kids." She pressed a button, and a printer began to whirr on the other side of the room.

"Do you have files on everyone?" Tom asked, astonished.

Pixie winked, picked up a glass of water from her desk and took a knowing sip. "Shall I call the mother and get an immediate appointment?"

Will nodded. "You're brilliant. And if the police come by, we weren't here."

Tom stared at him wildly. "You think I should run from the police?"

"Yes," Will said steadily. "For as long as we can keep you out of their way without it looking deliberate. In fact, turn off your phone."

"I've always fancied being on the run from the law," Pixie said wistfully. Tom tried to take courage from her absolute lack of concern. He fumbled his phone out of his jacket pocket and thumbed it off.

Will scanned the sheet from the printer. "Thank fuck! It's really close by. Thanks, Pix. Come on!"

He belted out of the door, Tom on his heels, and this time they both made for Will's car in the car park. As he started the engine, Will thrust Pixie's piece of paper at Tom.

"How do you know they'll talk to us?" Tom asked.

"Pixie's calling them. You don't say no."

Tom's weak smile dropped quickly. "What's the point, Will? It's just prolonging the inevitable."

Will shot him a glance and drove the car to the barrier. "We have a lead now. I still think the likeliest focus is you." He sounded almost evangelical. "Hansen assumes it's about Nick and his past. About revenge. But too much has been focused around you from the start. And every bit of information takes us closer, so…"

Tom said gently, "Will…"

"I know!" Will's voice was too loud, too desperate, and Tom understood then that Will was scared too. For him. For Tom.

"Okay," he said past the lump in his throat. "It's worth a try."

•••

Michael Rolfe's mother lived on the Bourne Estate, which was indeed, miraculously close. Will pushed the speed limit up Kirby Street and onto Hatton Place to Clerkenwell Road. Then it was a matter of ten minutes of ducking and weaving before they turned into a multistory car park close to Leather Lane.

It was long street and far from picturesque, but Leather Lane market had reputedly been operating for four hundred years and was now a hub for street food. So tourists buzzed around it.

Will strode along the street as if he knew exactly where to go, heading unerringly down a side street to a large open archway, once meant for horse-drawn carriages, presumably. They dipped past a white-and-orange traffic barrier.

Inside, the Bourne Estate would have reminded Tom of the kind of picturesque old English private school that popped up in the movies or on TV, if not for the floors of walkways above them with rickety bicycles leaning against their railings and draped with laundry. The buildings themselves were beautiful—red and yellow brick, with arts-and-crafts details, pilasters, decorative moldings. There were landscaped areas with grass shrubs and what looked like London plane trees, and it was almost bizarrely quiet and peaceful. The whole place looked as if it should belong to the wealthy, but obviously it didn't.

"I did some beat-time round here," Will volunteered as he took his bearings. "These are old local authority buildings. A new try at tenements. London County Council put them up before the First World War."

It certainly was the most beautiful council estate Tom had ever seen.

They had to buzz at the huge door of the building Will headed for, but after a couple of minutes' agitated wait they were allowed entry and trotted up concrete steps, following signs, until they found themselves on one of the walkways, outside a badly peeling navy-blue front door. It had an incongruously elegant fanlight.

Will rang the bell and the door opened almost at once.

The woman who peered out at them appeared to be in her forties, overweight and frazzled, wearing a large black T-shirt, lilac leggings and pink-and-white trainers. She took them in with a narrow glance.

"Are you the people who want to talk to Mum?" Her voice was cultured and not at all what Tom had expected from her appearance. "You don't look like private eyes." Touché, he thought wryly.

Will whipped out his wallet ID. "We are. Can we talk to you? Or your mother?"

The woman let them in with reluctance, but Tom detected anxiety there too.

"Someone talked Mum into this on the phone," the woman said. "She said…Carys was attacked. The police haven't told us that."

Will said in his police voice, "Carys is recovering in hospital."

The woman's eyes widened. "Oh. Well, I'm here to make sure Mum's okay. She rambles a bit. I just live on the other side of the estate, so…"

The flat was decorated in startlingly vibrant colors. The hall was bright yellow, and Tom caught sight of a lurid orange kitchen as they walked along into an equally bright-yellow lounge with a beautiful period window also painted yellow. Maybe they'd got a special deal on a big can of it. It couldn't be for the aesthetics.

The effect of that blaring color in such a small space was almost violent, and it was compounded by the smell of furniture polish and boiled fish into an assault on the senses.

The furniture in the room consisted of a blue sofa and two armchairs set round a coffee table and, across the room, a sideboard on which sat a bulky old-fashioned television, turned on to morning TV.

A woman with short tightly permed salt-and-pepper hair sat in an armchair not far from the window, a Zimmer frame standing next to her.

Shirley Rolfe, according to Pixie's notes—Michael's mother.

"I've just had my knees done," the woman said in the same cultured accent as her daughter. "So I'm afraid I can't stand up. Sally, would you go and make some tea, dear?"

The younger woman rolled her eyes but obeyed without a word. Tom and Will sat on the sofa, and Will launched in at once.

"We'd like to talk to you about your son's death, Mrs. Rolfe."

Shirley Rolfe blinked. "Michael? Not Carys? Michael took his own life."

Will nodded. "Can you tell us anything about Michael's state of mind before he died?"

"I don't understand," Mrs. Rolfe said.

"We think it may be linked to the attack on Carys." Will sounded so like a police officer on duty that Tom wasn't surprised to see Mrs. Rolfe succumb.

"Well…Mike was depressed, of course. To be honest, I didn't see much of him in the months before he died." Mrs. Rolfe hesitated. "About six months before he…he did it…he found out he was diabetic. That was such a shock because he'd been so fit, but Carys found it, luckily. And that was it. When he came to see me after that he was… I didn't like all the drugs Carys gave him."

"He was bipolar, Mum." Sally entered the room bearing a laden tray. It sounded like an old argument. "You can't blame Carys for that."

Mrs. Rolfe sniffed. "Well he didn't seem that depressed when he was diagnosed with the diabetes first. He said it was easy to live with if you were careful. Carys…"

"Carys had a lot to put up with." Sally sounded at the end of her patience. Her mother glared at her.

"A lot to put up with?" Tom prompted.

"He was a gentle soul," Mrs. Rolfe said, still glaring.

"He was having an affair!" Sally proclaimed. "It was devastating to Carys after how long they'd been together. I was furious with him but he wouldn't listen. He just said he loved this woman, but he was too scared to leave Carys."

"Scared," Tom repeated doubtfully.

"He was worried about her! Though not worried enough to stop seeing…that woman."

"So Carys knew?" Tom asked.

"Sally! It's not your business to wash our Mike's dirty linen in front of strangers," her mother snapped. "You always took Carys's side. Even at school."

"Why wouldn't I, Mum?" Sally returned angrily.

"They knew each other at school?" Will asked. He sounded as confused as Tom felt.

Mrs. Rolfe huffed and signaled imperiously for a cup of tea. Sally sullenly began to pour.

"We came from near Cambridge originally," Mrs. Rolfe said. "Then my husband got a job in Southampton, so we moved there. The children were teenagers then. Michael was sixteen, Sally was seventeen. They met

Carys and her sister at school...in the drama club. Carys's family had moved from Wales. When Mike and Carys married, I moved to London to be close to them after my husband died. And Sally was here too, of course," Mrs. Rolfe finished dismissively.

"Except Mike ruined it," Sally said with precise emphasis as she handed Mrs. Rolfe a cup of tea.

Tom thought her mother hadn't been exaggerating about Sally favoring her sister-in-law over her brother. But then Mrs. Rolfe had also obviously favored Michael over Sally. The joys of family life.

Mrs. Rolfe said, "He was your own brother, Sally. He must have been so unhappy to do what he did."

"And what about Carys?" Sally burst out.

Tom accepted a cup from her silently, not wanting to break the flow. It was like sitting in on a scene from a soap opera.

"Carys hasn't been to see us since Mike's funeral," Shirley retorted. "I thought, after losing him she wouldn't just forget us but she's shown how little she cares."

"She's *grieving*," Sally said. "She loved him *so* much! She had such a hellish time when she was a kid, and finding Mike dead...that must have been incredibly traumatic for her. On top of everything...reminding her! It was so *selfish* of him."

"What did it remind her of?" Will asked. Both women looked at him as if they'd forgotten he and Tom were there.

Sally took a steadying breath. "When we were at school. One of Carys's friends...murdered Emily, Carys's sister. Carys and another friend...saw it. Carys had a lot of therapy. But the boy who did it...he wasn't all there in the head. Carys actually visited him in prison! That's how good a person she is," she finished defiantly to her mother.

Tom blinked at her with open-mouthed shock.

Shirley countered, "*Michael* was the one who helped Carys through. They leaned on each other. Michael was close to Emily too."

"What was her maiden name?" Will asked. "Carys."

"Payne," Sally said. "With a Y. Seems pretty apt for her life."

Tom gulped down his tea to get rid of it, aware Will was doing the same, then they made their excuses and left as quickly as they could.

They waited to speak until they were both sitting in Will's car in the gloom of the multistory, engine running, ready to go.

"*Carys* is Glassy's friend?" Tom said, stunned. "I just assumed it was a boy."

Will said. "Me too. We need to confirm it but..."

Tom was already sure. "Glassy *was* the connection. Someone got revenge on Carys, the girl who testified against him. And…against the boy and girl who hurt him. Catriona and Nick."

"But why murder Max Perry?" Will tapped his fingertips against the steering wheel. "And why frame you?"

"Maybe Max saw something when he was watching me. Maybe we were right the first time—the murderer is doing this to me to toy with Nick. Make him ruin his own life." He pulled out his phone and switched it on. He really should call Nick, let him know he was okay.

"If it's Glassy he'd have to have someone working for him on the outside," Will said.

"Or someone seeking revenge for him, without him knowing," Tom suggested. "But…Dr. Wykeham implied he has no one." A thought struck. "Wouldn't Carys and Nick have known each other, though, if she visited Glassy?"

Will tapped the steering wheel. "Not necessarily. Wandsworth's a big prison, and we don't know if visiting arrangements at Red Moss were open."

"But it's a big coincidence," Tom said, and he didn't know what he was implying. "Nick and Carys—both with contacts in Red Moss."

"Don't forget Eddie Butts has too," Will pointed out dryly. "But yeah…Glassy does seem a possible focus. What he did to Carys's sister—drugging, mutilation, slashing wrists—the same MO as Catriona and Lily. Maybe even Michael. The insulin too…it's like a mash-up of MOs—David's and his."

"I don't know," Tom said slowly. "It just seems… Michael was having an affair, right? But Carys told me diabetes made him impotent and that was why he mutilated his penis before he died."

Will frowned. "When did Carys say that?"

Tom hadn't even told him. "I spoke to her the…"

Tom's phone buzzed. They both stared at it, as if a cobra had animated in Tom's lap.

The display showed several missed calls from an unknown number —the police, probably. But this call was from Nick. Tom put it on speaker.

"Tom." Nick's tone was flat, deadened. "Can you come to Greens? Christine'd like a final debrief."

"Okay. Nick…" Tom began.

"It's okay, Tom." The call cut off.

Tom said miserably, "A final debrief. He's going to do it. Glassy wins."

"Two more people have died, Tom," Will snapped. "And I'm not going to watch an innocent man go down for murder. Lawson's been operating without full context. Wasting resources... It's not reasonable. It's not fair! Hansen and her...civil servant have prioritized shielding Nick and their *investment* over everything. Well, it's past time they came clean. There's no alternative."

•••

Hansen was the only person in the room Nick had commandeered for the meeting at Greens.

The room was small and very narrow with dark-blue-painted paneled walls and a huge multipaned window. The only furniture was a brown leather sofa facing the window, and a round table for two in front of it, at which Hansen sat, her back to the light.

Tom and Will sank on to the long sofa facing her.

"Nick had to go to a meeting. He signed me in as a guest," Hansen said. Her cropped, platinum hair shone in the light coming through the window like a halo. "There's less likelihood of electronic surveillance here."

"Surveillance?" Tom repeated, horrified. But it made sense. "You think the killer...he's bugged my flat? And Nick's?"

"He's always ahead of the game," Hansen pointed out. Then, to Will, "I assume you have an RF detector?"

Will nodded. "I'll do a sweep of both places when I can." He said to Tom, "It's a radio-frequency detector. It can find any devices transmitting a signal."

Tom slumped down against the back of the sofa, absorbing the real possibility that the killer had heard everything he been doing and saying for—how long? Deeply personal things.

Fuck—could he feel any dirtier?

He focused fiercely on Hansen as Will recounted what they'd found at Max's house and what they'd learned about Carys and Glassy.

"So your money's on this...Glassy now?" Hansen's tone was sharper than Tom had heard it, but her career must be on a shaky peg too, given how far she'd gone out on a limb to protect Nick.

Will grimaced. "I wouldn't go that far. A lot fits but...like you said, the person who's doing this is always ten steps ahead. Cunning. Manipulative. Able to plan and plot moves...like a chess player. That doesn't sound like the Glassy we've been told about."

Hansen tapped her fingertips absently on the small table. "You need to talk to him. Trace anyone close to him."

"Only the police can push an interview with him. But my office have been trying to find out any of his known associates in Red Moss and Wandsworth for a few days."

Hansen gave a bloodless smile. "Good work, DI Foster."

"I was the one who pointed you at Max Perry, ma'am," Will said bitterly. "So not such good work."

Hansen shook her head. "He was the obvious suspect."

Will looked unconvinced.

"I'm going to be charged, aren't I?" Tom asked quietly. They both turned to him, and he could see how much they wished they could deny it.

Hansen said, "Lawson'll bide his time until SOCO tells him what they found at the Perry murder scene. Then…yes. I think he has enough circumstantial evidence to charge you. Tonight or tomorrow."

Tom nodded. He couldn't speak.

"But you *are* going to tell Lawson about Nick, aren't you?" Will demanded. "It's not fair to Tom or even Lawson to put Nick's anonymity first now."

Hansen raised a cool eyebrow. "Yes. I do understand that, DI Foster. But procedures have to be gone through. The minister in charge of the Public Protection Unit at the DOJ has been informed. She's briefing the Justice Secretary, then…we're clear to go." She sighed. "There's going to be serious political blowback if the whole story gets out. More questions in the House about the program."

"Having full police resources pointed in the right direction at last… That'll make a difference," Will said bracingly.

Tom couldn't stand their careful false optimism a minute longer.

"This is Lawson!" he burst out. "You know there's zero guarantee he's going to turn away from a solution that looks cut and dried, to follow something as messy and…and complicated as this. David Burchill and the Babes in Arms?" Tom made a harsh sound. "He's convinced it's me. It was set up to *look* like me. He might even say I knew about Nick and used it. I'm still the most likely to take the blame."

Will was trying to look skeptical, but Hansen appeared relieved that Tom had worked it out for himself. That he wasn't under the illusion he was about to be saved.

"You understand that apart from revealing Nick's identity to Lawson, I can't interfere again," she warned. "My intervention about Perry actually made it worse. Lawson now knows Perry assaulted and stalked you, and since he thinks you kill anyone who crosses you…" She sighed. "I'm not going to be in any position to oversee what he does anymore. It's purely up to him if he wants to use the new information. But…Nick wants to do it anyway." She sounded stoic, braced for what was to come.

But what Tom might be about to face… He wouldn't have believed he had the emotional resources left to feel scared. But he was. He was very scared of prison.

"You're both forgetting something." Will's voice was low and hard. "The killer is still out there. We don't know what his motivation is, but I don't think his endgame is just to put Tom in jail. *Maybe* we should be considering if his pattern is what he did to Carys. He killed the person she loved most. Then after she'd lived with that—suffered for a while—he went in to finish her off. With Nick…he killed Catriona and…"

"He's framed me to hurt Nick," Tom said.

"So his next victim could be either someone Nick loves, or Nick himself?" Hansen mused.

Will said, "Not Nick. Not yet. Up till now, the killer's focused a lot of effort on tormenting Tom. The way he took time to torment Catriona before…"

"All right!" Tom snapped. He felt freezing cold inside, as if his internal organs were going into hibernation.

But Will went on relentlessly, "Do not go to your flat alone, Tom. Or move around alone, until he's caught. Do you understand?"

Tom's face twisted with bitterness. "Well, that may not be a problem soon, since I'll be a guest of Her Majesty."

Hansen rose to her feet. For her the meeting was over.

"Nick'll come with me tomorrow to see DCI Lawson and make a statement. That's all I can do now." She slid the strap of her bag over her shoulder. "Good luck, Tom," she said softly.

Tom and Will waited in the room for a few more minutes, before following Hansen to the exit.

Outside the sky had turned to gray, the first break in relentless sunshine since the day Catriona's body had been found. The dull hammered-gray light felt far more suitable.

Tom glanced at his phone. It was barely lunchtime. Life outside—people sauntering by on the pavement—felt surreal.

"Give me a lift?" His tongue was thick in his mouth.

His phone beeped with an incoming text as they began to walk toward Will's car.

There were three unread messages from Pez: one asking him where he was; one reminding him about his weekly appointment at his salon, and about his shoot the next day for Boss; the third text told him he got the Mulberry job. He must have given Marina good "out of reach but not alienating" after all.

He looked down at the screen numbly, trying to take it all in.

"Actually," he said. Well, why not? Compared to all that was happening in the rest of his life, modeling and all it entailed felt down to earth and solid. He might even get to do the Boss job before Lawson locked him up. "Can you drop me on Brompton Road? I have to get waxed."

Will eyed him like a startled cat, and Tom laughed, though it wasn't really funny.

"You're not going home after that though? After all we just said?" They weren't really questions.

Tom managed a smile. Will still knew him. "Last night of freedom. Potentially. I don't want to spend it in a hotel. And Nick and Pez would fuss. The killer won't expect me to go back to the flat."

Will rolled his eyes violently. "That's one of the stupidest... Do you have a bloody death wish? You're coming to Leyton." He declared. "You shouldn't be alone."

Tom stopped walking.

Somehow, it hadn't occurred to him that Will would invite him again. Will's white-knight complex. Pity, perhaps.

He waited for the cosh of instinctive resistance to going back to there, to the house in which he'd almost lost himself. But what was the bloody point of worrying about that now?

He felt an adrenaline rush of perverse freedom.

"Can John come too?" he asked.

Will said, deadpan, "He's the only the reason I offered."

22

Tom emerged from his three-hour salon appointment, hair freshly highlighted, body waxed smooth and pores steamed, to find Will waiting for him in reception, reading a magazine, still dressed in his suit and tie and looking like an unusually attractive young businessman.

Tom briefly permitted himself to feel, not smother, the emotions the sight brought him. Pride, gratitude, huge affection, unshakeable attraction. The fantasy that it could always be like this. He hid it all.

From the salon, Will drove him to Notting Hill to collect John, John's things and his own dirty laundry. Nick wasn't in, to Tom's huge, guilty relief. Then they went to Shoreditch to fill an overnight bag, and on at last to the house in Leyton.

Will had bought it the year before he met Tom, as an investment in the belief that the area was about to be gentrified. And from the newly spruced-up appearance of a fair bit of Warren Road, Tom could see that he'd been right.

When he walked through the front door of the house, he barely recognized it.

The hall floorboards were polished now and golden brown, the walls pure white. When Tom had last seen it, there had been a sickly green carpet with a pattern of deeper ochre swirls, which looked as if it had lain there, tattered and ugly, for a century. The hall walls had been covered with stained, bile-colored wallpaper, which they'd planned to strip off next. The image was as clear in Tom's mind as if he were looking at a photograph.

"You've done an amazing job," Tom said, awed. He felt an unwanted tug of melancholy.

"Thanks," Will said from behind him. "Go on through."

The lounge had been equally transformed—snowy-white walls, varnished floorboards, a rescued fireplace Tom had helped Will manhandle from a salvage yard—himself fresh off the plane after a shoot in San Francisco. Will had been working on this room when they'd split, in fact.

There was a large, comfortable sofa—very similar to the one Tom had chosen for his own flat—and soft-looking, shabby-brown leather armchairs. It was a gorgeous room. Entirely Tom's taste.

Will told him to drop his bag in the spare room—a comfortable, elegantly masculine space painted in pale eau-de-nil. The message was clear. Tom was here for protection only.

But Tom just went with it. He didn't second-guess himself. Didn't do anything but lie down to doze on Will's comfortable sofa to the background mutter of the television, feeling bizarrely relaxed in a way he'd begun to believe he could never feel again.

John lay on his chest, delicious smells of cooking garlic and spices drifting though the open living room door.

One thing had become clear to Tom as he'd faced reality in that room in Greens. If he was about to be arrested and charged, if he was going to prison—or if the killer was going to stop toying with him and finish him off, one way or another, he didn't want to spend tonight pussyfooting around Pez or Nick, or going out to a club to do some recreational fucking, or reminiscing about his greatest campaigns…

He'd been given the chance to be exactly where he most wanted to be. In the place and in the company of the man he'd denied himself. He was basking in finally giving himself permission to enjoy it without fear of the consequences. He was going to allow himself to have that much.

"I thought we could eat in here and watch something."

Tom lazily opened his eyes to find Will standing by the sofa, holding a large wooden tray. He'd changed into light gray tracksuit pants and a white T-shirt, and he looked…young, Tom thought with a pang. Like a student Tom might have met in the Union back in the day, if he'd been very lucky.

John jumped off the sofa as Tom sat up and swung his feet to the floor. The tray, laid down on the low table in front of the sofa, bore an opened bottle of red wine, two glasses, and two bowls full of rice and meat in a sauce. The unmistakeable spicy perfume of curry.

"Did you make that from scratch?" Tom asked, impressed. "I didn't know you could cook Indian food." Will's previous forté had been Italian.

Will leaned down to pour rich, ruby wine into the glasses. "I went out with a girl whose family came from Uttar Pradesh. She and her mum taught me the basics." He handed Tom a glass.

A girl. Tom's small flinch of reaction hadn't gone unnoticed.

"Yes." Will sank on to the sofa, a cushion's width away. "Still bisexual."

A flush of shame raced over Tom's face and throat. It was none of Tom's business if Will had been seeing a woman, a man or a Shetland pony. Tom had been more than busy fucking around the world himself.

But…

"Sorry," he muttered.

"Still don't believe it's real?" Will picked up a bowl and fork. He didn't sound offended. More resigned.

Tom's blush deepened. "I *am* sorry. For the things I said then. I thought… Because only Des knew about us… I thought it was an excuse because you didn't want to tell people you were gay. I do know better now."

It was true. Tom's old anger at Will's self-declared bisexuality and his partial closet had been fueled in the main by insecurity and jealousy. It still was. He could admit that, if only to himself.

He finished with another weak, "I'm sorry."

"It's okay." Will shrugged and sighed. "I *was* dodging coming out at work. It was…too easy to hide behind the girlfriends they all knew I'd had. Asking you to keep it friendly the times you met my colleagues… It didn't seem all that important then, but it wasn't fair. If you'd moved in though… I *would've* told them."

Tom gave a weak smiled. His heart ached. "I know. I know you would. Maybe…I was just looking for something I could blame you for."

"Well," Will said bracingly. "As it turns out, I'm pretty sure now my… serious romantic feelings tend to focus on men. So maybe—in my case— you were almost right." He threw Tom a little smirk and turned his attention back to his food.

Tend to?

Tom took a bite of curry.

Had Will fallen in love again? More than once, even? With women or men? Because he hadn't been in love before Tom.

"What happened to her?" he asked. "The girlfriend who taught you to cook curry? It's great by the way."

"Why? You thinking of giving her a call?" Will gave a sly grin, but in a moment, the smile slid away. "I just...I was wasting her time."

They ate in silence for a few more minutes as Will fiddled with TV channels.

"You're brave," Tom blurted. "The way you can trust people."

"Not really," Will replied. "Not so much anymore."

Tom swallowed the lump in his throat. "I'm..."

"Don't. It's history."

But I don't want to be history.

The unwilling thought, clear and powerful, cleansed his mind of everything else. The shock of honesty. The impossibility of it.

Too late. Far too late.

Will engaged him in choosing a show to watch, and Tom went with it, being guided by Will's choices. So they ended up watching *How to Get Away With Murder* on Netflix which Will said was Mark's favorite show because it showed lawyers as ruthless amoral sharks.

Tom tried to concentrate on it, batting away the thoughts howling at the edges of his mind. Who would get to him first? Lawson or the killer?

And when the TV couldn't hold him, he fixed desperately on his surroundings. On the fireplace he'd helped wrestle into place, on floorboards he'd helped to sand. On the man sitting beside him, he'd never managed to force himself to stop wanting.

He told himself that his urge to cling to Will was just the vulnerability of fear, his usual defenses stripped away by all that had happened and what was coming. People did crazy things, when their life, as they knew it, was about to end.

But didn't it also concentrate the mind?

He forced himself to focus again on the TV show—a courtroom scene. He watched it for a minute or two.

"Christ." He gave a shaky laugh. "I hope Mark has someone as evil as her up his sleeve."

Will flinched and fumbled to pause the screen. "Fuck! I'm sorry. I didn't think."

"No, it's okay! Gives me hope my defense team won't have morals either."

Will didn't try to fob him off. Instead he said calmly, "Whatever happens, I won't stop until I've found the killer."

Tom held his solemn eyes. He forced a watery smile.

"I don't want you to put yourself in danger. He's…too clever." Will, for once, appeared at a loss. "Let's watch the end," Tom said.

Somehow, voicing his worst fears had helped, and Tom relaxed enough to concentrate on the show and the episode after it, until tiredness began to pull him in and out of consciousness.

"You're falling asleep," Will said softly.

Tom jerked back to awareness. "I didn't snore, did I?"

Will laughed. "No, you're just doing the nodding-dog thing."

Tom sat up and stretched. "Is it okay to take John to the spare room?" He didn't want to be alone.

Will hesitated for a split second, but it was enough for Tom to notice. What did he have to lose now?

He swallowed and took the chance. "Is that…where you want me to go?"

Will's gaze dropped. He frowned as he thought, and Tom knew he deserved rejection a thousand-fold in return for all the pain he'd paid out to Will. But it hurt all the same.

"No," Will said definitely.

Tom nodded. He'd expected nothing else.

But Will raised his eyes, large and golden-amber in the lamplight.

"That's not where I want you to go."

•••

Though it was after ten o' clock, the dim light of the London dusk faintly illuminated Will's bedroom—it was enough to see where the furniture was placed, at least.

Tom stood just inside the doorway as Will walked over to the far side of the big bed and switched on a large table lamp. The room burst into clarity. Tom moved slowly to the other side of the bed and switched on that lamp too.

Will still slept on the right. And Tom, through the past two and a bit years, had kept the habit of sleeping on the left. He'd never let himself notice that until now.

The room was simple and masculine like the spare room, softened by the ambience of the two bedside lamps. Polished floorboards, a wooden bed with a dark gray, discreetly patterned throw, a chest of drawers, a wardrobe. The walls were painted a soft mid-gray, with purple tones in this light.

It would be almost greenish in daylight.

"Purbeck Stone!" Tom breathed. He turned his whole body to Will and asked excitedly, "It is, isn't it?" Tom had picked it out when they'd been looking at colors, for the distant day Will could actually decorate.

"It looks amazing!"

Will cleared his throat and rubbed the back of his neck with little-boy sheepishness.

"It was the best color," he said with a defensive shrug.

Emotion was a huge, aching rock in Tom's chest, weighing him down. Regret. Fear. Awe. Love.

"Will," he whispered. "I'm scared."

Will was round the bed in seconds, hauling him in to a hug. Tom clung back just as hard.

Will muttered against the side of his head. "You need to sleep."

But Tom tried to burrow closer still. He'd climb inside Will if he could.

"I don't want to sleep," he said. "I don't want to waste it."

Will pulled back, and Tom could see his distress. He'd have had to be blind not to be aware that Will still had some feelings for him. And yet here Tom was, asking for something that would make it harder for both of them to let go.

Stupid. Selfish.

"I'm sorry," Tom rushed out. "I shouldn't have. You're right. Just sleep." Not least because an erection should be beyond him in his state of mind.

They were face to face, only inches apart. One of Will's big hands crept up to cradle the side of his face, and Will scrutinized.him—as if he were looking for clues, or trying to memorize him.

Will's eyes looked soft with sorrow and compassion. But he leaned toward Tom and gave him his answer. Brave, like Will was.

Tom let it happen for a few gentle seconds. The softness of Will's lips felt gossamer light, pressed sensually against his. But then, as if a switch had been pulled, all innocence blinked out of the touch, and the kiss became ravenous. Desperate.

Tom tasted curry spices and the coolness of red wine on Will's tongue; he felt the soft rasp of Will's evening stubble and smelled the echoes of Tom Ford on Will's skin. The combination was a blueprint for arousal.

When Tom managed to pull himself away, he stripped as if his clothes were burning him, hauling off his T-shirt, unbuttoning his jeans, heeling off his boots in a frantic race to feel skin.

Will, after a startled pause, did the same.

They hauled back the duvet together, and they were both naked when they sank onto the bed. Will rolled on top, and Tom welcomed him eagerly as if they'd agreed, as if every movement had been choreographed.

Like the last time, their swollen genitals rubbed against each other, until it almost felt to Tom as if, should he look down, he'd see visible sparks of ecstasy.

His ears buzzed with desire, his body pumped with it.

He writhed under Will's muscular weight, frantic for sensation; the friction of skin on skin a sweet shock until Will's hand lodged in his hair and held him still for another feverish kiss, greedy and rough and possessive.

When the kiss broke for air, Will tucked his face into the juncture of Tom's neck and shoulder and began to move his hips faster, more methodically. Waves of pleasure from the frottage were bringing Tom closer and closer to a point of no return. But when the realization of imminent orgasm took hold, when it seemed inevitable, rushing toward him like a floodtide in a tunnel, he made himself stop moving. Still as a corpse under Will's sweat-slick undulating body.

He couldn't stand for it to be just this. Not tonight.

"Do you wanna fuck me?" he breathed into Will's ear.

Will froze, face hidden in Tom's neck, as if a gun had been pressed to his head.

Tom urged recklessly. "You can fuck me from behind. Or...I can ride you? Would you like that?"

It had been a long time for Tom. Two years in fact.

When he and Will had been together, Tom had tried being fucked for the first time, and he'd loved it, as much as he'd loved fucking Will. Which had been—a lot. So he'd been amazed and disturbed to find after he and Will were finished that he didn't actually like bottoming as a simple act of sex. He just couldn't stand the intimacy; the sense of vulnerability. The trust.

Nick was versatile, and he'd always wanted desperately to fuck him, but Tom didn't allow it. Pez only liked to bottom. And after that one try Tom wasn't going to do it with casual shags. So in all his encounters, Tom was now exclusively a top.

Will raised his head from its hiding place. His eyes looked nervous, sick with lust.

"I've never done that...I mean with a guy."

He'd been ridden by a girl then. The image was a starburst of jealousy in Tom's mind. The urge to wipe that woman from Will's memory.

"Then you don't know what you're missing," Tom said.

Truthfully, Tom had never done it that way either from the top. But Pez had done it to him, so he had the basics. He braced his feet against the mattress and pushed up to topple Will flat onto his back beside him—their old game—momentum rolling Tom fully on top.

He grinned wildly. "All you have to do is lie there. Afraid you might nod off?"

Will gave a strangled laugh. "Nope. Terror will keep me awake."

"Glad to see you've still got some sense of self-preservation, copper," Tom purred.

He sat back onto his heels, bum pressed against Will's muscular thighs, and they smiled stupidly at each other. The connection between them, that Tom had worked so hard to forget.

"So…" Tom bit his lip lazily as Will's gaze roamed over him.

"So…" Will echoed. His reached up to stroke his palms over the muscular six-pack Tom sported. "You're smooth everywhere," he said softly. Before, Tom'd still had a treasure trail, a pubic bush, a tiny smattering of hair on his chest, like Will had. But all he had left now was a small patch of pubic hair, freshly manicured at the salon.

Will seemed to like it though, so Tom stretched deliberately, flaunting his body, reading everything in the greed in Will's eyes.

He lowered his chin and delivered his best sultry gaze from beneath his lashes. "So can I ride you? If it isn't too much bother. I appreciate you're a very busy man."

Will tried and failed to find a straight face. "Well…since I have a spare minute or two, I may as well help you out."

"Big of you."

Will's smirk widened. "Very"—he pushed up with his hips—"big of me."

Tom laughed and couldn't resist leaning down to kiss Will's smug mouth, but in the next second he landed on his back with a grunt, as Will slid off the bed to disappear into his ensuite. Neither of them got to hold the upper hand for long.

Tom lay on his back in the middle of the mattress, happy, wildly aroused, and in the stillness he allowed the rationality of thinking beyond the moment to slither in.

How stupid was it to do this? How could it possibly be fair to Will?

He stared blindly at the ceiling, feeling lust and excitement begin to drain away as fear and conscience pushed back in.

"You okay?"

Tom jerked and turned his head sharply on the pillow. Will was walking back toward the bed, big cock bouncing stiffly with every step. Lust flooded back in to drown doubt.

They both knew the score.

Will dropped two items on the sheet—a small bottle of lube and a foil square. That last 69 without rubbers had been crazy enough.

The mattress lurched as it took Will's weight on his knees.

"So...how do we do it?" Will sounded cautious now, as if Tom's mood had somehow transferred to him. As if he was waiting to be denied. Passivity was the opposite of Will's character, but he was leaving everything tonight in Tom's hands, and he read Tom so, so well.

Tom couldn't stand the careful neutrality of Will's expression, even as his body screamed his desire for sex.

Deliberately he beckoned Will toward him with a crooked finger, eyes hot.

Will paused then shuffled toward him, the sheet bunching and pulling beneath his shins as he moved. Tom rolled up lithely onto his knees, and then they faced each other, inches apart.

"You need to get me ready." Tom sounded coy even to himself. Provocative and sly.

Will's answering smile was just as challenging. "You're going to feel me inside you, tomorrow," he said, deliberately, his voice hot and thick. "Remember every minute."

Tom's eyes held on his and he could barely breathe.

In the old days, dominance and possessiveness from Will had been as unnerving to Tom as it had been arousing. Now, hearing it again felt exciting beyond words.

"Big talk," he whispered, and grinned.

He swiveled round and positioned himself across the bed on all fours, forearms braced in front of him, bum in the air. He waggled his arse for good measure.

And then Will wasn't playing anymore. He began to rub and stretch and lubricate Tom's hole, to push his long fingers inside, and it had been so long since Tom had felt anything like it. He hadn't even used a dildo to remind him. He'd forgotten the slide and twist, forced himself to forget how much he loved this. The perfection of surrender.

Will was patient, and clearly that patience was at some cost to himself. But he told Tom, low voiced, how amazing his arse was, how tight he was, the incredible sight of his own fingers disappearing inside him, and when they were both shaking with lust, he picked up the condom from the bed.

Tom craned his neck to watch over his shoulder as Will opened the foil and began to roll on the condom. He'd always secretly hated wrapping Will's cock, but they'd never reached the stage of fucking without rubbers. Tom was sure he never would with anyone.

Nick's wistful offer of exclusivity suddenly flashed, entirely unwanted, into his mind, like a dash of cold water.

He reared up on his knees and twisted rapidly round to face Will again. He wanted to see him.

Will looked tense and rigidly absorbed as he slicked lube onto the condom, close to the end of his tether. When his eyes met Tom's, they looked almost bewildered. He didn't resist Tom's palm against his chest pushing him on to his back. And he let Tom arrange him to his own satisfaction, lying flat, head on the pillows, prick ready to go.

Tom straddled him quickly, knees pressing into his sides, his own cock bare and rampant between his muscular thighs. And then, head down, long, pale blond strands of hair hiding his face, he slid back until he felt the light, damp tap of Will's erection against his backside.

He reached behind to hold the slippery, latex-covered shaft, holding it steady as he spread his thighs wider. Then he began to push down, feeling the first blunt pressure against the dip of clenched muscle at his anus.

He bit his lip hard and focused, feeling stubborn, tense resistance against the thick rounded head of Will's prick until, as he pushed down, the first inch burst through into slick tightness.

It hurt a bit. Of course it did, after so long. But everything hurt and this was the least of it—nothing at all, if it meant he could have Will inside him again. Feel how much Will still wanted him.

He glanced down, face twisted with the dull, stinging ache. Will's teeth were clenched, and Tom wondered if he was in pain too, cock squeezed too hard by the cramps assailing Tom.

"Tom," Will panted. "I'm hurting you. There's no point…"

But in that moment Tom had the control. Will was his.

He began a steady downward pressure, silencing Will as effectively as a hand slapped on his mouth. He could feel the trembling tension in Will's body as he fought to hold back, until, as if he couldn't help it, he made a tiny thrust upward into Tom's heat.

"Sorry…God, sorry…"

"No…just give me a second. It's been a while."

Tom closed his eyes and focused, and the cramping began to ease. He sighed with relief, rose up and pushed himself down lower, then up and lower still, until Will's cock was swallowed up inside him.

He wriggled helplessly on it, and they both moaned in unison as Will's hands came up to grip and knead the cheeks of his backside. Tom looked down at own swollen cock, back to full mast, jutting red and desperate from the manicured order of his ruthlessly trimmed pubic hair. No doubt for either of them, how much he was loving it.

He'd never used this position before Pez talked him into trying it from the bottom, and even then he'd got off a bit on the subtle confusion of submission and dominance. But now—the feel of sitting stretched and impaled on Will's sex, Will's beautiful face distorted with the effort of holding back, waiting for Tom to set the pace—which one of them was in charge?

The cock inside Tom twitched, and he moaned. The pressure against the walls of his channel was exquisite, nerves stretched and aching, waiting for stimulation. The sense of intimacy was almost unbearable.

"Tom," Will gasped. "Please."

Slowly, Tom began to raise and lower himself, fucking himself, slowly, then faster.

He reached behind to hold Will's thighs, above his knees, so that he leaned back, like Pez had done to him, changing the angle of penetration. "Oh *fuck*. That's lovely," he slurred. "That's so sweet."

But his hips never stopped pumping, his erect penis swaying with every movement, provocatively untouched. His head had fallen back, eyes closed, feeling the distracting brush of his long hair against the skin of his naked back, and he bounced on Will's cock.

Self-consciousness was abandoned to blazing sensation.

Finally Will snapped and began to power his hips up in time with Tom's graceful ride, and they moved together, moaning and panting, as if they were synchronized.

The pressure built in Tom's stretched thighs and his aching, swollen balls, bouncing and rubbing against Will's skin and pubic bush, feeling the exquisite push and pull of the big meaty shaft inside him. By silent agreement neither of them touched Tom's erection. Then Tom rammed his arse down hard one final time, hands still masochistically gripped behind him on Will's thighs, and he came, clenching spastically on the hard length lodged all the way inside him. His own neglected penis bobbed and twitched wildly as it spurted gushes of semen up into the empty air.

Seconds later Will let go too with a desperate groan, pulsing into the condom, and they were frozen—both of them—in their joint tableau of ecstasy.

They lay in tangled exhaustion for minutes afterwards, like abandoned puppets, panting and sweating, until Tom found the strength to push himself up on his arms and lift his tender bum off Will's now-deflated cock. He flopped sideways onto his back as Will peeled off and tied the condom.

Weariness kept them still and silent until Tom was able to drag himself across the space between them to cuddle in and put his head on Will's chest. Will accommodated him without comment, as if they'd been building to this closeness from the moment Will walked up to him outside Greens.

Tom lay staring into the gloom beyond the lamplight, eyes tracing lovingly over the rich gray of the walls.

He'd told Will the day they'd idly looked at paint shades—that this was the color he'd want on his bedroom walls if he ever got his own place. But when he'd bought his flat in Shoreditch, he hadn't thought of it.

"I'd forgotten how much I loved this gray," Tom murmured into the intimate quiet. Then, softly, "I painted my bedroom white."

"Tastes change." Will sounded totally accepting. Tom had moved on and forgotten things that had remained significant for Will.

Tom couldn't allow him to believe that.

"I didn't let myself hold on to it." He'd bundled the dream in with everything else and buried it all. "I didn't want to be…reminded."

Will said quietly at last, "I really envy how good you are at that. Denial."

No one's better at pretending than you, Tommy.

Tom raised mouth to Will's, to kiss his mind to silence, and they snogged, lying there peacefully, mouths moving with lush ease against each other, heads resting side by side on Will's pillow.

Eventually, Will pulled away and unexpectedly, given the atmosphere of wistful resignation between them, he summoned an enormous grin.

"I can't believe it!" It made him look like an evil schoolboy. "You're hard again. I mean I'm irresistible but…"

Tom refused to look down at his newly chubbed-up erection. "Maybe…" *It's what you do to me…* "I'm just filling my boots while I can."

Will's grin began to fade. Reality pattered in.

"I'm so sorry, Will," Tom whispered. "I'm so sorry you fell for a fuck-up like me."

Will swallowed. "We both fucked up." But he sounded uncomfortable, perhaps because he didn't enjoy discussions about emotions; perhaps because this would soon be yet another goodbye. Tom didn't know why he felt so shocked when Will went on, "Anyway talking of fucking… Do you want to do me?"

Tom stared at him across the pillow.

"I…wouldn't do it justice." He wanted it so much, but Will had given more than enough. "Another time." They both knew there wouldn't be one.

Will frowned. "You don't have to baby me. It's just sex."

Tom frowned back. The obvious lie somehow both irritated and steadied him.

"I don't get fucked often, so think yourself lucky," Will went on, with a smirk. "Only by people I really like." Then, softly, "I like you."

It was ruthless in its vulnerability, but Tom could only feel relieved that Will hadn't gone further. Because Tom couldn't say it back now any more than he could two years before.

Last chance, something told him.

But he couldn't do it. He couldn't do that to Will.

"I like you too," he said.

23

Tom blinked awake to the distant smell of coffee and the feel of sunlight shining on his face through thin white cotton blinds. The first thing he registered was that he was alone, then those beautiful grey walls.

He stretched luxuriously and closed his eyes against the brightness, caught in the aftermath of a dream that left a haze of sweetness behind it. But when he reached for the happy images, they slipped away.

The stretch brought memories with it. The delicious, hollow ache in his arse and thighs; a pleasant overworking of his back and stomach muscles, the sting of abraded skin.

He smiled and wallowed in delighted remembrance of Will under him. Clawing at his back. Moaning on his cock. But then he remembered what he'd chosen to forget when he'd taken up Will's invitation—that screwing him had always unleashed all Tom's unworthy, unwanted possessiveness. When he was fucking hard, hips pumping with all that need to own, Tom's low determined voice, telling Will that only Tom could make him moan like that. That he only belonged to Tom.

It was just sex babble, but maybe it had given voice to things neither of them needed to hear. It had been shitty of him.

But reality was shitty. Today would probably be the end of Tom's life as he knew it.

Lawson's dogged malice, or an ingenious killer out to finish him off. Which would get him first?

His stomach began to heave and writhe with distress.

On the floor, in his jeans pocket, his phone rang.

He froze, then plunged out of bed and darted for the bedroom door, pulse hammering wildly. As he pulled the door open, the ringing stopped.

He looked back at the pile of clothes for a second, then hurried to the kitchen, where the nauseating smell of good coffee and fresh toast assaulted him through the open doorway. He didn't feel as if he'd ever be able to eat again.

Will stood facing the door, behind a large dark-gray island unit, concentrating on the packet of cat-meat he was persuading into John's dish. John, meanwhile, sat impassively on the wooden floor at the side of the island, waiting. His litter tray was nestled against a far wall.

It was all casually, unreachably domestic.

"Will," Tom gasped.

Will looked up and took in his fear, alert at once. "What…?"

All Tom could think of to say was, "It's morning." Will's expression shifted into an awful sympathy. Tom took a deep, calming breath. "My phone rang."

"Was it the police?"

Tom laughed and it sounded hysterical. "I don't know. I ran away."

Will managed an answering laugh as tribute. "Well, I appreciate the view."

Tom realized only then that he was naked, cock out and plumped up from fear. Ridiculously, instinct whipped both his hands across to cover his genitals, and Will's grin became more genuine.

A phone rang again.

Tom whipped back to the still-open doorway, hands falling from their protective cup, but he realized that the sound was coming, not from the bedroom, but from Will's phone, lying on the white marble top of the island.

Tom turned and gazed at it, then him, with huge, horrified eyes.

Will picked it up and glanced at the display. He said stoically, "It's Des."

Time then. Tom had to face it. Will's expression was fierce as he raised one finger to his lips and pressed it there in warning. Like the car.

"Des. How're you doing, mate?" Will pushed a button and laid the phone carefully on the island tabletop.

"Ach ye know," Des said from the speaker. Des's full Ballymena dialect was in play, as Tom remembered it had always tended to be around Will. Possibly, because Des trusted him that much. "'Bout ye, Guv?"

"Oh. Fine."

Des sounded in a buoyant mood. Tom couldn't help but feel betrayed by that.

"You at home?" Des asked.

"Uh…yep." Will sounded relaxed somehow.

"Good," Des returned. The doorbell rang. "I'm at the front door."

Tom drew in a sharp, terrified breath.

Will ended the call, and Tom could see the effort he was making to conceal anything other than absolute calm. Will said, "Go and get dressed."

Tom obediently raced back to the bedroom and behind him he heard Will head for the front door. He shut himself in and pulled on clothes from his bag, hearing voices, then nothing, as they moved to the living room or the kitchen.

When he was dressed, he slipped back into the hall and stopped for a second, listening. The voices were in the kitchen.

The kitchen door had been left half-open, and Tom could Des's strident voice clearly as he crept to hide behind it.

"...like that slate on the floor. An' the extension an' all...you've really transformed it, Guv."

"Thanks, mate. You still take milk?"

There was a short silence as, Tom had to assume, coffee was presented.

Then Des said with dry economy, "Ye'll have heard all about Max Perry. Since ye were at the scene an' all."

Will sighed loudly enough for Tom to hear him. "Yep."

"Is Tom here?"

Tom put his hand over his mouth. "Nope, sorry," Will said. "Haven't seen him since we gave our statements yesterday."

God. He was lying to the police as well. Tom wondered if Will had ever even considered doing it before.

"Aye, well." Des sounded unperturbed. "Ingham at South Ken had to give Perry to the gaffer. She didn't have a hope of holdin' on, mind. Perry's number three. That makes it a serial."

Tom's trembling hand pressed harder against his mouth. *Serial.* He stared at a knot in one of the polished floorboards in the hallway.

"I gave a statement there, Des," Will said curtly. "I don't have any more information."

Des laughed. "Guv, I'm the one with the info. I just thought ye'd like to know we got the bastard."

Tom heard Will's stunned, "You *got* him?"

"Oh aye," Des crowed. "He wasn't as clever as he thought. Nothin' anywhere else, washed the wine glasses, but the eejit left a print on the label of the bottle. They all fuck up sometime."

"Who is it?" Will asked. Hushed, as if he didn't quite dare to believe it.

Tom felt exactly the same, the gush of incredulous relief leaving him nauseous.

A miracle. At the eleventh hour.

"Peter Brownley," Des enunciated. "The gaffer's off to lift him right now. I found I had a vital errand, and I somehow mysteriously ended up in Leyton."

For a merciful second or two, the name meant nothing. Then realization hit. Tom burst through the kitchen door. "No! Des. *No!*"

"Ah, so ye're there after all, Tom," Des said, unperturbed, as he turned to greet Tom's explosive entrance. "Now there's a wee surprise." He'd positioned himself between the door and the island unit, coffee mug in hand. Will, behind the island, looked resigned.

"Actually," Des went on. "We've been closing in on him since we managed to trace the IP of the computer that sent the hate mail to Mrs. Haining. It was in Echo's offices."

Tom struggled to parse it out. How could it be over, and still be worse?

"You've been investigating *Pez* all this time and not me?"

"Aye well…" Des ran an awkward hand over his ginger hair. "Not till yesterday, to be honest. The VPN company…Foxy…finally gave us the IP address. Then SOCO came through on the Perry crime scene. An' Brownley doesn't have alibis for any of the murders."

"That's not true!" Tom exclaimed. "Pez was *my* alibi for Catriona's death!"

"Ah, but he wasn't." Des waved his mug at him. "You told us. He went off and left ye in the club. When we checked up, some people thought they saw ye, cuz ye're…memorable, though there wasn't a definitive ID. But Brownley told us he was with you all night."

"He'd have been *trying* to protect me." Tom groaned. Hadn't Nick said they should all lie to help Tom? Only—Tom, in his aggressively confident innocence, hadn't lied, and he hadn't thought to tell Pez not to. "This is Pez! You *know* he wouldn't hurt a fly."

Des raised an eyebrow. "Aye, that's what the guy said in Psycho. Look, Tom. Apart from the performance at yer office, yeah? I met him a few times when you were…you know…with the Guv. An' to be honest, he seemed to be angry all the time. Hiding it behind that bitchy-queen act." Des look at his mug then back at Tom. "He wanted you, an' he hated the Guv. Any eejit could see that."

Or, Tom thought resentfully, Des was extrapolating from the night Pez and Tom had staged their treacherous kiss.

Tom turned desperate eyes to Will, but Will's expression had closed.

"Ye know the boss had an Assistant Commissioner in to see him yesterday," Des said nonchalantly. "To tell him *Max Perry* should be the prime suspect." He snorted. Tom spotted Will's quick grimace, behind Des's back. "The gaffer's thrilled she made an arse of herself. He's not a fan. Anyway. Tom. How'd ye like a wee lift to the station?"

"The station?" Tom repeated. He sounded out of it.

"The gaffer'd like a wee word," Des said, but his tone gentled. "As a witness."

"He'll be in later," Will said flatly. "And he'll have a lawyer with him."

Des whirled round in protest. "But I told you he's not a…"

"He's not setting foot inside Lawson's station again without a brief, Des."

Des gave a showy sigh. "Ach, ye're still a mother hen. All right. It's your money, Tom. How soon can I tell the boss you'll be in?"

"I don't have to go with you now?" Tom asked.

"What d'ye mean? I'm not here. I'm phonin' ye."

Tom gave a pale smile of gratitude. "An hour or two?" he asked.

"Grand," said Des. "An' after that it'll be over."

24

"Pez didn't do it," Tom said the moment Lawson and Salt came through the door of the interview room, both carrying blue cardboard folders. Beside Tom, Mark Nimmo shifted discreetly, which was the interview room equivalent of an elbow in the side.

Mark had told him forcefully in station reception how he was meant to deal with the interview: "I know he's your friend but he's also the *only* reason Lawson hasn't got you in the cells on a triple murder charge. So *my* advice—in this position—is to say as little as you can get away with and do *not* question the arrest."

Lawson didn't speak as he sat down. Des raised a meaningful brow at Tom and switched on the recording device.

"So you don't think Peter did it, Mr. Gray?" Lawson asked jovially after they all identified themselves. Tom was "Mr. Gray" again then. Pez was the one now without respect. Lawson sounded as if he were humoring a child, or a fractious old lady. "'Ave you got something to confess?"

Mark very pointedly cleared his throat. It meant: *Told you so.* Or: *Shut the fuck up.* Probably both.

"No," Tom said quickly. "But I know Pez, Chief Inspector." His knee started to bounce. "He's straightforward. He's a loudmouth! He'd never in a million years get involved in anything like this!"

Mark kicked Tom's ankle under the table. He flinched and barely contained a yelp.

"You've known Peter, 'ow long?" Lawson asked.

"Three years." Tom ran a hand back through his hair. "He's my best friend as well as my first agent. I *know* him!"

Lawson made an acknowledging movement of his head. "I see." His mouth set in a tight, considering purse. "Peter has admitted to sending 'ate mail and unpleasant objects to Mrs. 'Aining."

It took seconds to sink in then Tom said, very sure, "He's lying. He's trying to protect me because he must think…"

"As you can see, Chief Inspector," Mark said smoothly. "Mr. Gray is in some distress at this news. Perhaps we should recess to…"

"No!" Tom snapped. "It's fine."

"Peter knew the contents of emails we 'adn't revealed to anyone outside the investigation," Lawson went on. "And he knew the identity of most of the objects posted through Mrs. 'Aining's letterbox." Lawson raised his eyebrows. "It was 'im, Mr. Gray."

Tom gave an agonized moan. "But…*why*? Did he say why?"

Lawson sounded almost avuncular. "He claims he was motivated by love." His voice hardened. "Funny kind of love. Did you know he has strong feelings for you?"

"I…" Tom pressed an anguished palm against his forehead, but he couldn't bring himself to answer. *Jesus, Pez!* How terrified must he be? "Has he admitted to murder though?" he asked desperately.

Lawson gave him a narrow look but didn't say a word.

No, then. And Lawson had transferred his conviction that Catriona's harasser had to be her murderer from Tom straight to Pez.

"Why's Pez saying any of this stuff? Shouldn't he be…remaining silent?" Tom turned to Mark. "He should have a lawyer!"

Mark, after a ruffled second, said, "Mr. Haining hired my boss. But not before Mr. Brownley agreed to be interviewed by the Detective Chief Inspector here, without legal counsel."

"Peter said he wanted to get his story on record," Lawson said with an innocent smile. And Tom knew that without Mark, that would have been him. Lawson would have thrown away the key after Lily's murder, and if Max hadn't been killed the same way, he'd never have looked any further. "Peter *claims* the reason he harassed Mrs. 'Aining was because you weren't listening to him when he urged you to end your relationship with her 'usband. He said, you kept saying you would, but you didn't. He thought you were bein' manipulated to settle with Mr. 'Aining an' ruin your career. So he acted in desperation. To save you from yourself."

Tom regarded him with silent shock.

Lawson looked satisfied. "Catriona Haining already 'ated you and was trying to get her 'usband back. Peter was sure she'd never come to us to avoid a scandal damaging her business, but he thought she'd show her 'usband an' he'd leave you in disgust. Then everything would go back to normal, because they'd never kick you out of the agency. Or you could leave together."

"I…that's…*ridiculous*." Tom sounded dazed; he could hear that himself.

"Mr. Brownley didn't think so," Lawson said precisely. "There have been three linked murders. Catriona 'Aining, Lily Adderton and Max Perry. They're all individuals who crossed you."

In his peripheral vision, Tom saw Mark straighten in his chair.

Lawson continued, "I 'ad thought that pointed to your door. But I think Peter got frustrated and scared. Catriona didn't tell her 'usband. She told her friend Lily. An' Lily was urgin' her to report you to us. It's in her emails. When Catriona died, Lily was out of control. And then there's Perry… In your statement at the murder scene, you said he drugged, assaulted and stalked you." Lawson eyed Tom with something approaching curiosity as he dealt the killer blow. "It was all for you, Mr. Gray."

Tom's throat prickled, but he would not allow these men to see his tears. "No," he said definitely.

"I think he wanted to protect you. In his own way."

And God, Tom thought, that did sound like Pez. "Even if he did harass Catriona," he said desperately. "There's no proof he killed anyone."

"He had access to Mrs. 'Aining's username and password, so he could leave the fake suicide note. His print was at Max Perry's murder scene. *And* he's diabetic," Lawson finished. "That would put insulin at the front of his mind for murder."

"No. Pez isn't capable of killing anyone," Tom said with certainty. "And he wouldn't play…sick games like these murders… And the mutilations… The cat! He's squeamish about things like that!"

"One thing I've learned doing this job, Mr. Gray…" Lawson said. "Is that we never really know anybody." Tom stared at him, speechless at last. Lawson asked, "Did you and Dr. Carys Rolfe have any kind of misunderstanding Peter knew about?"

Tom said, horrified, "No!" Didn't that put a hole in the theory? But Lawson shrugged.

"Is Dr. Rolfe all right?" Tom asked, subdued.

"She was lucky," Lawson said. "He misjudged the amount of chloroform needed to keep her unconscious long enough for the other drugs to work. An' bein' a doctor, she knew what to do. Her memory's 'azy but we're 'opeful it'll come back."

Tom didn't say anything.

"You've been investigating parallel to us." Lawson didn't mention Will, but Tom knew that was the root of his question. "You 'ad no suspicion Peter was behind it?"

Tom closed his eyes. "No. And I still don't believe it." Then, "What'll happen to him now?"

"Peter has been remanded in custody pending further investigation," Lawson reeled off.

"Can I see him?" Tom asked quickly.

"We don't allow visitors in police custody suites," Lawson said. "The best thing you can do Mr. Gray, is go 'ome. And thank God it's done."

•••

For the first time since the case began, Will had ventured into Southwark police station. When Tom and Mark were shown out into reception from the station interior, he was sitting waiting. And beside him—faithful, constant Nick who'd never left Tom to face any of this alone.

Will, Nick and Jena; Hansen, James Henderson and Tom. They'd created their own little secret society, leaving Pez on the outside.

Tom thought about the string of texts on his phone from the last few days, most of them unanswered.

"How did it go?" Will asked.

"Apart from the fact he kept trying to fall on his sword," Mark said with acid economy. "Fine."

Tom glared at him with agitated frustration. Because, yes, Tom may have been reckless in Mark's eyes, but how could he listen to those claims about Pez without saying something?

"How long can they keep him?" he asked.

Mark shrugged. "Twenty-four hours, but they can apply for an extension since it's a serious crime. Something to remember, Tom. Pez may be denying the rest, but he *admitted* harassing Mrs. Haining, pretending to be you."

Nick made a startled sound.

Mark went on relentlessly, "He allowed you to become the prime suspect in a murder investigation. Bear that in mind while you're agonizing."

Mark spoke as impatiently and tactlessly as if Tom were a tiresome child—a different man from the impervious, glib professional Tom had first met. He wasn't acting. And that realization brought with it renewed sharp suspicion that maybe Mark was angry with Tom because of Will. Because Will really was more than a buddy fuck to him.

But then again—what Mark had said was true. Tom was trying not to look at what Pez *had* admitted to doing. Not while Pez was being accused of serial murder.

When Mark left, Tom, Nick and Will walked to the same café as they'd used after Tom's last interview, and Tom filled them both in. What Pez had admitted. What Lawson believed. What Lawson still didn't seem to know. When Tom trailed off to silence, Will went outside to make a phone call to Hansen.

"Ask her to help him," Tom pleaded as Will left the table.

Nick and he sat then, in fragile silence, until Tom broke it.

"Thanks for getting him a lawyer," he said.

Nick shrugged. "It's Pez." But he looked shell-shocked. "I just...I can't believe he'd deliberately harass and frighten Cat. Just to break us up...you and me? I had no idea he hated me that much."

"He doesn't hate you," Tom said tiredly. He could see, though, that Nick didn't believe him.

They sat for another silent moment or two, then Nick ventured, "At least you don't have to be scared anymore." He laid his hand over Tom's on the pale green tabletop. "Did you sleep?"

Tom flashed back on the night before. Like some physical prod to his conscience, his arse twinged. "A bit."

Nick sighed with resignation. "You went back to your flat, didn't you? Despite everything." *I know you did*, his tone said.

Tom cleared his throat. He wanted to be honest. "I went to Will's."

He glanced up in time to catch a flash of feeling on Nick's face, but Tom had no wish to understand it.

The bell on the door jangled, and Will came back into the café. It took all Tom's willpower not to wrench his hand away from Nick's.

Will slid into the booth beside Nick. "She's okay with it." Tom saw his glance at their joined hands.

And then Tom understood what he'd said, and he did pull back his hand, in outrage.

"*Okay* with it?" he repeated. "But Pez knows nothing about the Babes in Arms *or* who Nick is! And the murders were committed to mimic..." The tight expression on Will's face finally got through to him. He trailed off. "She doesn't care, does she? She doesn't care so long as Nick keeps his anonymity, and her part in it stays secret. So long as the *Justice* Ministry isn't exposed to scrutiny."

Will said carefully, "There are good reasons stalkers and harassers are looked at first in cases like this. She's ready to accept that Pez may have found out about Nick and Catriona's past. She's going to try for a plea deal. A reduced term in return for...for Pez's silence."

"Twenty-five years instead of thirty?" Tom parroted venomously. "Pez won't even know what he's promising to stay quiet about. He didn't fucking *know*!"

"But Catriona knew," Nick said shakily. "She trusted Pez. She was close to him, even though he was your friend. If he got her drunk... That's must be how he got her password. And if she got really drunk and upset, she could have told him out of spite."

"But Pez said they *weren't* close," Tom countered, but it sounded plaintive, like a child unable to believe he'd been lied to. He felt betrayed. "And...what about the Rolfes? What motive would he have for hurting them?"

"Only Pez knows that," Nick said. He played compulsively with his mug, twisting it back and fore on the tabletop. "Maybe...Cat told him how Dr. Rolfe's husband died. Maybe that gave him the idea in the first place."

Tom stared at him with hurt disbelief. "You think he's guilty!"

"I don't *know*." Nick's mouth twisted. "His confession has thrown me, I admit that. Look, I just know I'm glad it's not you in there. I thought today...that might be it."

So had Tom. But the price for taking away that burden was too high. "Will," he pleaded. "You don't think...?"

"I need to run some background on Pez," Will said. Tom couldn't read his expression. "See if there were any previous instances of extreme behavior."

"I've put out feelers to sell the business," Nick said.

"What?" Tom breathed. Another shock, though this one felt like a pinprick compared with all the other blows that had landed.

"I thought...if I have to expose my identity, or someone exposes me, it'd be best to be ready."

Well. It was the logical thing to do. But stupidly, Tom hadn't expected it so soon.

In any event, he didn't have time to brood. "Can I come with you?" he asked Will.

"Tom!" Nick's tone was sharp. "You have the Boss shoot this afternoon."

Tom eyed him with disbelief. "How the *fuck* can I...?" He met Will's neutral eyes across the table.

"Come on, baby!" Nick said bracingly. "You haven't let any of this push you off-course. You have to keep going."

Will began tapping numbers into his phone, as if he was trying to give them privacy.

"If Pez goes to jail for murder and Echo gets sold off, I'll be more than off-course," Tom snapped.

Nick sighed. "I may not have to sell." He didn't mention the fact that Pez's conviction would spare him exposure and save Echo. "But…you can go to any agency out there." He smiled. "And…whatever happens, I'll be right with you. Backing you all the way." He put his hand on top of Tom's again and squeezed tight.

Tom couldn't stand it.

He couldn't stand the too-familiar weight of gratitude for Nick's loyalty. Couldn't stand the even more naggingly familiar feeling that all he'd achieved…all he was vying for…was trivial, now he'd had his nose rubbed in bloody life and death.

But his career was—deliberately—the focus of his being. How could he deny that?

He looked desperately at Will, still on the phone, but Will didn't look back. He was listening, smiling to the person at the other end of his call, and by the way that smile tugged uneasily at Tom's gut, he thought it was likely a conversation with Pixie. Or Mark, perhaps. Tom loathed his own useless, compulsive jealousy along with everything else.

His old phone,which Des had handed back to him, beeped quietly to a new text. The number gave no clues to the author, so he pulled his hand from under Nick's again and opened it.

This is my new number. I had to change it. Alistair won't stop messaging and calling. You really should take him in hand. It's embarrassing. Richard and I'll be in Monte Carlo for the rest of the month. Saw you in French Vogue yesterday. Kiss kiss. Anya.

Anya. Angela Gray, actually. But like everything else in his mother's life, her name hadn't been glamorous enough to be acceptable. He read the message again carefully, allowing the old rush of empathetic humiliation for his father to sweep him along, stronger today than it had been since he was fourteen years old, watching his dad impaled on the dagger of unreturned adoration.

Tom had honestly thought himself inured to it by time and weary experience. But his mum's message, at this precise moment, just like the news on the Armani contract—came like a nudge from the cosmos. Maybe someone up there was looking out for him.

He fumbled the text closed. But as he was backing out of the app, he spotted an unread message which must have come in while he was in the interview room.

GQ cover's looking nailed on since Armani word got out! SO proud of you. You're the name on everyone's lips! Champagne dinner on me when you get here. We'll get you boozed enough to see sense and come to mama. WAIT till you see the apartment Juana scoped out for you. Bring your fucking cat. XOXO

Melanie's timing was once again impeccable.

Tom reread the message—the routine push to move to New York, but with more "not taking no for an answer" determination.

Just over a week ago, his answer *would* have been no. But in the space of that week, all Tom's professional and emotional certainties had crumbled around him.

No one close to him in London remained untainted. There was no one here he could trust anymore with the person he needed to be. Nowhere he could feel safe.

And in London, a killer seemed to have targeted his sickness on him. Maybe that killer was even his best friend. Or he could still be out there, pulling his strings.

So how would he react if Tom just…removed himself from the game?

New York really could be the answer—to that and everything else—a new start, a new stage, away from the emotional carnage of his life in London. An escape from the mess of entanglement and obligation smeared over his commitments at Echo. From the insidious, undermining need for Will.

Tom was going to New York anyway in a couple of days for the Armani contract. He could go with the intention of signing that apartment lease. Get John shipped over; get someone to pack up his flat and ship his stuff too. He could help Pez as much from New York as from London.

His sudden sense of wild relief told him everything. It was like finally spotting an exit from a trap.

He looked up.

First things first.

"All right," he said to Nick. "Can you get someone to text me the details."

He didn't look at Will.

25

It was probably the worst shoot Tom had ever done. Worse even than the last one.

Normally he could focus on the mechanics of it. On what Bill, the very successful photographer, wanted—though in this case, Bill obviously wanted into the knickers of Pearl, the female model, while she in turn, was all over Marcos, the second male model. At least the drama allowed Tom to keep largely to himself.

But he sat through hair and makeup in a fog, and when the shoot began, he couldn't seem to pull it back.

They were on location for the shoot in Whitechapel in the East End in various evocative locations. Bill had managed to resist the Whitechapel cliché of Jack the Ripper's old stomping grounds and went with other iconography in an area heaving with life and color: Brick Lane, packed end to end with Bangladeshi curry houses; the Blind Beggar Pub where notorious gangster Ronnie Kray had gunned down a rival gang member in the sixties, to enter pop culture with his twin, Reggie; the frontage of the one-time Whitechapel Bell Foundry where the Liberty bell was struck; Petticoat Lane markets.

Bill's crew, Tom, and the other two models, slogged round his list of locations obediently.

Tom and Marcos, apart from their compulsory likeness in physique were opposites in looks. Marcos was Portuguese, and had short, black hair, a darkly tanned complexion and stubble. Pearl was English—the requisite height and very thin aristocratic and blonde. Pearl and Marcos were both quite new, and this was a huge shoot for them. But though Tom was unquestionably the star name, he was aware Pearl might well be earning more than him for the afternoon's work. It had long since stopped bothering him.

It wasn't a demanding shoot, other than the location changes, multiple setups and gawping passersby, but Tom, however hard he tried to fix his concentration on the job, found himself glazing over. Thinking about Pez. The increasingly compelling idea of moving to New York. Nick. The unsolved case. Will. The appalling suspicion that as much as he needed Pez to be innocent, part of him secretly also wished he were guilty, because then Tom could stop being afraid.

At least no one could see his eyes behind the designer sunglasses he was trying to sell.

His love and fear for Pez gnawed at him constantly, but they warred with his disbelieving disgust at what Pez had admitted. And since Nick had voiced his doubts, inconvenient memories kept pushing through, like insidious little parasites worming their way into his brain.

Pez—constantly nagging him to end his relationship with Nick, as he'd nagged him to leave Will. Himself, dragging his heels in the scarred aftermath of Will, letting Nick sink deeper into his life for comfort, without ever actively making a choice. Pez's furious frustration with him.

The day after Catriona's death, Pez using her end and the police pursuing Tom for Pez's actions—to push him again to leave Nick.

That first day at Greens, Pez pointing them toward Max as someone who'd set Tom up, instead of coming clean.

And the cruelty of the harassment campaign when Pez must have known how vulnerable Catriona was if he was close to her.

If Pez could do all that…

"That's great," Bill said loudly, his accent pure Essex. He'd posed Tom, Pearl and Marcos together outside a Jewish bagel shop. "Give me something enigmatic, Tom. Yeah, lovely! Make me wonder what's going on behind those shades! Pearl, sweetheart, that is *beautiful*. Chin up a bit and to the right. Yeah! Marcos, try to give me *something*."

Tom thought, when he glimpsed some of the shots on Bill's laptop as they prepared to up sticks for the Blind Beggar Pub, that all three of them looked pissed off and superior. But Bill saw moody and aspirational, so that was all right.

Tom texted Will in his first brief break, because he couldn't help himself.

Just like Dad, he thought with disgust, but at least, unlike his father, Tom was forcing himself to stop.

Find anything? he sent.

The answer came as he waited at the saloon bar inside the Blind Beggar, the actual scene of the 1960s murder. The room was lit by huge, ornate chandeliers hanging from a glossy, blood-red ceiling, and the walls were pale and red brick. For this shot, he was alone.

Nothing so far, Will replied.

When the time came Tom leaned on the dark wood bar, with his arm propped on an elbow in front of him, hand held up casually, displaying a watch with a huge face and a light-brown leather strap. On the wall in the background, Bill had included Kray memorabilia in the shot.

"Something different this time, Tom, yeah?" Without his lust for Pearl, or his resentment of Marcos, Bill was professional with Tom. "Show me peaceful. Like you found the secret to happiness, and it told you to buy this watch. Channel the last time you felt content."

Tom's mind went at once, treacherously, to the night before. Waiting for the axe to fall, but still—his head had rested on Will's chest, listening to the steady thump-thump of his heart and he'd been…happy.

"Oh yeah, baby," Bill crooned. "Exactly that."

•••

He had an excuse. A valid excuse. But Tom wasn't sure whom it was aimed at.

Will or himself. Who was he trying to fool?

While he watched Marcos being set up for an eyewear shot outside the Bell Foundry, Tom pulled out his phone and texted before his conscience could talk him out of it.

I have to get John. Or can I stay over again? Maybe not a good idea to go home. Plus I need to talk to you.

When Tom left him that morning, John had been in the kitchen, sleeping on the sun-warmed slate floor, completely at home. And as Tom sat in a foldaway chair by the side of the set, watching Bill bully Marcos for daring to be more attractive to Pearl, he let himself drift to thoughts of the house. The kitchen with its big glass doors into the garden, the lounge with that long, squishy sofa he could stretch out on, the bedroom with its walls of Purbeck Stone, and he felt a longing so acute it could almost be homesickness.

He thought of Will—the dangerous flutter of wild joy and safety he always inspired.

If Tom were a different person, he could welcome it all.

But he wasn't a different person. He was fucked-up, neurotic Tom Gray, and he was going to leave his feelings for Will Foster far behind where they couldn't control him. Bury them deep again before they ruined him. The way obsessions did.

His phone beeped.

You'll need a key. Where are you now?

"Won the lottery?" Pearl's bored drawl drew his attention with reluctance from the phone screen. She sat in the canvas chair next to him, huge light-green eyes fixed on him with the attitude of someone so bored that any distraction would do, even talking to another model she didn't expect to bone.

Tom looked at her quizzically.

"The way you were looking at your phone…" she explained. Then a thought visibly struck her, and her lethargic try at interest flipped to avidity. "Did you get a new job? Something big?"

Tom flashed an enigmatic smile. Since the only thing she thought worth excitement was a big contract, he could see his standing with her had risen further. And suddenly he envied her fiercely. He wanted so badly to get back that uncomplicated greed for success.

He sent his location and rough finish time to Will, then waited, insides squirming with tension, for a reply.

Text me when you're almost finished. I'll come and get you.

The rest of the shoot went in a blur, and by just after five they were back at Bill's studios—also in Whitechapel. As the cork popped on the first bottle of Prosecco, Tom made his excuses and darted outside to meet Will, scrubbing off his makeup with a wipe as he went. And his trepidation was easily overwhelmed by that old unkillable excitement.

Will's lips twitched as Tom got into the Passat, and without comment he reached across Tom's body to pull down the passenger's sun visor. In the little mirror, Tom's face was patched and streaked with foundation, like beige warpaint, and his mascara and kohl eyeliner were blotched round his eyes. Still without saying anything, Will pulled open the passenger glove compartment to display a whole packet of wet wipes inside.

Tom laughed and began to wipe, and the drive to Leyton passed in companionable silence. Tom knew that if Will had found anything on Pez, or the case, he'd have told him at once. So he indulged himself imagining, just for the length of that drive, that this was his life, going home with Will after work the way so many couples did. The way he and Will had done a few times when they were together and Tom had been working in London. It was pure masochism.

John was vocally pleased to see them, and while Tom fed him, Will went to get changed. From there, the evening mirrored the one before. Will cooked an Italian dish his mum had taught him this time, they watched TV and went to bed. The epitome of dull suburban life. And Tom relished every second, as he secretly had all the times he'd been with Will for real. It felt to him as if both of them were playing bittersweet roles that evening, of how it might have been.

In a way, it was like the night before had been, but this time, he wasn't indulging himself with the fantasy that he had the courage to choose this, given the chance. He'd lost that ability long before he met Will.

He was well aware, of course, that he wasn't coming out of Will's return to his life unscathed. Maybe…the shiny things he'd used to distract himself before this couldn't shine for him the same way. Maybe he'd no longer be able to convince himself they made him happy. But at least his distractions were controllable and safe. And he'd always keep his pride and his independence. That was all he'd needed or wanted, since he was a kid.

He followed Will to his bedroom without discussion, when the time came. Will didn't ask him what it meant or what he'd wanted to talk about or where they stood. He seemed willing to take it on its own terms. Tom was certain that he knew there was no future for them.

They each undressed themselves like a couple comfortable with each other, then slid naked into bed from their own sides. Tom didn't hesitate to wriggle across at once to hug Will, wasting not a second in maneuvering back into that position he loved, head on Will's broad chest.

They lay in silence for a while, and Tom wondered if they'd just slide into sleep like that. Just…rest together.

But he couldn't stand that. It was time for truth.

"I told you I needed to talk," Tom said at last. His voice was soft. He was glad he didn't have to look at Will as he told him everything. "I wanted to tell you myself. I'm…going to go to New York, Will. Permanently. My flight's booked for a big shoot the day after tomorrow, and I don't… I'm not planning to come back unless it's for…work. Now and then." Tom could feel under his cheek the moment Will tensed. The moment he let it go.

"What about the case?" Will asked mildly. Tom could feel his eyes filling already. How many goodbyes had he said to him now? And every one felt more like amputation.

"I'll pay for the best defence for Pez. But…I want you to let the case go, Will." Tom didn't dare raise his head to look at him. "I can't stand the thought of you taking any more risks when I'm gone. If the killer isn't Pez…I'm afraid for you if you get too close."

Will sounded very careful when he said, "*If?* You were sure it wasn't him this morning. You wanted me to keep going. You'd leave Pez in jail on multiple murder charges? Though you don't believe…"

"Christ, Will! You make it sound like I can change it! Like *you* can! As if either of us can stop it, when it feels like all we've done is make things worse. Whoever the killer is…I think we've done everything he wanted us to. Except this. Except—this pawn removing itself from the game."

Will didn't say anything. That interview technique of his, Tom reminded himself.

"I know you think I'm just running away and maybe…maybe that's what it is. But I'm doing nothing here but walk into every trap he sets. I just hope the bastard didn't put the care into framing Pez for murder that he put into framing me."

Silence. Then Will said, "Yeah. Maybe it's wise. If Pez didn't do it, it'll be safer."

Honesty.

"It's not just the case. I'm destroyed about Pez. Echo's probably done for, one way or another. Nick has to stop living his life for me when he's never going to get what he wants. And…"

Will must have felt the increased tension in every inch of his body.

You. Most of all. I have to get away from you. He might as well have said it aloud.

"I'm sorry," Tom said softly. "I just…I can't be with anyone, Will. I'm…a lost cause."

The last thing he expected to feel was Will's hand rise to gently stroke his hair, and the compassion in the touch almost finished him. His eyes were blurred with tears he wouldn't shed, as he gazed out across Will's chest into the lamplit gloom.

"You're just afraid, Tom," Will said at last. He sounded exhausted. "You hurt yourself to try to prevent being hurt. But it is what it is. It's your business now not mine."

"What if you got bored?" Tom blurted out.

"Bored?" Will asked. "With what?"

"With me." Christ, he sounded pathetic... But Tom pressed on blindly. "If you ever..."

If you decided I wasn't enough...what would I do? How could I recover from that?

Will didn't manage even the semblance of surprise.

"I know," he said. "It's not your career. Your career's just somewhere you hide. It's your mum and dad. You've allowed your whole life to be defined by them. To see love as obsession and loss."

Tom opened his mouth to deny it. But he'd let his guard down.

"I won't be him," he said.

"So you're her instead," Will returned softly.

The insight shamed Tom beyond bearing. The selfishness of what drove him.

In his defensive panic when he'd left Will, he'd refused to acknowledge that he was doing what his mother did to his father, before Will could think of doing it to him.

And Nick...Pez...

Tom stared at the curtained window across from him. He squeezed his eyes closed.

He understood then that Will had given up on him, maybe a long time ago. Maybe when he'd seen that Tom was too damaged and afraid to bank on. The moments they'd had together since they met again had been the last spasms of a corpse.

It was what he'd needed to happen, but still, the sense of loss was unbearable.

He heaved himself up onto his elbow and leaned urgently over Will, and the odd innocence of Will's startled reaction inflamed him. Tom kissed him with all his loss and want, and after a moment of surprised adjustment, Will kissed back. It blinked into desperation in a second.

Will's arms came up to pull him tight against him, as their tongues did slick, velvet battle. Tom made himself pull back to pant, "You want to?"

One for the road.

He thought Will would push him away in disgust but to his surprise Will instead gave a slow, frowning nod, and that was enough to dive back at once into the kiss.

Tom's attention was so much on the feel of Will's slippery tongue in his mouth, his soft, full lips, that he was barely aware that he was rubbing his aching shaft urgently against the hard silk skin of Will's hip.

He wanted to devour him.

He tore his mouth away.

It felt no different, and yet entirely different, from the last time. It felt like everything—the same insane, incendiary reaction he always had to Will, overshadowed by the sure knowledge that the clock was ticking, but this time all the responsibility was his alone.

Will's eyes looked dark and liquid in the lamplight, but he didn't say anything, as if he knew it was pointless. He hooked a hand round Tom's neck instead and pulled him in for another kiss.

Tom almost fought against it, his mind roaming restlessly around all that they'd said—the background riff of imminent loss—but instead he surrendered and rolled on top of Will until simple sensation blurred everything out.

Will's hands slid hungrily up and down the length of his back, the dip of his waist, the steep swell of his buttocks.

Eventually Tom had to pull back for air, and because his aching cock felt ready to spurt, molten lust thrumming in his balls and his belly and his thighs.

He looked down at Will's face, eyes shut, body moving restlessly underneath him, and he wanted all of it for himself this last time. Will's pleasure, Will's thoughts, Will's focus. Will.

The possessiveness that he'd never succeeded in nailing away.

"Can I have you?" he breathed into Will's flushed cheek, then pulled back to see.

Will's eyes sprang open. His pupils had almost consumed his pale hazel irises, and he looked vulnerable as Will so rarely was.

Because there was a finality to this. No ifs, or maybes. No reprieves.

"The stuff's in the bedside drawer on your side," Will said hoarsely.

Tom stroked his cheek, desperate to give comfort, but Will closed his eyes again, and when Tom rolled off him to reach the bedside cabinet, Will rolled too, onto his front away from him. Tom pulled back to look, taking in his wide, well-muscled back, the curve of his sculpted arse, that flawlessly smooth olive skin, his thick, silky dark hair. Tom thought Will would always be the most beautiful man he'd ever know.

He'd always loved to see Will's face, the moment Tom took him—another memory chucked into the pit to bury.

But Tom couldn't blame Will for wanting to make this as impersonal as he could. Plain, simple sex.

But it wasn't.

"Will? Are you sure you want this?" His voice sounded thick with tears. Not exactly sexy. But though Will didn't look back at him, he nodded his head definitely on the pillow.

Tom forced himself to savor it. He spent a long time kissing over Will's shoulders and down his spine to the dimples at the base, into the dip at his waist. Will tried to stay still underneath him, but Tom bit the smooth skin of his arse, marking him, staying away from the cleft, until Will began to writhe under him.

Finally, he pulled the full smooth cheeks apart and licked in, absorbing the musky smell, the bitter taste.

"Fuck!" Will jerked with shock and tried to pull away. "I haven't showered!"

"I want to taste you," Tom said thickly. "And smell you and feel you."

And memorize you.

Tom lowered his head again to begin a slow torment with his tongue, licking and tickling until any taste was gone. Then he circled the tip round Will's anus, small and pink and tight, coaxing and pushing with his tongue until he got inside.

By the time he lifted his head, Will was quivering under him like a dog ready to hunt. But Tom took his time preparing him with his fingers, generous quantities of lube.

When Will was ready Tom slid up the length of his body to cover it with his own, the smoothness of his chest rubbing sensuously against the equally smooth skin of Will's back, his erection stroking damply in the cleft of his arse.

He kissed the back of Will's ear, the side of his cheek, all he could see of his face. But Will's eyes remained closed.

Tom slid on a condom carefully, afraid that any touch might make him shoot before he could get near Will's arse. He pulled Will up on to all fours.

Will's head hung low between his shoulders. His braced arms hid any expression, but Tom saw with relief that his cock was hard, hanging almost parallel to his stomach.

Tom shuffled into position, erection held in his hand, and rubbed the head tantalizingly against Will's hole. Then he began to push inside, gently at first, then harder, and at that moment Will pushed impatiently back. It happened all at once.

"Will..." A helpless kind of whine, as his cock slid relentlessly in.

Tom began to fuck, sliding his cock in and out, in and out of the dark, clenching perfection of Will's arse, trying to angle his thrusts, picking up speed, as Will pushed back hungrily to meet him. And the sight of it—watching it—was almost too erotic to bear.

He bent over Will's hunched body and tried to reach under him to grasp his cock, but Will batted his hand away, and he didn't have the mental capacity to argue. Already he felt too close, hands digging hard into Will's hips as he fucked, knowing he was leaving finger bruises. Glad of it.

He tried to make it last but Will squeezed his arse muscles deliberately, and released—squeezed again—and the massage of rippling, velvety muscle on Tom's bursting shaft felt so insanely good that he knew he couldn't go on.

"Will," he groaned in warning. "You gotta stop that or I'm gonna come."

But Will panted, "Come then." And Tom couldn't have held it back if he'd had a knife at his throat. He began to shoot into the condom, driven so high he felt as if he were having a stroke—loving that this was Will, wishing he could plant his seed.

When he came round from his sex daze though, draped over Will's back, sated penis still embedded in his arse, he understood at once from the quivering tension in the body still holding his up, that Will hadn't come.

He groped round underneath Will's braced body to try to help, but again his hand was batted away.

"Pull out," Will ordered. He sounded as if his teeth were gritted, at the end of his tether.

"Will?" Tom ventured. With dawning horror, "Did I hurt you?" He backed away, dragging out his sated cock, as he held on to the condom, scanning it anxiously for blood.

The second he was free, Will twisted round and pushed him flat onto the bed, on his back.

"I want to finish inside you," Will announced without emotion. He stretched over Tom's body to extract another condom from the bedside drawer.

Tom stared up at the picture he made.

Will's muscular body glistened with sweat, his cock looked huge and scarlet, balls drawn up tight. He looked like a fantasy man.

One to remember, his treacherous mind threw in.

"Over you go," Will said, and Tom understood with a lurch of pain that Will still didn't want to have see his face. So he rolled over onto his stomach, and let Will at it.

Will was efficient this time. He didn't talk or coax or praise; it was as if Tom were someone he didn't know. And Tom hated that, though he understood it.

As it happened, Tom was so relaxed after his bone-hollowing orgasm that it wasn't a hard job to loosen him up to take Will's fuck. But though he expected to almost fall asleep in the aftermath of his own release, instead his prick engorged against the sheet, aroused just by Will's twisting fingers. After a time, Will's arm slid under his belly, urging him up on to all fours, as he'd done to Will.

He waited, head hanging, peering down at his reawakened erection dangling between his legs, almost as if it didn't belong to him. Then he felt a large hand on his back, and the press of Will's latex-covered cockhead against his hole.

"Tom." It was a helpless kind of groan, almost involuntary, as Will's cock skewered him.

He felt Will's tension, as he tried to hold back to allow him to adjust, and Tom recognized hazily that he must be in an agony of denied orgasm by now. But as Tom gathered his wits to urge him on, he felt the first, restrained back and forth pumping inside him, almost rubbing—awkward at first, then more definite, stroking something achingly sensitive, and thought barely existed anymore. His arms collapsed like overcooked noodles, and his arse was held up in Will's hands for screwing.

"Fuck me," he moaned. "Will."

And that was like a trigger being pulled. Will went at it as if he couldn't control the rhythmic driving of his hips, his hand stroking and controlling Tom's erection.

Tom tried to move in concert, but Will's hands held his arse still to take his fuck. It was total submission, and maybe that was why Will had always loved putting him in this position, creating the illusion of complete ownership. And why Tom hadn't been able to stand to do it with anyone else.

It was giving himself away, and there had been no one else he could do that with.

Tom felt Will's slick body shudder against him, and he wished so hard and possessively in that second—as he had in Will's position—that he could feel his seed spurting into him, something to take with him.

Will's last desperate thrust pushed him over into his own shuddering climax.

And then it was over.

Done.

26

Will was still asleep when Tom woke. Lying on his side, facing him.

Will's face was squished against the pillow, his extraordinary lashes spread like bruises on his cheekbones, resting on the blue shadows underneath. Tom's heart ached with love.

He'd refused to give it that name, like a superstitious child closing its eyes against reality as if that would make it disappear.

Pathetic.

He made himself slide back a bit and then a bit more, until his feet touched the floor, then he padded quietly to the ensuite to wipe himself down, staring at his own hollow eyes in the mirror.

He was moving to New York at last, as he'd always known a successful model should.

But instead—Tom had stayed in London. Was that because subconsciously he'd clung to the idea that Will was there, potentially just around the next corner?

Well. He'd played with fire again. And now look at him.

When he'd ever imagined a New York move though, he'd always assumed Pez would come with him whether Mel liked it or not—conquering the Big Apple side by side. Now he had nothing but himself to worry about. Just himself and John. Tom Gray—supermodel-in-waiting, about to conquer a strange land.

Tom's ice-blue eyes reflected only unhappiness back at him.

Will was still sleeping when Tom came back into the room and collected his clothes from the floor. He stood at the end of the bed, staring at him.

He almost found himself pulling out his phone to take a photograph, but that would be…brutally counterproductive. The point was to forget.

Yet he couldn't stop looking, like a man gulping water, knowing he was about to be denied it. Trying to imprint the image of Will, asleep in his bed like a boy, in his perfect gray bedroom.

Wake up! Stop me from going!

At last, Tom turned away. His eyes were prickling again, his throat tight and raw.

Will would understand. Tom was sure of that.

He'd let Tom slide away and exit in peace.

And Nick? He still had to tell Nick he was leaving him behind too. Pez—how would he ever talk to Pez again?

Tom closed the bedroom door behind him with a quiet snick. His heart was a vast, tender bruise in his chest.

He dressed quickly in the kitchen then went about gathering John's accessories into their own big bag. Finally he managed to corner John against the big glass doors and put him, squawking with protest, into his cat carrier. It didn't escape him that John seemed to want to stay.

He used his phone to order a cab. But the second he ended the call, the phone rang. Instinctively he looked at the closed kitchen door, but it was paranoid to expect the sound to carry all the way to Will's room.

"Hello," he said quickly. He sounded strange. Strangled, like he was trying not to cry.

"Tom…is that you?" The voice was hushed and urgent, and it took him a second, but Des Salt's accent identified him.

Tom frowned impatiently. "You just called my phone," he pointed out. Then, as Des's tone registered, "Is something wrong? Has Pez done something to him…?"

"Where are you?" Des snapped.

He blinked. "I'm at Will's."

He heard Des's hard intake of breath over the phone. "Is he there?"

It was almost a whisper. Playing hide and seek from his colleagues again.

Tom closed his eyes, searching for calm, ready to tell Des to just fuck off. He wasn't about to bring the phone to Will, not for anything. He couldn't face him.

"He's in bed," he said, tone firm. "And I've got…"

"*Listen* to me," Des cut in, still in that sibilant whisper, his accent stronger than Tom had ever heard it. "Ye have to get outta there. Now!"

Tom stared at the closed kitchen door, and something primal caused his chest to tighten, his heartbeat to start to pitter-pat faster. And faster. It made him instantly annoyed. He was beyond tired of being afraid.

"What are you talking about?" He was hiss-whispering now too.

"Tom! Don't. Fuckin'. Argue. *Go!*"

"Is this supposed to be funny?" Tom spat. He tried for outrage, but his voice shook.

And he asked himself, terrified—what more could happen? What more could go wrong?

"Jaysus! Why won't ye just…? All right!" He began to speak very slowly, carefully, as if Tom were an idiot. Still, all but whispering. "Carys

Rolfe remembered the identity of her attacker." He paused. "It was the Guv, Tom. It was Will."

Tom heard the words. He heard Des's barely concealed distress. But the idea was too ridiculous to process. His stomach was cold, though, as if it understood when his mind refused, as if he'd swallowed a bucket of ice, and his legs seemed to have lost strength. He stumbled backwards until he could prop himself against the seat of one of the tall chairs in front of the island.

"No!" But he was shaking. "That's not true. Is someone making you say that?"

"For fuck's sake, Tom." Des sounded close to tears himself. "She was attacked. She almost died. Why would she lie? What reason? You *know* how I feel about him. But he fits, for every one of the murders. He has no alibis…we just didn't look at him."

Tom put a shaking hand over his mouth. He could feel sobs shaking in his throat, wanting to escape.

He was having a nightmare. That was the only rational explanation. He was going to wake up next to Will in that big cozy bed.

"That's insane." His voice shook with rage and pain. "He has no motive…"

The kitchen door creaked open. Will stood in doorway, naked and sleepy and painfully beautiful. He walked into the room, a step or two, then stopped, visibly coming to alertness as he took in Tom fully dressed on the phone; the bag packed with cat accessories; John sulking in his cat-carrier on the floor.

"You," Des said in his ear. "You're the motive. We got that right. Just the wrong suspect. It's all about you."

Tom's gaze held Will's uselessly. But instinct saved him.

Blank. He could always do blank.

"Look, we're on our way there now," Des said. "But you have to get out, Tom. He's dangerous. Maybe most of all to you. He fooled all of us."

Tom pressed the red button to end the call.

Will gave a stoic little smile.

"You're going," he said. Stating the obvious. He must have put Tom's obvious distress down to guilt.

Tom couldn't speak.

Because looking at it with clear eyes, Will had every possible reason to hate him. To want vengeance. They'd both been caught in an obsessive passion, but Tom had coldly sacrificed Will over and over to escape it. Last night he'd done it again.

It all fits.

All this time.

Did he have alibis? Did he? Tom didn't even know. But Des would know and he said…

"Tom?" Will frowned at him with concern. "You don't look well."

"No. Yeah," Tom said. "I'm…fine. I'll just…"

He felt dead. In fact. Numb to his core.

Will.

Will had caused all this pain? *His* Will—the man he'd loved and hurt, the man who'd still managed to forgive him—wasn't real at all.

He didn't know who was peering out at him from Will's body.

"I have to go."

He turned and fumbled up the bag and the box.

He had to pass Will, get within touching distance.

If this hadn't happened, if Des hadn't called, would he be changing his mind now? Would he have been able to resist another touch? Another kiss?

No. Probably not. Probably, he'd have crumbled, if Will had asked him to stay.

He couldn't help gazing compulsively at Will's carefully neutral expression. Concealing what? Just a few minutes ago, he'd have assumed it was pain, dealt to him again by Tom.

But how angry must he be? How long had he wanted revenge? Or—to get Tom back in his power?

Tom's head felt ready to explode, like an overstretched balloon. His guts were water. But he managed a model's empty smile.

"I'll call you," he said dismissively, and walked toward then past him.

Had that been a mistake? A provocatively cold goodbye, even by Tom Gray standards.

He tensed for a disabling punch from behind, to the kidneys. A chokehold. As he got further away, a tackle to drag him down to the floor. Planning countermoves in his head.

It wasn't far to the front door, but Tom felt every step. He moved at a steady pace, letting his grimace of terror show only now, when no one could see it. He thought he heard a noise behind him. He was sure Will was in the hall too.

He pulled his leather jacket from the peg on which he'd hung it the night before. His bike was still parked in SFN's car park—since the day he'd found Max Perry and Will had ridden to the rescue. Except Will had killed him. He'd hated Max and he'd killed him and framed Tom. And then comforted him.

Tom turned the latch and pulled open the front door.

His black cab was already waiting, double-parked. He choked down a sob of relief and stepped out onto the stone doorstep. Without looking behind him, he pulled the door closed.

Outside it was another beautiful unwanted day. He could smell the sweet vanilla scent of the little white flowers that overflowed from a pot beside the front doorstep. Nemesia, Will had called them, when Tom had commented yesterday. Will liked plants.

Tom was safe now. He walked along the path, away from the house he'd loved, for the last time. But as he pulled open the gate, he heard a scream and huge crash behind him—inside the house. It froze him in his tracks.

He took another sobbing breath. He'd have turned back, before. Run up the path and hammered on the door, if he'd heard that sound of agony.

Now he knew it was rage.

He put his belongings into the back of the cab and climbed in after them, ordering the driver urgently to just…go. "Notting Hill," he said. Not Shoreditch, because…what if Will went after him there, and he was alone?

The moment the car turned out of Warren Road, Tom let his stoic mask drop.

He raised his hands to hide his face and let his tears come. He didn't care what the driver might see in his mirror. His pain and loss felt incomprehensible.

It had been Will? All this time?

Murdering. Tormenting him. Playing him. Terrifying him. Framing him and then Pez with that fucking fingerprint. And he'd told Will he was leaving for good. What would he have done, to stop him going?

Tom was in love with—had just had sex with—a serial killer who'd manipulated him and toyed with him all the way.

He made himself sit still to take that in, and make it real. Force himself to accept this reality. Make himself feel the utter repulsion he should feel.

But he couldn't accept it. His mind slid instead to Will's tender hand stroking Tom's hair as Tom broke his heart.

He'd thought.

Did Will have a heart?

You're just afraid, Tom. You hurt youself to try to prevent being hurt…

Tom grabbed his phone.

"Listen to me," he said, the moment Will picked it up. His voice was terse. "Carys remembered. The police are on their way."

"Remembered?" Will repeated. He sounded suitably bewildered. "Remembered what?"

"Remembered you fucking attacked her, you bastard," Tom snapped. "It was you all along." He ended the call and threw the phone violently onto the seat beside him.

He shouldn't have done that. Christ! He knew he shouldn't!

But it was Will, and it was unbearable.

He'd warned the man he thought he knew. The man he'd punished for being the love of Tom's life. And it was fucking insane, because he'd been leaving him in any case. Choosing safety over love—again—and hadn't he just been fucking vindicated in every way?

But tears were still coursing down his cheeks, because it felt like the end of everything that truly mattered. After everything, *this* was the worst thing.

Even though he'd thrown it away again and again, the reality that there could never be a way back, that his Will no longer existed, felt like the worst punishment in the world.

•••

"God, baby! I've been so worried!"

Nick was already standing at the front door of his house as Tom climbed out of his cab and began to haul out his things. He looked frantic, in fact.

Tom had phoned ahead to check Nick was home as opposed to in the office, but hadn't allowed any more conversation.

He paid the cabbie and trudged up the path, clutching his belongings. Then he stood rigidly, still holding his bags and the cat carrier as Nick hugged him.

Tom didn't need a mirror to know he looked distraught.

"Who told you?" he asked without expression.

Nick pulled back from the hug. He sounded almost apologetic as he said, "DS Salt. He called me to see if you were here. He didn't want to try your phone, in case you...were with him." He read Tom's flinch. "Oh God. You were!"

Tom looked away. "Yeah," he said bitterly. "Des called me anyway."

He didn't even know why it angered him. Would it have been better if he'd stayed in ignorance until the police burst in? Des had done him a kindness in sparing him that particular scene. Otherwise...maybe Lawson and Des would have interrupted a reconciliation.

"They needed to get you out before they arrested him," Nick said. "They had to avoid the possibility of a hostage situation."

Tom stared at him in disbelief.

The sound of the crash. The furious, throat-ripping scream behind him after he left Will's house.

Tom swallowed the sourness of bile in his throat.

"Jesus, Tom! What if he'd tried to kill himself and take you with him?"

"*Kill* himself?" Tom breathed. The world shifted sideways. White lights flickered around his vision.

"For God's sake, DM!" An anxious female voice. Jena. "Get him inside. He looks ready to pass out."

Tom didn't protest as she took the cat carrier and the bag from him, and Nick slid an arm round his waist to lead him into the hall, then on into the lounge.

The familiarity of it, the vile purple chair—he wanted to scream.

He freed himself from Nick's arm and sat on the sofa directly facing the wall unit, his back to the door. His and Nick's usual sofa.

It took a moment or two for his dizziness to pass, and as Tom sat there, John, freed from his carrier, jumped up beside him,

"They're wrong," Tom said clearly, even though he'd cried tears of acceptance in the cab. He'd said the exact same thing about Pez.

But here with other people, his defensiveness of Will felt overwhelming.

Denial? Who the fuck cared? He'd hang on to it as long as he could. "He doesn't have a motive."

Nick sat gingerly beside him and took his lax hand. Tom resisted the urge to pull it away.

He didn't want anyone's touch at that moment.

Except Will's. But *his* Will, not the other one.

Jena crouched in front of him, her face creased with pity. "I'm so, so sorry, Tommy."

He swallowed again and again, tried to swallow the bitterness in his mouth.

"Tell me what Des Salt said," he demanded, with narrow fury.

Jena's expression became even more distressed. "I'll make some tea," she muttered and scampered out of the room.

Nick clutched his hand tighter. "DS Salt said…when you left him, Foster started drinking. And he was…volatile. He screwed up an operation and people died. Afterwards he hit a superior officer."

"I knew that already. And he wasn't the one who screwed up. Will told me all about it." It felt good to say that.

"But Salt said he changed after you left. He got bitter and angry, even before he blew up his career."

"That's not a motive for murdering people! Any more than it was for Pez. And Will…Will would *never* kill that way. No. Not with…with drugs and mutilation and…mind games." If Will ever killed—and yes, Tom knew anyone could kill—it would be some untouchable villain in broad daylight. Not this.

"This is insane. It has something to do with Red Moss," Tom finished doggedly. "Glassy."

"But that's what Will led you to believe, wasn't it?" Nick said sadly. "He was the expert investigator, baby. He led you by the nose to that conclusion."

Tom froze. His certainty wavered. Had he?

"*No.* The murders…the cutting, the insulin. They mimicked your case and Glassy's."

Nick shook his head and ran a hand over his smooth hair.

"I've been thinking it through since DS Salt called. Will studied my case; he studied me. And if he had you under surveillance, I think he saw me with you—and he recognized me. You finished with him because he got too serious. But maybe if he watched us, saw I'd left Cat, he might have thought you just hadn't wanted it with him. And he's…some sort of narcissistic psychopath."

That fucking word again.

"Tom, I hope you don't mind, but Dr. Rolfe is coming by." Jena carried a tray full of mugs into the room. "I visited her in hospital because Cat liked her so much. They've let her home, but she's very shaken and she's off work. She hates being in her house alone now. When I heard all this happened today, I called her to see she's okay, but she wasn't okay so… I hope you're not angry. It's not her fault. " She set down the tray and looked at Tom anxiously. She handed Tom a mug. "Come on. Drink some to please me."

He didn't want it, but he sipped it anyway.

"Pez was the one who harassed Cat," Nick said eventually into the silence. "But…everything else was Foster taking advantage of the situation. Once they bring him in, he'll reveal my identity. I know that."

Tom regarded him coldly over the rim of his mug, a shield. He couldn't muster even a glimmer of concern about Nick's precious anonymity, or Echo, or New York.

Tom's phone rang. An unknown number again.

He pressed Accept, with a sixth sense of who it would be.

"Tom, where are you?" Speak of the devil. Des Salt, and sounding impatient too. "You can't…"

"I'm at Nick's," Tom cut in, tone icy. "I left Will at his house."

"Well he wasn't there when we arrived."

Because I warned him. The knowledge brought a dyspeptic churn of pride, relief, shame and guilt. He heard Des speaking to someone, presumably beside him, voice muffled.

"Tom." Des spoke into the mouthpiece again. "Stay there. Don't go out, and make sure you're not alone at any time."

"Why?" Tom demanded, although he knew.

"Because if he knows the game's up," Des said, "you'll be his final target."

•••

"So Will's still loose?" Jena asked.

Tom nodded. His stomach surged up to his throat.

"I just…I need to go to…" He stumbled upright and darted for the sanctuary of Nick's large bathroom, halfway down the hallway. By the time he made it to the cistern, he'd managed to control his urge to vomit.

But he stayed kneeling there, swallowing hard, because the feeling he was going to throw up didn't go. In the distance, he heard the doorbell ring.

He should leave, shouldn't he, if he was putting the others in danger? Will would hate Carys too.

He sighed and slumped round into a sitting position, shuffling to the side until he could sit supported against the black-painted clawfoot bath.

Everything in the house was tasteful, but Tom never had found out whose taste it was. Not Nick's, certainly—some designer who was paid to make people look stylish.

His head fell back, clanging dully against the bath.

The bathroom in Will's house had been beautiful. A clawfoot bath like this, but painted scarlet on the outside, the only color in a room of wood, plaster, porcelain and stone.

He drew a wavering breath, tears pooling again behind his eyes. He'd never cried much before this last week. Now he couldn't seem to stop.

He couldn't even say he'd lost something, when he'd thrown it away himself.

But now his love had all been proven an illusion, he didn't feel vindicated or relieved, or free. He found he wanted it back, more than anything else in his life. He wanted it to have been real. Even the gray walls in Will's bedroom—even that—he had to view now through the prism of sick obsession, not yearning. Not…love.

Grief rose again in his throat and his eyes, his face twisting with it— with despair and regret and longing.

"Will," he whispered.

There was a tentative knock at the bathroom door.

"Tom?" Jena, sounding concerned. "Tom, are you all right, sweetie? Did you throw up?"

Tom grimaced ferociously and slumped lower. He knew she cared but he just wanted to be left alone.

"No, I'm fine." His voice was too hoarse. "I'll be out in a minute."

"Dr. Rolfe is here. Maybe she can give you something, to help you feel better."

Tom let gravity pull his head down onto his chest. "I'll see."

She muttered a platitude, then he heard her steps disappearing along the hall.

They'd talk about him, try to work out a way to buck him up. Whatever it was, he didn't want it.

A phone began to ring, and it took him a solid two seconds to understand it was his. He'd held on to it without realizing, through everything. He pulled it up to look at it, a strange kind of anticipation in his chest.

Unknown number. Instinctive, desperate hope burst, like a bubble on the ground.

Des again.

"Yes," he answered tiredly. "What?"

There was a startled pause. "Tom?"

It took a moment to recognize the voice, talking softly.

"James?"

"I got your number from records." The call was clearly surreptitious. "I heard Lawson's gone after Will."

Tom let out a sound that mixed relief and pain. Because James Henderson, at least, had liked Will. Understood him. Even Des was hunting Will now.

"Look," Henderson said, voice close to a murmur. "I tried his number but...obviously...no reply. I left a message for AC Hansen too. I'll keep trying. I don't know what the hell is going on but it felt maybe... There was nothing on the search terms for 'red string' on HOLMES. Will asked me to look."

Had he? Tom said weakly, "Okay." Why the fuck did Henderson think that mattered now?

"The thing is, Alec, one of our sergeants, knows everyone on the force and that's barely an exaggeration. I asked him if he's ever heard of anything and...he knew a guy who retired a few years ago who worked a case that involved red string. But that detail was held back from the press in case of copycats, and it wasn't on HOLMES because the case notes were sealed years ago. That's unusual. But this was a huge case, and a famous..."

"The Babes in Arms," Tom cut in. He sounded dazed.

There was a cautious pause. "Yes. Red string tied round both victims' wrists when they were found. So I started to think I may be getting an idea what this is about. DCI Lawson's investigation…the MO involves insulin, *like* the Babes in Arms. And the murderer—a guy called David Burchill—he's out on license with lifetime anonymity. Lawson doesn't have a clue about any of it."

Tom said nothing, but he didn't deny a word.

"Right," Henderson said slowly. "Call me if you need me, Tom. Program this number in to your phone. I'll keep trying AC Hansen."

Tom obediently created a contact.

When Henderson rang off, Tom sat and stared at the wall in front of him, trying to think. The wall was pale blue, and though it had a pleasant purplish undertone, somehow the effect, even in the bright light streaming through the bathroom window, was cold.

Another connection between the cases. Red string.

Why would…?

Tom sprang to his feet, fumbled the lock and tore open the door.

"Nick!" He raced into the hall and burst into the lounge. Nick had taken the purple chair, Jena and a very subdued Carys Rolfe sat on the sofa, perpendicular to the TV unit. They all looked up with shock and alarm. "Will can't have done it!"

Nick's eyes widened, before his expression settled into sad, resigned weariness.

"Tom…" he began carefully.

"Red string!"

Nick blinked twice. "What?" He looked nonplussed, but also at last the beginnings of anger. Tom supposed his denial must seem perverse… desperate, to Nick.

"We didn't even mention it to you, did we?" Tom went on. "Because we didn't know it was important until after Max was killed. And then Pez was taken in and everything was… Listen! There was a piece of red string tied round Michael's wrist *and* Max Perry's." He looked wildly at Carys, who in turn regarded him with startled concern.

"Mike?" she said uncertainly. "But that was his Kabbalah string."

"I'm sure there was red string in Catriona's bedroom," Tom pressed on desperately. "We need to find out if it was at Lily's murder scene too." The need for discretion finally hit him. "Nick. I just got a call. Can I speak with you in private?"

Nick rubbed a hand over his face. He looked exhausted. "Since it's all going to come out now anyway," he said with a heavy sigh. "I just told

Carys about everything, since she was hauled into this without any say in it."

Weren't we all? Tom thought in a burst of bitterness.

Carys gave an uncertain smile. She appeared shell-shocked, the way Tom remembered he'd felt on meeting David Burchill. Though Carys had once had her own brush with murder.

"There was red string tied round the wrists of the Morton babies too," he said to Nick. "Did they ask you about it when they questioned you?"

Nick looked stunned, as if he could barely keep up. "No," he said blankly.

"Then…no one else knew, except the cops who worked the case, and *Morton* who found them. Nick! It's not Will. It *has* to be Morton!"

Silence.

He looked around the room. Jena and Carys Rolfe were staring at him as if Tom had just embarrassed himself publicly. When he searched Nick's face for validation, all he saw was sympathy.

It maddened him.

"Think! How would Will know about it? It's not on the police database, the files are sealed, and it was never made public."

"Okay," Nick said. "Why don't you come and sit down, and we can talk about it?"

"Sit? We can't just sit! We need to tell someone. Hansen! Fuck, I should call Pixie!"

Nick stood up. "Tom. Come on," he coaxed. All three of them were looking at Tom as if he were unhinged. Nick raised his hands—vertically, palms up—like someone trying to appease a maniac. "This isn't helping. Please, baby. You're overwrought. Just sit down."

Was that how Tom seemed to them? Just…hysterical?

Tom hauled in a deep, deep breath. He had to appear calm, and he had to convince Nick somehow, because Hansen seemed to only listen to him. To care only about Nick's well-being.

And only Hansen could control Lawson—if they could persuade her to do the right thing. Surely the case was too shambolic now for anything else to advantage her.

Tom gritted his teeth, rubbed his nose hard and pushed his hair behind his ear. Then he walked to his usual sofa and sat down, seething with resentment.

"Here," Jena said to Tom with an encouraging smile. "We cracked out the hard stuff." She handed him a mug of what looked like coffee, but he could smell alcohol in it. "Go on."

Tom clenched his jaw but he forced himself to take an impatient gulp.

"So will you listen to me, now?" he demanded.

"Okay." Nick sank back in the purple chair. "Tell us again."

Tom went through it once more as methodically as he could.

"Tom," Carys said tentatively, when he finished. "I don't know about the rest of it, but... Will Foster *was* the man who attacked me."

"Buy why *would* he?" Tom asked desperately. And Jesus! How had he forgotten in his defensive zeal, that the actual witness against Will was in the room with him? "You might have made a mistake. I mean it was dark. I mean... did he speak to you?"

Carys frowned as if she were trying to remember. She had bruises on her face, and to Tom, she seemed diminished, somehow. Less confident.

"I don't think I made a mistake," her voice quavered. "I saw a glimpse of him. He didn't have a mask or... I don't know *why* he'd attack me, Tom. But I'd seen him before he came in to the surgery with you, outside the practice. That's why I recognized him that day you both came in."

Tom jolted with unwanted recollection. He remembered Carys's reaction had annoyed him—stupidly possessive of Will even that first day.

"He was in a car mostly, but the first day I noticed him he was leaning against the side of it, watching our building, as if he was waiting for someone. He's a very handsome man. Very...striking. I remember Catriona had an appointment that day. And I've thought—since he attacked me— he must have been following *her.*" Tears slipped out of her brown eyes. "But he'd have no reason to hurt Michael," she said earnestly. "Michael had nothing to do with Catriona. I *know* what happened to Mike. I lived with him. I watched it happen and I couldn't stop it. Mike killed himself, Tom. I live with that every day. And I'm sorry if it doesn't fit your...theories." Her voice shook into silence.

Tom rubbed his free hand over his mouth.

He felt ashamed. And yet. Michael Rolfe fit the others. It had just been a coincidence?

Maybe...maybe Will had been watching the practice for a case. And Carys mistook who attacked her. But...

He took a desperate gulp of alcoholic coffee, trying to hang on to belief.

"But how would Will know about the red string?" he repeated doggedly.

"He was a policeman," Nick reminded him, "He may have known someone who worked the case, or someone who knew someone. It's obvious, baby. I know you don't want to believe it."

"But that'd be a ridiculous coincidence and someone—told me—" He swallowed hard. "There's no such thing as a coincidence…in a murder case. I'm supposed to believe Will happened to meet one of a tiny handful of officers who knew about a withheld piece of evidence, *and* would talk about it when he shouldn't; *and* he knew you from studying you at uni *and* he happened to see you when he was stalking me. What are the odds of all of that happening together?"

"You think I'm lying," Carys quavered, appalled. Her expression was devastated.

Tom caught Nick's reproving expression.

"No," Tom said quickly. "Of course not! I just think…you may have misremembered. You'd been given chloroform. Injected with insulin and—"

"Tom…" Nick said.

"Morton knew about the string, Nick," Tom said. "And he knew you very well. If he saw you recently and recognized you. That's one stroke of luck—chance—to believe in, not…four. And if he wanted to torment you." Tom chewed his lip, trying to piece it together. "Or—it could be Glassy. You testified against him," he said to Carys.

Nick said, "What?"

Carys's eyes widened with shock.

Of course—if she hadn't been in contact with Michael's family, she wouldn't have realized Tom knew what had happened in her childhood.

"Carys's sister was the girl Glassy murdered," he explained sheepishly. "She visited him in Red Moss?"

Nick and Carys eyed each other with sudden wariness.

Nick said, "I barely went in to the Visit Room. Jena was my only visitor and she couldn't come often."

Carys said, "I just visited Martin a few times. I didn't know you were there."

"Glassy…*Martin* had reason to hate you and Nick *and* Catriona," Tom said to Carys. "Maybe he and Morton are working together! Or Morton used his history as a red herring!"

Jena frowned. "So you think Morton took the opportunity of what Pez did to Cat, and what Lily did in reporting it, to start to framing you for murder? To use you to torment Nick. Using Max Perry's presents and his stalking…Killing Max because you'd had a fight with him. Framing you, to make Nick suffer? Because Nick loves you."

"Yes!" Tom said. "We've been playing round the edges of that theory all along, haven't we? And Morton's tall, like Will. You could have mistaken him?" he asked Carys with hope in his voice.

Carys stared at him, then glanced at Jena uncertainly, as if for reassurance.

"Morton genuinely thinks Nick murdered his sons. He lost all three of his kids because of what happened. His wife sounds like she's barely hanging on. That's a cause for the vengeance of a lifetime."

"Why not, DM?" Jena asked suddenly. "If he recognized you it would explain a lot."

Tom turned to look at her with relief, then back, eagerly, at Nick.

Nick sighed and dropped his head, then looked up again.

"Foster ruled Morton out himself," he said. "He told Chris that the officer working with him inside the Met checked where Morton was the night Cat died. He was at a Rotary Club dinner with his wife when she was murdered. There were multiple witnesses."

Tom felt the shock of panicked disappointment, like being pushed into thin air.

He had worked himself up to genuine hope, and Nick had just… stamped on it.

He wanted to scream. He wanted to hate him.

"Fuck," he cursed shakily, with a false laugh. "An unbreakable fucking alibi again. Everyone who needs them has them." He squeezed his eyes tight shut, then forced them open. He couldn't give up. "It must be Glassy then. Someone working for him. Everything leads back to Red Moss."

He sat back on the sofa and shook his head to try to clear it. It felt thick, as if it had been stuffed with cotton wool. Alcohol on top of high emotion.

He closed his eyes in despair.

Perfect fucking alibis all round.

He forced his eyelids open and focused on Nick's pile of DVDs as he'd done so often. He fought the slide into drunken exhaustion.

Bogart. Huston. Hitchcock. Wilder. Welles.

God. He still had to tell Nick he was definitely moving to New York.

His mind drifted, defying his willpower.

"How much did you use?" A murmur in Carys's distinctive accent.

"Shhh," Jena. Then, louder, "You need sleep, Tommy."

And he understood. They'd put something in his coffee to knock him out. Nick had done the same thing before, taking away Tom's agency. All for his own good.

Outrage fueled a burst of adrenaline that thinned the heavy weight of sleep creeping over his mind, like clouds inexorably covering the face of the moon.

It all came back to him—Tom fucking Gray. Like a fucking albatross.

Pez…Will… Doing insane things because of *him*. Because they loved him and he hurt them as naturally as breathing. His fault. Lawson had seen that from the start. The very first person Lawson's instinct had fixed on, and he'd been right. In a way.

"There are good reasons stalkers and harassers are looked at first in cases like this…"

Will had said that but… *Most cases…* What was niggling at him? *Think!*

His lecturer said in murder cases the victim's partner was the first suspect, because they were likely to have the most reason to kill them. But hadn't been relevant because Nick…

He fought for clarity. Tried to shake the weight of drugged thickness from his brain.

Because…Nick had a perfect alibi. Like Carys when her husband died. Did Lily's husband have one too?

There was a sudden, violent noise behind him, like a door bursting open and hitting the wall.

His name. *"Tom!* You have…!"

Then—sounds. Panting and grunting. Bitten-off words. Women's voices. whisper-shouting.

A scuffle.

Tom hauled himself round as far as he could on the sofa, dragging stone limbs into place, until he could slump against the back and see over the top of it.

Will!

It was Will. Struggling with Nick, who seemed to be trying to press a hand to his face to silence him. Will holding him off, then…

Nick pressed his other hand against Will's chest and held it there.

Will froze as if he'd been stabbed. Then he screamed, a horrible shout of agony, and began to jerk violently, like an out-of-control puppet, while Nick held his hand with grim determination against Will's heaving chest.

It went on for what felt like minutes, but could only have been seconds, until Will crumpled like weighted paper to the floor and lay, twitching spastically, as if he were having some kind of fit, with no control over his own limbs.

Tom moaned. "No. What did you do to him?"

"The stun gun the police gave me," Nick panted. "For fuck's sake, Tom, I had to! He came to kill you!"

Tom stared, mesmerized, at Will's twitching body, his face twisted grotesquely into a grimace of pain. Tom met his agonized eyes. They were aware. Desperate, before they shut.

But Tom didn't see hatred.

His own eyes began to close, and his head drooped, face half pressed on to the back of the sofa.

"Is he out?" Carys sounded calm. As a doctor she'd have to be, Tom supposed. He was drifting away.

Tom felt a gentle hand brush back his hair from his forehead. "Yeah. Looks like he is," Jena said tenderly.

"How long will the stun hold?"

"Fifteen minutes maybe." Nick sounded agitated. "He's big. Fit."

"I can't give him anything that'd show in his bloodstream." Carys again. "Zap him again. Same place. It might hold him for longer."

"That could also kill him." Jena's voice. Stern.

Alarm, gut fear, prodded Tom closer to the surface. He forced open his eyes again. Nick and the two women stood over Will's body—Will lying as he'd been, eyes closed, limbs twitching. No threat to anyone.

"Call the police now," Carys said.

"No," Tom moaned and pulled himself further up the sofa back. As if they were joined together by a wire, all three heads turned to him, startled. They looked almost shocked he was there.

Awake, he thought with furious resentment. They were shocked he was awake.

"Tom," Nick repeated reasonably. "He came to kill you. We have to restrain him till the police come."

"You want to hurt him again." He sounded drunk, or ill. His tongue felt far too big for his mouth.

"No!" Nick protested, wounded. "I saved you from him!"

Tom gazed at the helpless man on the floor, surrounded, like a stag waiting to be finished.

"He doesn't...even have...a weapon," Tom managed, through his teeth.

Carys eyed him for a second, as if he were some odd, new species then she bent down, and from behind Will's body, picked up an evil-looking long-bladed knife with a wooden handle. In the same hand, she clutched a transparent plastic bag, dangling, to display syringes with orange tips, and a collection of little purple-capped bottles.

Tom stared at the objects with hopeless misery.

But still...there was...something. Something he was missing. But he couldn't drag his mind into action to pinpoint what it was.

He felt his muscles give, and he slid back down on his side against the sofa back, head once more resting on top.

"Will," he moaned again. It sounded plaintive. His head had twisted forward, eyes focused on the wall unit in front of him, forcing himself to list each individual object, compel his mind to work.

He could hear them talking behind him, and more grunts…the sounds of effort. Will was being dragged further into the room.

Tom drew a sobbing breath. He fixed on the DVDs again, tried fiercely to read the titles but he couldn't focus his eyes well enough to do it.

But one spine protruded further than the others, and he made himself concentrate on the picture until he remembered it in flashes of memory. Hitchcock. Two men on a train. Laughing with Nick about how homoerotic it was. The perfect crime.

His eyes opened.

Each man was meant to do the other's murder. Nothing to connect them. The one who had the motive wasn't there when the crime was committed. An ironclad alibi.

His heart was beating faster and faster.

That was just fucking…ridiculous.

He heard a soft thump behind him.

He twisted painfully until he could peer over the back of the sofa at the scene. Will now lay further inside the room. His violent tremors had lessened, but he seemed to to be unconscious. Nick, Jena and Carys still stood around him, frowning down at him like an unwanted object. Jena was to the left at Will's feet, Nick beside her, slightly in front of Will's body and Carys at his head.

It took too long for Tom to register that the plastic bag holding the syringes and bottles now rested in Will's lax hand. The knife lay close beside it.

He understood then, what he'd seen, but failed to process.

Carys hands were covered with thin beige gloves—doctor's gloves. When she'd held up the clear bag of bottles and syringes, she'd been wearing them too.

As if she'd known. As if she didn't want her fingerprints on the bag.

And in that moment, he knew he was right.

"*Strangers On a Train*," he said with wonder. All three of them stiffened and turned to look at him. And the mixed emotions on their faces— shock, amazement, dismay, annoyance—told him all he needed to know. They'd written him off again. "You did it for each other."

He swallowed with effort. His head drooped under its own weight, and his mouth was desert dry, but his outraged mind was holding on.

"But you weren't strangers," he forced himself on. "Is that where you got the idea? From the movie?"

"Christ, Ava!" Carys barked. "How little did you give him?"

Suddenly her accent sounded a lot less charming.

On the floor between their legs, he saw Will's eyes crack open, a sliver of amber, and his fear lessened just from that.

Will was there. And Will was who Tom had thought he was all along. Relief gave him courage.

It occurred to Tom's slowed brain that he'd been very stupid to say it aloud. That he might die now. But he had to draw them away from Will. Perhaps he'd always been meant to be a victim, or a scapegoat, like Will.

Nick hadn't been the passive, patient lover after all. Maybe he'd been seething all along, plotting vengeance for every rejection.

He knew that even if the police burst in now he could prove none of it, but nothing was going to make Tom sit by like a beast waiting to be led to the abattoir. Or let them hurt Will.

He hadn't drunk all that much of the coffee Jena had given him. And concentrated terror was working for him, fighting off the fog.

If he could distract them long enough to let Will recover, they might have a chance. Maybe Carys was right, and it wouldn't take fifteen minutes. Will was strong.

"You had Michael killed," he said to Carys, but his voice was so distorted only the cold gleam in her eyes told him she understood. "Did you kill your sister too? And you," he slurred to Nick, all pain and betrayal. "God. You killed those children. And you had Catriona murdered. You removed...inconvenient people for...Carys Rolfe, and she did it for you. A fucking *transaction*. And you melded your sick...signatures in every murder."

"No!" Nick exclaimed. He was in front of Tom in seconds, both hands cradling his face, staring with desperate horror into his eyes. "Tom, no! That's crazy. I don't know who killed the twins. But *Will* killed the others. I've never hurt a soul in my life. Jena, for God's sake, call the police now!"

With all his weak strength, Tom jerked his face away.

"Tom!" Nick sounded distraught.

Almost. Believable.

"He's telling the truth!" Jena shouted. "He's never killed *anyone*."

"You need...to open...your eyes," Tom slurred with disgust. "You can't cover for..."

"Tom!" Nick said again, stunned, betrayed, as if he couldn't believe Tom had worked it out.

"I believed all the shit...you spun..." Tom gritted out somehow. "About your *innocence*...and you destroyed...a whole...family." Every word was a fight. "For...nothing."

"No!" Jena snapped. She raised trembling hands and pushed her fingers into her pink, feathery hair, gripping hard. "Bethany was humiliating him. She was a smug bitch. Everyone was mocking him. All over the school. It was *unbearable*. She had to pay a price that meant something."

"Jena!" Nick's voice sounded weak with horror and disbelief. "For fuck's sake…"

Tom squinted at him, then at Jena, trying to process what she'd said. But his brain was so sluggish. Had she just admitted that Nick did it? Or…?

"*God!*" Jena screamed at Nick, her perfect calm blinking out of existence. "What has he *done* to you? Wake! *Up!* I've tried *everything* to give him to you. But it didn't *work*. He won't…!" She stopped, teeth clenched and raised her palms in a gesture of culpability. "I know I should have made sure he was out. But it's *done* now. It's like *fate* that he heard. It was *never* going to happen. Not with him."

"Birdie. Come on now. Calm down." Nick's tone was exaggeratedly appeasing, as if he were talking Jena down off a ledge. "Tom's under the influence of whatever you gave him to help him get a peaceful night's sleep. That's why he's making crazy accusations. But you need to stop saying these things." He turned to Tom. "I'm calling the police right now." He gestured at Will's slumped body. "He has to be taken in to custody. The police have *evidence*! Fuck, Tom, he came to kill you. Everyone's losing it! This is bloody insane."

There was a short, dramatic pause, everyone frozen in their uncertain tableau, then from nowhere, Carys laughed and followed it with a gusty sigh.

"C'mon now, David. You know Ava's right. The damage is done." She sounded exactly like a mother coaxing her child to do his homework. "I'm not being funny but we can't really take the chance on either of them now, can we?" She looked at Tom and smiled with that warm, dimpled approval Tom found so appealing. "Who knew there was a brain behind that face, ay?"

She cocked her head and raised her untidy eyebrows at Tom in the universal grimace of "Oh well. Never mind."

Then she turned and strode across the room to the large-paned Victorian window and picked up a medium-sized black bag from the floor in front of it. A doctor's bag.

She walked over to pick up the pocket of clear plastic from Will's limp hand.

"Carys," Nick said warningly. "I said *no*."

Carys clicked her tongue. "I'm not your sister, David," she said sweetly. "You don't boss me."

She snapped open the black bag, pulling out a small paper and cellophane package with a large hypodermic syringe inside, much bigger than the ones in the plastic bag. In her other hand, she held one of the little glass bottles with a purple cap.

Insulin.

She tore open the syringe bag with her teeth and pulled out the syringe. Then she uncapped the needle and held the syringe up to the light, drawing back the plunger to its fullest extent.

"Think with your big brain," she lilted to Nick. "What d'you expect to happen, ay? We have two witnesses who'll back each other up. They have to go." It all sounded so businesslike, so logical. She shook her head chidingly at Tom, all false regret. "Shame you had to be so clever."

"You. Don't. Touch him." Nick's voice was low, dangerous.

"This is how it's going to go." Carys worked the purple cap off the bottle. "We're not here. We went out, and Tom said he was going to bed. Our murderer…" She nodded in Will's direction without removing her eyes from the syringe, attached to the bottle. "Broke in, and killed him. Poor Tom. Foster was still at the scene when we got back, and we had to fight him off, stun him…then the knife got in the way. Maybe he fell on it…all very tragic." Her eyes swung to Tom, narrowed in happy calculation. "Actually I think I may add in some chloroform for Pathology… that'll be a nice touch. Make it more likely he could be overpowered by an attack from behind."

Tom's disbelief was slowly melting into dread. The matter-of-fact enjoyment she took in it all, her easy assumption that nothing could stop her. Because nothing ever had. Tom took in her sturdy frame, her competent, eager determination.

Tom's limbs felt like cloth. He couldn't really hope to defend himself. And he realized that Nick, a murderer, and Jena, his accomplice, were all that stood between himself and Will—and Carys's determination to end them.

He shot a compulsive glance at Will, to find him staring back with wild urgency in his eyes, as if he'd been trying to communicate by force of desperation. He was aware, at least. Forgotten in the drama playing out above him.

Tom looked away sharply. He *had* to distract attention from Will until he could recover.

"Nick, don't let her," Tom said. His tongue was getting heavy again, clumsy, his words stumbling. Somehow he levered up a limp hand to brush Nick's arm, pleading. "I know I'm difficult and…I panic…but… you must see…I love you."

Nick looked startled. "You never put it into words. But…" He smiled. "I thought you did deep down."

"He's 'putting it into words' now because his neck's on the line," Carys said flatly. She dropped an empty insulin bottle to the floor and broke the top of a new one, plunged the needle in. "Come on, David. Man up! Are you really going to put Ava at risk after all she's done for you?"

Carys pulled out the hypodermic and took another out of a large package, to repeat the same actions. Pulling back the plunger, injecting air into the bottle and sucking out its contents. Then on to another bottle, with a different label.

They all watched her businesslike preparations, mesmerized.

"Look, I'll make sure he won't say anything," Nick blurted.

"No, David." Carys pulled the full syringe out of the bottle. "*I* will."

Tom looked wildly at Jena for aid, but she was standing beside to Nick, as if she had no part in it. She met Tom's eyes but her expression told him nothing. Perhaps he saw regret. But it was worthless.

He felt no better—woozy and not in control of his limbs. Only desperation—adrenaline—was holding off unconsciousness.

"Are you going to call the police now?" he slurred to Nick desperately, but his eyes slid compulsively back to Carys. "I'll say…I'll tell them Will attacked me." He sounded breathless, afraid, even to himself. "If we all… say it… They won't believe him…and…"

Carys began to arrange her three full hypodermic syringes in a neat row. She pointed to the one on the right. "This is a sedative. Lorazepam. Makes it nice. And then the insulin. For completion's sake." She looked at Tom as if she expected his admiration for her foresight. "*And* some GHB. We have to be consistent, don't we?" Her bright lilt sounded obscene to Tom now. Carys smiled kindly. "There's worse ways to go," she comforted. "I'll save the chloroform to the end, maybe. It might make you sick if we did it now." Then she said cheerfully, all brisk Matron on the Ward, "Let's get this in first, shall we?"

Tom struggled backwards from the sofa cushion, to his feet. His legs barely held him, but he was not going to make it easy. He drew a deep breath,

"You're not fucking touching me…" he managed. "You murderous bitch."

Carys raised her eyebrows. "Rude. David, are you going to help or…?"

There was sudden, violent movement. Nick and Jena both staggered, as if the ground had moved under their feet. And Tom understood.

Will had tried to scythe their legs from under them, and he began to try to push himself up onto his feet. Tom stumbled to the side of the sofa past Nick who was on his knees. But Jena was solidly upright again.

She swung round and snatched something from a small table behind her.

Will had one foot and one knee under him, levering himself painfully upright.

Jena was on him at once.

She flung herself at him, her momentum toppling him backwards, her sturdy body on top, and she pressed her hand hard against his heart.

The awful spasming jerking movements began again.

"Stop!" Tom screamed. "You'll kill him."

But Jena didn't stop...gave it more long, long agonizing seconds before she rose and faced Tom. Her eyes looked wild.

"Right!" Carys said with a showy sigh. "This is getting messy. Let's get the unpleasantness over with, shall we?"

Nick pulled himself upright, and to Tom's vast relief, he sidled over to stand beside him.

"You don't touch him," he said.

Carys tapped her foot with impatience.

"Are you really going to try and stop me, David? You're choosing him over Ava? You know what'll happen to..."

Beside Tom, Nick suddenly made a garbled noise, a strangled yelp of agony, and Tom turning toward him couldn't understand what was happening.

Nick's eyes bulged from their sockets, his face puce and straining. Then he collapsed, bumping against the side of the sofa as he fell.

Jena stood behind him, holding the stun device. Tears coursed down her pale cheeks.

"He'll forgive me," she told Carys. She looked afraid, before it hardened to defiance. "He's too besotted to see sense right now. But he'll realize...I did it to save him."

And then Tom was alone with them.

Slowly, Jena edged toward him, holding the stun device ready in her hand.

"Nice," Carys approved, like a teacher to a proactive student. "We can say...Will found it in the flat and used it to disable Tom while he worked on him. Save the chloroform."

Tom backed away toward the wall.

Carys had edged into position between the sofa and the coffee table.

Tom was almost within her reach. She was almost within his. He could try a blow. But he had no faith that he could land it in his state, and if he fell off balance, he'd be worse than carrion. She could lean across right now, grab him—and he had almost no strength to resist.

Tom couldn't reach the door, but the window...?

"Did you...and David...swap techniques in Red Moss?" If he could keep her talking, boasting, maybe Will or Nick might come round... Delay was all he had.

"Never spoke to him," Carys said. "Ava though... I recognized her from seeing her in Visiting back then. I really did meet her on a train, just like the movie. It was like an Act of God. I gave you a couple of little clues though, Tom, didn't I, that first day? The train and Hitchcock? Gave you a fair chance? Anyway Ava's the one with the balls, aren't you, cariad?"

Tom didn't take his eyes from Carys. But still he almost sobbed the word, "Jena?"

"I *told* you Nick didn't kill anyone." Jena sounded angry and upset, tearful. "He wouldn't. He protected me. *I* used Mum's insulin and...I gave the babies a Kalava each, for protection on their journey."

"Kalava?" Tom repeated but he still didn't look at her. He couldn't stand to.

"A sacred thread. I loved watching Hindu ceremonies when I was small. I studied it."

Jena. His friend. Jena was the killer. A child who'd killed children and was killing still. Tom squeezed his eyes shut, then forced them open again. He didn't have time.

Carys's watchful smile mesmerized him.

"The red string and the insulin," he said to her. "That was hers. But the mutilation. That was all you... Your first kill." His clouded, frightened mind followed through with the thought. "You're going to cut me."

Carys's expression shifted to concern. "You just realized. I'm afraid we *do* have to keep up consistency for the police. So they can tie up their investigation." Tom couldn't wrench his eyes away from her. "Aw. You know already, don't you? You cheated on poor Will, didn't you? So... well...what would he cut off?" Carys tilted her head sadly.

Castration. She was going to castrate him, like Max. She looked more closely at him, feeding on his horror. "Aw, don't worry, cariad. I don't think you'll feel it. Though maybe...hmmm..." She played hammily at reconsidering. "An angry, rejected lover would want you to, wouldn't they? We have to think of realism for the postmortem, you know? Anyway it'll be over soon enough. Shock and blood loss. You wouldn't be needing it anymore anyway."

Tom made an incoherent sound. Pure fear.

Carys smiled. Tom shuffled back against the wall unit, sidling along it.

"Mr. Foster's not going to be quite so lucky," Carys went on. "Once he kills you, he's going to fall on his knife accidentally, when one of us stuns him. Not such an easy way to go—gutting yourself. But…you can't have everything, can you?"

Tom hand groped desperately behind him on the shelves and fell on bronze. A statue.

He grabbed the nearest shape. His fingers recognized it. Ganesh, the elephant god, so heavy when Tom pulled it off the shelf, it dragged down his weakened arm.

"Are you going to hit me with that?" Carys asked roguishly. "I don't think you can lift it high enough, do you?"

Her eyes sparkled, and her bruised skin had flushed a light, attractive pink. She looked aroused, relishing every second of the kill.

Jena moved behind her into Tom's eyeline. He couldn't see enjoyment, just stoic determination. Set to her task.

Behind them, Will, with agonizing effort, had pulled his phone from his pocket and dropped it on the carpet, fumbling at it with useless sausage fingers. If one of them turned and saw him…

"Why did you kill your sister?" Tom gasped out.

Carys hestitated for a second, then she laughed. She appeared delighted, and it was because he was dragging it out. Giving her more fun.

"Oh, I do like how you're making this last." As if she'd read his mind. "We're going to make it really like the movies, are we? Confess our sins in the last reel? Well. Why not? We have a few minutes. So…I was at the point where I had to decide if I wanted to be a doctor or an actor, see? I'm brilliant at acting, if I say so myself. So I needed to know if it was worth the extra work to be a doctor. If I'd enjoy it enough to be… worth the while, you know? The power of life and death. So I needed a test subject, like every scientist does. And well…Emily'd been trying to steal Mike from me, hadn't she?" Carys shrugged. "She…presented herself. Like Bruno says in the movie—'Some people are better off dead.' I have the whole script in my head, you know." Tom looked into her avid eyes, and his guts threatened to turn to water. He hadn't actually believed evil like this could exist, and he stood no chance against it. Self-aware, relishing, unapologetic evil, still wearing a kind face.

Over her shoulder Tom could see Jena, waiting in reserve with the stun device in her hand. He thought she seemed lost.

"Jena, please," he said.

"I tried everything to give you to him, Tommy. To break you down. To make you see you needed to depend on him. His object of desire." She gave a bitter, watery laugh. "He always chooses the elusive ones. But you were never going to be caught by anyone, were you?" She began to cry silently. Somehow that helped.

It was over. Tom knew it. But he was fucked if he'd go down without a fight.

He took one last step toward the big window and raised the hand holding the statue as far up as his weakened muscles would allow.

Carys was right. He couldn't muster the strength to lift it properly, but he could swing his body round, pulled by the weight of the bronze, until his arm swept to the end of its arc, and he let the statue go. Its momentum carried through the glass and wood of Nick's huge front window and out into Durham Terrace, propelling shards everywhere, some of them landing on his skin, pinpricks of invisible pain.

A cry for help that no one would hear.

It was his last gambit. Carys was on him at once, her sturdy body pressing him back against the surviving panes of glass. He felt the needle penetrate the side of his neck, and the burning pain of the liquid inside it entering his flesh.

"Naughty boy." He had the satisfaction of hearing anger in her voice. Maybe her plan was no longer quite so neat. "Such a waste though," he heard her croon in his ear, her lovely Welsh lilt full of cold sympathy. "So pretty."

Over her shoulder, he saw Will on the floor behind the sofa, trying to rise, unable to force his paralysed limbs to do it.

Will's eyes were wet, tears streaked his cheeks. Tom held them with relief, grateful that Will would do this for him. Not look away. He loved him for it, for making sure that he wasn't alone in these last, awful moments, though he'd chosen loneliness all his life. He regretted so much. Wished for so much. He tried to show what he felt. That even now Will made him feel safe.

Another needle slid into his neck. Another burning, poisonous rush. He smelled the familiar blend of lavender and metal.

Consciousness began to slip away. Blackness was a numbing prickly tide, sweeping over his face and head like tar water, submerging him, and he was grateful for it, knowing what was to come at Carys's hands.

He thought he heard Jena sob. Then he imagined a voice. A man's voice, shouting and hysterical. A noise, sharp and booming, like a shot. But even if it was real, it was too late for him.

27

Tom felt light before he saw it, and he hadn't opened his eyes. The light shone through his lids to turn the blackness red. A man, still shouting. Orders, he thought. He was flying, the air rushing against his skin, though his legs and arms were still. It felt peaceful. Wonderful, in fact. And yet, there was something…

One last thought.

Will.

•••

The black slowly turned red again, and the strange feeling of nothingness remained. He thought he could hear rustling, but he didn't know if it was worth forcing open his lids. Then he felt something. His legs were immoveable, pinned, but his helpless hand lifted.

Exhausted curiosity, rather than fear, forced open his lids.

Everything was bright white. He'd expected that.

He realized there was a figure in silhouette against the light that slowly resolved into something small and blue.

He tried to speak, driven by some…urgency. This time the figure noticed.

"You're awake," it said. Female. "I'll just get…"

He slid into the black, glad of it.

•••

Something was weighing down his left hand. It was hot. Sweaty. He couldn't raise his eyelids, they weighed pounds each.

A voice. "I have to go home soon, to get some sleep. Did I say I'm in charge at the lab this week?" Recognition came. His father. "I'll try your mum again. I think she may have changed her number though…" Then, "I love you, Tom."

He drifted away, anxiety following.

•••

Noise woke him, a clattering in the distance. It sounded like a trolley, full of dishes, and with too many wheels.

He opened his eyes. It was bright again. Daylight. The ceiling was ugly.

He tuned in on voices murmuring nearby and turned his head slowly to the sound, amazed that he could make parts of his body work to his will.

He lay in a small room on an elevated bed. Rough white sheets and a pale blue blanket were tightly tucked around his legs. And—equipment beside him, some attached to him. A drip ran into his arm.

At the end of the bed, in front of a large window, two people stood talking intently, blonde and black, dark and blue.

Tom's focus was still floaty, but eventually he was able to understand that one of the people was Christine Hansen, wearing full uniform, and a plump woman he didn't know, in a dark blue dress with white piping on it.

A nurse.

Fear hit before he could remember why, and he jolted helplessly on the bed.

It made a shocking, crashing noise and emphasized to him how completely imprisoned his lower half was by the tightly tucked bedding.

Both women's attention turned to him, and his wild panic intensified, though he couldn't remember why he didn't feel safe with them.

"Will," he pleaded, but it barely made a sound.

"It's all right, Tom." Hansen sounded both surprised and relieved. "You're in St. Mary's. It was the closest A & E. You've been out for three… three and a half days. It's Friday."

Tom blinked at her, trying to get a grip on his jittering alarm. His mind felt strange—tender and bruised, as if it had been thrown about inside his skull. Images blipped in and out of his mind, like sunlight flickering through leaves.

The nurse, who introduced herself as Sandra, was suddenly everywhere, taking his pulse, poking and prodding him.

"Would you like a drink?" she asked.

His mouth felt like ashes. He nodded and tried to pull himself up, but he didn't have the strength to fight the sheets.

Sandra picked up a control near his hand and the top part of the bed rose until he ended in a near-sitting position. She held a glass to his mouth.

"We need to run a routine test or two, Tom. I'll be back soon."

One professional smile, a nod to Hansen, and she left.

Tom sank back against the pillows. He felt less vulnerable sitting up, all in all, even if he couldn't manage it on his own.

A memory brushed across his mind.

He tried to lurch upright. How much had he dreamed? How much had been real?

"Where's Will?" he croaked.

Hansen jolted forward, as if to stop him. "He's fine, Tom. He was admitted for a checkup, but he's out of hospital."

"I don't know…what happened?" He sounded pathetic. Like a little boy. Tom's skin heated. Hansen's bracing smile vanished.

"A total bloody shambles. That's what happened. Saved by dumb luck." Her uniform really suited her, Tom noted absently, and her pale pink lipstick was impeccably applied. "You had a stalker after all," she said with a bitter smile. "Or Nick had. Former Superintendant Morton. He took the number-plate of DI Foster's car when you visited him, used his contacts in the force—illegally I might add—to trace him, and by watching him, he found Nick. He started a surveillance so he was outside—*watching*—when you smashed the window. And since he was carrying his legal firearm at the time, he was able to blow the lock open and…" She sighed. "Subdue Rolfe before she could inject you with her final dose of drugs."

Tom's mouth hung open. "*Morton* saved us?"

Hansen's whole face twitched. "In more ways than one. His wife's taken several overdoses…the most recent was Lorazepam. So he knew GPs carry a sort of antidote to it in their bags. Flumazenil. He got a shot from Rolfe's supplies and… You were so far gone he risked giving it you, to keep you alive till the ambulance arrived."

Tom's eyes began to fill—physical weakness and pent-up emotion.

"Jena murdered his children." Hansen's expression blanked. Tom stumbled on. What if Hansen somehow didn't know? "Morton's children. And she murdered people for Carys. And Carys killed for her."

"Jena confessed everything," Hansen cut in stiffly. "Rolfe still thinks she's cleverer than any of us, and she'll talk her way out."

"They…met on a train." Tom sounded breathless. "Like the…"

"Like the film," Hansen interrupted. "They saw it as…serendipity apparently. They both needed help. Nick was desperate to leave Catriona for you, and Jena was sure Catriona would expose him and ruin them if he did. And Rolfe's old friend, who'd helped her frame Martin Holmes, had got religion and a conscience. She told Rolfe she was planning to confess they'd both lied about what they'd seen. That and Rolfe's husband had got another woman pregnant and was preparing to leave her. Rolfe had a whole hit-list ready. Jena says she didn't trust Rolfe not to expose Nick unless she agreed, but I'm more inclined to believe she was…wholeheartedly involved. Catriona had to be silenced anyway. So they both made a deal to carry out three murders each of people they had no personal motive to kill, while the person who'd gain created an iron alibi for themselves. Carys killed Catriona, Lily Adderton and Max Perry. Jena killed Maxine Blunt up in Sunderland, then Michael Rolfe, and finally his lover, Molly Cole, the day after Catriona."

Molly. The very first time Tom and Will met Carys—the receptionist weeping for her friend. Carys giving them her own crocodile tears.

I'm brilliant at acting, if I say so myself.

"Once they agreed," Hansen went on, "Jena removed Maxine first as a matter of urgency before she could confess. Then, she introduced Catriona to Carys. Jena'd found out about Brownley's campaign of harassment, and she intensified it and used it along with prescribed medication and some 'counseling sessions' from Rolfe, to keep Catriona in line till they were ready. Meanwhile Rolfe deliberately misdiagnosed her husband as type 2 diabetic and then as bipolar. So she was able to give him him a cocktail of drugs that affected his mental state. The insulin she gave him was replaced with water initially, so it didn't kill him too early, but the antipsychotics were real."

"God. And Michael's family thought Carys adored him."

"She did, apparently," Hansen said. "Until he chose someone else. She introduced him to Jena, as a friend, went off on holiday, and Jena 'popped by' one day while she was away."

It was incomprehensible to believe that she'd prepared for his death so callously, watching his struggle every day. But Tom recalled the look in Carys's eyes as she prepared to finish him off. The fathomless depth of busy, happy evil.

"Jena claims she only had Catriona on her list, so she agreed a kind of IOU against Rolfe's three solid targets. Then events persuaded her to call in the other two murders. Lily had to go because she was out of control. Jena couldn't talk her out of bringing the press down on you, so she lured her to the hotel in Paddington where she ended up having a drink with Carys Rolfe."

"Dear God," Tom said softly.

"Max Perry had been watching you, and having you watched. And Jena heard that recording. Heard him imply that that he knew about Nick. Plus he was pushing into your life."

Tom remembered Jena, sitting texting busily next to him in Nick's lounge, after Tom had obligingly announced where Max lived. Texting Carys then.

"After Perry died, they moved to tie it up. Rolfe had never cared who carried the can. But Jena arranged from the very beginning for it to be Will Foster. They faked the attack on Rolfe together, just after Rolfe killed Perry. She knew exactly which dose of insulin to take, of course. Jena left the body of a cat and a package from Max, to drive you to Max's flat with luck. Find the body. She wanted to frame Peter Brownley first to force his confession and discredit him with you. But DI Foster was always going to be the final patsy. He was supposed to have been arrested and brought down by the eyewitness testimony of Carys Rolfe. It's what she did to Martin Holmes, and he's still in custody."

"But why bring Will into it?" Tom said in anguish. "I hadn't seen him for two years?"

"Because Jena believed the reason you wouldn't commit to Nick was because you'd never got over DI Foster. So she used the harassment allegations against you to pull him back in to your life and the case. The endgame was meant to be life imprisonment for him and a cure for you, which would allow you to turn to Nick wholeheartedly."

"She killed the Morton kids to bring Bethany into line," Tom said doubtfully. "And…framing me… That was meant to do the same?"

"People are like pieces on a board to her. But my God, she can plot and strategize like a grandmaster." Under Hansen's impeccable makeup, Tom could see her exhaustion. "She seems to be pathologically obsessed with her brother. With getting him whatever he wants. Punishing…manipulating anyone who denies him or hurts him. Psychiatrists are going to have a field day with her. Rolfe…Rolfe's just a common or garden homicidal maniac."

Tom flinched. "Everything we found then, Will and me…they meant us to find. We really were just puppets?" He didn't know why that felt so humiliating, after everything else.

Hansen protested. "No. No, Tom! Remember no one's going to react exactly as they're supposed to. Jena says she put in an anonymous call to lead you and DI Foster to Catriona's old identity as the first step. You were meant to become part of Nick's secret. That was part of the plan. But you weren't meant to find Martin Holmes, or work out the red string connection or connect anything to Rolfe. That was luck and brilliant detective work."

"But Carys said she gave clues. And they even…combined their old signatures. Why would they take that risk?"

"The Babes in Arms signature was important to what Jena wanted to do. Rolfe insisting on including hers? I think she wanted that satisfaction. Like…signing a work of art. It's not uncommon. Rolfe's pretty much a classic serial killer. And in her line of work…medicine…that's like a fox in a henhouse. We're checking back through her patient lists now."

Tom flashed back to his first meeting with Carys. The warmth and empathy that had so impressed him when he'd needed kindness. How willingly he'd been gulled by what he wanted to see. How many people had fallen under that same spell?

"I think she and Jena recognized each other in a way," Hansen said. "When they met. Their essential…alikeness. They'd both killed as children, both left symbolic marks on their victims. That's very unusual. Together, they made a lethal blend."

Tom trained his eyes on the large sunny window as he tried to process it all.

When he looked back, he had to concede that he *had* felt closer to Nick as Jena's plan played out—more guilty, more responsible. Grateful. Vulnerable. But his feelings for Will had overwhelmed everything.

He said, almost in reaction, "If Jena and Nick hadn't forced you to tell me about David Burchill, you'd have let me swing to protect Nick's secret, wouldn't you? The way you'd have sacrificed Pez."

Hansen's frosted pink mouth parted in what looked like shock; the first time Tom had seen her really discomforted.

"There was solid evidence against Brownley," she said defensively. "And anyway, I'm not sure…"

The door squeaked open, and a man shouldered his way into the room, balancing two lidded paper cups, one in each hand. He stopped dead when he saw Tom semi-upright on the bed, then his startlement slid effortlessly into delight.

"You're awake!" Nick said. "How are you feeling?"

Tom stared at him with blank horror. "Oh Christ. Why aren't you…?" His voice gave out.

Why aren't you in jail with your sister?

Nick's joy and relief evaporated. Caution and bewilderment took their place.

They stared at each other in awful silence.

"Nick's been here every day." Hansen sounded uncertain.

"It's all right, Chris," Nick put in quickly.

Chris?

Tom glared at Hansen with betrayed disbelief, then back at Nick. Nick looked down at the floor.

When he raised his eyes again, they were sorrowful, waiting, like some sacrificial victim.

Are you going to tell?

"I'll leave you two to talk." Hansen picked up her shoulderbag from the floor. "I'll be in touch, Tom."

The atmosphere in the room when she left felt thick with a sticky, dirty silence. Tom felt anxious again. Unsafe. But anger surged to save him.

"The police don't know you helped her?" Tom accused. "*Covered* for her? Or is Hansen covering for *you*?"

"No!" Nick looked horrified. "When Morton broke in, I was on the ground too, remember? And…Will didn't…say anything."

Tom's agitation grew. He wriggled up the bed to try sit up straighter. But his limbs still felt pitifully weak.

"*Why?* Why didn't he say?"

"Why didn't you?" Nick asked with miserable logic.

Tom stilled. Why hadn't he? He and Will had heard the three of them—Jena, Carys *and* Nick—colluding. Nick should have been charged with aiding and abetting at the very least.

"I tried to save you," Nick said. "I'd have died to save you."

Was that why? Because at the end, Nick, even if he'd been more than ready to sacrifice Will, had tried to fight for Tom? Or because Nick—an innocent man—had already served years in jail?

"Please," Nick went on. "I know…*I know* it's not easy. But it's over. I have a buyer for Echo, and the Justice Ministry'll help me set up again. Maybe abroad this time. New York."

Tom stared at him, a rabbit in front of a snake.

Nick sighed. "Tom. Please. *Try.* We *fit*. Will and you were never going to work. But I've known you were for me from the day I met you moping in the lifts."

And that finally broke through Tom's mesmerized stasis.

"I can't *believe* you!" he yelled. "You *helped* her. She murdered…so many people. You *let* her organize the murder of your own *wife*!"

"No!" Nick looked appalled. But how often had he lied with total conviction, to Tom's face?

"She's a killer!" Tom said, tone unforgiving. "And you *knew* she was a killer, when she murdered those kids."

Nick flinched. "She was a little girl."

Tom shook his head fiercely. "A little girl who killed babies. *You* let her go on murdering people. Both of them. Her and Carys."

"No, Tom! I didn't know they'd do it until after I found Cat, and then I thought it was over. I didn't expect Lily. Or Max Perry! Jena just kept telling me she'd make sure you weren't in any more trouble. That your career would be safe. She thought she was trying to help us."

"*Us?*" Tom's voice shook with exhaustion and righteous rage. "You mean *you*! All her life she's played God to give *you* what you want. People died, and *you* enabled her, because you were too weak to stop her! Or did it just suit you that she was trying to hand me to you on a plate?"

Nick froze as if he'd been struck. "You think I'm *weak*?" He sounded stunned.

Tom could barely believe that nothing else he'd said, no other blow, seemed to have landed, but that one.

"Yes!" Tom goaded, for that exact reason. "What the fuck else can you call it? You let her run amok! You were going to stand by and let her frame Will!"

Nick spat, "Better him than you!"

"Better *neither* of us! Better the actual murderers! Your fucking *sister* tried to kill me."

"Only because she thought there was no alternative! That you'd tell the police," Nick shouted back in anguish.

It struck Tom suddenly, that through everything, through all the time he'd known him, he'd never heard Nick raise his voice at him. Any more than Tom had ever yelled at him. They'd never fought, because that would have been too real.

"Damned right I'd have told the police!" Tom hissed, "There's loyalty and there's criminal stupidity. You're like some...spineless...*assistant* covering up anything she did."

Silence fell like a stage curtain, so sudden and complete it seemed to echo. Even distant hospital noises had stilled.

Tom regarded Nick warily. Nick, in turn, looked utterly shell-shocked.

"Darling Malik," he said, dazed. "That's me. She's Naukarani. Like Cat was. *I'm* Malik."

Tom shook his head slowly. "I don't give a fuck what you call each other." His voice was low and poisonous. "I don't care about your secret names or your fucked-up relationship. Peck fucking *peck*! You spent years of your life locked up to protect a child killer, so she could kill again. You are responsible, Nick. Yes, you're *weak* and criminally stupid."

Nick's eyes were black holes in his white face, burning with emotion.

"Don't call me stupid," he said softly. "Don't ever call me weak."

"I don't want to see you again." Tom's voice was implacable. "Just be fucking grateful I don't tell Hansen everything."

Nick's expression wiped to blankness. Whatever was going on behind his eyes, he hid all of it.

The door opened behind him.

Sandra swept in, followed by a stocky, balding, bespectacled middle-aged man wearing a checked long-sleeved shirt. A stethoscope hung round his neck. Tom could have snogged them both with relief.

"Good morning, Mr. Gray!" the man said with crazed, professional cheer. "Back with us, I see! Sorry to keep you waiting. We need to do a few tests. I'm afraid your visitor's going to have to..."

"I'm just going, Doctor," Nick said with a poised smile, as if he were off to chair a meeting. The smile didn't slip when he turned back to Tom.

"Well," he said. "Bye for now, Tom."

But Tom wasn't having it. "Enjoy abroad," he said coldly. "I won't have time to see you before you go."

Nick's opaque mask of social unconcern remained impeccable. Without another word, he turned and left.

And Tom, staring at the closed door, felt both powerfully relieved and unnerved, as if he'd just said goodbye to someone he didn't know.

28

Tom slept again and jerked awake, eyes wide open, to the feel of a needle sinking into his throat.

It took him a second to distinguish reality from nightmare.

Will stood at the end of the bed, watching him.

Tom thought for a second that Will was part of the dream. But he didn't disappear, and as Tom drank him in greedily, he felt that familiar rush of brilliant relief, like a kid whose parents turned up, despite denials on all sides, to save him from trouble.

Tom beamed at him. After a startled moment, Will smiled politely back.

"*Will*," Tom breathed. "Are you all right?"

Will nodded. "No damage. How about you though?"

"I'll be fine." Then Tom said honestly, "But...I don't know if I'll ever forget the feeling of the needle going in." There was no one else he could admit that to.

Will's expression twisted, then smoothed. "We thought you were dead, before the ambulance came. Morton was..." He shook his head with forced levity. "Let's just say, if ever a man deserved a fruit basket..."

Tom snorted an equally unamused laugh. "I'll send him a van. A van of fruit." Then, "Nick was here." Will's expression closed. "Why didn't you turn him in, Will?"

Will grimaced. "I thought it should be your choice. I assume you didn't either?"

It felt like a reproach.

"It's just..." Tom tried to explain what he barely understood himself. "He already served so much time for the Morton murders and..."

"It's all right." Will looked away and down, then, as if he were forcing himself, back up at Tom. "Thank you. For calling to warn me…when you knew I'd be arrested."

Tom's unease began to root and grow. Will sounded so distant, as if they were back outside Greens again—that first reunion.

"Of course," he said urgently. "I had to."

Will gave a small lopsided smile, oddly bitter. "Even though you obviously thought I'd done it."

"Well." Tom flushed. "Des believed it and he hero worships you and he told me…"

"It's all right," Will cut in with a reassuring smile.

"I was all over the place, Will," Tom said urgently. "But…I knew. I knew in my gut it couldn't be true."

Will's smile softened. "It's really okay. You were under unbelievable emotional strain. Terrorized. Gaslighted. *Anyway* in the end—you worked the whole thing out. *Strangers on a Train.* How did you get that?"

"The fine edge of desperation," Tom said. "And…we solved it together. We're a good team." But he could hear the beginnings of tears in his own voice. He knew what was coming.

Will smiled, his pale hazel eyes twinkling with light. "Yeah. We were." Past tense.

Panic began to bubble in Tom's abdomen. "We need to talk," he said.

"We did," Will replied gently. "I think we both know what happened was the kind of thing that happens in wartime, yeah? Extreme circumstances. Time taken away from reality."

Was this what it felt like then? What Tom had run from all his life? Was this how his dad felt?

"Is that all it was?" Tom's voice shook.

Will frowned. "You've said it over and over, and you're right. Our lives don't fit. New York City and Leyton. The Met Gala and…B&Q." He tried a smile then looked away. "But…" He looked back and met Tom's eyes. "This time we're friends. No anger or bitterness. And that's good."

Tom took him in, in all his upright beauty, and the sharp agony in his chest and throat were so great it felt as if his heart were physically breaking apart. His tentative, terrified overtures had been useless, and he had no courage for any more. It was far too late.

It made no sense to feel so devastated and abandoned.

He was the one who'd wanted Will to accept how things were, and Will had absorbed his lesson. Tom was a free spirit with the world at his feet, never to be tied down. Ever since they'd met again, Tom had made sure that Will accepted they had no future. And now Will had no desire left to risk another crazy experiment in blending incompatible lives with a fuck-up like Tom.

"Yeah," Tom said quietly. And that was that.

"AC Hansen has *suggested* I go back to the Met," Will volunteered. "Repeatedly. Over and over. And over." He slipped his hands into his trouser pockets and smirked.

He was trying. Tom should try too. "Is it working?"

Will raised a wicked eyebrow. "I don't think Joey Clarkson'd be very pleased," he said. Tom managed to grin, loving him so fucking much. "But it is."

"Tom?" The voice was as familiar as his own, but timid, and timidity was all wrong. As was the version of Pez who edged round the door of Tom's room, makeup free, wearing a plain black T-shirt and dark jeans. He looked like Pez with all the joy and bravery stripped from him. He looked like Peter Brownley.

Will made a little movement of his mouth, like acceptance of inevitability.

"I'll be off then."

"*No*," Tom burst out. "You don't have to…"

Pez, behind Will, looked at the floor as if Tom had hit him. He must be assuming that Tom didn't want to be alone with him. Or maybe Pez just saw he couldn't bear to let Will go.

"Thanks, Will," he forced out. "Thanks for everything."

Will's face twisted, and Tom could see a quick sheen of emotion turning his eyes liquid, that dark curtain of lashes dipping to hide it.

He swallowed, then gave Tom one of those swashbuckling, cock-raising grins.

"Best fun I've had in years," he said. And then he was gone.

•••

It was impossible to concentrate.

And that was wrong, because Pez was sitting beside the bed, confessing his sins as if Tom were his parish priest.

But the truth was, Tom didn't care.

The devastation of those first accusations by Lily felt so long ago, and so pale. Just the first meek chapter in some epic of disaster, ending in shock and misery.

He certainly felt miserable now. Will had been gone for fifteen minutes.

"Pez," he said, fighting to keep irritation out of his tone. "Let it go."

Pez raised his tearful face. Without his usual eye makeup, he looked puffy and very young. "I can't let it go, Tommy. I look back now and...I think I must have lost my fucking mind. What I did...it was vile."

"Yeah. Yeah, Pez, it was. I don't know what the fuck you were thinking. But in the end, it didn't kill Catriona, and it didn't put me in prison. Compared with everything else that happened it's...it's peanuts now."

"I would have come clean," Pez assured him anxiously. "If they really had charged you over Catriona, or Lily. And I didn't send some of the things the police said she got—the worst things...some of them... I thought she was tough as hell, Tommy. That's all I ever saw from her. I had no idea how damagaed she was. But I told Jena everything. The very first day, when you went in to the station, but she said to leave it. Then she said I should point the investigation at Max because he deserved it."

"She knew about Max all along?" Tom asked, startled. "Even before you announced it at Greens?"

Pez looked even more shamefaced. "I used to tell her everything... cry on her shoulder. I trusted her."

"Yeah I know." He hadn't known, but Jena had been pulling all their strings. "Please. If I can let it go, can't you? Just...I need to know we can be friends though, Pez. *Just* friends. Can you accept that?"

Pez's bloodshot green eyes fixed on his. He looked so tragic, so hurt and remorseful.

Tom knew exactly how he felt, because he was feeling it too, just... for someone else.

He wanted to hug him and be hugged back. But he had to make sure this time that Pez knew how things stood. No false hope.

Pez though, was still brave.

"I'm thinking of asking Mark out," he said.

Tom gazed at him, startled. "Mark...Nimmo?" He tried to imagine it—Mark and Pez—but his nerve failed him. Then, "Aren't you scared he'll outbitch you?"

Pez gave a huff of a laugh. "He can only try." He sighed. "I don't know what's happening with Echo now, but...assuming I'm still...your booker, I brought your schedule along. Mel's been hysterical for days about the Armani shoot. Here's the contract you were meant to sign." He held out a small pile of papers, took a deep breath, and tossed his head stagily.

It was like watching the old Pez flounce back in to take possession. "*Frankly* I didn't know it was possible to stay at that pitch of diva for so long. You missed the flight *obviously* but she forgives you, because it reached the press. And you're a hero and a victim. Which is *peak* promo."

Tom closed his eyes.

"I told her I thought you'd make it in maybe five days," Pez went on relentlessly. "You *definitely* need a good salon treatment *and* a wax."

He held out a pen, and Tom, without further consideration, signed the contract.

"Five days," he said. "Tell her I'll make it."

Pez nodded doubtfully. "The Gardiners have John. The Cap took him over there." Tom's eyes shot to his. It felt like a knife in his ribs. Unbearable. Will had looked after John.

Pez, studying him, gave a sad little smile. "You never did let him go."

Tom felt his face crumple.

Truth all round.

•••

"Tom? Time for supper, Tom."

Tom blinked groggily and peered up at the nurse already maneuvering the movable table attached to his bed, into place. The tray sat there waiting, with covered plates and a cup topped with cling film. Tom pulled himself into a sitting position reluctantly. Even if he'd been feeling hungry, this wasn't going to be pretty.

The nurse laughed. "It's not that bad. You could have chosen the boiled fish."

Tom gave her a wan smile. She wasn't Sandra. Younger. Cheeky. He seemed to recall she'd identified herself, in one of his hazier moments, as Julie.

"You mean steamed fillet of sole," he reproved sourly. He'd been fooled by the menu once.

Julie grinned. "Exactly. *You* had the gumption to go for the boeuf bourguignon."

"The beef stew rather than the boiled fish."

"Yup," Julie said. Then, briskly. "*More* flowers came." They both glanced at the windowsill groaning with vases filled with extravagant bouquets from fans and industry people. "We'll keep them at the nurses station, okay?" She clearly didn't expect an argument. "Plus a couple more three-feet teddy bears and an even bigger stuffed giraffe. Send them down to the children's ward?"

Tom nodded dumbly.

"This was left at the nurses station." Julie set a small white bag with string handles on the bed beside his hand. "All the cards that came with the prezzies are in there too. They can help you through the beef stew." Julie took her exit line and sailed out of the room.

Tom scowled and pulled the tray toward him. Minus its metal lid, the boeuf bourguignon challenged him with lumpy brown blandness.

He sighed, stomach twisting with nerves, the way it did every time he thought about the massive decision he was taking. But it wasn't really a decision anymore. It had become a necessity rather than a choice.

He grimaced restlessly and opened his wrapped pack of cutlery. He was going to have to at least try to make a dent in the beef. Show he'd made an effort.

He eyed it but put down the cutlery and picked up the white bag instead, fishing blindly inside until he felt some small florist's gift envelopes, which he extracted first. They all had his name and ward number on the front, and they came from fans who followed him one way or another: sweet, encouraging "get well soon" messages.

And among them, one he didn't understand: *Have you looked up the words yet?*

Tom put a fork of food into his mouth and chewed thoughtfully. *The words?*

An unwanted memory slid in—of Nick white-faced in the heat of battle, banging on about his childish codes with Jena.

Tom had to force the food in his mouth down his throat, past his outrage.

Nick sent him flowers? Despite all Tom had said? How much clearer could he have made his contempt for Nick's enabling weakness? Was Nick deluding himself that Tom would forgive him, just because Nick loved his homicidal sister?

Tom dropped the card as if contact with it contaminated him, almost ready to ask Julie to pick out the flowers Nick had sent and torch them. But still, some inbuilt urge for completion—for *knowing*—found him reaching surreptitiously for his phone. According to Tom's search engine, the words he thought Nick had said were Hindi. Naukrani meant "handmaiden". Malik meant "master".

Tom chewed his lip, furious with himself for taking the bait.

He narrowed his eyes on his congealing plate, and memory resolved again into Nick's expression of shocked disbelief.

"Darling Malik. She's Naukarani. Like Cat was. I am Malik."

Tom's eyes shot back to the card. He stopped breathing.

DM and N.

She's the handmaiden. I'm the master.

Nick had been so disbelieving, so outraged, because Tom thought he was the follower. The one picking up after Jena. And all the time… had it been him? Never getting his hands dirty, but Jena, serving him, until the end?

The two of them, growing up and reaching adolescence together in that little house, with no adult to care, or control them. And David, had he been grooming Ava to be that…his handmaiden? The way he'd groomed and shaped Denise into the woman he wanted? Until he'd grown bored and moved on to Tom?

Except, Tom had refused to comply so Nick and Jena had set about breaking his independence?

But, Tom thought desperately—that didn't fit David taking the fall for Ava, if his whole persona was manipulating someone else to do his dirty work like…some mafia don.

Unless—unless someone at the time had pushed the same button as Tom had.

Accused David of weakness and gullibility before his stronger sister? Like blindly tripping a switch?

He lay there and took stock. He'd learned, at least, how not to panic.

He couldn't prove this meant anything at all. No one had heard Nick say it to him; no one knew what it might mean. *Might* mean. Maybe it wasn't even true! Just Nick getting in one last jab, wanting Tom to know his version of the truth—because he couldn't stand to be seen as Jena's hapless instrument rather than the puppet-master who'd controlled all of them.

Tom shifted restlessly, and the bag tapped against his hand. When he picked it up, it felt almost weightless but when he tipped it upside down, an object dropped out.

A part of him thought he was dreaming.

A small square box, covered in brown wrapping paper, dyed scarlet. A label: *Tom Gray, Echo Models.*

Echo. Why hadn't he ever made that connection? The nymph who'd been ruined by Narcissus.

It was meant to be over. But they'd got it wrong.

The gifts hadn't been from Max. The break-in hadn't been Max. The package beside the pathetic corpse of the cat. The sense of relentless invasion…hadn't been Max.

Jena and Carys had no interest in him even if they somehow had the ability to locate him and send something like this, from behind bars. This didn't come from either of them.

Nick hadn't lied.

Tom ripped off the paper to find a red jewelry box inside, emblazoned with gold: *Cartier.*

His face twisted into a grotesque grimace of disgust, horror, terror.

A printed Cartier card inside the box told him that the ring, nestled in black velvet padding, was made of white gold with eight diamonds embedded, to a total of 0.19 carats. A wedding band. And inside the ring, when he rolled it round in its velvet setting—the Cartier name, and one other word, engraved.

The memory crouched there, waiting for completion. *So you will… always be…*

Mine.

Tom didn't take out the ring. Like a fairytale, he wouldn't grant it that power.

Instead he snapped the box closed. He didn't pause to second-guess himself.

He lifted up his phone, and made an against-hospital-rules call to Christine Hansen.

29

Four days later, Tom stood, clutching John's cat-carrier tightly in his right hand and rang the doorbell. His packed holdall lay on the doorstep beside his feet, and he stared down at it as if it bore the answers to the universe. Behind him he heard the purr of his dad's car pulling away from the pavement, leaving him to his fate. Or maybe, waiting out of sight further down the road, just in case. It was a hot, muggy-thick early evening, and the only noise Tom could hear was the low roar of traffic on Leyton High Road.

The door opened. Tom looked up sharply.

Mark Nimmo stood in Will's open doorway, eyebrows reaching for his hairline as he took in Tom, then his big bag, then his cat carrier. Tom stared back at him, and he felt as if he'd been whacked in the stomach, leaving a nauseous mess of shocked humiliation.

Well, what had he expected, exactly? That Will would be pining?

He tried to order words in his mind to apologize for the interruption, but Mark didn't give him the chance.

Instead, he yelled over his shoulder, "You owe me seventy-five quid," and brushed past Tom to march down the path and out of the gate.

Tom turned to gape after him. Then he heard "What?" shouted from the back of the house—Will's voice—and his stomach clenched again.

Mark's presence had undermined his determination, and fear was beginning to get the better of him again. But, he told himself, for the thousandth time—that was no longer acceptable.

Time to grow up. No one had guarantees.

He'd learned some things were worth the risk. They were worth any-thing.

Tom walked inside and closed the door behind him, putting his be-longings down in the hallway, breathing the house in. He remembered his last, awful exit from it, and how much he'd longed for it, lying aching and miserable in his hospital bed.

As if he could read Tom's mind, John began to mew impatiently.

Tom glanced down at the box, then on impulse, he opened it and let the cat out. John took a few moments to survey his surroundings, stretched extravagantly, and slunk down the hall to the room he'd favored when he'd stayed here—the kitchen, where Tom could hear activity. The door was half-open. John slipped inside.

Tom waited. His pulse hammered with apprehension.

He heard, after a good half a minute, "*What the fuck? John?*" Then the kitchen door was wrenched open, and Will stood there, staring at Tom as if he'd beamed down from a mothership.

Tom drank him in.

Will wore a faded lemon-yellow casual button-up, complementing his olive skin, and pale blue jeans, a dishtowel flung over his shoulder.

"Hi," Tom said. All his speeches, rehearsed repeatedly, had vanished into the space in his head.

"You told Hansen about Nick," Will said, as if no time had passed since their conversation in the hospital. It sounded almost accusing. "She asked me to corroborate what we heard at the flat, before she went ahead and arrested him. She wouldn't tell me anything else."

Tom grimaced. "I got another...*gift* at the hospital. A wedding ring."

Will froze.

"I think...Nick's...*ego* needed me to know that Jena did what *he* wanted not the other way round," Tom said. "I think that applied all the way from the murder of the Morton twins. But when it comes down to it, it's my word against his."

"Maybe Carys will testify against him," Will said. "And Hansen has our evidence. If she charges him even just as an accessory, there's a good chance he goes back to prison."

Tom nodded. Hansen had told him. But none of that was why he was here.

"You didn't contact me," he said. "When you heard about Nick."

"You're meant to be in New York," Will said, and frowned as if that had only just occurred to him.

Tom managed a fair try at a smile. "Delayed again because of this, so not for a couple of days yet. And…just for the shoot." He bit his lip and finished in a rush, "I'm not moving there."

He saw the response to that statement immediately in Will's body language—wariness—and Tom's mad surge of confidence deflated instantly, like a pricked balloon.

"I just…" He pushed on. "I'm staying in London."

Will swallowed. "I…Tom…"

And Tom knew that tone. The brush-off, like the hospital. But this time he was going to fight. He fumbled in the pocket of his light jacket and proffered the paper he pulled out.

A signed confirmation that Tom would begin his deferred postgraduate degree at UCL in October. The deadline to apply had been 31st July. He'd just made it.

"I needed you to see this. In case…it changes anything?" His whole body was shaking.

Will took a second to accept the paper, cautious eyes never leaving Tom's face, then he opened it and skimmed it. He looked back up, and his expression held incredulity, mixed with suspicion and frank horror.

Tom's hopes began to wither.

That had been it—his best play. The decision he'd made—the thing he'd begun to plan, in his hospital bed. Proof of something.

"You can't be serious," Will said.

"I can," Tom returned mulishly. "I'm starting next term."

Will looked down at the paper again, as if he couldn't believe his eyes. "*Why?*" he asked, and Tom realized painfully that he was just as appalled as Pez had been when he told him.

"Because it'll give us a chance." It felt like the bravest thing he'd ever said.

"No!" Will said fiercely. "You've just made it to the top of your career. You've *worked* for it. It's everything to you. You can't sacrifice that for anyone."

"I can still do bits of work when I want. I have the status now to…"

"That's *not* what you've worked for."

"So I won't be a supermodel. *Fuck. That.* I don't *want it*! I don't know I ever did, except to beat the challenge. It's been something to do, because I thought I should. Not a thing I love. I want to finish university. And I *want* to be with you."

Will's eyes were anguished. "You've been through a trauma, Tom. Huge trauma. You're not thinking straight. You'll be on billboards in

Time Square next month! Ads on TV. Magazines. You can't give up what you've achieved for..." he gestured at the dim hallway, "...for 'ironing in suburbia.' You'd resent me in no time. Like last time."

"It's *my* choice, Will." But Tom knew he was losing the argument. And that old reflexive fear was beginning to gnaw at him, making him want to bolt away from being on the wrong end of loving too much.

What if Will just didn't want to tell him the truth? That those few shags had been fine, but he was long past the point of wanting permanence with Tom? That Tom had pissed him around once too many times.

So, throw it all out there then. Take the risk.

"You *know* my career wasn't why I left," he said, fighting his voice to steadiness. "Or...why I fought this so hard. I *love* you. I've *been* in love with you pretty much since I met you, and you were right, I was terrified of it. I've been running away from myself, more than you."

Will's wide eyes searched his face, though in bewilderment or horror, Tom couldn't tell.

"So," Tom went on firmly. "This is what's going to happen, whether you say yes or no. I'm going to enroll for my postgrad in forensic science, like I would have if Pez hadn't spotted me in the park. I'll fulfill my modeling contracts—and I have quite a few—and do jobs on the side when I have time, and if clients still want to hire me."

Will looked no less stunned, no less alarmed.

"But the question is..." Tom finished, with his last thread of courage. "Do *you* want me? Anymore?"

All his vulnerability was laid out, like a cloak at Will's feet. But Will's expression was far from delight. He swung around, facing into the kitchen again, hand shooting up to cup the back of his neck.

Over Will's shoulder, Tom could see John had settled in his old position, beside the window, at home.

Tears burned Tom's nose, his eyes, his throat.

"I'll always fucking want you." Will's voice sounded tormented. "That's the problem."

Tom stilled. He could only see the back of Will's head, that hopeless hand gripping his neck.

"Then have me," Tom said. "I think you're the only person who ever will."

Will dropped his arm but he didn't turn round, as if he was afraid to, and Tom couldn't stand that.

He stepped closer and pressed his palm against Will's back, a touch after so many days without, then he slid round to stand in front of him, face to face...

Will was frowning, eyes lowered, lashes thick and sooty.

"Please, Will," Tom said. "Whatever else, I've never lied to you." Will's eyes rose to his. "I'm still terrified. But I've learned. I won't turn away again. I won't let you down."

Their gazes held. Then at last, Will let go a breath Tom hadn't known he'd been holding.

"You can't stop waxing," Will said, with resignation. "I like the waxing."

Tom took a second or two to understand, still caught in the atmosphere of tension and fear between them. And then he did.

He gave a shaky, elated laugh. "Okay. The waxing stays."

"And now I owe Mark seventy-five pounds."

Tom grinned, weak with relief. "He bet you I'd come crawling back." It was a statement, not a question.

"I bet against it."

Tom took in the implication at once, and his grin faded slightly. "Why seventy-five?"

"I'm just a detective. I couldn't afford a hundred."

Tom laughed again. He'd never felt happiness like it, like he could burst with it. They still hadn't really touched.

"Do you have enough dinner cooking to feed me too?"

"I see you brought a bag," Will pointed out dryly. Yes, then.

"All I've been dreaming of," Tom said truthfully. "Is you cooking for me again. And the two of us watching a movie, cuddling on the sofa."

Hardly an erotic fantasy. But Tom thought he saw some hidden tension in Will begin to loosen. Will's expression didn't change, though, from solemnity.

He said, "As long as it's not Hitchcock."

•••

"Mr. Gray?"

The eager voice came from just behind him.

Tom looked up from his contemplation of his phone, and almost bumped into a girl slouched close to his left, also studying her phone and—surreptitiously—him.

Tom had been standing on the pavement outside the Department of Security and Crime Science, trying to decide whether to brave Oxford Street, which would inevitably be purgatory. But then it *was* December. And he had to do his Christmas shopping sometime.

It took a few seconds, in his preoccupation, to identify the man, bundled up in a green anorak and woolen hat in the clear frosty air, smiling at him with bizarre satisfaction. Because he was entirely out of context.

Their last meeting felt like a bad dream, long ago, but so did everything from that hellish part of the summer. Except what Tom had got out of it in the end.

"Mr. Glanville." Tom kept his voice neutral. "What a coincidence."

Glanville smiled amiably. "Well, it's not really a coincidence. I came to see you."

"Oh? What about?" But Tom was sure he already knew.

"Well." Glanville's voice lowered. His dark brown eyes were alight with excitement behind his spectacles. "It's about…David," he whispered. His breath puffed out, whitely visible in the icy air. "You didn't say you knew him when we met," Glanville continued, with half-scolding reproach.

Tom drew himself up to his full height, forcing Glanville to crane his neck to look up at him.

Whatever Glanville saw on his face, it changed his expression to caution. He went on quickly, "But of course I understand why you couldn't." He waited for a moment, then he burst out, "I *knew* there had been a miscarriage of justice. Just like now. David was protecting Ava all along."

It took all Tom's willpower not to show his disdain. Of course, Glanville would view the claims in his book as validated and David as victimized. Sickeningly, a lot of people did now.

In the end Jena had pleaded guilty as Ava Burchill to three counts of murder, and to the murder of the Morton children.

Carys had denied everything and gone for a jury trial, but on remand in HMP Bronzefield, she'd suddenly changed her plea to guilty too. Tom was cynical enough now to wonder exactly what she'd been promised in return for not making too many scandalous waves.

Nick had denied almost everything to Hansen, claiming Tom had been in no condition to understand what he'd said. But he'd admitted to assisting an offender—to save Tom the need to testify, he told her. He was still awaiting sentence.

The identity under which he'd pled guilty, though, had to be that of David Burchill, which of course had heightened the media furor, since it was now accepted that David Burchill had been innocent of murder. "Nick Haining" and Nick Haining's assets remained his, to carry on his life when he got out.

Glassy had finally been freed from custody and was probably due substantial compensation, but Tom thought it was probably far too late for him.

Hansen had emerged without a stain on her record; in fact, she'd taken most of the credit for helping put the insulin murders to bed. Lawson wasn't mentioned. Echo had been sold, it was rumored, but never confirmed, for millions. Pez joined another agency and found a stableful of new clients as well as full-time comfort in the arms of Mark Nimmo. Tom still couldn't get his head round that.

It really was over.

Except, perversely, Tom's mysterious withdrawal from the modeling scene to study forensic science, just as he hit the very top, had only increased his value. That, along with the fact that the main tabloid focus on the case had been the near-death of a supermodel, had also served to significantly up Tom's Instagram followers.

It had all made him more interesting, more elusive, more the ultimate object of desire. At least that's what Mel in New York had said, after she'd stopped threatening him. People always wanted what didn't want them back.

So Tom did only the most lucrative jobs now—ones that didn't take him away from home or university for long.

"I visited him in prison," Glanville said. "It was a great pleasure. I haven't talked to him since we were preparing the book."

Tom vaguely recalled Nick's dismissal of Glanville's unwanted career suicide, but he didn't comment.

He said, "Uh-huh. And why did you want to see me?"

He pulled his gloves from the slanted pocket of his leather motorcycle jacket and slid in his phone instead.

"Well, he told me to look for you here to tell…"

"He knew I'd be here?" Tom interrupted sharply.

"Well, yes. Obviously. Anyway." Glanville moved to the right, in front of the last glare of the setting winter sun, which was disappearing behind the trees in Tavistock Square Gardens. "He said to tell you that he's doing very well, and he knows how to be a big beast in the jungle."

Tom recalled the reference at once—Nick explaining how he'd managed in jail the last time.

"He also said to tell you that he knew this would be the price he'd have to pay to make sure you knew the truth. And that he's doing it for you."

"For me?" Tom found anger easily. Repugnance. Knowing that Nick was trying to touch him the only way he had left.

"Are you all right, Mr. Gray?" Glanville was studying him closely. To report back probably.

"Listen," Tom said, all tolerance gone. "Back in Red Moss…in a place like that…did you never ask yourself how a *reasonable* boy held sway?"

Glanville looked startled. Tom thought he didn't like the question, but he didn't pretend to misunderstand.

"Well." He sounded defensive. "David always had a way about him. The others wanted to please him, and…they kept the peace when he told them to. It made the unit more pleasant for everyone, especially for the staff."

Tom smiled thinly.

It was so clear. Other people enforcing David's will. Ava on Bethany. His acolytes at Red Moss on Glassy, on anyone who stepped out of line. Glanville, to cast doubt on his conviction. Then Jena on Catriona. And here Glanville was again. David's eager instrument.

"Has it never occurred to you, Mr. Glanville, that *you* 'like to please him' too?"

Glanville drew in breath, almost a gasp. "I should let you get home," he said stiffly. "It's very cold."

"It really is," Tom agreed and pulled on his gloves. "And Mr. Glanville?"

Glanville looked very cautious. "Yes?"

"You and I don't need to see to each other again," Tom said.

Glanville looked as stunned and hurt as if a stranger had hurled abuse at him in the street. He began to back away, all wounded dignity.

"I'll pass on to David how you were when I see him." He gave one last betrayed glare. "He seems very fond of you."

Tom raised a gloved hand in an ironic wave, and Glanville walked away.

Tom watched him go until he disappeared among the knots of people on the pavement.

Stray memories hit of lying in Nick's bed in the Notting Hill flat, being worshipped. Nick's touch, his patient mouth, his voracious dark-blue eyes—it made Tom want to be sick. The knowledge that Nick still thought he could slither into Tom's mind made him want to be sick.

But his days as a pawn in Nick's games were over.

He turned to his left and strode along the grand terrace of Tavistock Square, then along Woburn Place to Bernard Street, to reach his bike. Without another thought to Christmas shopping he set off, music blaring in his helmet speakers. His mind was back in the muggy, relentless heat of the summer. He took the bike on his usual route out of Bloomsbury through Clerkenwell and Canonbury to Leyton.

Tom had given up the Shoreditch flat with little regret, because he hadn't wanted to mess about anymore. He'd lasted a month, in fact, before he found himself asking Will if he and John could move to Warren Road, even though it would practically double his travel time to the department in Bloomsbury. Will had been wary, perhaps because of the disastrous outcome of his own invitation to move in two and a half years before. But Tom talked him round.

Tom loved it all and took none of it for granted. His new life. University. Modeling on the side. The house. And most of all, being with Will Foster, every second he could. And right then, they had a lot of seconds, because Will was at home having finished at SFN at the end of November, ready to start with the Met at his old rank of DI in January. Hansen was adamant he'd be a DCI within nine months.

The trip home took Tom three quarters of an hour, and it was dark when he turned in to Warren Road, the ground glistening like Lurex under orange sodium streetlamps. It even smelled cold.

The window of their living room was unveiled, and welcoming lamps were on, there and in the hallway, visible in the fanlight over the front door. Tom wheeled his bike up the path, unlocked the side gate, and took the bike inside to prop it up and padlock it against a back wall.

The kitchen was fully lit up, golden against the gloom of the winter night, illuminating the patio in front of it and part of the frosted garden. Through the glass doors, Tom could see Will in the kitchen, making tea by the looks of it. John, Tom guessed, would be by the fire.

Will wore a black jeans and a black T-shirt, and Tom smiled just watching him move, because he couldn't help it. Three years after spotting him for the first time, and he still couldn't see past Will Foster.

They were going out that evening, he and Will, to meet James Henderson and Ben Morgan, for dinner in Fulham. They'd become friends in the past months. They had a bit in common.

Tom pulled off his helmet and tapped his fingers against the glass until Will looked up, smiled and strode over to slide open the glass.

"You ducked out on shopping again? It's just going to get worse the more you put it off," he warned. Will's was all done, of course, and probably wrapped.

Tom managed a sound of amusement he didn't feel. "I have an excuse. Brian Glanville pissed all over my Christmas spirit."

Will's stunned expression was some kind of compensation.

Tom told him everything Glanville had said; the man's willful blind innocence as he delivered Nick's message of continued obsession. Or perhaps it had been a threat. Who knew? Talking about it, putting it into words, made a tide of rage and disgust rise up again.

"I'm thinking about him," Tom said venomously. "Nick. Sitting in there, reading all those…sympathetic opinion pieces about a cunning, dominant psychopathic sister controlling her poor, weak brother." Tom pulled off his gloves with unnecessary force. "He must be at the end of his tether already. He's not even a celebrity killer any more. He's just the sidekick."

Will hugged him hard, trying to squeeze the fury out of him. Tom's leather jacket creaked under the pressure of it.

"He's looking at the top end of three to ten years." Will sounded totally certain. He pulled back, holding Tom at arm's length, hands grasping his biceps to look into his face. "He's admitted assisting a serial killer. His own fucked-up brain made him do something so stupid he's ended up back inside, just like the first time. And his sister has all the glory now. He lost, Tom."

"But…" Tom shook his head. "He spent years in jail for two murders they think he had nothing to do with. You know that may change his sentence…"

"And it may not," Will cut in. "They believe he covered for her twice." He pulled Tom closer again. "I love you, you know. And I will always keep you safe."

Warmth began to fizz through his veins, like a drug, an antidote. Will didn't often make declarations—probably because of how Tom used to react to them.

I'll do the same for you, Tom thought. Aloud he said, "I love you too."

Now that Tom had started saying it, he couldn't seem to stop. "And as sick as it sounds…I'm so fucking grateful they chose you as their scapegoat. Because I got this. I got you back. I got a second chance."

It had sounded better in his head.

But Will understood. He shook his head in mock despair.

"That's a bit…narcissistic, isn't it?"

Tom laughed, pure joy.

"I'm a model," he said.

ACKNOWLEDGEMENTS

A huge thank you first of all to my editor, Nicole Kimberling of Blind Eye Books, who again wielded the Kimberling Axe with awe-inspiring precision, and has believed in this book and encouraged me through all kinds of ups, downs, wobbles, doubts etc. It's an exhilarating thing to work with an editor who actively encourages you to try new things, to take risks, to not always take the safe or familiar option. Plus she's patient, kind, scarily clever and very funny, but don't tell anyone.

A massive thank you as well to the brilliant and intrepid Anne Scott who trudged through the manuscript and produced another forensic, insightful copyedit. And to the uber-talented Ginn Hale for kindly casting her eye over the book and giving her advice.

I'd also really like to say thank you to all the readers of my first book, *Bitter Legacy*, who contacted me as a new author and encouraged me to keep going and/or just generally messed about with Dal Carrington Colby Dexter on social media.

And finally thank you to my family, who put up with me when I periodically disappeared down the rabbit hole (and occasionally the plug hole) for this project. Love you forever.

ABOUT THE AUTHOR

Dal Maclean comes from Scotland. Her background is in journalism, and she has an undying passion for history, the more gossipy and scandalous the better. Dal has lived in Asia and worked all over the world, but home is now the UK. She dislikes the Tragic Gay trope, but loves imperfect characters and genuine emotional conflict in romantic fiction. As an author, and a reader, she believes it's worth a bit of work to reach a happy ending. Agatha Christie, English gardens and ill-advised cocktails are three fatal weaknesses, though not usually at the same time.

Her first book, *Bitter Legacy* was a 2017 Lambda Literary Award Finalist for Mystery and an official selection of the American Library Association's Over The Rainbow reading list.

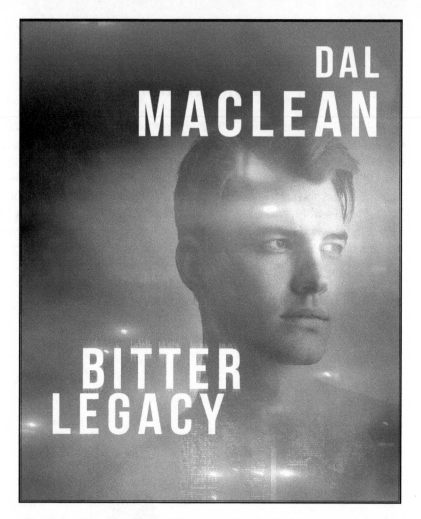

DAL MACLEAN

BITTER LEGACY

Detective Sergeant James Henderson's remarkable gut instincts have put him on a three-year fast track to becoming an inspector. But the advancement of his career has come at a cost. Gay, posh and eager to prove himself in the Metropolitan Police, James has allowed himself few chances for romance.

But when the murder of barrister Maria Curzon-Whyte lands in his lap, all that changes. His investigation leads him to a circle of irresistibly charming men. And though he knows better, James finds himself enticed into their company.

Soon his desire for photographer Ben Morgan challenges him to find a way into the other man's lifestyle of one-night stands and carefree promiscuity. At the same time his single murder case multiplies into a cruel pattern of violence and depravity.

As the bodies pile up and shocking secrets come to light, James finds both his tumultuous private life and coveted career threatened by a bitter legacy.